SAFETY NET

DEANNA GREY

Developmental Editor: Victoria Jane

Proofreader: Bancy

Beta Readers: Muddled Ink Editorial, AJ (AJ's Author Club), Layna James, Paula

Sensitivity Reader: J.S. Jasper

Cover Artist: Treshell Fisher

*To socially anxious Black women.
You deserve to have a voice, to share your story, to experience
unconditional love, to be unapologetically you.*

CONTENT WARNINGS

Mention of parental neglect
Depiction of social anxiety and repetitive thoughts
Minor injury that includes brief description of blood
On-page sex scenes

CHAPTER ONE

LINCOLN

was twenty-five minutes late for my 'you-honestly-might-be-going-on-academic-probation' meeting. If I did deserve a but (which I'm well aware I didn't), it would look like this: But it was Thursday. And Thursdays were time sinkholes for me.

One moment, I was bidding in an online auction, going toe to toe with strangers for first edition copies of obscure mystery paperbacks. Next, I was at an estate sale, talking to a couple who (almost) convinced me to buy a couch the size of Texas.

Now, I sat down in my academic advisor's office, overanalyzing a textured painting of the midnight sky.

"Who's the artist?" I picked at the flaky varnish finish on my chair's armrest. Now that the conversation I should have had weeks ago was here, I scrambled to think of more excuses for delay.

Jonah, my frowning advisor, shrugged. It took him a second to settle in his squeaky desk chair. He buttoned his cleanly pressed suit jacket. Summer heat and a crappy AC system didn't dare threaten his commitment to professionalism. "It came with the office."

"Name of the piece?" Whenever I didn't grasp at straws, I felt like I was wasting resources.

Jonah studied me over the silver metal rims of his glasses, mouth in a thin line as he repeated, "It came with the office."

"Ah." My shoulders sagged at his refusal to humor me even a little. "Nothing a little research can't fix."

The oil-painted stars reminded me of my roommate's best friend, Celeste Able. There were stars in the corners of her eyes when I first met her. Small, hand-drawn stars. Barely noticeable, barely there. But once I saw them, I couldn't stop marveling.

Those stars were delicate work, worthy of close examination but almost hidden. Who did something that special but attempted to hide it?

It was safe to say Celeste was an artist. I've always gravitated towards artists. Their attention to detail was enviable. I've tried to hone that kind of dedication to craft with no luck. It was difficult for me to commit to things. Not in a destructive way, but in an 'I'm ready to get this done and move on to the next thing' way.

The mindset served me well as a hockey goalie. Up until recently, I didn't think I needed to change. Now? I suspected my life would improve drastically if I took cues from an artist.

"Lincoln." Jonah's firm voice was a hook, hindering me from swimming deeper into my thoughts of Celeste. "How about we pretend you're at the rink? This office is your goal."

I straightened. "Sure. I love a good visualization."

"I figured. And since that's the case, I'd appreciate it if you'd give this conversation as much patience as you'd give a game."

There went the knots in my stomach. "Right. What I'd give a game…"

Hockey was my safe harbor, the only place that accepted my impatience. Rewarded it. After last season's forfeit, I wondered whether I should address said impatience.

Since last season's premature ending, I've done some deep, reflective thinking. I had a lot of time on my hands while not playing hockey and all. After finding out the Hawks were out of the playoffs, I realized I might not walk across the stage at graduation.

"Victory Lap" was what Jonah called it.

"Sounds fun," I had joked because, well, it did. Heaven knew I wasn't in store for victory on the ice anytime soon. I might as well take one somewhere else.

"Not in this case," Jonah had promised with a frown. My advisor wasn't much of a smiler. His unbothered brow made me antsy.

Jonah looked like he could be my brother if my folks liked kids enough to have more than one. Our brown skin was nearly the same medium shade. Our hair, equally curly, buzzed at the sides and left to grow longer on top. He was at least a decade older than me and possessed the soulless stare of a man unfulfilled.

As much as I liked him, I feared him. His advisor gig didn't appear that soul-crushing. But he knew something I didn't. Sitting across from him felt like looking into a bleak future.

"You plan on going pro?" Jonah asked.

"In hockey?"

He released a sigh. "Yes, Lincoln. In hockey. Do you plan on playing in the NHL?"

I chuckled and adjusted in my seat. The cold wood was far too hard and slippery to be a place where one made life-changing decisions. "Only a few of us are drafted out of the NCAA. Lucky few. Since I didn't get a deal my senior year of high school, my odds are slim. So, I don't plan on anything because it's been out of my hands since I got to Mendell. I could try being a free agent, though."

"Okay." He nodded and typed something. "And if that doesn't work?"

I shrugged, my gaze straying to the photos on his desk. Jonah was a cat dad. "I'll figure something out. Hey, you know, I heard cat people are especially empathetic because of their constant exposure to rejection. What's your take?"

His jaw ticked. "Irrelevant. Let's visualize life after college. After hockey."

Jonah tipped the cat photo over with a slight nudge of his pen when he realized I was still staring. "What does that look like?"

I took a deep breath and closed my eyes for a second, trying to put in some real effort. But as soon as my imaginary world came into focus, I was face-to-face with a blank canvas. The world around me hollowed out as everyone moved on, while I stood in place.

Breathing became a feat. I could barely hear my thoughts over my pounding heart. My eyes shot open. Jonah's frown deepened at my jerk back into the present.

I cleared my throat and readjusted my collar. "Maybe I'll move back home for a bit."

I needed to pace. Jonah didn't like when I did that, so I remained glued to my seat. "Maybe work for my grandma."

"She owns a chocolate store, right?" Jonah scrolled through his notes as he recalled the tidbit. "That sounds interesting."

I nodded, trying to swallow and not look as lightheaded as I felt. "I wish it were more Wonka and less Hershey, though. There's no whimsy. She sells your typical bars. I'm trying to convince her to branch out. Rebrand."

"Okay, that's the makings of a plan. Are you interested in the business side of things? Perhaps we could incorporate a business course? Intro to finance, too. Maybe graphic design for rebranding ideas?"

"Business is not a long-term interest. I have a more casual investment in the rebrand," I said. "I want to make something that'll impress my grandma, then move on."

"We need to add courses that spark long-term interest. You're seriously behind on your credits. And your GPA isn't where it needs to be."

"I'm working on that. All that. It'll be fine." Grades had never been my strong suit. Sitting still for hours and listening to a lecture was mind-numbing. There was little room for tangents or rabbit holes. My learning style was based solely on tangents and rabbit holes.

Jonah steepled his fingers and pressed them to his chin. "You've been saying that for three semesters. Lincoln, you do know you're one failed course away from being on academic probation in the fall, right? And with the added attention on the hockey team, the school can't continue to overlook 'fine' grades. They want you to represent what Mendell could be. Or they'll use you as an example of what they won't tolerate."

"Better late than never, I suppose," I said under my breath.

"All lenience and goodwill have been burned through. You understand how serious this is? How you decide to show up could set the tone for the rest of your life. The foundation you lay here will be the one you have to stand on for years to come."

I swore my shirt collar had shrunk since I sat down and developed some self-heating capabilities. I tugged on the fabric, trying to experience some of that crappy AC. "Yes, I understand."

I took this seriously. I just didn't like to think about it often. There wasn't much I could do about past grades. Grades in the future, well, that'd be a different story. I was ready and… my phone buzzed. Someone outbid me for the rare paperbacks. It was now up to two hundred dollars. Damn it.

"Lincoln," Jonah said firmly.

"Committed," I finished out loud, stuffing my phone back into my pocket. "I'm committed."

"I sure hope so." Jonah leaned back in his chair. He scrubbed his hands on his face as he tried to figure out how to save me. My favorite thing about Jonah was his genuine care for his students. He hated his job, but the thought of failing students probably kept him up at night.

"I got this." I leaned forward to pick up his cat photo and turned it to him in hopes it would remind him there was something happier and more peaceful out there than dealing with my ass. "I won't bring your counseling into question. Trust me."

He blew out a calmer breath, the wrinkles in his forehead fading. "Weirdly enough, I do trust you're going to come back from this. I've seen students recover from worse. And you have a good support system."

"The best." I leaned back in my chair. "I'm recommitted to not doing a victory lap…because that's a bad thing, correct?"

"It is," he affirmed with a hint of an amused smile on the horizon.

"So strange," I mused under my breath.

"Like we agreed, you're going to use this summer semester as time to catch up." He reached for his mouse, refocused on his task. "We'll give you a nine-credit course load. Think you can handle that?"

"It'll be cake," I promised.

My issue had never been the work. It'd been the motivation to do the work, finding the drive to finish a degree I wasn't going to use. I didn't have a natural inclination to focus on the future. Why would I when the present was far more entertaining?

But the visualization of the empty canvas lingered on the edges of my mind. The taste of anxiety was so new; my system didn't understand how to digest it. If I didn't want to be left behind by my friends and didn't want to contend with these nerves constantly, I'd have to figure out how to hunker down.

"I know you're not stressed about post-grad," Jonah said. "And in some cases, that could be a good thing. But you should make concrete plans. There's a whole life after college. If hockey is what you want, you need to bring your GPA up to be eligible to continue playing in your senior year. You could potentially transition into an assistant coaching position. If you want to do something in Criminal Justice—"

"I enjoyed the courses," I said. "But I'm not interested in the career. Unless it was fictional."

I had chosen my major because it was the most exciting option. It combined my love for questions and my itch to find answers.

"I don't know what that means," Jonah said.

"Like, fiction. Novels, games, movies."

"You want to write about crime?"

"No, not professionally. I just like mysteries. So, if I could be inside a, oh, I don't know, Agatha Christie novel professionally, I would."

Jonah stared at me, silent for a second, and then laughed. I'd never seen him so light and unbothered. "I don't know what to do with that."

"Neither do I." I smiled, but something twisted in my stomach. I flexed my fingers, attributing the discomfort to skipping lunch for this meeting.

"Well, since we're in the same boat, we'll work little by little together." Jonah turned his screen so I could see the classes available for enrollment. "Let's start by picking some electives. Whatever interests you."

The class titles blurred together like some nonsensical child's drawing. I blinked, trying to refocus. The gap between wanting to be better and the patience to do so widened with every breath I took. I bit down on my inner cheek, willing myself to see through the fog. To work a little harder on this future planning and foundation-building.

"So?" Jonah's brows pulled downward, confused by my sluggish response.

My jaw tightened. The titles never came into focus. I couldn't stare at them forever and waste Jonah's afternoon any more than I already had.

I pointed out some random lines that included a few 3000-level courses. None of them would disrupt my early mornings or my afternoon workouts.

Jonah rubbed the back of his neck. "You sure?"

"Of course." I nodded without hesitation. The longer this dragged on, the more I felt utterly useless. "They'll meet my elective requirements, right?"

"They will," he confirmed as he turned the screen back to him.

"Then, let's do it." I drummed my hands on the armrest, ready to get back to my bidding war. I hoped another fifty bucks would declare me the winner. Now that was satisfaction. That was a victory. "Sign me up."

"You barely looked at the descriptions."

"That's the fun of it. Isn't the point of an elective to broaden horizons? Can't do that if I'm researching what the class will be like."

"It's not research; it's basic information—you know what, never mind. Maybe you're right."

"Going in blind is my preferred method for most things."

Jonah sighed but nodded. "Alright, Lincoln. We'll try this your way. But at the slightest sign of struggle, ask for help. Deciding things at the drop of a hat will only get you so far."

"I hear you." I gave the screen a final look. "I need to choose one more, right?"

He shook his head. "The hockey program strongly encourages all players to enroll in our Community Development course. Honestly, it's an unspoken requirement."

I frowned. I rarely (if ever) appreciated being forced into

doing something. "They think we'll feel less likely to take part in a gambling ring if we volunteer on the weekends?"

Jonah shrugged. "It's worth a shot. I recommended therapy, but the committee wanted something group-focused."

"And public enough to take photos of," I filled in the gap. I especially hated doing something to further someone else's agenda.

"Group-focused," he repeated, though the knowing look he offered confirmed my suspicions. "The course should be easy. Just do your best to find a project that gives back to the community, meet with your professor regularly for updates, and the credits are yours. After that, you'll only have two semesters to go. Then, you're free."

"Sounds like a plan," I agreed, in a voice confident enough to mask my doubts.

"You've got this. Keep focusing and you'll walk across the stage with the rest of your friends next year."

A simple smile and nod were enough to convince him that I believed in myself, too.

CHAPTER TWO
CELESTE

There was nothing like being stuck on the side of the highway, with cars blurring past you at eighty miles an hour, to make you come to a decision.

"I think I'm going to stop having social anxiety," I shouted as a semi-truck that failed to switch lanes barreled by.

Naomi's black braids whipped at her cheeks. Her brown skin beaded with sweat from the evening heat. She crouched at the front of my car, inspecting the tire that had decided to delay our journey home. "Come again? Couldn't hear you over the roar of potential death."

I waited for a break in traffic before I rolled over the spare tire. It had taken some elbow grease and a YouTube tutorial refresher, but we managed to get the car jacked up.

"Social anxiety disorder," I said, now by her side. "I'm over it."

She laughed and held out her hand for the wrench tucked in the waistband of my skirt. "Took you long enough."

"I know." I rolled my eyes. "Been dragging my feet for years. But you know how we are."

"Obsessed with one another." Naomi finished removing the lug nuts I'd loosened.

"Enthralled. It's toxic." I got into position to help her remove the tire. Dirt and grime from the rubber stamped our fingers. Between the summer sun and the dry air, we were huffing and puffing, trying to get the spare into place.

"What made you finally come to terms with this long-overdue breakup?" Naomi made a face as we struggled to align the tire's holes with the wheel's bolts.

I took a deep breath, readying myself before ripping off the band-aid. "My parents withdrew their financial support for school."

Her hands fell from the tire, and I moved to the center to keep it in place.

"*What*?" she asked, louder due more to frustration's sake than highway traffic interference. "When?"

"When they realized they weren't getting a refund for the classes I dropped last semester. I missed the add/drop period." I was usually better about that.

I was also better about curating my classes, so nothing stood in the way of completion. Unfortunately, ProfessorsScores.com failed me. Dozens of students there assured me the professors for my English and Art History courses didn't require presentations. And if they did, I could convince them to let me write a ten-page paper instead.

Maybe the professors had new requirements. Maybe they were tired of reading ten-page papers. Maybe they didn't like my timid email request. Whatever it was, they hadn't budged. I tried to stick it out in the first few classes. Because perhaps there was a chance I could conquer almost twenty years of crippling anxiety in the span of a week.

It turns out, I made things worse. Now, I had an aversion to the sidewalks leading from the English building to the nearest working restroom. I also scared a group of touring high school seniors with my panicked throwing up, but I couldn't dwell on the nitty-gritty details...not when they made my stomach churn with aftershocks.

"So, what does this mean?" Naomi searched my face, confused at my nonchalance. What I hadn't shared was that I cried for weeks about the situation. My best friend had enough on her plate—no need to add my deteriorating college experience to the combo.

"It means," I said, grunting as I finished aligning the tire. It was my turn to hold out my hand in request for the wrench. "I don't have enough money for the rest of my courses."

"Celeste." Seeing a frown on her face was foreign. "How long have you known this?"

"Since last semester."

Her eyes widened. "You've kept this a secret that long?"

"It wasn't a secret." I almost pulled my bicep trying to tighten the first nut. Naomi noticed the struggle and leaned in again to help. She placed her hand over mine, and we tugged the wrench together.

"You could have asked for help," she said.

"With what? Coming up with thousands of dollars in the span of four months?"

"I have a head for numbers."

That she did, along with two part-time jobs, twelve-credit course load, and a whole life I needed her to enjoy.

Naomi was the kind of friend who'd douse you first if you were both on fire. And then, she'd insist her third-degree burns were of no concern until you were salved up. It took true investigative work to learn she was homeless after the death of her mother. And hours of convincing her to come live with my family and me while she got back on her feet.

"And I have a head for obsessing over solutions," I said.

"So, you've been ruminating. And how does that set you on the path of this grand anxiety breakup?"

When I didn't answer, she sighed. The grease on her fingers transferred to her jaw as she tried to flip her braids back. I itched to hold my own hair off my neck, resisting because of the grime under my freshly painted pink nails. It was a terrible day to forgo my protective twists. My brown coils were a heavy blanket on my skin, shrinking by the second from soaking up my sweat.

"You want to know my solution or not?" We were on the final nut. I waved her hand away so I could finish tightening it myself.

"Fine." Naomi huffed and gave up crouching to sit on the burning concrete. She winced in discomfort but toughed it out because if she felt anything like me, her knees were killing her. Her legs were far longer than mine, so she had to scoot back to extend fully.

"I'm going to stop having social anxiety," I said.

"Ha ha." She wiped her hands on her jeans. "Be for real now."

"That's just step one."

She raised a brow, catching on to the seriousness wrapped in my absurdity. "Step two?"

"Ophelia Lawrence is coming back to Tinsel," I said.

Naomi's mouth parted in awe because, of course, she remembered my favorite songwriter. "How long have you known this?"

"Only a couple of days."

"And you've been sitting on this information? We were just doing the world's best rendition of *Every Single*. I was this close to hitting the high note in the chorus."

"So close," I agreed, laughing at the fact I'd gotten her deep enough into musicals that she knew every word to one of my all-time favorites.

"I would have liked to know one of the greatest songwriters of our generation was coming here."

"I'm sorry," I said, still laughing.

"It'll all be forgiven if you say we have tickets."

"Tickets?" I asked.

"Is she not here for a show?"

"No." I shook my head and tested all the nuts once more.

Everything felt tight enough. "She's here to announce a mentorship program at the playhouse. Aunt Kiera and my mentor, Nola, gave me a heads up and a chance to look at the application before it goes live next week."

My aunt was the manager of Tinsel's Playhouse. She'd gotten me into musicals as a kid, always convincing my parents to let me tag along with her and my cousin whenever a new show was in town. And Nola was my school-appointed mentor. She wasn't particularly one for inspiration, but she gave brilliant critiques. Her ear was unmatched at Mendell's School of Music.

"Ophelia's going to mentor you?" Naomi reached out to grab my arm, but thought otherwise when she remembered her hands were filthy. She settled for air-pinching my cheeks. "Oh my God, are you kidding?"

"Whoa, hold on. We do not know that yet." My stomach jumped, restless at the thought of how low the odds of me getting the mentorship were. "I have to apply. And for the application, I have to submit something incredible. Something that will impress a genius musician who's written Tony award-winning musicals and Grammy-winning soundtracks. She's the only Black woman to compose an entire film for a Disney princess. And she did all that before thirty-five."

"And you'll be writing for Broadway by twenty-three." Naomi shrugged. "I don't see the problem here."

I released a low, disbelieving laugh.

"I'm serious," she said. "Celeste, you're talented. Anytime I'm in the music building, someone's singing your praises. Pun intended."

I scoffed. "It's stiff competition. The winner gets the chance to join her in New York for a season. All expenses paid. I'd work under her for a few months. Learn far more than I could at Mendell. And then, maybe...I could clean up my musical. I want to apply for a grant. With Ophelia's recommendation and notes on revisions, I don't know... I could use it to finish school and get started on doing this writing stuff for real."

I chewed on my inner cheek. This all sounded ridiculous. A fool's dream. Did I really think I was going to come up with something brilliant enough to impress someone like Ophelia over the course of a summer? My skin burned at how silly the plan was now it existed outside my brain.

Naomi huffed in disapproval, already anticipating my train of thought. "Nope. You're doing it. Regardless of whether you need the money, you're applying. When are we starting?"

I shook my head. "I don't expect you to help."

"Girl, stop." She pushed herself off the ground and offered me a hand up. Cars continued to speed by as we plotted out how I would achieve all my hopes and dreams.

"So?" Naomi placed her hands on her hips. "When? And how?"

I took a breath and went for it. "I need to stand out. I can record demos and sing all the parts, but that's what most people will do."

I couldn't possibly know who all would apply. But I was familiar with some of my competition because they'd come from our school. The very school that didn't put much stock into funding the arts. Neglected art programs made hungry students. Hungry students were a force to be reckoned with—especially hungry musicians. There was a kind of fire in our belly that wouldn't be tamed, no matter how many "you should get a backup plan" comments were thrown our way.

"Everyone in my department will be incredible," I insisted. "I have to be better."

Naomi rubbed her hands together, dying for my solution. "What have you got for me?"

I swallowed, taking a beat before explaining, "I want to put on a musical. A real musical, with singers and musicians. On stage and everything."

My goal was out there in all its silly, impossible, hopeful glory. I gnawed at the bit, waiting for her response.

Naomi tried to press her lips together to keep from smiling too widely. "Are you talking about the musical you started writing in middle school?"

"It's gone through the ringer since you've heard it," I was quick to promise.

"It's brilliant," Naomi insisted.

I laughed, thankful my biggest fan was so sure. "You don't know that."

"Ophelia better watch her crown."

"So, you don't think the idea's too ridiculous? Too risky?" I chewed on my bottom lip.

"It's perfect, Celeste. The timing couldn't be any better. Ophelia here with a once-in-a-lifetime mentorship right when your folks stop financially supporting you? The stars have aligned. It'd be too risky *not* to do it."

I breathed a sigh. "I'll need a crew."

"Of course." Naomi nodded. "I... I'm drowning in work, but I can do weekends and nights."

I shook my head. "I'd love your help, if you have any extra time, but you're not giving up your sleep schedule and off days for me. I need to find other people. I have performers in mind; I just need people to work backstage."

Naomi hummed. I knew that look on her face. The setting sun made the air slightly less torturous. And the traffic had thinned, so standing on the side of the interstate was half as dangerous.

"What?" I asked.

"You have to really give it a chance," she said. "Because it's a match made in heaven."

"*What?*" I pressed.

"You need a right-hand. And I know a guy who needs a good community service project for a summer course. He'll handle the interactions with performers so you can focus on any final music tweaks."

My stomach turned. I knew where this was going. And, unfortunately, it did sound like a good idea.

"You really think he'd say yes?"

Naomi smiled and nodded. "There is no world in which Lincoln Hill would ever turn down a chance to work with you."

CHAPTER THREE

LINCOLN

"Wow, am I finally worthy?" Sam asked sarcastically when I picked up his call.

"You are lucky you," I said with a smile. I lifted my shoulder, holding the phone in place against my ear. "I'm a very busy guy, as you know."

My hands were full with two crates I'd bought from a yard sale. A family down the street had been offloading all their Halloween supplies. Never mind it being the wrong season; I would have our rental house decorated by the time the guys and Naomi returned. It was never too early to do a practice run for a Halloween-themed murder mystery dinner.

"You better stay busy and ensure you're at the rink tomorrow. Six AM sharp," Sam said.

"What's this for again?" I teased. The ladder Finn used to clean out the gutters rested on the side of the porch. I dumped the boxes at the bottom of the stairs and dragged the ladder to the side of the house, where I'd start what I'd call an art installation. Years ago, I learned labeling my projects as art helped my best friend, Henrik, accept things out of the ordinary.

Hen liked to color in the lines. The guy wouldn't go

outside without a tidy bedroom and an even tidier appearance. Christmas trees were for Christmas, pumpkin pie for Friendsgiving, and Halloween movies should never be spoken of before October 1st or after November 2nd. However, I had a vision that defied the concept of time. And Hen had an undeniable respect for art.

"Stop messing around, Lincoln," Sam said as if he could see the wheels turning in my head. "Don't screw this up."

"Didn't plan on it," I promised, swallowing a far more cutting response. I resolved to channel my irritability about his nagging into my project.

I couldn't fault Sam for anticipating a grievous lapse in judgment on my end. He had known me since high school, where I would often skip classes out of sheer boredom.

But hell, I'd appreciate fake trust. The low probability of my failure to rise to the occasion constantly haunted my thoughts. I didn't need it hammered into my skull from an external source when my internal team had things covered.

I opened the ladder and positioned it under the roof. The installation involved rigging the ghosts to fall when someone opened the side door. I'd have to figure out how to make a clue to fall along with the ghosts as well. A sign tied around the ghosts' necks might be the easier option. But a note swirling to the ground would be far more theatrical.

Sam exhaled. "I can hear you right now. You're doing something you're not supposed to do."

"Something I'm not supposed to do?" I chuckled. "Who are you? My father?"

"I hear cars going by. So, you're not inside studying or at the rink."

"Why would I be studying? The semester doesn't start for another week." I grunted as I repositioned the ladder. Its legs wobbled enough to be a red flag. But if it had held a guy as heavy as Finn, it should be stable enough to house my weight.

"That doesn't mean you can waste your time," Sam said. "And you're definitely not going to waste Anthony's time. I stuck my neck out for you. He's driving down early because I convinced him you were dedicated."

"Sam, relax." I put the phone on speaker, resting it on the porch railing before climbing. The ladder swayed but remained upright. "Once I meet him, I'll prove I'm worth the drive up. Give me some credit."

"Credit? Lincoln, you filed for bankruptcy years ago."

"That was the old me, young and naïve. Fallen prey to shark loans. And living in your shadow," I joked. "I've taken on the responsibility that was forced on me per your abandonment."

Sam's laugh was looser. He sounded more like himself.

My captain—ex-captain, now rival, eternal friend—was about three hundred miles away at a school with an angel as a mascot and one of the best hockey championship records in the country. He had transferred out of Mendell for a few reasons, one large, eclipsing one being his girlfriend, Aderyn: another captain, another leader, another person who got the short end of the stick.

Aderyn's ex-stepfather – our former athletic director–got a little too comfortable with his gambling habit and decided to take his betting to new heights. Accusations were made (and proven), investigations were opened (and closed), and people got hurt (and recovered as best they could).

And so, the landscape of hockey and all other sports programs at Mendell shifted. We couldn't undo the harm, but we could learn from it. We had a committee dedicated to athletic well-being. It was unfortunate it took a scandal to implement it, but still, it was a nice change.

Not finishing out the season during my junior year due to no fault of my own bred a special kind of disappointment. Four hockey seasons were equivalent to the blink of an eye. I'd learned as much in high school. So, cutting a season short and letting all that momentum go to waste left a hole. Not having control over a massive part of my life, a part I once felt the most stable in, stole a decent chunk of my inner peace.

Sam was also no stranger to a lack of inner peace due to the scandal. Though he was gone, he still felt a responsibility to help his team. Help me. I appreciated his willingness. It led him to connect me with a former NHL goalie, Anthony Baker, who agreed to train me during my senior year.

"Anthony's dedicated to what he does," Sam said. "I think you can learn a lot from him if you take this seriously."

"What did I say about the new me?" I'm at the top of the ladder now. Finn did an incredible job on our gutters. There was plenty of space to latch a few hooks up here, along with my trip wire.

"I mean it." I leaned forward, trying to get a better look at the shingles and a concerning dark splotch that could be mold.

"What's going on?" Sam asked. "I can't hear you that well anymore."

"I said—" I cut myself short when the rung beneath my foot gave out. I'd been so focused on the ladder's legs, I hadn't paid attention to the rungs. The wood had rotted thanks to the undoubted years it spent in the elements. The Ables (who happened to be Celeste's parents) were the couple we rented the house from and were notoriously bad at maintaining much of anything.

I reached for the edge of the roof, trying to hold myself in position. But the rung underneath my other foot cracked too. Before I could inhale, both completely broke in unison. A coordinated attack, if you ask me.

I landed on my knee first. The sharp pain traveled down my shin too fast for me to react. I bit down on my inner cheek, trying to focus on anything but the broken, bleeding skin.

"Lincoln?" Static from my pain muffled Sam's voice. "Are you still there?"

I inhaled, feeling a throbbing ache as I tried to brush it off and stand. When I attempted to push off the ground, I noticed a cut on my hand, the blood painting my palm and sliding down my forearm. Fuck, that burned.

"Don't move yet," a soft, concerned voice said.

I looked toward the end of the porch. Celeste Able stood a few feet away. Her hands were full of reusable bags that she dumped before coming to my side. I thought it was a dream because her gentle touch on the back of my palm made all my pain vanish for a moment.

The wind picked up her perfume; the soft, floral scent teased my nose and triggered memories of all the times I'd volunteered at the community center just to say 'hi.' Just to see her for a second.

Celeste kneeled, examining my hand and knee. I smiled at her despite the pain making my mouth taste of copper. She stared back, uninterested and unfazed, like she usually did, and damn it, my heart hammered. Wanting someone I couldn't have was the only pain worth focusing on.

"Lincoln?" Sam's voice called out again, disrupting whatever stare-off Celeste and I were having. "Are you good?"

"He fell," Celeste answered while I remained frozen in shock at her presence.

"What?" Sam asked. "Who's that? You're talking too quietly."

Celeste dipped her head, embarrassed. She cleared her throat and tried again. "Lincoln fell from a ladder."

"What are you doing here?" I finally recovered enough to speak again.

She didn't answer, and I realized how accusatory I sounded. But this was unprecedented. Celeste only came around when Naomi was home. Her visits were brief, and she avoided interacting with anyone outside of her best friend as much as possible.

"I was…" Celeste shook her head, unable to meet my gaze

as she tried to respond. With her head dipped down, I could see the stars I loved so much in the corners of her eyes. So precise. So beautiful.

Her brown skin glowed underneath the sun, the light turning her eyes a golden brown. Usually, her dark hair was in twists, but today she wore it loose, the coils reaching well past her shoulders.

Celeste had wide-set eyes, big and bold enough to make her nerves more noticeable. I'd learned in the past year there was not much that wouldn't set off her anxiety. And yet, I still resolved to try. I wanted to be someone she felt safe enough to talk to—or at least tolerate. I could live with tolerance. Maybe even thrive because this was Celeste—a wildly creative human being who loved her quiet corners and her art. I was attracted to the gentle flow of it all.

"I was… dropping off some things for Naomi," Celeste finally managed to get out. Her gaze stayed trained on the ground as she asked, "Can you stand?"

"What's that?" Sam's voice interrupted.

"I can stand," I assured before checking in with myself to see if it was accurate. As soon as I moved, an involuntary hiss escaped my lips. The nerves in my knee made a case for stillness. I clutched my thigh, trying to get my muscles to relax long enough for me to calm my breathing and reach a verdict.

"How bad is he?" Sam asked.

"He's having problems getting up." Celeste lifted her head high so her voice would carry. "And he's got a cut on his hand. There's a lot of blood."

She examined the cut, unblinking. Celeste was far calmer around the injury than I was.

"What the hell were you doing, Lincoln?" Sam asked.

"I'm fine." I winced at my hand. The bleeding had slowed, at least.

"Can you help him up on your own?" Sam asked.

"Um…" Celeste studied me. She was almost a foot shorter than I. There wasn't much muscle on her, either. "I could try."

"It's fine," I said. "Hang up on that nerd and call one of the guys for me."

"Aren't they in Richport?" Sam asked.

"Still?" I cursed.

"Finn said they were looking for places to eat dinner," Sam said.

"Wow, so it's official. Everyone's abandoned me." I tried to get up again and winced at the pain. Celeste tucked her hand under my elbow, steadying me as I attempted to stabilize. The piercing spark that ran along my skin had nothing to do with my injury.

"Stop moping," Sam said. "You're not alone. I'm guessing that's Celeste?"

"Y-yes." She swallowed, and we were close enough I could see her neck bob. Her fingers were cold against my skin, and her long nails scraped me lightly anytime she adjusted her grip. She held onto me like I was drying paper mâché.

"Are you sure you can get him up?" Sam's tone indicated he was in problem-solver mode.

"I can." Celeste's voice was a little louder this time. Her hands shook, but she sounded determined.

"Alright, good," Sam said. "If it's a lot of blood, depending on what he cut himself on, he might need to go to urgent care."

"It's fine," I insisted. "I'm fine."

"Is he really?" Sam asked.

Celeste froze, not expecting a request for assessment. She studied me, looking for any sign that I would go into some kind of shock due to my wounds. Going into shock due to her closeness was more likely. My chest about caved in when she twisted her mouth to the side, focusing on how to help me.

"I'll get him inside and get the first aid kit," she decided. "After we get everything cleaned up, we'll go from there."

"Perfect, so you're all good?" Sam asked, making sure everything was handled before he hung up. "You don't need me to call in reinforcements?"

Celeste nodded, a determined glint in her gaze as she stared at the phone like it was my friend in the flesh. "I got him."

CHAPTER FOUR
CELESTE

'd spent all morning pep-talking myself to get out of the house and drive over to the rental. Spent all afternoon doing a final rehearsal of what I wanted to say.

All that rehearsal amounted to nothing because quicksand may as well have laid the walk up to the front door. My lungs felt clogged with concrete, and my fingers wouldn't stop trembling.

I knew Naomi and the other guys were gone. And Lincoln would be on his own, and that made for a less intimidating exchange…allegedly.

Before I could knock on the front door, Lincoln's deep voice came from the side of the house. The buzzing in my ears cranked up a couple of notches because why not go for gold? I took a deep breath, breathing in a million more nerves.

"You got this," I whispered. "Just talk to him. With words. Normal words. And he'll respond. And you go back and forth like that until you understand each other."

With another less-than-helpful deep breath, I turned the corner. I saw the mistake before it unfolded. Lincoln trusted a ladder that was over ten years older than me. It had survived an absurd amount of rainstorms and blizzards.

"I don't know if—" I tried to get out before the wind stole half my words and the splitting of wood claimed the rest.

Gravity yanked Lincoln to Earth, uncaring and unbothered. The loud thud of his body hitting the porch, along with the appearance of bright blood, forced my anxiety aside. Worrying about impressions didn't matter much when faced with pain and danger. I went to Lincoln's side without hesitation, leaving shyness at the front door for me to pick up on the way out.

Now, his arm was over my shoulder, our sides pressed together as he avoided putting too much weight on his knee.

"I could wait here," Lincoln said when I struggled to find my balance. "Until you get the first aid kit."

I shook my head. "It's too hot."

Harsh sunlight bathed the porch. My lower back was already soaked.

I'd be lying if I said I hadn't considered leaving (after calling someone for him, of course). I could tell from how tense his jaw got with every slight move of his hand that Lincoln was in more pain than he let on. I didn't have anything to say that might help brighten the mood. No silly story to distract him from the pain. I wished to be witty. To be able to start a conversation of interest for once in my life.

"We'll go slow," I whispered because we were close enough to feel one another's breath. My arm wrapped around his waist, stabilizing us as we took a tentative step forward. I could feel his heartbeat, pounding from the adrenaline of the fall. I attributed the speed of my heart to talking to him for the first time in months.

Our text thread died sometime earlier this year when I couldn't figure out how to keep up with his energy. I left his last message without a response, and days turned into weeks and months. Lincoln's lack of messages had been a relief...at first.

Sometimes I went back to the thread and re-read every time we'd found an odd sort of rhythm. Conversations were a lot like music; there were ebbs and flows. An improv of sorts. Attempts at harmony. There were pockets where our duet had been interesting. Nothing extraordinary, but still nice. Almost sweet. And I'd given it all up because I'd overanalyzed every note I decided to play. The point of improv wasn't perfection, but I've always been slow to realize those sorts of things.

"Well, this is embarrassing," Lincoln said once we passed the house's threshold.

"Really?" I asked, surprised at the idea of Lincoln being capable of embarrassment. I'd seen this guy dance on a table at a house party, pretend to be animals for children's entertainment at the community center, and welcome the attention of hundreds at the hockey arena.

"Terribly." His deep, warm laugh filled every corner of this old house.

I got him to the couch and held onto his arm while he lowered himself. The transfer of weight could have been smoother. What started as a careful seat ended in a quick fall onto the cushions. I slipped in the process, heartbeat picking up a few more notches. My knee landed in the middle of Lincoln's legs. I caught myself, palm resting on the cushion behind his head. His hand reached out to steady me. Lincoln's fingers folded around my waist, unaware I had managed to find my balance again. Our gazes met for a second. While his eyes were calm, mine were wide with shock. I yanked out of his grip, cheeks burning and mind wishing for the safety of my bedroom.

"Sorry," I muttered, not sure if I was apologizing for the stumble or pulling away so fast. It wasn't like his grip was awful. In fact, weirdly, I enjoyed the warmth of it. It was a reminder he was just a person like me.

"You're good," he said, trying to meet my gaze without any luck.

I was miles away from "good." I'd been talking to him for less than ten minutes, and my body was already giving way to social exhaustion. How did people do this daily?

The most shameful part about my anxiety wasn't the racing heart, sweaty pits, or awkward responses. It was the reality that being this conscious of perception placed me in a glass cage of my own making. Being visibly anxious gave people my deepest secret (my desire and failure to be perfect) on a silver platter without me having to say a word. The disorder that evolved from my need for protection gave away the soft, most sensitive part of me to strangers.

"Is the first aid kit still in the kitchen??" I tugged at the hem of my shirt, looking for some relief from feeling shrink-wrapped in my own skin.

"We moved it to the upstairs bathroom." Lincoln winced as he tried to get into a comfortable position. "Underneath the sink."

I hurried to retrieve the kit. While in the bathroom, I caught a glimpse of my wide-eyed panic in the mirror. I took a second, closed my eyes, and tried a breathing exercise my therapist taught me.

"He's just a human," I whispered to myself. "Like you."

A kind, friendly human who probably thinks you're a strange, head-empty loser, the little monstrous version of me goaded. I tried the breathing exercise again, but the voice was too distracting. I was in an even worse state than before when I returned to the living room. My need to avoid perception had multiplied tenfold.

I sat on the couch in silence, leaving a cushion between us.

"Alright," Lincoln said when I rummaged through the supplies. "Alright, you got me. I'll tell you."

"Tell me?" I almost dropped the antiseptic and gauze when he interrupted the quiet.

"Since you're so interested in why I was on that ladder," he teased.

My cheeks burned because I was supposed to ask. That was what someone with passable social skills would have done, right? Ask a person why they fell. Start a conversation to fill the silence. The topic had been such low-hanging fruit; I didn't know how I missed it.

Ask why, I noted internally. I would add it to my "talking to people cheat sheet" in my journal as soon as I could. Most of the entries on the sheet were things I'd observed from hanging out with Naomi. She spoke to people as if it were as simple as watching the sunrise.

"Why were you on the ladder?" I poured the antiseptic onto the gauze. Lincoln offered me his hand without my having to ask for it. He didn't so much as wince when I pressed it to his skin. It was hard to swallow being this close to him, but I tried anyway. My loud gulp convinced me never to try again.

"Doing a test run for the entertainment for our Halloween party." Lincoln reached for some gauze, using one hand to pour some rubbing alcohol, and started cleaning his knee.

We worked quickly and managed to avoid making skin-to-skin contact again. It was a careful dance I committed to because I had enough physical contact after helping him inside. Touching people I didn't know was low on my list of social aversions, but it was still present nonetheless.

"Halloween?" I remembered the misshapen ghost at the base of the porch.

"Yeah, I won a coin toss to be in charge of it this year, thank god." He smiled, excitement lighting up his face. His hair was the longest it'd been since I met him. The dark curls stretched toward the ceiling. Lincoln's brown skin was a few shades lighter than mine and far less textured. What he lacked in acne, he made up for in birthmarks. Three created a triangle on one of his cheeks. An oval-shaped one peeked out of his collarbone when he turned his head. I knew these marks well. I studied them when he was busy talking in the large groups he always found himself in. There was no denying he was a cute guy. There was no denying that was part of the reason talking to him was so difficult.

"Did I cut my face, too?" Lincoln reached up to touch his cheek.

I hadn't realized my observing had turned into staring. "No...you...umm... what's the entertainment going to...be?"

My skin burned, but Lincoln didn't miss a second.

"An immersive murder mystery set in a haunted house."

I nodded and reached for a bandage. Lincoln loved hosting parties, especially ones involving the games he created. He liked puzzles and getting everyone around him involved in solving them. It was the one thing that made him a little less intimidating to me. His special interest reminded me of how intense I could get with musicals. How, if I weren't socially awkward, I too would host themed parties about my favorite things.

I wanted to ask him something, anything about the event. But the words didn't leave my mouth. I was overwhelmed by what questions to ask and the appropriate way to ask them.

"You should come," Lincoln said. "I don't think you got the chance to play last time."

I tried to smile. The last time I'd pushed myself to come to one of their house parties, I ended up overstimulated. I had a panic attack in my car afterward. It took me days to feel like myself again. I couldn't handle being around anyone, not even Naomi, for more than ten minutes. That was when the texts between Lincoln and me came to an official end. He'd checked in, and I'd left it unanswered.

"It's okay," I said, meaning it was okay that I didn't get to play, not that I didn't want to come. Lincoln assumed the latter.

"No worries." He smiled and pulled his hand away since I had finished bandaging him.

"I meant...I hadn't been ready the first...time."

"It's not everyone's cup of tea." Lincoln focused on patching up his leg.

My mouth remained open as I tried to come up with something to say. The anxiety that had made my stomach sour turned into frustration. If I couldn't correct a simple misunderstanding, how in the world did I expect to ask him to work with me? Or anyone to work with me, for that matter?

Say something, I willed myself. *Anything.*

At this point, I'd settle for a dry comment on the weather. My brain had other plans.

"Who's your favorite mystery author?" It was random but not too out of left field... I hoped.

"Too difficult to narrow down." Lincoln smiled, his bright energy returning. "Will you settle for my favorite one at the moment?"

"That works." I nodded; the weight in my chest loosened because I'd done something to push the conversation forward. It was a small, pinky-finger, minimal-effort push. But a push, nonetheless.

"Zoey Carter. If you happen to look her up, don't believe the reviews," he warned. "She's ahead of her time; I promise."

I raised a brow. "Why...uh...do you like her?"

"Her plots are a perfect blend of real and nonsensical," he said, moving his hands as he spoke. "Every time I finish her books, I'm more confused than when I started."

"And that's... a good thing?"

"The best. It makes me feel a part of it. She doesn't spell

everything out, and it's exciting trying to fill in the blanks. It's like I'm writing the story along with her, you know?"

I nodded, trying to wrap my head around it. I didn't know how I'd feel reading something that left me with more questions than answers. It sounded stressful. I already had enough internal anxiety to overcome. But something about the way Lincoln's energy skyrocketed while he talked about it was enough to sell me. I tucked the name in the back of my mind, vowing to read something from the author. And if I did, I'd have an in with him—something easy and sure to talk about.

"Do you...have a particular book of hers you'd recommend to a new reader?" I asked.

"Oh, for sure—" Lincoln stopped short when there was a loud knock at the back sliding door. We turned. A guy with long, curly brown hair and sunburned cheeks stood there with his phone pressed to the glass. I couldn't make out whatever was on the screen, but it was clear that he wanted Lincoln to see it.

"You can't ignore me all week." The glass muffled his stern tone. His posture more rigid than a telephone pole.

"This guy." Lincoln sighed, unfazed by his new guest's icy glare. "Sorry, excuse me for a second. I've gotta take care of this."

He got up, limping a bit as he went to open the door.

"Get in, hurry, hurry," Lincoln said with renewed vigor as he rushed the guy past the threshold.

He stepped inside, brow wrinkled with confusion and concern at Lincoln's sense of urgency. His dismay grew when Lincoln scanned the backyard before closing the door behind him.

"What's going on?" the guy asked. When he didn't get an immediate answer from Lincoln, he glanced at me for an explanation. I was as lost as he was; my nerves spiked now there were two people I had to try to figure out how to interact with.

Lincoln made a show of closing the blinds and curtains. He still favored his leg but did an impressive job of getting around. "I can't have the neighbors seeing you. They have a bad habit of wanting to introduce themselves when they see people come over."

The guy shook his head. "What are you going on about?"

"Since the Incident, they've obsessed over Mendell's hockey team," Lincoln explained in a stage whisper. "If they find out you play, they'll ask for your jersey number. They've memorized every player."

"Okay, and?"

"I kind of told them my name was Jack Whitfield."

I blinked, still not on the same page, but this seemed to mean something to the guy.

"Things could get a little dicey when they figured out I lied," Lincoln continued. "Can't have them complaining about lying college students to the HOA. They're big on neighborhood trust and whatnot. We've gotta keep this lease for another semester."

"Why would you tell them you're me? And why would they believe you? We look nothing alike."

It was true. Jack was a white guy with gauges in his ears and wore black from head-to-toe. He had an unapproachable demeanor I doubt Lincoln could pull off even if he wanted to.

"I said they memorized names and numbers. Not faces." Lincoln peeked through one of the blinds, ever dramatic. I pressed my lips together, trying not to smile because in small bursts, I could ignore my nerves and appreciate his amusing overreactions.

Jack's skin got redder. "Are you going to answer my question?"

"I don't like the idea of people like them having my real name." Lincoln pulled away from the blinds. "It doesn't sit well with me. They're up to something."

"You can't be serious," Jack said. "So, you're willing to give them *my* name and not a fake one?"

"They'd know it was fake." Lincoln scoffed like it was apparent. "Don't worry about it. I'm forty percent sure they're not planning to use your name in their next séance. And if they do, I'm forty-two percent sure they need to know what you look like to succeed in a hex."

"They're witches now?" Jack asked.

"No, unfortunately not. They're Westbrooke fans." Lincoln sighed. "If we miss the winning goal next season, or if you lose more teeth than usual, we'll know why."

"Are you fucking with me?" Jack asked.

"Time will tell. Anyway, glad to see you got up the walk okay." Lincoln patted his friend's (?) shoulder. "You're a little breathy, though. Off-season not treating you well? You should hit the gym with Hen, Finn, and me. It'll keep you competitive."

He shrugged Lincoln's hand off. "You're unbelievable."

I tried to think of a good excuse to leave. I felt like I'd interrupted something even though I was there first.

"It was just a suggestion," Lincoln said. "If you want to lift weights in your lonesome, I won't stop you."

I parted my lips, getting nothing but quiet air out.

"I didn't come here to get an invite to a workout session." Jack shoved his phone in Lincoln's face.

"I should probably…" I tried again. Lincoln noticed my attempt at an exit.

"Oh, no," he said. "Jack's just dropping by. Right, Jack? Thanks for the 'hello.' Bring food next time; that's always a good way to get on someone's good side."

Lincoln tried to herd him to the front door, but Jack matched his strength. He wasn't as tall as Lincoln, but he was a bit more built.

"Good side attempts are your job," Jack said. "Since I'm

getting burned alive on social media, thanks to you and your big mouth."

Jack shoved his phone in Lincoln's direction again, and this time, Lincoln took it.

"You told reporters you think I divided the team. Lincoln, *divided*?"

Lincoln frowned as he read whatever was on the screen.

"What else would you call it?" Lincoln's voice had lost any semblance of go-lucky.

My back straightened as I tried to get a better look at his face. I'd never heard Lincoln speak so low or seen his shoulders sag as if he harbored regret. I wasn't sure I liked Jack and how he barged in here, disrupting the atmosphere.

"I'd call it complicated," Jack said.

"Sorry, but I don't find consistent betrayal that complex," Lincoln said.

"Oh my god." Jack ran his fingers through his hair. "Are you—wait, are you bleeding? Why the hell are you bleeding so much?"

The bandage on Lincoln's hand had opened. I had done a poor job of securing it. I grabbed a fresh one and stood up to fix the problem.

"He fell...and he should probably get some rest." I didn't make eye contact with Jack. I couldn't. But I did try to make my voice harder. My tone, final. I didn't want to leave unless Jack did too. Heaven knew Lincoln didn't need someone standing up for him. And yet, I had the urge to do just that... in the only way I could. But of course, my small voice was like a tiny dog trying to protect its owner from a Rottweiler.

"What were you doing? Don't you have that mentorship thing tomorrow?" Jack asked.

"Don't worry about it; it's fine," Lincoln said to Jack, and to me, "Thanks, I've got it. Sorry about all this."

And there went my opening. My window of opportunity to pitch the volunteer position had closed the second Jack joined… okay, maybe I shouldn't blame it all on him. I'd been stuck in limbo long before he showed up.

"It's literally my job now to worry about it," Jack said.

When Lincoln's brow furrowed, Jack added, "The accountability initiative. You don't remember?"

"There have been so many initiatives over the last few months; it's been hard to keep track of them." Lincoln's sigh reminded me of my own when overwhelm threatened to nudge me off a cliffside.

"Well, for better or worse, I'm your partner." Jack closed his eyes for a moment, clearly still grappling with this fact. "Which means the least you could do is stop talking to reporters about me. We're supposed to be building team trust."

To his credit, Lincoln's lips pressed together with remorse. "He wasn't a reporter; he was a journalism student working on a paper. I was trying to help."

"He works for *the* paper, genius."

While they were busy biting one another's heads off, curiosity got the best of me. I unlocked my phone and pulled up the school's newspaper website. The sports headline read: *Believe in nothing, fall for everything: Mendell's hockey boys aren't so golden.*

I skimmed the rest. It was riddled with clichés, but overall, was a well-written piece. The author condemned the athletic department while also throwing the players under the bus. Most of the piece delved into how the school invested money in the hockey program instead of distributing the funds to other programs. I felt bad for agreeing with some of the opinions. But I did wish Mendell invested even a sixth of the money they put into hockey toward the music program. Our department was small, with limited practice space and resources. We shared music stands, an auditorium without AC, and seats that were peeling.

"Did they get you to sign up for that community outreach course?" Jack's question brought my attention back to them.

"Of course." Lincoln finished rewrapping his hand. "An uninspired attempt to make us look good."

"Have you picked your project?" Jack asked.

"Why? Do you plan on copying me?" Lincoln teased.

"Yeah, that's the whole point. How are we supposed to be accountable to each other if we're not together?"

The playhouse was a part of the community. And my aunt signed volunteer slips all the time. She could even write them an official letter. Lincoln, needing to do community outreach, made asking for his help that much easier. He wouldn't have to do something just for me, the lonely girl who left him on-read.

The puzzle pieces were coming together, and all I had to do was open my mouth.

"If…" I started, and they both looked at me, waiting. Before I knew what was happening, I ended it with a rushed, "I have to go."

"Okay, thank you for helping me back inside and with all this." Lincoln held up his hand. "Maybe we could—"

"Of course." I blinked every other second, holding back hot tears and heavy embarrassment. "See you around."

I cursed myself as I rushed out of the house, not even waiting to hear a goodbye. My nails dug into my palm as I sucked in air through my mouth. Pathetic. I was absolutely pathetic.

I knew asking was going to be hard, but after that failed attempt, it felt downright impossible. I didn't have enough time. If I didn't figure out how to speak to this guy soon, then I'd have to go back to the drawing board.

CHAPTER FIVE
CELESTE

"You ready to try again?" Naomi sat on my bedroom floor, cross-legged. She sorted through a pile of Gameboy cartridges my brothers had given me to pass on to her.

I lay on my bed, my legs stretched out over the headboard, and my gaze focused on the script in my notes app.

I'd written down everything I needed to say for the next time I spoke to Lincoln. It'd been a week since my initial failed attempt. Once Naomi heard about it, she decided we needed to come up with a game plan. We practiced a couple of hours each day for the entire week. She played the role of Lincoln, which allowed me to smooth out any kinks in my delivery. There seemed to be more issues popping up the longer we went on.

"Yeah, one second. I need to figure out a better transition from 'hi' to 'will you be my assistant director for two months, even though you can count on one hand the number of one-on-one conversations we've had alone.'"

Naomi nodded. "Valid. By the way, Finn's on his way to pick me up. I could get him to be Lincoln. It'll feel more realistic. Especially since you two can also count on one hand how many times you've spoken to one another alone."

I almost dropped my phone on my face. "I can't do this with Finn."

Naomi pulled her attention away from what she'd dubbed a retro gamer's dream. The bed dipped underneath her weight as she climbed on.

"He won't mind if you stumble on your words. He does the same thing all the time." She grabbed my phone, holding it out of reach when I stretched for it. "You don't need the script anymore. You have it memorized from top to bottom."

"You know what?" I sat up, lightheaded, my ears buzzing from the abrupt movement. "I think that's enough practice for today."

"Celeste," Naomi said firmly. "You only have a few more days left to confirm what you're going to do. Have you even asked your cousin about the casting?"

"I have." I perked up, proud to have done something right. "He's in and he's working on convincing his skating partner to play the lead. Which is perfect because that means they'll already have chemistry."

"Great." Naomi nodded. "Now, tell me, do you plan on doing all the prep, set design, and rehearsals by yourself?"

I made a face. "No."

Her phone buzzed as if the universe heard a predetermined cue. Naomi raised a brow, seeking permission. She wouldn't force me, kicking and screaming.

"He can come up," I said. "But ask him first, please. I don't want him to feel like he has no choice."

"He'll be more than happy to help." Naomi smiled, gave me back my phone, and then hurried off to let her boyfriend in.

It didn't take long for her to bring him up. Finn was a solid guy. Literally and metaphorically. He was large and quiet, with dark, curly hair and pale skin that burned a deep, tomato-red whenever Naomi flirted with him. His skin was that shade now, but there was no amusement in his eyes. Naomi once told me she thought he was shy. Shyness made Finn appear hard and mysterious. His quiet drew people closer, a lighthouse of sorts.

My shyness made people think I was rude. Uppity. It repelled people, warning them of something strange within. I wondered if it was his maleness, whiteness, athleticism, or a mix of all three that made his quietness more accepted.

I was in elementary school when I learned being quiet wouldn't always work in my favor. At home, silence helped me avoid the verbal sparring my brothers and parents found joy in. Disagreements, even the teasing kind, left me anxious and confused. My nervous system regulated when I didn't have to share opinions and thoughts that would ultimately be picked apart until there was nothing left but scraps.

But in a bright, colorful classroom, my teachers found silence a damning fault. One in which they responded with threats of lower grades (to this day, the mere mention of the phrase "participation score" sent my stomach turning) and limited opportunities. Once upon a time, I had worked my way up to being in the highest-level reading class. I reveled in the status symbol and shiny 'I am a reader' pin.

That all came crashing down when I got demoted to the lowest level. My reading teacher could never convince me to do the dreaded, throat-tightening, vomit-inducing, hand-raise. I preferred to redo all the assignments I finished that year instead of answering a question out loud.

"Hey," Finn greeted. His expression was stoic. Without Naomi's footnotes, I would insist he didn't like me. And maybe even hated me on principle.

"Hi." To "meet" his gaze, I used my trick of staring at a person's forehead to feign eye contact. Baby steps toward participation marks. Baby steps.

"Alright, remember," Naomi said as she sat on the edge of my bed. "You're Lincoln. Be Lincoln."

Finn frowned. "How does one be Lincoln?"

"Loose, bold, unfinished," she said. "An ellipsis."

"What does that mean?" I wondered while Finn simultaneously said, "I feel like I'm going to need a little more time to adjust, considering I'm clearly a question mark."

Something passed between them, and I felt like an intruder in my own room.

Couples were cute when they were coupling in their own space—conceptual, theoretical couples. Couples too far away to remind you you were probably going to end up in a house by the sea alone…though honestly, that didn't sound too bad. I couldn't imagine myself entangled with someone long enough to want to share a house by the sea with them. So, knowing deep down that I couldn't envision being someone's "other half," witnessing romantic love firmly placed it on my list of awkward social experiences I preferred to avoid.

"You're right." Naomi got up from the bed. "A question mark through and through. New plan."

"New plan?" I clasped my hands together, massaging out the nerves running through my veins. I was still struggling to accept the old one.

Finn's shoulders relaxed. "New plan."

"We're Lincoln." Naomi hurried past me to stand behind Finn. He tried to turn around to get a good look at her, but she held onto his shoulders, keeping him steady and facing me.

"I feel so silly," I mourned when I realized I needed two people to help me feel comfortable talking to one guy who probably hadn't given me a passing thought since we last spoke.

"Don't feel silly," Naomi said. "This isn't silly. This is you trying to get better. Now, take a deep breath and be yourself."

I took the breath. Being me was the more challenging exercise.

"Hi… Lincoln." I winced.

"Hi… Celeste," Finn said in a tone that gave my stiffness a run for its money. Oh, God, we sounded like cardboard cutouts trying to mimic real humans.

Naomi whispered something, and Finn added, "I'm glad we're finally getting a chance to talk."

"So am I?" My shaky voice exposed my full-body tremors.

"Surety," Naomi reminded me.

I cleared my throat and repeated ten percent steadier, "So am I."

"What's…uh, going on?" Finn shook his head, red burning at his own unsteadiness.

Knowing that I wasn't fumbling alone made it easier to smile a little at him. "I'm working on this project… It's for a mentorship program. Or rather, an application for a mentorship program… It's a musical. Or rather, it will be…"

"Wait, sorry." He frowned, his voice a little less disapproving and a little more curious. "You wrote a musical?"

This was Finn speaking. The impressed nature of his reaction was genuine.

I rocked back and forth on my heels, smiling a bit wider. "I did."

"What's it about?"

My heart was in my throat as I realized I was going to have to share this with him. With Lincoln. With dozens of other people, if I planned to go through with this. If I wanted to succeed, I'd have to be seen and heard. It wouldn't all fall on the music, even if I thought it should speak for itself.

"It's not anything new or—"

"I'm going to stop you right there." Naomi peeked her head out from behind Finn. "Don't diminish your work before you've given him a chance to enjoy it. Let him decide if it's good for himself."

"I was managing expectations," I said.

"Not your job. You're busy enough as is." She disappeared behind her boyfriend once more.

Finn's gaze softened, and he almost offered me a smile. "Managing expectations feels like a decent way to protect your ego; I get it. But she's right. Let Lincoln and others decide if they enjoy it."

I nodded, adding their advice to the laundry list of things I needed to internalize. It was exhausting trying to keep track of everything. And even more so to attempt implementation, but I willed myself forward.

"It doesn't have to be something new," Finn added. "People love things that remind them of what they love."

"It's a nod to *The Nutcracker*," I said.

"That's a ballet? Right?" he asked. "What's it about?"

I brushed off my surprise, remembering that not everyone was familiar with theatre. Especially not a guy who was recovering from a brain injury.

"It's about a girl, a Nutcracker who comes to life, and their adventures in a fairytale world."

"Sounds whimsical," Finn said. "Lincoln loves whimsical."

"I hope so."

"Even if he didn't, he would look forward to spending time with you," he assured.

My cheeks burned. Even faking eye contact became too much.

"I'm sure the same goes for you," Finn said.

I shrugged. "I don't know him well enough to say…"

I dared to look up in time to catch Finn's brow wrinkle. "But you want to? Know him that is."

Did I? Of course. But not in the way Finn may be alluding to. Not in the way Naomi insisted Lincoln wanted to get to know me.

I'd never felt the pull to know anyone in that way. And I

hadn't thought too much about how different my sentiment was until last year, when Naomi found Finn. She would fantasize about spending time with him and all the touchy-feely, sexual stuff that came with it. I didn't mind talking about love or sex. I never minded watching movies depicting whirlwind romances and happily-ever-afters. In fact, sometimes it fascinated me how people fell into love or lust so easily. Because I never looked at someone and imagined cuddling with them. Fantasizing about being in bed with someone was anything but thrilling. Why would I want to kiss someone I'd just met? Let alone sleep with them. It all seemed impractical and uninteresting. Like a task, a checklist of things to get through so the other person felt seen and comfortable. Kiss here. Entwine fingers there. Stare into their eyes like nothing else mattered when, in fact, there are a million other things that mattered as much.

My stomach churned; my heart rate was steady in its uptick. I didn't know how to explain all that in a succinct way that was easy to understand. I've never had to because it never felt imperative for others to understand.

Naomi whispered something in Finn's ear. She sensed my tension and his confusion becoming something unsettling for both of us.

"I'm not giving Lincoln, apparently," Finn said apologetically.

"It's okay." I tried to smile. "I'm not giving…"

Anything good. Anything hopeful. My hesitation about Lincoln would be a red flag for any friend, especially if said friend believed Lincoln was still interested in me, which I could and would refute if given the opportunity. I'd burned that bridge long ago. Between the anxiety and my standoffish nature, I was shocked most days even Naomi chose to stick around.

The most interesting thing about me was my music. And even that only went so far.

"But you got the conversation flowing for a little while there," Naomi jumped in as she moved from behind Finn. "It sounded natural. You two were learning about each other without needing a prompt from someone else."

"We should try again," Finn said. "I'll do better now I know what you all are looking for."

"No, I think…" I shook my head. "I think this has been more than helpful."

Naomi's smile vanished. "You sure? We haven't even gotten to the part where you tell him about benchmarks. That's your favorite part!"

I tried to smile as I picked at my nail beds behind my back. "Best not to overprepare. It'll make the whole thing sound too stiff, right?"

Naomi tilted her head side to side before her reluctant, "Right."

"One more piece of advice?" Finn asked. "It's something that helps me."

"Sure," I said, shocked he'd even offer any.

"When you talk to Lincoln, you should focus on your purpose," Finn said. "When I had to get used to being around people again post-accident, I struggled a lot with getting what I thought and felt out. Especially when it came to talking to Naomi, so I started practicing small talk with anyone I could. While I practiced, I thought of the big picture: connecting with Naomi. That purpose was a north star. Whenever I felt overwhelmed about saying the right thing, I'd think about her and how my practice was helping me connect with her. The goal stabilized me."

"That's…really helpful. Thank you." I'm shocked by how much he shared. It's the longest I've heard Finn speak. He massaged Naomi's hand, glancing at her throughout as though he was still thinking of ways to get closer to her and still seeing her as his north star.

"When you're ready to talk to Lincoln, don't think about

planning every word. Think about what you're trying to share. Where do you want to be when the conversation is over?"

It was easy to smile at Finn when he sounded so sure I would succeed. "Thank you."

"Did it help? Really?" He looked hopeful.

"A lot," I promised.

"I'm glad." He seemed pleased as a soft sigh fell from his lips. "Could I ask you a favor?"

Naomi looked as surprised as I felt. I nodded for him to go on.

"Whatever happens, whenever you get comfortable with him," Finn said. "Be honest with Lincoln about how you feel about him. He can handle it."

It wasn't a warning, but it wasn't something he wanted me to take lightly either. My skin was so hot it probably burned at the touch. If there was one thing I never wanted to do in this lifetime, it was to take advantage of someone's feelings toward me.

"I will," I promised. "Don't worry, I will."

CHAPTER SIX
CELESTE

Once Finn and Naomi left, Finn's advice about purpose was immediately written onto the Post-it taped to the first page of my journal. I spent a moment writing, hoping it would help me get closer to figuring out my purpose in conversing with Lincoln.

The cloth-bound journal that housed all my boring secrets had entries dating back to middle school. I hadn't taken writing in it seriously until university. Classes made me realize my problems would be the death of me if I didn't filter them out somehow.

My therapist suggested brain dumping. *Typical,* was the first thought I had about the assignment. Therapists always suggested writing things down. I never liked spending extra time in my head. I lived, ate, and slept within the four walls of my mind.

Vital, was the tune I now sang after a year of scribbling down every inconvenience, no matter how minor. Stubbed toes led to musings on life feeling like a sharp edge just waiting for me to trip up. Rainy afternoons breed terrible poetry on nostalgia.

The journal became a collection of my most cringe-worthy

thoughts and fears. It was my prized possession. My reason for sanity.

Finn's suggestion echoed in my head as I tried to work through my lingering fears about connecting. My knuckles strained from how tightly I held the pen. I tried to manage the frustration and impatience coloring every word I wrote down.

Lincoln has this energy I'll never be able to match. Where does his ability to just share what he feels and thinks out loud, no matter how mundane, come from? I want to learn how to obtain even a fraction of that kind of bravery.

And there it was: a purpose. A north star to guide me when it came to talking to Lincoln. I wanted to learn from him.

I pulled out my phone, looking for the note I'd taken down about his favorite author. If I hurried, I could make it to the bookstore downtown before it closed. A quick search showed they had multiple copies on their shelves. I could order online, but that'd take days, and another test of my social skills wouldn't kill me. Besides, bookstores were a low-tier anxiety threat.

I did my version of a light makeup routine: BB cream, brows, pink blush, a sharp wing, and glossy lips. I stamped on a star at the tip of my liner because it made me feel like a magical girl, and *Sailor Moon* had been my safe place since kindergarten.

"You headed out?" Eli, my older brother, asked as soon as he saw me clear the stairs. His starter locs stretched toward the shaggy carpet as he balanced on his hands. Our eldest brother, Luka, held up his phone with a timer on the screen.

This was what a physical therapist and a dentist did on their vacation.

"I have to pick a book up downtown." I grabbed my keys off the counter.

The TV was on low in the background, playing an old summer movie about neighborhood kids and their undying love of baseball. Our living room looked trapped in the time of the film with our floral-patterned couches, wood-paneled walls, and one too many table lamps equipped with tassels.

"Can I come with?" Eli asked, while Luka said, "I'm making dinner; should I set you a plate?"

"No," I answered Eli, and to Luka, "Yes, please."

"Why not?" Eli asked. Despite our two-year age gap, he was the tagalong. It was nearly impossible to be a tagalong to someone who barely left the house, but Eli loved defying the odds. It started as his way of looking out for me. He noticed how harmful my anxiety had gotten before anyone else in our family had. Much like him, I could read between the lines and understood he hid his protective worry inside the illusion of being an annoying brother who didn't mind his own business.

"Because I'm working on self-improvement," I told him as I rummaged through my tote bag, confirming all my going-out essentials were there. "And I won't be able to improve if you're there doing all the difficult stuff for me."

Eli moved out of the house years ago, but every time he came back, he resumed his role. I only recently started pushing back when I realized without my brothers and Naomi around, there was an endless list of things I couldn't do.

"I promise I won't do the difficult stuff," Eli said.

I raised an eyebrow. "Really?"

"Fine." He sighed. "I promise I won't do *all* the difficult stuff. Come on, Celeste. Work with me."

I stood my ground. "Hard pass."

Luka laughed, rubbing his hand across his thick, prematurely salt-and-pepper beard. "Good for you, Cel. Before you go, how do you feel about chicken tonight? Grilled."

"Mom hates chicken," I reminded him.

"Well, Mom isn't joining, so…" Luka said.

"Neither is the old man. We're free to get a little wild," Eli teased, still balancing and talking, voice steady as ever. It was impressive. "Might throw in some mashed potatoes and gravy. Now there's a real party."

I scoffed. "What was it this time?"

"A house in Richport?" Eli asked, looking at Luka for confirmation.

"Nah, I think it was that apartment in Lake City," Luka corrected. "Ground floor. Flooding."

My parents often ran around town during the weekend to manage what we all knew was a burning legacy. Dad inherited ten real estate properties from his father. His only experience with buildings was being a construction worker on a crew that built beautiful houses for cheap.

Cue Grandpa. A man who hated all three of his children (and six grandchildren) without prejudice. Dad was the least hated, so in the final will, he inherited six houses, three commercial properties, and an old community center.

"Think they'll come to their senses?" I wondered out loud.

Luka snorted. "You know those two are too prideful to call it quits. They'll drown in their narcissism together. I'll be counting the days until they do. Good fucking riddance."

Eli's chuckle almost resulted in a dismount. He was at five minutes now.

As soon as my brothers were able to move out, they did. And whenever they came home, their focus was one hundred percent on me or one another. I didn't think they'd bother making the drive down when (or if) I ever got the chance to move out, too. I didn't blame them, but I also felt a pang of sadness for a version of our family I'd never experienced.

We didn't have a mantle littered with childhood photos, plastic trophies, and finger paintings. The closest thing we had to a tradition was an argument on the eve of any holiday about who was cooking what and when. Sometimes, when we convinced ourselves to try our hand at lighting the fireplace, it emitted dark clouds of smoke we'd inevitably have to extinguish. It was almost as if, even when we tried to be a cookie-cutter family from the suburbs, the universe was there to remind us, 'No, you just look like one.'

"You sure you don't want company?" Eli asked.

I smiled, grateful to have them, to know them, and to have them want to know me. "I'll make you a deal: you stop asking, and I'll make my lemon cake."

"You better shut the hell up," Luka warned. I could never tell which one of them was more obsessed with the recipe.

"Fine, fine," Eli conceded. "Will it have the drizzle frosting, though?"

"Duh," I said.

"Then I promise, my lips are sealed." He finally dismounted. "Until next time."

I laughed. "Nice to do business with you."

———

Mountain Pine Books was nestled in the heart of Main Street. According to the plaque above the front door, it was the only building on the block made up of its original bricks from the early 1900s. Inside, the air smelled of coffee and pinecones, courtesy of the on-site café and the burning candles placed rather boldly throughout the store. The abundance of windows on the ground floor welcomed in a healthy dose of sunlight. Heat from the rays meant the AC and fans above worked overtime.

"Welcome to Mountain Pine. Let us know if you need help finding anything," a worker behind a stack of new hardbacks greeted. She didn't even look up as she waved in my direction.

I murmured a thank you; my heart drummed as I dipped into the closest aisle. The weathered wood floors groaned underneath my sandals.

My fingers ran over the mix of old and new spines as I took a couple of deep breaths. In for five, hold for three, out for five. Repeat. My lightheadedness subsided. The shaking of my hands was still present, but scrolling through my phone for the list of books would help.

Carter had a vast catalog to choose from. I looked up at the wooden signs hanging from the ceiling, which indicated the location of each genre. The mystery section was on the back wall, filling most of the built-in shelves.

The bookstore was nearly empty. My shoulders relaxed as I browsed without worrying about getting in anyone's way. I found Carter easily enough. The first one I laid eyes on was a tattered used paperback with yellowing pages on sale for a dollar. I read the synopsis and was surprised to find a murder mystery set in the Wild West sounded interesting. I moved on to Doyle next. It couldn't hurt to work in a classic, too. I'm sure Lincoln would appreciate discussions about more than just his favorite author. As expected, there was a whole section dedicated to Holmes.

"It was brilliant," someone's muffled voice could be heard a few shelves over.

"Hardly," the other person scoffed. "Lazy writing, lazy premise, lazy characters."

My back stiffened when I realized footsteps were approaching. I did my breathing exercise again and repeated my mantra: *No one's focused on you. You're a side character in their story.*

Monstrous me threw her opinion in the ring: *Or you're a silly joke they'll share in passing. The girl in the bookstore nearly passed out while trying to browse.*

I tried ignoring her, drowning the voice out with thoughts of how the used books felt dry and fragile in my hands, how they smelled of old ink and aging fibers. I kept my gaze locked on Holmes as the voices neared, hoping to find support in the timeless detective. The colorful illustration of Sherlock stared back at me, aloof and unfazed by my panic. Everything I knew about this character I learned through TV. Despite not knowing his original story, I was confident enough in my knowledge of Sherlock to confirm he wouldn't be able to stomach my constant bouts of sky-is-falling rhetoric, which put me in an even deeper state of unease. Not even a fictional character would be able to deal with me. This wasn't something to get worked up over, and yet, I found a way.

"That's what makes it fun," the original voice insisted. My throat tightened at the low chuckle that followed the statement. There was no way it was him. The odds were... decently high considering this was the only bookstore in town that carried Carter's books, and he didn't seem like the type to order online. Lincoln liked being outside.

"Kid, that's what makes it a dud." The older Black man Lincoln debated with came into my peripheral vision. He wore a plaid newsboy cap and a Mountain Pine Books gray tee. There was a set of thick glasses hanging from a brown neckband that he picked up to place on his nose as he stopped in front of the mystery section. His arms were full of books. Not only was I in the way of his reshelving, but I was also in Lincoln's direct line of sight.

My jaw clenched as I wondered if I could escape upstairs and hide out until the coast was clear. But that'd go against every goal I had in mind today. I couldn't keep putting this off. The universe had given me the perfect second chance.

Yeah, no. You're not ready for this. You need more time. Please, run. Abort mission and run.

The stairs weren't far. Four, maybe six steps until I could

reach the bottom of them. They'd creak underneath my shoes all the way up, but Lincoln was so deep in conversation he wouldn't even notice.

My planning cost me valuable time. Before I could take one step, Lincoln said, "You're just jealous because your stack of Lee novels hasn't sold, but my tip on stocking Carter paid off. Look, someone's picked something right now—good choice, my friend."

Lincoln gestured to the paperback under my arm. "You're going to love it. It's one of my..."

He paused when he met my gaze. I tried to smile. I hoped my mouth responded to orders because I knew my lungs didn't.

"Favorites," Lincoln finished in a quieter voice. "Hey."

The guy with him raised a brow and removed his glasses to get a good look at me.

I swallowed. "Hi."

CHAPTER SEVEN

LINCOLN

wasn't supposed to be at another bookstore today. But something about Mendell's campus bookstore unsettled me. The shelves were too glossy, the lights too bright, and the air reeked of cleaning supplies. The books I needed for this semester lost half their value as soon as I swiped my card. The visit was a necessary evil—a rite of passage to becoming a serious student. I often delayed buying textbooks until after the first week of classes. But between Jonah's concern and Sam's skepticism about my ability to pull it together, I needed to try. I needed to break my bad habits.

So, to make up for the torture of being an adult, I went to my favorite bookstore directly after stuffing my textbooks into my gym bag. I knew the old book smell would cleanse my palate, and Lenny was going to be on shift.

My new friend was an ex-retiree who knew all about the lore of Tinsel and hated how much I loved new-age mystery stories. Lenny preferred keeping things old-school and non-commercial.

"Not Doyle," he would huff when I assumed. "And do not speak of Christie in front of me."

"Oh, Len, you're breaking my heart," I lamented. "What did my girl Christie ever do to you?"

"Nothing. That's the problem."

See, Lenny was a fan of ultra-stuffy writing that waxed poetic about the meaning of cloudy summer mornings. There was a time and place for all kinds of literature (in my humble opinion). But God, if I contemplate the meaning of blue curtains again, I might quit reading for good. And that'd be terrible considering I started to develop a decent enough attention span for it.

While getting my weekly "bug Lenny" quota in, I also got to inquire about Carter sales. Sometimes I worried I was the only person keeping Mountain Pines' mystery section alive. But then, I ran into Celeste.

She stood in the middle of my favorite section. My heart raced when I saw my favorite Carter book tucked under her arm and my favorite Holmes book in the other hand. The orange glow pouring in from the windows gave her quite the halo effect. Celeste's smile was small, and her gaze was distracted, as if she were looking for something or someone else besides me. Maybe Naomi? She even seemed to prefer Finn's presence. My mind began its familiar game of how to say the right thing to Celeste without fucking it up.

"I need to get a cart. Took too many books by hand again," Lenny grumbled. He could read a room, and to be honest, wasn't exactly working at the bookstore to make new friends. I just happened upon him like a stain on his Sunday's best or a stub on the toe in the middle of the night.

"Need help?" I called after him as he shuffled away. He gave me a look and rolled his eyes before continuing.

I laughed and told her, "Believe it or not, I'm his third-best friend."

"Oh?" She hugged the books to her chest, and they doubled as a shield. I stepped back a half foot to give her space and glanced at the shelf to offer her some sense of privacy. I touched a few spines, feigning interest. It's difficult to fake the need to look at books when she was here. Celeste was in my favorite store, holding my favorite book, and wearing my favorite color ribbons around her jean loops. Every time I've seen her in jeans, they include some type of bow. Today's color was green. The ribbons reminded me of a jersey, and I couldn't help but wonder what she'd look like in a Mendell Hawks hockey jersey. My jersey.

It was an embarrassingly attractive fantasy that made me lightheaded with want. A couple of minutes in Celeste's presence already had me forgetting how to breathe. And I liked the struggle. Got high off it in some weird, pathetic, 'I think this crush will consume every part of my self-respect' way.

"Who's one and two?" Celeste asked.

I barely heard the words. I replayed the sentence in my head a couple of times, but the meaning still didn't click. I got distracted by her hair. It was braided in two, the green ribbons woven in there as well.

When we'd met a year ago, and I learned my typical nonsense wouldn't capture her attention, I set off trying to figure out what would. The investigation didn't get me much closer than an occasional polite greeting or rare smile. But it did confirm Celeste held the key to triggering a fire in my veins. She had a peaceful confidence about her. It was in those small details. The things that set her apart from me, Lenny, and every person I'd ever encountered. In her quiet, Celeste was her own person. She didn't have to run her mouth like yours truly to be seen or heard. I couldn't imagine her walking into a room unnoticed.

"Sorry." I shook my head, trying to stay on task and not admire how pink her cheeks were. God, she was so beautiful. So out of my fucking league. "What do you mean?"

"Oh…" She looked down at the floor for a second. "You said you were number three. Maybe I misheard. I thought…"

"No, you heard right." My assurance came quickly, paired

with a wheezy laugh. "Ms. Lane works as a cashier here during the night shift. She can get him to smile within two minutes of talking to him. And Andy, the delivery guy, is number two. The man is an incredible trumpet player, and Lenny likes being reminded of his old club days, back when they had more live bands and fewer stereos. I don't know much about music, but I'm sure Andy's one of the best out there."

Celeste nodded with a small smile. The gentle quiet returned. She shifted from one foot to another. I scratched the back of my neck.

Though I enjoyed the entertainment of a back-and-forth, silence wasn't always terrible if you liked the company you were in. If it were anyone else, I would have said my good-byes and forgotten about the whole exchange. I'd never do that with her. Any second Celeste had to spare, I selfishly wanted.

The bookstore grew warm, despite the constant turn of the dusty fans overhead. I tapped the side of my thigh, fingers restless as I tried to come up with something I knew she would feel comfortable sharing. Nerves squeezed at my throat, unfamiliar and taunting as words got stuck there. I tried to swallow, but my mouth was drier than scorched earth.

"You're into music, right?" I blurted, hopeful. I knew she was into music. I'd seen her scribble down notes in the lines of a notebook behind her desk at the community center. On campus, Celeste was never without her pink flute case strapped to her like some cartoon character, wearing the same thing day after day. I pretended not to know in hopes it'd give her a comfortable excuse to share.

"Mm." She nodded and looked at the floor again, adding, "I'm studying it."

"I've seen you carrying a case around campus," I said, and then quickly added (so I didn't sound like an absolute creep),

"Music department's close to the Liberal Arts building. I had most of my courses there last semester."

Mendell was big, but not so big you didn't run into people on campus. Every time I saw Celeste, it was the product of a happy accident. Or, maybe (as I liked to imagine) the universe making our paths cross over and over, so we had ample chance to talk. Just like now, she was here and actually conversing. Asking me questions (or, maybe just one question, beggars couldn't be choosers) and it was thrilling. I had too much to say. Every thought I've wanted to share with her over the course of the last year bubbled to the surface. I continuously reminded myself, *slow down*.

"I play the flute." There was a slight spark in her eyes when she said it. I took down a mental note to look up facts about flutes. Some funny ones, preferably. The possibility of making her laugh made my chest heavy with anticipation. I needed to make the most of our small window of opportunity, and the one way I figured I could was by eliciting a laugh.

"That's incredible. I can't keep a beat to save my life. All my music teachers hated me. I couldn't for the life of me remember which note was which on the...what's the line thing where the symbols go?"

Celeste smiled, amused at how I mimed the lines in search of the term.

"Staff."

I snapped my fingers. "Right, the staff."

"It's difficult to get the hang of at first." Celeste nodded. "Did you...um, ever learn the mnemonic for remembering the notes?"

I shook my head. Maybe I had at one point, but that knowledge had fallen to the wayside along with thousands of other things my teachers attempted to impart.

"The common one is Every Good Boy Does Fine for the treble clef—those are the five lines," she said. "E's at the bottom… and g-go up to F. And between the lines—they're called treble clef spaces—is FACE."

"That would have been a lifesaver in middle school. I made a fool of myself in front of an auditorium of extremely bored parents. We got booed. Talk about traumatic."

"I bet." Celeste's stance had softened, shoulders curved down, and feet hip distance apart. She still glanced down at the floor now and then, but when she looked up, she didn't look away anymore. Her gaze maintained contact with mine, and her gentle smile inspired me to keep this up. I couldn't put a finger on exactly what I was doing right, but whatever it was, I needed to keep doing it.

I rested my hand on one of the shelves above our heads, using it for stability. My heart continued to race. Learning to manage the lightheaded excitement I felt from prolonged conversations with her was going to take some time.

Celeste's gaze flickered to my arm, and I realized its position made our conversation seem far more exclusive. I'd created a barrier for us, blocking out the bookstore. For a second, I considered putting my arm back to my side, but when she shifted a little closer, I left it. Was it possible she was interested in a world of just the two of us? Could she envision it as clearly as I could?

Our abandoned text thread said otherwise. I'd never been one to take things too personally, so Celeste's eventual silence hadn't pierced my core. It was successful in planting a seed of doubt about the possibility of an us, though. I wondered if that seed would survive after this change in energy.

"That's my favorite Carter. The one I wanted to tell you about before Jack interrupted." I tapped the cover lightly with two fingers, an excuse to be close to her. The book was between us, but I swear I felt the warmth of her skin through the soft cover.

She looked down, gaze more on my fingers than the cover. "Yeah?"

"I'm obsessed with the detective. She's a badass ex-marine biologist who solves crimes of the sea. It's like if Ace Ventura and *Murder, She Wrote* had a baby. Do you like poodles?"

Celeste blinked, trying to keep up. "Poodles?"

"The detective," I explained. "She has two of them. They are half the reason why the crimes get solved in time. One's best friends with an orca—a surprisingly heartfelt relationship. I may have cried during the last few chapters when those two had to part ways. Goodbyes always suck—oh, shit, my bad, spoilers. Sorry."

"It's fine." Celeste laughed. It's far more melodic than I could have dreamed. I leaned against the bookcase more because the noise almost knocked me off my feet.

"Sorry," Celeste added quickly. "I wasn't laughing at your... crying. I was...I've never heard of something so nonsensical."

"Carter lives and breathes nonsense. I think we may be long-lost twins."

"Could be." She nodded, playing along.

"What about you?"

Celeste blinked. "I...don't follow. Sorry."

"No. It's my fault. I'm a tumbleweed."

She shook her head, still confused, still smiling. Another laugh was a hair's breadth away, and I live for its proximity. Yearning for a laugh was a new high or low, I couldn't decide which. My body could decide it wanted to feel her laugh. The vibration of it against my chest. The taste of it on my lips.

"It's what my grandma calls me. Just rolling forward," I said. "It's a compliment...I think. At least I take it as one. Anyway, your favorite detective?"

"I don't know many," she said softly.

"You already have a good start." I gestured to the books in her hands and then looked at the shelf, trying to see if I could recommend any more to her. "Damn."

"What?" Celeste asked, sounding genuinely worried.

I looked over my shoulder toward where Lenny had disappeared. "He stocked the latest books in this series and didn't tell me about it. Okay, Celeste, these are incredible. I haven't read them all yet, but everything this author puts out is gold. Five kids driving in their minivan across Canada to solve old ghost stories. Paranormal cold cases."

I studied the new illustrated covers, ready to buy the whole set.

"Sounds fun." Celeste tried to get a peek at the artwork, so I moved over to make it easier for her to see. The feel of her body heat reminded me of how real this conversation was. Dry mouth was back with vengeance.

"This entire series deserves the book equality of an Oscar," I said hoarsely.

"Pulitzer?"

"Bless you," I murmured while still staring at the familiar characters on the page.

Celeste laughed again. "No...um, the Oscar for books. I think it'd be a Pulitzer."

"Ah." I nodded and smiled at her.

She cleared her throat and turned her gaze toward the shelves again. I forced myself to move back a bit, too.

The air didn't smell of ink on paper anymore. It smelt of citrus and clover. Of her. I wanted to be closer. Not just physically. I wanted to be like we were now, talking about books and finding interest in something together. I didn't think I was lonely before, but with her here, I wondered if that had been the case. If all along, I wanted someone to get lost with in a bookstore.

"I think...I got everything I came for," Celeste said quietly as she lifted her books.

My heart sank, but I smiled.

"Me too." I grabbed the rest of the series. "Can we walk up together?"

Her flighty gaze was back, straying to the front of the store. "Okay."

"I started coming here more since school's been out, so if you ever need company, feel free to let me know," I offered as we started to check out.

Celeste didn't respond verbally, but I think she released a soft hum of acknowledgement. I'd take it.

There was no line at the register. I greeted Kasey, and she gave me a tired smile. Most days, she ran this place on her own.

"Those, too." I gestured to Celeste's stack. "If you don't mind?"

I directed the question to Celeste, who looked confused at first.

"You don't...have to," she whispered.

"I know. It's my way of getting someone I know to read my favorites, so I have someone to talk to about it," I said and offered my hand for her books. "It's pretty selfish of me, actually."

"Thanks." Celeste let me bag the books.

"I was thinking maybe..." Celeste started. "You could walk me to my...car?"

"Of course," I said without a second thought. It's an unusual request that made me feel like an eleven-year-old getting to hold hands with a girl on the bus for the first time.

I grabbed our bags and opened the door for her. The sun was setting, painting the town a pink and orange hue. The streets were mostly empty, foot traffic down thanks to most people fleeing to beachside cities for the summer.

"I'm just over there." Celeste pointed to the on-street parking a few yards down.

I inwardly sighed at how close it was. It'd take us a minute, two tops. How pitiful was it to be annoyed at the short length of time it'd take for me to get her to her car?

"Are you a fast reader?" I asked as soon as she said, "I have something to ask you."

"Go for it," I said as she said, "No, not really."

We shared a laugh. It's such a simple thing I would think about for weeks and months to come because she looked up at me and was comfortable enough to stand mere inches away. And if you knew her, you knew sharing something like this was rare.

We were in front of her car now. Celeste didn't move to retrieve her keys. She picked at the thin, paper handle of her store bag.

"I heard you're looking for…" She took a deep breath and closed her eyes for a second. "A volunteer project. Something for your community outreach class?"

"Sure." I ran my hand over the back of my head. I'd put the ticking time bomb that was my academic career in the back of my mind during this entire conversation. Escaping its clutches had been fun.

Compartmentalizing was second nature to me; it was how I got through growing up. My parents spent months out of the country, leaving me behind with my grandmother. They sent back a plethora of shiny postcards and posed photos. Whenever they came home, it was on their own time, without warning. Whenever they left, it was on their time, without warning. The constant ebb and flow of in and out, goodbyes and hellos had me breaking down my expectations and disappointment, dropping them into separate boxes.

"Might settle on highway clean up," I said. "Jack didn't seem to hate the idea, so that'd make our sentence together more tolerable."

"I may have something you guys could do," she said. "Something…in AC. And maybe with snacks?"

"You had me as soon as you said I," I joked (but not really). "Is it at the community center? Because I fully planned on still coming to the tutoring sessions outside of school."

She shook her head, her picking at the paper ramped up. "It's at the playhouse. I'm…I'm working on a project—something to submit for a mentorship program. And I need…a crew. I have an actor. Well, two. Maybe more if Ellis – he's my cousin—can convince more of his friends to join in."

I tilted my head to the side. "Ellis is your cousin?"

She raised a brow. "Do you know him?"

"Yeah, sort of." Our crowds overlapped. Ellis was a hardcore party guy. Incredibly fun to be around, but I often struggled to keep up with him, and that said a lot. "What's the project?"

Celeste could say we were going to regrout the tile in the playhouse's bathrooms, and I'd say yes.

"It's…" She looked away for a second, pressing her hand to her cheek. "A musical. Mine. My musical. I write music."

She'd written a musical? Oh, yeah, there was never a world in which I didn't pine for this woman. "You know, you should always introduce yourself with that. If I wrote musicals, people would never hear the end of it."

She laughed, looking a little less like she was going to bolt at a moment's notice. "Thanks…but in most circles it's kind of considered odd."

"You're in the wrong circles," I promised.

She pressed her lips together, considering for a second. "Maybe."

"I'm honored you'd invite me," I said. "I'm a yes, obviously. And Jack will be too since we're chained together."

"You don't have to say yes immediately. I was going to pitch the story to you." She rummaged through her tote bag for her phone.

"No pitch necessary. If you made it, I know it's amazing."

Her laugh was a bit dry this time, unconvinced by my flattery. "Sure."

"It's in the details," I said quickly, trying to prove I wasn't all-in simply because she was beautiful, and my heart sped up every time I knew she was in the vicinity. "The colors you choose for your eyeliner. Rainy days are yellow. Sunny days are pink. Purple when there's something big happening in the community center. That's when I know an event's coming up and you're in charge of prep. Then there's…"

She stared at me like I'd grown another head. Or, just revealed how closely I'd been paying attention to small changes in her routine. Fuck. This was, without a doubt, not the way to talk to her to reduce the panic.

"What I meant to say…" I shrugged, trying to figure out how to run that back. "You seem like you make good art."

You seem like you make good art? What the hell was wrong with me? I have crushed on dozens of people in my lifetime. Never have I ever struggled this much to flirt with them.

"I don't know about that, but I hope I will one day." She played with the end of one of her braids. "So…do you think you'd be free to set up a meeting to decide initial plans for the project? I have a PowerPoint that'll help you prepare."

"Love a good PowerPoint."

"Oh, and my aunt's the manager of the playhouse, so she can sign off on any form you need for your class. The hours won't stretch outside of what the class requires, I swear."

"Sounds good." It was probably best that I kept my responses concise for the rest of the conversation or risk further awkward overly-detailed reveals.

"Good." She lifted herself on the balls of her feet for a second. It was a small move I'd seen her do with Naomi whenever she got excited over something they were talking about. I smiled because I was even hooked on her tiny expression of joy. The motion made her braids sway, and I imagined touching them, the softness between my fingers as I held them off her neck.

"I'll text you," she promised.

"I'll answer," I said, in awe and out of it because this was really happening.

Celeste dipped her gaze down; her bottom lip pulled between her teeth in embarrassment. And I immediately realized what I'd done.

"I didn't mean it like that," I added quickly. I really, *really* needed to go home. Reset or something.

"Okay," she said and moved her focus toward fishing out her keys. "I'll see you…soon?"

"Soon," I promised. And better than whatever the hell this was.

CHAPTER EIGHT

LINCOLN

As soon as the frigid air of the arena hit my nose, my body felt like it'd shed an itchy layer. I had no clue where my life was going. Where I was supposed to end up. But I knew for sure now, I loved being on the ice. Everything fell into place here.

Maybe this could be my future?

I laughed at myself. It was a little late for those kinds of thoughts, though. I was always a little late.

Henrik knocked his hockey stick against mine to claim my attention. We were the only ones in the locker room, getting ready for practice. Without gear on, Henrik would never be mistaken for a hockey player. He was the smallest guy on the team, with a lean body built more like a long-distance runner. His dark hair was cut short, always brushed off his forehead in as perfect a condition as when he first got it cut. Henrik's pale skin was unmarred by adolescence, a key evidence he was born to be a middle-aged man and came from a time when people wore pocket watches and three-piece suits to dinner.

"I'll talk to Sam for you," he offered. "If you really don't want to work with Anthony."

I didn't have a problem working with Anthony. I'd said a one-off comment at breakfast about my heavy summer course load, impending volunteer hours at the playhouse, and Henrik took it seriously.

"I'm not afraid to stand my ground with Sam." I finished lacing up my skates, grabbed my helmet, and stood up.

"Oh, really?" Henrik asked. He took longer than me to get ready, probably holding out hope I'd give in at the last minute.

"There are worse things in life than disappointing Samson Morgan," I said.

"You really think so?" he teased.

"Plenty." Like ending up alone. Dead ends in life. Never actually finishing anything of importance. Never getting the chance to know how it felt to see Celeste and have her see me.

I shook out my shoulders, trying to rid my mind of everything that would weigh me down on the ice, and started toward the door.

"Thanks for coming, Hen. But I need you to let this go and focus on getting a puck passed me. We both know you can't do that yet, so it's good you're spending the summer practicing too."

Henrik's laugh echoed. "You live in a fantasy world."

I knew good and well Henrik could smoke me any hour of the day. I also knew, deep down, underneath all his politeness lay a hardened competitor. That's why he got to be Sam's right hand man, why he could keep up with Finn's speed. Why did he opt to be here with me during break, even though our typical off-season schedule didn't require (and, in fact, discouraged) any ice time?

"When's the last time you did it?" I lingered in the doorway.

He opened his mouth and closed it again as he paused, deep in thought. The current version of Henrik couldn't tell a lie (teenage Henrik would be appalled).

"Exactly." I tapped the door frame. "See you out there. Preferably with game."

Henrik tossed a glove in my direction. I chuckled when it missed me and headed out to the rink. I thought I was a little early and would earn some points from Anthony. But some guy was already waiting on the ice.

"Lincoln Hill." The monotoned greeting felt harder than the ice he stood on.

"Anthony Jackson." I smiled. He didn't return it.

Anthony was a stocky guy with dark brown skin and blonde-tipped locs that barely reached his shoulders. He squinted at me as I stepped onto the rink and made my way over to him.

"I expected you'd be here well before me and already warmed up." He tossed down the last of his cones.

"My bad?" I couldn't tell if he was joking or not. "I could have sworn I was on time."

"On time is late. Your bad cost us twenty-five minutes." He held up his watch, showing me the timer I was apparently on. "Practice starts at eight AM. That means you're already warmed up and ready to go."

"Honestly, all I need is a couple of these." I swung my arms back and forth. And did a few (admittedly shallow) lunges. "And I'm good to go, boss."

Anthony frowned, unimpressed. We were quiet for a second, an awkward standoff between strangers who somehow already had one-sided beef.

"Finish a real warm-up and come find me when you're done," he said finally.

I opened my mouth to apologize, but snapped it shut before I could. From the deep-set frown he wore, that was not what he wanted to hear. After years of training, playing on varsity teams, and heeding coaches, I knew how to mold. I learned how to fit myself into any box for small periods.

Anthony wouldn't take an excuse. In fact, he would probably find it one of the most offensive things I could do.

"Yes, sir," I said, hoping some show of respect would make up for my mistake. Sam hadn't been kidding; this guy was all-business.

I started my usual warm-up routine, glancing in Anthony's direction in the box now and then. He scratched down something in a small, worn notebook. His gaze never once strayed from the pages to check my progress. Henrik joined me halfway through, already sensing bloated tension on the quiet rink.

"Serious?" Henrik asked.

"Deathly." I tried to catch my breath from the most intense sprints I'd ever done. Anthony had called from the sidelines once, asking, "Is that really as fast as you can go?"

I wouldn't take that lying down, even when my knee started throbbing in protest. It'd taken longer than I expected to recover from the fall from the ladder. Bouncing back at twenty-one wasn't as easy as it'd been at thirteen.

"Nice, maybe you'll learn something new," Henrik noted.

I snorted. "Better. He's costing my folks seventy-five an hour."

"Speaking of payment." Anthony surprised us both by no longer being in the box but a few feet away. His skates barely made noise on the ice. It was almost like he floated above it. Maybe that was his problem. With the ability to float above everything, surely one would become too humorless to let something as simple as a warm-up slide.

"Who are you?" Anthony asked Henrik.

"A friend." Henrik pushed himself up to give him a proper greeting. "I'm Henrik Olsen. I thought I'd be a body if you guys needed it."

"You're on the Hawks with Hill?" Anthony asked with a raised brow. He looked Henrik up and down, assessing his smaller build.

"I am." Henrik stood as straight as he could with pads on his shoulders.

Anthony studied him for a moment before finally saying, "I guess if you have the free time, I could use you. This works better if Lincoln has more than one opponent."

"I'm all yours," Henrik said and waited for a beat before adding, "Sir."

I scoffed under my breath at the telltale rise in his voice.

"You two finish up and we'll get to work," Anthony ordered before going back to the sideline.

"You really love your age gaps," I teased in a low voice.

Henrik shot me a look. "Be quiet and stop messing around."

"Just an observation." I held up my hands in defense.

"Observe yourself stretching." Henrik shook his head and tried to pretend like he didn't want to smile.

There wasn't a muscle in my body that didn't ache after my session with Anthony. But pain came secondary to spending time with Celeste.

I took my time climbing the steps to Mendell's music building. I had to stop halfway to stretch out my calf. Someone passing by asked if I needed help the rest of the way up. And you know what, I was tempted to accept the offer. But I was also known to be a bit of a baby when it came to stuff like this.

"Go on without me," I told the kind stranger. "I have a high chance of making it on my own. And if I don't, well, these stairs look freshly power-washed so sleeping here doesn't seem too awful."

They didn't look convinced but left me to my theatrics. It took me another couple of minutes, but I managed to conquer the rest of the stairs. The inside of the music building was warm, and the smell reminded me of my second-grade class-room: plastic and fresh markers on a whiteboard.

I pulled up the text Celeste promised to send, and I promised to answer (I cringe at the memory).

CELESTE

Are you okay meeting in the Music building? I have a reservation for one of the rooms.

sounds like a plan!

CELESTE

Alright, it's room 203. On the 2nd floor. Try not to take the elevator unless it's necessary.

The screaming of my thighs made elevator use feel like an absolute necessity. My training session had been more than brutal; it'd been disheartening. Was I really this out of shape? According to Anthony, in addition to not being ready to prac-tice, I didn't understand a single thing about being a goalie. Everything from my stance to my philosophy (or lack thereof) needed fixing. By the end of the session, he'd asked,

"Why are you here? Honestly?"

Between my burning lungs and heaving breath, I didn't have a good answer for him. I was still searching for one when I stepped into the elevator. The door dinged as if it were going to shut, but it remained open. I mashed the close button about six times before it finally gave in and let me have my way. After it closed, the groaning started. It was a low, horrific noise. I was the asshole in the horror film who did the one thing he'd been warned not to and who would now crash to their untimely death, and wake up in some demon's court-room. I wondered if hell offered free legal counsel. Could I, in turn, pay it forward, counselling the next unlucky fool to take the elevators after they ignored a reasonable warning,

By some miracle, the elevator began to move. Up, thankfully. Its slow ascent had me reaching for my phone, readying a text to send to our group chat.

> If you don't hear from me, I may be in Dante's Inferno. The entrance is in the basement of the music building. Only come looking for me if you're sure you can get me out. Otherwise, it'd be a waste of time and energy.

FINN

Got it.

He was the only one to answer. I took it as a sign I needed to give them a refresher on how many laughs they could credit to my presence alone. It was hard work being the primary source of entertainment for the friend group. It downright saddened me to think of how little they were laughing at this very moment because I wasn't there.

The elevator door finally slid (3/4ths) open on the second floor. I hurried out in case it changed its mind about its judgment on my soul.

Our meeting room was easy enough to find. My ribcage might have been bruised from how hard my heart hammered in anticipation of seeing her. I wiped my palms on the back of my jeans, trying to get rid of nervous sweat.

The door was unlocked, but no one was inside. I went in anyway, checking the time to see if I was early. The clock showed I was ten minutes late.

The room was small, with two wall-to-ceiling windows on the far end, facing the bright green lawn at the front of the building. There were plastic chairs neatly arranged in a half-circle. In the middle stood a black podium that hosted a stack of sheet music.

Celeste's pink tote rested on one of the chairs, weighed down by bag charms and a fully stickered water bottle. Next to the bag was a flute. The silver metal reflected the yellow overhead lighting.

She was nowhere to be found, so I took a seat next to the flute and drummed my hands on my thighs.

"Hi," I said to the flute, realizing I hadn't offered a greeting. "How's it going?"

This was the closest I'd been to an instrument since my abysmal middle school recital. Seeing one wasn't as triggering as I expected. I rested my elbows on my knees and looked closer. There were so many buttons, each one shinier than the next. I tried to resist the childish urge to touch, but I felt like I was in a museum. And I'm a tactile person. Plus, the knowledge Celeste had held this instrument made me even more tempted to touch. There was a chance for adjacent touch here. A chance to place my fingers where hers had been and experience a bit of what she did.

The metal was cold. Each button curved down, making a perfect little space for finger pads. I dared to press down on one, and when it closed, the door opened. I snatched my hand away. The sudden movement disturbed the flute, and I scrambled to stabilize it once more.

"Hi." Celeste's greeting was low, and her gaze on my hand holding her flute. I didn't know much about musician etiquette, but I did realize touching someone's instrument without permission was considered taboo.

"Hi." I snatched my hand away once more, now that the flute stopped rocking. "Sorry. I was just thinking about middle school, music, and forks in the road. What if I had killed it in band and learned how to read music instead of learning how to block pucks? Then the flute was shining in the lights. I thought, Wow, I haven't seen an instrument in person in years. That's weird, right? Music is such a big part of most people's lives, but we rarely know how to play instruments and never see them."

Celeste remained silent as she came closer. She picked up her flute and inspected it. A wave of shame washed over me as I realized it probably cost her a fortune, and I'd gone and treated it like a toy.

"Have you held one before?" she asked.

I raised a brow. "No…"

"Would you like to?"

"Uh…"

She offered me a small smile then. "You just seemed curious. And I don't mind."

"In that case, yeah." I nodded. "I've always wanted to hold one. Or a clarinet. Or…what's the one that looks like a clarinet but has the weird long spout?"

Celeste laughed. "A bassoon?"

"Bassoon." I nodded. "One summer, I begged my grandma to put me in band because I'd thought I'd fuck up a bassoon."

Her laugh was brighter and lasted longer. I need to drown in it. To be so entwined that I didn't know my end and its beginning.

"Really? People aren't usually interested in wind instruments. Not when pianos, guitars, and drums are around," she noted.

"Those are much too obvious if you ask me," I teased.

Celeste moved a chair over so she'd have enough room to stand beside me. She offered me the flute. When I hesitated, she said, "Don't worry, you won't break it."

"I've been known to break even the most unbreakable things."

"Just don't go whipping it around," she joked. "And you'll be fine."

I accepted the instrument she placed in my hands. It was lighter than I thought it'd be.

"This is the mouthpiece." Celeste pointed to the long part

on top, which had an oval-shaped hole. "Don't worry about that, it's kind of gross cause I've had my mouth all over it."

I chuckled. *She doesn't know how unbothered I am about that.* My pulse quickened at just the thought of my mouth anywhere near where hers had been. I fell further on the pathetic scale when she adjusted my fingers.

"You space them out on the keys like this. Level it and stabilize it with your thumbs on the bottom." Celeste instructed me, focusing on getting my positioning right. My body buzzed, overstimulated with every new sensation. Her fingers were soft and warm on mine. The star-shaped necklace she wore dangled between us, the warm metal brushing my skin as it swayed. She smelled like how a good daydream felt.

"I'm going to teach you a note. The fingering for this one…" Celeste started.

And there it was: I was hard. Damn it. Fingering? Not imagery I needed right now.

"Requires you to lift your pinkies and the pointer on your left hand," she said.

"Okay." I nodded, trying hard not to breathe heavily like some asshole.

"Hold it steady."

I followed her instructions, gripping the instrument like my life depended on it.

"There you go," she praised. "You're a natural."

I laughed at how easy the encouragement fell from her lips. I was thrilled to have done something right in her presence.

"Do you want me to…show you? Like how it sounds? I don't know if you care."

"I care," I said, genuinely curious how it sounded.

She moved completely behind me. I wasn't ready for how close her face was to mine when she leaned over my shoulder.

"Don't move," she whispered.

I was as still as a rock. And still as hard as one too when she placed her hands on my shoulders, fingers barely touching me as she blew into the mouthpiece.

A beautiful note pierced the air. Celeste stopped short, laughing when I hummed in awe.

"Incredible," I said. "The beginning of an angel's chorus."

As she laughed, she briefly dropped her forehead, pressing against my shoulder. I stayed utterly still, terrified of ruining this moment. Celeste pulled back when she realized how close she was.

She cleared her throat. "Sorry."

"I don't mind," I whispered.

"That's...um...that's a D." She took a deep breath and readjusted my hands, so I only held down three fingers on my left hand, my thumb, and my right pinky. "Ready?"

I only trusted myself to nod at this point. She blew again, the note low and soothing. I felt the vibrations of her breath, which made the sparks flowing up and down my arms more intense.

The note slowly changed, high in frequency. I looked down to see if my fingers had slipped due to my struggle to stay focused. They hadn't, thank God.

"G in the first octave was the lower one," Celeste said when she pulled back. "G in the second octave was higher."

"You change your airflow to get a different sound?" I asked, taking a closer examination of the mouthpiece.

"Right." She moved beside me again, beaming at how I'd caught on. "A lot of notes on the flute have the same fingering and the sound depends on how fast or if I blow at an angle."

"You're a great teacher." I would have learned a lot if she hadn't been so close and so her.

"Thanks." She dipped her head, shy as she grabbed a seat to move in front of me. "Ready to get down to business?"

I carefully placed the flute down. "I am if you are."

She reached for her bag and pulled out a couple of folders. Celeste handed one to me and kept the other for herself.

"This is an outline of how I hope everything will go." She opened a folder, and I followed suit, marveling at how organized everything was.

"I mainly need help in the set design department." She pointed to page three, indicating I should go there when I was still stuck on the index.

"You and Jack will be in charge of sorting," she said. "I don't have a budget, so we're using old set pieces from the playhouse storage. It's stuff from the shows they put on every year. I made a list of things you guys should look out for. Must-haves and maybes."

I nodded, scanning the items. Seemed straightforward enough.

"And…" she hesitated. "If you're up for it…"

I looked up. "I'm up for anything. Between Jack and me, this task will only take a couple of days—no more than four. And we need more volunteer hours than that. I like this hands-on stuff." Tutoring kids at the community center had become one of my favorite things during the month, but having to model patience by sitting in one place for long made me fidgety. I like how active this musical was going to have me.

Celeste picked at the edge of her paper. "I was wondering if you'd be like…my assistant director. Interact with the performers. Relay information. Basically…be my mouthpiece."

I blinked, surprised by the request and, honestly, honored she'd trust me with something like this. "You want me to do all the talking?"

"Basically." She paused for a second, pressing her lips together as she thought. "I really admire how you communicate. You always make everyone feel included."

That was the highest compliment I'd ever received. And a slight indication Celeste had noticed me.

"I need you to know, I was born for this kind of work," I said. "I won't let you down."

She smiled. "I know you won't."

CHAPTER NINE
CELESTE

learned to play the flute at the age of eight, thanks to a free summer music program at my school. After two months of practicing how to direct my air flow to hit a note properly, I fell in love.

Growing up, I rarely spoke a word at school and only a couple of times at home. Selective mutism was what my school counselor called it. Dramatic was what my parents dubbed it. I'm not sure if I believed in nature or nurture. What I did know was I didn't remember a time when I wasn't afraid to speak. But as soon as I had a flute in hand, I couldn't stop making noise.

So, I believed in music. I believed it was my native language. As soon as I mastered it, I didn't want to be silent. Why stay quiet when I could tell such beautiful stories through the notes?

My aunt, Robyn, noticed my love and decided to take me in as her own. Whenever she went to the theatre, I got to tag along with her and her son, Ellis. We'd always sat in the mezzanine, lap full of popcorn, and cheap, tiny binoculars that never failed to make Ellis and me fall into fits of giggles. I didn't feel like I was the only outsider when I watched *The*

Phantom of the Opera. The Lion King made me brave enough to ask Aunt Robyn to take me to auditions…we didn't make it out of the parking lot. *Annie* was my favorite, a girl my age who ended up with a happy family despite a rough start.

Whatever problem I had could be solved by listening to *Defying Gravity*. Whatever loneliness I felt would fade whenever I pulled on my headphones, mimed the flute parts of the overture from *Rodgers and Hammerstein's Cinderella*.

After immersing myself in musicals for years, it felt like the natural next step was to write my own. So, in middle school, I started scribbling one down on loose-leaf paper. At first, it was a hodgepodge of all my favorites—Frankenstein's musical monster. But as I got older and more skilled, the arrangements became my own. The story, though still inspired by my favorite fairytale, evolved into something unique.

Currently, it was nowhere near perfect. I didn't think it could be with who I was now: timid and unsure. But I would make it the best it could be before presenting it to Ophelia.

The only place I could get real work done was in my treehouse. My brothers built it for me one summer after losing track of me one too many times in the woods behind our house. It'd been their job to watch me, and they figured the perfect way to do so was to build a place I didn't want to leave.

They'd done a good job for teenagers. The treehouse stood the test of time. It was large enough for a chest full of art supplies and blankets. I'd hung princess curtains in the windows, strung fairy lights on the outside and inside. We'd rigged a bucket where I could request snacks to be sent up without having to climb down the ladder. It would always be the safest place to dream and create.

I delved deep into edits for hours on the weathered, wooden floor. The late evening air caused sweat to form my armpits and the back of my knees. Despite the slight discomfort, curling onto my worn beanbag brought me a sense of calm.

The middle part of the musical sagged. My songs there were overly sentimental, harping too long and hard on the overall themes. As a viewer, I loved a good sad beat. But there was such a thing as dragging it out.

It'd been hours since I spoke to anyone when my snack bell dinged. I pulled off my headphones, confused. Eli and Luka had gone out to dinner with old high school friends. I hadn't heard the noisy sedan pull back into the driveway. And my parents never ventured into the backyard. They only went outside when it was a necessary transition point to a car.

I pushed back the curtains, peering down to find Ellis waiting with a bag of fast food.

"I don't think it'll make the trip up." He tried to put the bag into the basket, demonstrating how it'd surely topple over.

I laughed and gestured at the ladder. "You can come up."

"I'm not allowed. You banned me six years ago."

I frowned, trying to remember. "Did I?"

"I left loose gummy worms on the blanket Grandma gave you for your thirteenth. It was the hottest summer since the nineties. The wash made the yarn fuzzy, and you couldn't get Grandma to make you another because she'd moved on to wreath-making."

I clicked my tongue on the roof of my mouth, remembering. "Oh, right."

He shrugged. "Honestly, the punishment fits the crime. I would have made you crochet me a new one."

"Who says I still won't?"

"My apology fries and shake from Raven's?" He held up his bag. "And an update on your dream cast for your upcoming award-winning musical."

I nodded. "You've served your sentence and paid your fine. Come on up."

Ellis gave the treehouse a once-over when he cleared the ladder. "Was it always this tiny?"

"We're adults now," I reached for the bag of food. I couldn't remember the last time I ate. It'd been before the sun came up. Now, it was setting.

"Damn it." He bumped his head while trying to move around.

"Knees, it's the only way," I said around a mouthful of fries.

"I'm trying to preserve them for next season."

I scoffed. "One crawl won't ruin your chances to finish your program."

"Maybe not, but to lift?" He sighed. "That's a whole other story."

While I marveled over musicals, my cousin found his place at the ice rink. He was tall, lanky, and the most graceful person I'd ever met. He was conscious of perfect lines before he put on skates. Determined to accurately mirror the ballet dancers in *Swan Lake* before he'd even taken a class. Like with me, his mom saw potential and fed his flame. He started competing and winning in middle school. And now, he was on track to place on the Olympic team...if his injury was adequately cared for.

"What have you got for me?" I wiped salt from the corners of my mouth.

"A go for Halle," he said. "All-in. I had to give her full control of all our music choices next season to get the yes, but it was worth it."

"Thank you, thank you." I grabbed him for a hug.

"Don't get too excited." He laughed, hugging me back. "She wanted the last word on our costumes, too. I told her you had a story to tell, and she promised she'd adhere to it if it didn't include too much pink and too little sparkle."

"Deal. The woman can have whatever her heart desires."

Halle was a performer, through and through. I'd never

been brave enough to try to befriend her, but from every interaction we had, she'd been kind. Very quiet. But not my brand of quiet. Halle spoke when she had something to say, no more, no less. She was the kind of silent I wish I could be. While nervous energy swirled around me whenever I spoke, a steady calm and confidence buzzed around her.

"Perfect," Ellis said. "Now, for *my* demands."

Here we go. I offered him a fry in hopes a delay would evolve into a distraction. He turned it down. "How are my chances with Naomi looking these days?"

I gave him a look. Ellis had a crush on Naomi for years. She never returned his feelings but did have a soft spot for him. They bonded most when we were teens, and they both became more comfortable with talking about their bisexuality.

"She's locked in."

"Same guy?" he asked.

When I nodded, he groaned and fell back onto one of my pillows.

"They were roommates," I reminded him. "He knits her cardigans and fixes stuff around the house for her. He built her a desk and has plans on building a custom display case for all her games and streamer gear."

"Shit." He sighed, placing his hands behind his head, and stared up at the glow in the dark stars on the roof. "That's cute. And he plays hockey?"

I nodded. "He's shy. And holds her hand whenever he gets anxious."

Ellis sucked the back of his teeth. "I can't compete with that."

"You truly can't, and I'm sorry." I rubbed his shoulder. When I offered a fry this time, he accepted it.

"I'll get over it…one day," he said. "He's on the team with Lincoln, right?"

"Yeah, do you know him? Because he said he knew you." I

watched my cousin's face closely, trying to pick out the tell-tale signs of a crush. He had been in as many relationships as I had, but something about the fantasy of it all really hooked him. Ellis said he didn't go past the first date because he didn't have time. Figure skating was an all-consuming sport. But, still, there was something more to it.

"We've seen each other around," he said with a one-shoulder shrug. "He's cool. Sometimes hard to keep up with in conversation, but fun."

I nodded, and a weird sense of relief blossomed in my chest. I credited it to the project. If Ellis liked Lincoln and we all had to work together for the summer, things would inevitably start to get awkward. I wondered if I should consider implementing a no-dating policy for the cast and crew until after the musical was over.

"Celeste?" Ellis' voice brought me back from outlining a no-fraternizing clause.

"What?"

"The music." He gestured to my headphones. "Let me hear it?"

I tightened my grip on the headphones. "It's not ready."

"It never is," he sang.

"You really need to start rehearsing," I said deadpan. "You're flat."

He chuckled. "Shut up. I can't rehearse without content."

"You can rehearse with anything."

"Come on, give them here. I'll give you notes. We need to have this ready by next week. Halle wants to start practicing. It's her first musical. You know the woman is a perfectionist."

I took a deep breath and looked down at the MP3 file I'd been tweaking all day in my editing software. "Don't laugh. It's a demo."

"I never laugh."

My nose wrinkled at the blatant lie.

"I laughed one time." He held up a finger. "But it was a good laugh. The kind of laugh you want from an audience."

"It was a break-up ballad."

"I happened to find break-ups funny, I'm sorry."

I sighed, knowing I had to rip this band-aid off sooner or later. Besides, Ellis was the best person to share this with–despite his strange sense of humor. He'd known me since birth and had been familiar with music since birth.

I handed him the headphones. Once he had them in place and gave me a thumbs-up, I clicked play. Ellis closed his eyes as he listened, trying to immerse himself and escape my nervous energy. I chewed on my nail, watching the track play. As soon as it finished, Ellis tugged the headphones off. He kept his eyes closed. I covered my mouth, stomach turning as I considered maybe it was truly horrible. A small part of me had some hope, but now, I had to consider it could be a delusion.

Holy crap. I've assembled a team of talented people to waste their summer feeding my delusion.

"It's so good, I can't believe it hasn't been made yet." Ellis opened his eyes. "You know? Like you hear the song of the summer and don't remember a time when it wasn't on your go-to road trip playlist."

I gasped. "Shut up."

"See, I knew being your cousin would get me somewhere."

"Shut up." I fell back on the pillow next to him, laughing. "Ellis, are you for real?"

He was, because here's the thing about my cousin: he loved poking holes in things. He was the kind of person who would critique movies while watching and had notes on the decor of every room he entered. He was ninety percent cold, brutal critique thanks to his unrelenting experience with a skating coach who barely let him breathe without commenting on the slightest finger out of place or unsteady landing.

"You could kill this." He held up his pinky. "Like, blow it out of the park, if the rest of the music is like this."

I squealed, so giddy I could barely breathe. I hooked my pinky around his. "This one's the worst, El. I just finished fixing it."

"Oh, shit." Ellis laughed, eyes wide in awe. "That's your worst? You're going to kill this, Celeste."

I smiled so hard I wanted to cry. Because he was being honest, and for the first time in forever, I felt ready.

CHAPTER TEN

LINCOLN

"We're not on the ice today," Anthony said… as soon as I stepped onto the ice.

He sat on the sidelines with his notebook open and pen in hand, already writing something down.

"Loved the heads up." I pulled off my helmet. "Always looking out."

"And we won't need your assistance today," he said to Henrik, who was at my elbow, equally confused. "But feel free to stick around if you want to learn something."

"Thanks," Henrik said. "I think I will."

He was a better man than me. I was practically salivating for an excuse to get out of practice and work on some things for Celeste. Her expressed admiration still reverberated in my brain, sending shockwaves of excitement through my veins.

"Alright, let's get to it." Anthony finished writing down one more thing before getting up and leaving the arena.

Henrik and I exchanged looks before we started removing what we could, then followed him. Anthony led us to the office section of the building. I usually didn't come here unless a coach or trainer had some bad news to share or it was mandatory check-in time. So, my associations with the cold air and burnt cheese smell toggled between not fun and rather dull.

"Why don't you have a seat?" Anthony's suggestions all sounded like orders.

Henrik and I slowly sat in two chairs placed in front of the desk. Everything in the office looked new, from the sparkling glass desk and empty bookcase to the photo frames that still had placeholder shots of random families hanging on the walls.

I wondered if all those families were actors. Or did those companies buy actual family photos? Were the images being licensed out by photographers? Or did the families offer them to companies themselves? Was there such a thing as a family photo agent? Someone who only offered contracts if the family was a packaged deal. A company either took on all of them or none at all.

"Do you have something to write with?" Anthony pulled a laptop out of one of the desk drawers.

I snapped out of my musing to look at Henrik, who somehow, someway, already had a pocket notebook and pen out.

"*What the hell?*" I mouthed. "*How?*"

He shrugged and clicked his pen, at the ready.

"Well?" Anthony's stern gaze was on me, judging and waiting.

"I have my phone." I fumbled to get it out of my back pocket.

"Too distracting." Anthony gave me a disapproving frown and was quiet for a second. What did he want me to do? Conjure up loose-leaf paper?

"Here." He reached into the drawer again, grabbing a legal notepad.

"Thanks," I said. "Just need—"

Henrik offered up a fountain pen. The thing looked like it cost more than our rent.

"Where are you getting this stuff?" I accepted this pen, looking him up and down for some hidden bag.

"Alright, eyes on the screen," Anthony said as he pulled up a video. I didn't have to look at the paused image long to realize it was of one of our games. I winced. I hated seeing myself in motion. Everything on the ice felt epic when I did it, only to turn out looking like desperate flails and last-minute splits. Somewhere on the official Mendell Hawks social media page, there was a compilation of all my flubs edited to what I can only describe as chaos clown music. Whenever I thought about it, I reconsidered every decision that led me up to this point.

"Lincoln, I want you to tell me everything you did wrong," he said.

"Got out of bed this morning, for one," I muttered.

"Huh?" Anthony gave me a look that told me he'd heard me perfectly.

I cleared my throat. "Sure, boss. I'll take notes of my many flaws. Thought you'd never ask."

"Figured you might appreciate the break," he said flatly. "From the way you've been dragging yourself through practices, sitting seems more your speed."

Well, damn. I hadn't been on my A-game, sure. But who was in the summer when everything else besides work was appealing? I'd literally watched videos of paint drying (in my defense, it was a DIY channel and bonding time with Naomi and Finn) before I even considered doing the extra drills and conditioning Anthony wanted me to do outside of practice.

Anthony clicked play on the video, and almost immediately, Henrik wrote something down. I leaned over to see what he possibly had to critique so early, stopping when Anthony glared at me.

Right.

Focus.

I looked for myself on screen, noting posture and position.

This game had been against the Amber Titans. A decent team that consistently ranked somewhere near us during the season but could never quite get past the first round of play-offs until last year, when we weren't in them.

Besides a few scratches on the paper, it was quiet as we watched. Anthony paused after the video was a quarter of the way through.

"Okay, what have we got so far?" he asked.

I chewed on my inner cheek and tried to hide my blank page by pulling the notepad to my chest. They waited for me, and I waited for them. The standoff wasn't too long before Henrik raised his hand. Anthony shook his head and pointed to me.

"Uh…" I sat up straight, understanding I wasn't getting off easy. "So many things."

"Name one," Anthony challenged.

"Well, I'm pretty lazy," I said. "Let my guard down when I thought I was in the clear. I follow the players, not the pucks, most of the time. I butterfly slide far too much for it to make sense…are you going to stop me on one thing or are we tackling them all?"

Anthony smiled. Genuinely smiled at me. And I may have sensed a bit of shock and pride. The approval sent a surprising sense of joy through my body.

"So, you are self-aware," Anthony said. "You just choose to lack common sense. Got you."

And joy faded. It was nice to get a taste, even if only for a moment.

"This is a good thing," Anthony assured. "It means I can work with you. If you work with me."

"I thought that's what we were doing," I said.

"Everyone gets a trial period, Lincoln. You're still in yours," he said. "Now, let's keep going. Henrik? What have you got for me?"

Hen looked down at his page. I whistled at how it was

almost entirely covered in notes. This may be even more grueling than being on the ice.

We spend two hours dissecting every move I made over the course of three different games, from three different points in the season. Henrik and Anthony were high-energy and detailed. I tried to keep up, head spinning as I took note of whatever problem they pointed out and then whatever solution they suggested. By the end of it, I was so tired that even the thought of glancing at the goal at the end of it made my head hurt.

"He's good," Henrik said on our way out. "I think this could be a real turning point for you."

"Yeah…" My brain was basically mush.

"Lincoln?" He waved his hand in front of my face. "You okay?"

"Better now." I let out a breath. "That was a lot."

"But necessary."

"Agree to disagree."

"Come on." His smile faded when he realized I wasn't joking. "Are you serious? Wait, no, don't answer that. You're not. Why would I think otherwise?"

"I'm not good with that much data in one go."

"I get that," he said, empathizing a little. "But come on, you're getting personalized feedback…if you don't want that, why ask him to stick around?"

When I didn't respond, Henrik asked, "What's wrong?"

"Nothing." My uncertainty about my capability flashed on my face. It was only for a split second, but Henrik knew precisely how to catch it before it disappeared. "I just have some prep to do for our first rehearsals."

"Right." Henrik didn't sound convinced.

"Some of which you agreed to help with," I reminded him.

He laughed. "I know, I know. But are you sure you're ready to take more notes?"

"Never been more ready," I promised because this time, it'd be for fun. And it'd be for Celeste.

———

The tabs upon tabs of set design research inundated my laptop. One tidbit about creating atmosphere led to wrapping my head around color theory. Colors opened the door to materials, leading to a whole new world, as I then started considering the influence of texture.

The rabbit hole was bottomless, and I was a dedicated diver. My focus became lasered, and time became slippery as sand. Halfway through an article on collaboration and unity with other departments, I considered how well Celeste and I communicated…which could use some work.

Thus began the great pivot. I'd started looking up ways to communicate and support someone with social anxiety disorder. Before meeting Celeste, I'd never heard of it, and a couple of hours online left me in even more admiration of her than before.

"She asked me to do a lot of the social labor, which you know I don't mind at all," I told Henrik as he set up the supplies. "But I was always reading this article about supporting partners with anxiety—"

"Partner, huh?" he asked with a smile.

"It was a natural progression of my research," I promised. "I'm not that presumptuous."

"Sure, sure," he teased.

I scoffed. "Moving on. One of the suggestions was that whenever possible, I should help provide tangible means of comfort."

Tea was high on the list—especially those known for their calming benefits. And Naomi had shared Celeste preferred tea brewed at home. Making a cup seemed straightforward enough. But when I'd attempted it on my own with Henrik and Naomi's combined collection of loose-leaf teas, I'd made something that could be found in a backed-up ditch after a thunderstorm. There would be no calming Celeste if I handed her a cup of my monstrosity.

"There's a handful of teas to help with anxiety. Peppermint, chamomile, and lavender are the most popular," Henrik began. He placed his hand on each tin as he explained. "I've personally found lavender to be most successful for me. But I do remember when Celeste was over one night, Naomi got her to try my peppermint tea, and she seemed to enjoy it."

"Show me how to make both?" I asked.

"Of course." Henrik nodded and picked up a metal orb that swung from a chain. "This is an infuser."

Then he picked up something with a handle that looked like the orb cut in half. "And this is a strainer."

"You're starting the lesson already?" Finn came into the kitchen with his keys and a bag from a hardware supply store in hand. "I thought you were going to wait for me."

"I was going to do part two," Henrik promised. "I knew you were busy today and had to pick up Naomi tonight."

"I have a small window now." Finn set his things down and took the spot on the other side of Henrik.

"You're learning, too?" I asked.

Finn nodded. "Naomi really loves it when Hen makes a cup. I want to figure out how to do it right."

"Alright, so, heads up, Naomi likes her tea extremely sweet," Henrik said. "But Celeste seemed to appreciate less sugar."

I wrote that down in my notes app. Finn set up his camera and pressed the record button.

"Oh, shit, smart." I pointed to the phone. "Send that to me later?"

Finn nodded, and Henrik laughed. For the first time in forever, I was not in on the joke.

"What?" I asked.

"Nothing, nothing," Henrik said. "I just really appreciate the effort you two are putting in."

I grunted and gestured for him to continue. "Come on, small window, remember? We need to stay on track for Finn."

Henrik went into detail about loose leaf tea, the proper way to let it steep, and how to serve it.

"And if you want to get real fancy." Henrik went to our cabinets and got out a glass teapot. "You can serve with this. But never put it on the stove or in the microwave."

"Okay, so, how are we supposed to warm up the water?" I asked, poking the teapot because it seemed sturdy enough.

"You heat the water in the kettle like I showed you," Henrik said. "And pour it in here."

"Is this just for aesthetic purposes?" I asked.

"This one? Maybe. But there are plenty that include strainers or keep the tea warm—that reminds me, you could knit a cozy for this, Finn," Henrik said. "It'll keep the tea warm for a bit longer."

"Noted," Finn said.

"So, what are we thinking? Ready to give it a try?" Henrik asked us.

I rubbed my hands together, enthusiastic to finally be in the hands-on portion of this lesson. Finn seemed a bit nervous, but willing nonetheless.

While I buzzed through making my cup, Finn was meticulous, starting over twice when he wasn't sure he got the right portion of leaves into the strainer.

When I placed my finished cup in front of Henrik, he scrutinized it with a single brow raised.

"Had a little problem with straining, but otherwise, it was a breeze," I said and gestured for him to taste.

"Little?" Henrik murmured.

"Did you strain at all?" Finn asked.

"I did," I promised. "Don't be so dramatic, there are only a few leaves."

"Did you give it a taste?" Henrik asked.

"Nope, that's all you." I smiled and nodded for him to sip. I didn't like tea, no matter how many times Henrik gave me a different cup to try. For most of the first year, he'd practiced his skills on me, bringing me different variations of what I could have sworn were the same, lightly flavored water. It wasn't until he started giving the cups to others I realized he was actually good at it.

Henrik took a tentative sip, remained quiet for a second to feel it out, and then took another.

"Yeah, as expected." Henrik nodded.

I raised my hands in celebration.

"Horrible," he finished.

Finn tried to hide his chuckle, and I stopped in mid-celebration.

"Oh, fuck. Seriously?" My shoulders sagged, heart dropping along with them. "It's not even a little good. Like an after kick that shows promise?"

I'd actually tried to slow down. Do everything right. This was something simple I could do to support Celeste. I needed to get it right.

"The aftertaste is the worst part," Henrik said point-blank.

Finn picked up the cup and took a sip. The wrinkle of his nose and immediate cough and curse were as expressive as I've seen him in almost a year.

"I think I poisoned him," I murmured in horror as Finn went to the sink to drink from the tap.

"I'm fine," he said after a while. "Just have a sensitive gag reflex."

"So, I'm at risk of making her lose her lunch now? Great."

Henrik laughed and gave my shoulder an encouraging squeeze. "You have a lot to learn. Can't rush it. But you're on the right track. I promise, I'll have you making Celeste the perfect cup in no time. Now, let's try it again. This time...a little less leaves, yeah?"

I nodded and shook out my shoulders, committing to the lesson. "A little less leaves. "

CHAPTER ELEVEN
CELESTE

The playhouse was booked up this weekend, so we scheduled our first musical practice outside at Mendell's amphitheater. It was a small, half-oval stage that was only used a couple of times a year for indie artists' concerts and open markets. The tiered, stoned seating that curved around the stage was covered in grass, perfect for blankets in the summer and lawn chairs in the winter. The greenery and floral carvings framing the stone seating made the theatre reminiscent of something stumbled upon in a fairytale set deep in some mystic forest.

Lincoln did all the prep work to ensure we could practice here without violating any campus rules. I was the first to arrive. I'd changed my outfit six times and my hair twice. My hands wouldn't stop shaking, and I considered taking something before remembering I'd stopped my anxiety medication last month because of how exhausted it'd made me. And since then, I'd been trying to find another psychiatrist who didn't make me feel like I was lying when I talked about how speaking to people physically hurt.

I self-soothed with cold water and my noise-cancelling headphones. The *Wicked* soundtrack played on repeat as I tried to trick my body into believing I was in the safety of my room.

Halle arrived ten minutes before rehearsals with her cousin, Kaya, in tow. In the group chat Lincoln had placed us in and facilitated, he'd explained that Kaya was on board to play the supporting role, thanks to Halle's convincing.

"Hey," Halle greeted in her soft voice. She wore a blue romper that emphasized her short, toned frame. A long braid stretched down her back, elegant as it swayed with every step she took.

"Hi." I snatched off my headphones, dislodging my scrunchie in the process. "Hello."

She didn't seem phased by my double greeting. Halle dropped her bag on the floor and sat crisscrossed in front of me. "This is Kaya. I don't know if you've met."

"I..." We had. At the party last year. But Kaya shook her head, not seeming to remember. And I was too embarrassed to remind her.

"Celeste, right?" Kaya's voice was louder than her cousin's. Stronger, too. She possessed the kind of muscles that undoubtedly required rigorous upkeep. Her hair was shorter than it had been last year, the tight coils colored a dark red. Her skin was the same dark, unblemished brown of her cousin's.

"Celeste," I confirmed, accepting her hand. Her shake was firm, and I did my best to keep my expression neutral. "Thank...thank you guys for doing this."

"Of course!" Halle waved her hand. "I love doing stuff like this between seasons. It's a nice break. And I've never done a show by a Black woman who wrote it for a Black lead."

"Yeah." Kaya nodded in agreement, tone not as enthused. But from what I could recall, she didn't seem impressed with anything that happened around her, so I tried not to take it personally.

I offered them a shaky smile. I wanted to fill the gap in the conversation with something witty or funny, but nothing felt good enough.

"Look at this!" Ellis called from the bottom of the stage, pausing for dramatic effect to frame us with his hands. "Three beautiful ladies ready to make history."

I let out a soundless sigh, grateful for his interruption and the attention it drew.

"You didn't send me the script like you promised," Halle scolded as she watched him come up on stage.

"You didn't get the script?" My eyes went wide in horror. That'd set us back. I'd thought they'd been able to do a couple of readthroughs. My cheeks burned when I realized I should have followed up in the group chat when I thought of it. But I'd gotten too nervous about being pushy and eventually let it go since Ellis promised he had it covered.

"Relax." Ellis offered his fist to Kaya for a dab, but she scoffed and gave him the finger instead. They smiled at each other, so I didn't have to worry about issues in the cast just yet...I don't think.

Ellis had been known for letting things roll off his back. So, if there was real tension between the two, would I be aware of it? Should I ask to get ahead of it? Like I should have done with the script?

My thoughts began to spiral, and we hadn't even officially started.

"You're a natural, my love. You're going to pick it up in no time." Ellis sat behind Halle and pulled her into him, allowing her to relax against his chest. She wrinkled her nose, but her frustration seemed to cool down when he rocked her back and forth.

They've been skating partners since their freshman year of high school. The intimacy in their movements was fascinating.

I'm envious of how they could rely on each other. Regard-less of whether it was platonic, like Ellis insisted, or otherwise, the relationship was sweet to witness. Watching them reminded me of my daydreams of being close enough to someone to lean my back against their chest and know they would support me without question. I don't think I'll ever meet someone I'd trust to hold me that intimately. Melancholy stung in my chest.

Kaya caught my gaze and offered me a small smile. There was a knowing look in her eyes, a sense of camaraderie in the third wheel fatigue department. That smile promptly vanished when Jack came on the scene.

"Hey, Celeste," he greeted and opted for the spot next to me. "And...everyone else."

They all muttered a greeting. I could tell Ellis wasn't serious, but the girls seemed annoyed with Jack's arrival. Great. Another potential conflict.

"Got this for you." Jack handed me a sheet of paper. "It's the inventory I took this morning."

I raised a brow, accepting the paper. "This morning?"

"Your aunt let me in early. I had to get started on my hours because I have a family thing later."

I scanned the sheet, taking in the level of detail. He'd even gone the extra mile and added notes on the quality of each item. Some were in brand-new condition, and quite a few were in such terrible shape he noted them as hazardous. "Wow, thank you...really, this is amazing."

"I know someone who can get your aunt new lights, by the way." Jack pulled out his phone. "I forgot to give her the number. I'll get you the details in the group chat."

I smiled, grateful. Our first impression wasn't great, but he'd been under stress, so I was more than willing to overlook it in favor of this smoother experience. I glanced over at the others; they didn't seem to be as forgiving. I caught Ellis' gaze and gave him a questioning shake of the head. He shrugged, indicating he wasn't interested in getting into it.

"Sorry, I'm late." Lincoln climbed onto the stage, with a

gym bag slung over his shoulder, holding a green travel mug labeled "Mendell U." His hair was wet, freshly washed, with curls shining from product. He smelled of spring, and I immediately wanted to go over to him to discuss the group tension, the scripts, and my nerves about our timeline. I did no such thing, of course, keeping my seat and waiting patiently for his attention.

I don't think I've ever wanted someone's attention more than now.

The curious change came from my realization that Lincoln wasn't some scary, overbearing person. Sure, his run-on sentences often threatened to incite a rash whenever I spoke to him. But he was kind. The type of person who read body language and backed off, asked opinions, and genuinely waited for answers. I anticipated his attention because I trusted I'd be heard. And now, more than ever, being listened to was what I needed.

"Did you bring enough for the class?" Halle teased, nudging her chin to the steaming mug.

"When the class proves they're going to kill it, sure," Lincoln said. "For now, the only person worthy is our director."

"Oh...thank you." I stood to accept the cup. Warmth spread throughout my palm, coaxing my muscles into a state of temporary relaxation. The surprise I felt when receiving the drink merged nicely with the relief I gained from his presence. I was off the hook for relaying plans and dallying out orders.

"Lavender, one sugar, and a splash of oatmilk." Lincoln turned completely to me as he spoke, blocking out the others. For a moment, we had some privacy as they started talking amongst themselves.

"That sounds...perfect." I pulled the mug into my chest, grateful to have something to do with my hands besides holding them limply at my side.

Lincoln smiled and added in a voice only loud enough for me to hear: "Hope it'll provide some calm amidst the storm."

My smile came easily. His whisper sent a warmth far more comforting than any cup of tea could produce through my body.

"It will." I nodded, more confident in that than in anything else that would happen today.

"I made it myself." He scratched his jaw as if he were unsure he should have shared the information. "Because Naomi told me you prefer it homemade."

I raised a brow, the gesture turning into something even more thoughtful. I didn't know how to react. Instead, I took a sip and it was…

"Alright?" Lincoln shifted his weight from one foot to another, eyes bright with hope and excitement. When I hesitated for a second to force down the intense, leafy mouthful, he added, "You can be honest. I'm learning."

"It's alright." I coughed a bit and used the back of my hand to wipe at the corner of my mouth.

His shoulders sagged. "I can take it."

I looked up at him. The sun shone through his hair, making it a lighter brown. His easy smile remained despite impending negative feedback. Lincoln had made me tea when there were about a million and one cafes between here and his place. Him taking the extra step made me feel even more thankful. I had this strange urge to squeeze his hand.

"I like when the drink's almost half oatmilk." My voice was low, shaking as I offered feedback. "And not so many… leaves."

He winced and pulled out his phone, taking down a note. "I got you—learning curve. You don't have to drink that, by the way! I wouldn't be offended in the slightest. In fact, I could throw it away for you. Get you something from the cafe? I'll be quick."

"It's fine," I said quickly, pressing the cup against my chest, keeping it out of his reach. "It's still comforting."

"You sure?" His forehead furrowed, unconvinced.

"Positive," I promised. Between the drink and talking to him, my head stopped spinning. Heart rate calmed down to a slow, steady pace.

"Okay, then, ready to get this show on the road?" Lincoln waited for my nod of permission before proceeding.

He gave me one more smile before turning to everyone else. "Alright, so, Ellis. You lead in the script readthrough. Jack, you read for the part of Harris. We're still trying to work on getting one of Ellis's buddies to play that role, but there are contract issues."

"We have to sign contracts?" Kaya frowned. "I thought this was recreational."

"There are no contracts," Halle assured with an amused roll of her eyes.

"There may be contracts." Lincoln pressed a hand to his lips and glanced at me for confirmation. I slowly shook my head.

"I just got news from the high-ups that there aren't any contracts," he amended.

Ellis chuckled. "You don't say."

"So, you all get to work with your quick readthrough. Do some vocal warm-ups and whatnot while Celeste and I take a sidebar." Lincoln gestured for me to follow him to the other end of the stage while everyone else got to work.

I grabbed my bag and hurried after him.

"So, how are you feeling about your first day? Excited?"

"I feel…" Like I was pinned underneath a tidal wave. Spinning in the middle of a current, stretching up and out to a surface I wasn't strong enough to pierce. I considered going with 'alright.' That was simpler and less likely to freak him out. No one wanted to be around someone whose first response to anything was sheer panic.

"Honesty, remember?" Lincoln searched my eyes for the truth underneath all this water. "We'll figure it out from there."

The 'we' gave me pause, the catalyst for a flower of warmth to unfold in my chest. There was sincere earnestness in how he looked at me. I could tell Lincoln I needed to figure out how to conquer the world in the next hour, and he'd probably promise to see every moment through alongside me. I almost laughed at the thought of asking just to tease him. I knew he'd appreciate it. I didn't know much about him, but I knew enough to believe he was safe enough to be silly around.

Instead of going in for the joke, I decided to keep on task because I'm not yet confident enough to commit to the bit.

"Overwhelmed," I said. "I'm still fixing songs and finalizing the music. And I'm catching…a vibe."

Lincoln frowned. "A vibe?"

"Yeah." I subtly nudged my chin toward our cast. "Between those four."

"Oh, yeah." Lincoln waved dismissively. "Don't worry about that. The love square doesn't affect them all the time. They'll focus. I know they don't look like it, but they're surprisingly professional when motivated."

I laughed a bit, still confused. "Love square?"

"It's a whole thing," he promised. "I'll catch you up later. In the meantime, what do you need from me today? I'm yours. More tea runs. Handling the speakers. Offering acting techniques. I'm your man."

"Could you just…keep doing what you're doing? Leading?" I asked, feeling useless for having to ask him to take the steering wheel on my project.

"I got you," he said without hesitation. "What's the goal for today?"

"I need them to get familiar with each other and the

music," I said. "Get a feel for how things flow and if they need to change anything to suit their voices."

"Got it, captain."

"And…um…" I rummaged through my bag, pulling out my Carter paperback in the process.

"You're tabbing it?" he asked with a smile.

"Yeah…" I nodded and let him take it from me. "I marked some of the scenes we texted about. I was trying to… understand your headspace. It felt like a smart thing at the time, but now that I'm saying it…"

I felt like a creep. Was it creepy to tab all the things he'd mentioned? Did it make me look obsessive? Once I'd started reading, the world and all the absurdity in the storytelling drew me in. The book felt like it was a mashup of *Alice in Wonderland* and *Sherlock*. And every time I reached a part Lincoln said he enjoyed, I felt like I was learning a secret about him and becoming privy to something he didn't always share with the public. And I'd found an unexplainable joy in that feeling of exclusivity.

"Could we trade copies one day?" Lincoln asked as he flipped through the book. "I would love to read your thoughts. Understand your headspace, too."

He didn't think it was weird. I released a sigh of relief. I bit on the inside of my cheek, trying not to smile too much. My breathing slowed as I imagined what our exchange of thoughts might look like and how he would smile and listen intently to every word, as he had in all our conversations thus far.

"Celeste?" Lincoln asked in a tone that indicated it wasn't the first time he'd said my name. "Everything okay?"

I blinked. I'd been staring at him longer than intended. Despite the awkwardness of staring, the daydreaming made me smile.

"I'd like that. Sharing. I don't have many interesting

thoughts, but yeah… I'd like that." I picked at my nail, trying to focus on not blankly staring at him again.

He shook his head, disagreeing with my self-deprecation. "An artist like you will have a myriad of insights. I'll be lucky if I can keep up."

I'm having trouble keeping eye contact, flattered he'd even think that. Let alone believe it.

"Is there anything else you need from me?" he asked, closing the book and handing it back to me.

"No, I think… you've been more than helpful."

"I aim to please. And I'm here if something changes. Don't be afraid to use me."

I nodded, numbly, as he gave me a small smile that sent off an unfamiliar thrill racing through my veins. I didn't know what it meant, but I chalked it up to being supported and said, "I won't be afraid."

"Swear?" he said, half-teasing.

"I swear."

CHAPTER TWELVE

LINCOLN

"This is all for a one-night show, right?" Finn looked over the crude sketches I'd laid across the kitchen table. I stood across from him, eyes dry from my lack of sleep and fingers drumming on the counter, waiting for something else to sink my time into.

This musical planning was a blast. I'd spent the weekend watching clips of all the musicals Celeste had referenced in her conversations with me. Some of them were hard to get through. Others were wildly addictive. I loved *Annie*, didn't realize I could enjoy *The Lion King* any more than I already had, and was deep in the *Into the Woods* subreddit.

"Yes." I pointed at one of my sketches. "See this arch; it'll be in the opening. We start in the woods—"

"This thing is supposed to be twenty feet tall." Finn raised a brow. "And covered in real moss."

"You're right; I'm thinking too small." I picked up my pencil and chewed on the eraser. "We could easily do another five feet. That'd matched the scope of things. And I checked the playhouse's ceiling. It's well over fifty feet tall—"

"I'm not building a twenty-foot archway, Lincoln," Finn said. "Do you know how long that'd take?"

"You just built our coffee table and gazebo." I gestured to our backyard. "In two days, Finn. You built a gazebo in two days; imagine what you could do in two months?"

He frowned. "You can't be serious. I assembled it from a kit. It came with step-by-step, illustrated instructions."

"Did I not draw you illustrated instructions?" I grabbed the plans for the archway and studied them myself. They're not professional-grade blueprints, sure. But all the information was there. "You're more than capable of doing this. I've seen your skill, and I believe in you. I think it's high time to believe in yourself."

"It's not self-belief I lack."

"Then what is it?" I wondered, genuinely willing to do my part to help him do his part.

"Patience," he grumbled. "Time."

I held my hands up. "Easy. I could help you with that."

"Lincoln." Henrik appeared in the kitchen entryway. As soon as I looked, he tossed a tennis ball toward me. I tried to swat it away with my pen, but missed it. The ball hit my chin, and the pen slipped from my grip.

"Ow." I picked up the tennis ball and threw it at him. He caught it without blinking an eye.

"Did that look like the reaction time of a starting goalie?" Henrik asked Finn.

"Sadly…no." Finn frowned, disappointed in me times two. I would have taken offense if I hadn't spent the past few days channeling all my energy and excitement into Celeste's project. Who cared about reflexes when the beautiful girl you wanted to spend all your time with needed your help with something? I had more important things to prove than how fast I could block a puck.

"I don't have time for your surprise attacks," I said. He'd been pelting tennis balls at me all week under the guise of helping me keep my reflexes fresh. Honestly, I think he was trying to get me to react. Push me far enough to say what I've been leaving unsaid since Sam left.

"Make time," Henrik said. "It's painful watching Anthony nearly push you to your breaking point every session."

Finn studied me. "That's why you were asking about my painkillers?"

"You're fishing for painkillers?" Henrik crossed his arms over his chest.

"You two are being very dramatic for no reason. I take an Advil every once in a while, alert the media," I picked up my laptop and moved to the living room...which, unfortunately, didn't give me much separation considering our open floor plan.

"Sure, it's just once in a while?" Henrik's skepticism made Finn concerned enough to go to the cabinet where he stashed the last remnants of his prescriptions from his accident. I scoffed.

"You two are reaching. I know the summer's been slow and boring because I've been busy, but I promise I'll be back home to entertain as soon as I can," I said.

"I think you should consider freezing practices," Henrik said. "What's the point of doing something you don't want to do? Especially when that something means reinjuring yourself to the point where you're taking painkillers daily."

"I'm not taking painkillers daily." I swallowed a frustrated sigh. If I'd wanted a talking to, I'd call up Sam.

"Mostly because I wouldn't give you any," Finn noted as he picked up another of my drawings.

Henrik followed me like a shadow, sitting beside me on the couch. I scooted over, putting a cushion between us. On a typical day, I preferred an invasion of personal space. Growing up an only kid did that to me. However, this invasion demanded my attention and heart, two things that were occupied for the foreseeable future.

"I'm not interested in painkillers...anymore. Working is

more than enough of a distraction." I said while I searched to find out how much wood we could get affordably. Our pockets weren't deep. So, realistically, we could only buy enough to make another coffee table.

Finn and Henrik continued to talk. Their back and forth became as non-consequential as lo-fi music. I typed up a few emails for our upcoming fundraiser. Finally, I called the one person I knew could change our financial situation in a heart-beat—if I played my cards right.

"Hey, Mini," she answered on the first ring.

"Hey, Grandma," I said.

The guys stopped talking. Henrik raised a brow, and Finn followed suit—only interested because of Henrik's interest.

"What's the matter?" she asked.

I laughed. "Nothing."

"You don't, hey, Grandma, me for nothing," she said.

"Let me talk to her after you?" Henrik asked. I shook my head and flipped him off, knowing exactly what he would say if he got her on the phone.

"I, hey, Grandma, you every time," I defended.

"No, you tell me why I shouldn't make mint chocolate or lecture me about outsourcing," she said. "I pick up this phone knowing you're going to talk my ear off about something you know nothing about."

I laughed. "Oh, come on. I'm just trying to be helpful."

"You're just trying to piss me off enough, so I'll spill the beans on our next reveal," she said. "Pain in my ass."

"I love you, too," I said with enough endearment to pierce her frozen heart. Grandma lived a long life of fighting for what was hers. She'd almost lost our family's chocolate company three times over the past few decades. She'd had three husbands and one wife and now lived unattached, with the occasional partner moving in and out of her world. She didn't bend for anyone but made the occa-sional exception for me, her only grandchild...and the guys, her pseudo-grandchildren, who often got better treatment than me.

Exhibit A: Henrik calling Grandma on his own phone. She told me, "Hold on a second. I got someone else on the other line."

Henrik moved back to the kitchen. He set his phone on the island and put it on speaker so Finn could participate in the conversation.

"Morning, Grandma Hill," Henrik said.

"Morning, Henny," she said, a voice sweet enough to give someone a sugar rush. "How are you? How's school? Did you all get my care package?"

I shot daggers at a man who turned his back on me. Henrik sweet-talked my grandma, earning his way into her good graces the second they met. I didn't mind their bond; I wanted nothing more for my best friend. But his ability to capture her attention proved annoying on days like this one. These days, I want nothing more than to stay on the right track. Being this laser-focused was an oddity. I needed to seize the moment before it gave way to something else.

"I'm good. School's fun. We loved the care package," Henrik said. "Did you receive ours?"

Grandma laughed. "I did. That was unnecessary but sweet. I've missed your baking. Your new recipe for oatmeal cookies is heavenly."

"I'll send more soon." Henrik tried to shoulder-check me out of the way when I came over to grab his phone. "I've been wondering if Lincoln has checked in with you about his summer training."

Grandma tsked. "That boy talks about everything but what he does on campus. Why? What's wrong?"

"Nothing's wrong," I yelled over Henrik's attempt to respond. "Other than you hanging up on me to answer someone else's less important call."

"Both calls were important, Mini," Grandma promised.

"But I know I'll get actual updates when Henrik calls. It's called prioritizing."

Henrik gave me a wink. I huffed a breath of disbelief and joined him at the island. If they wouldn't let me have my conversation, I'd have to settle for crashing theirs.

"So, what's going on?" Grandma asked.

"I'm volunteering to help assemble a musical," I said.

Henrik answered simultaneously, "I'm worried about Lincoln's training."

"Musical and training," she said. "Let's start with training. I refuse to have your senior year end like this one did. What's this private coach doing? Samson said he was the best."

Grandma didn't know anything about hockey, nor did she have much interest in the sport until I came home after my first day of middle school and told her I wanted to go out for the team. After that, she made my dream her mission. She researched the best coaches, schools, and opportunities. My one-off comment and growing interest incentivized her to make my dream a reality.

When she heard about how our last season ended, she became the embodiment of fury. She even went as far as to threaten to sue the school for damages. Being well-acquainted with lawsuits, she had a decent chance of making some noise. But that fire was doused when her lawyers explained how long it'd take and how the outcome would most likely end in a settlement outside of court. And by that time, the world would have moved on. The damage wouldn't be undone. The school's declining reputation was as damaging as any lawsuit that could be brought against it.

"Anthony is the best," Henrik said.

"But…?" Grandma asked.

"But I don't know if he's the right choice. At least, not now. It's a lot of work on top of summer classes."

"Lincoln's enrolled in summer classes?"

Henrik looked at me.

"Oh, now, I finally get a chance to speak?" I asked, only half-teasing.

"The floor is yours," Henrik said. "For now."

I scoffed and picked up his phone to claim a monopoly on the microphone. "Look, Henrik's scared because I'm dealing with a minor injury. Anthony's a hardass; he won't give me a break. But I'm handling it and the classes. I know how to handle everything."

My impending academic probation and failing performance on the ice swirled in my brain, taunting me. Knowing how to handle everything was what she needed to hear, though. Guilt pinched at my stomach, yet I remained unmovable. I couldn't have her learn all her efforts in giving me the life I have had been a waste because of something as trivial as my lack of focus.

I had no leg to stand on in terms of excuses. Finn had struggled with a brain injury and had still managed to get better on and off the ice. Sam had been weighed down with the burden of leading the team, with the odds stacked against him. Henrik was ostracized from his (so-called) family because of his sexuality. And though he pretended not to be bothered by their lack of acceptance, I could see it gnawing at him every holiday he spent at home with us. They had valid reasons to waver, to feel the weight of the world on their shoulders and want to take detours to escape the pain.

"Is it working? The practice?" she asked. "Does it make you more confident for next season?"

I hesitated for a second. Finn and Henrik watched me closely. I was tempted to use that opportunity to confess. We were just missing Sam and Naomi. If I told these guys the truth, they'd pass the information along, so I wouldn't have to repeat it if I didn't want to. Maybe my academic probation wasn't as bad as I'd built it up to be. Perhaps it wasn't the cry for help Henrik would make it out to be. I'd made a few questionable choices. Went to a few too many parties. And skipped a few lectures too many. Typical. Common even. I was so common that I bored myself to death. I was a stereotypical jock who couldn't hunker down long enough to make something of himself.

"The practice is working." I set the phone down so I would have my hands free to fidget with the paper on the table. Before I could continue, Grandma jumped in.

"Good, then focus on that," she said. "I don't know why you're taking summer classes. You get good grades, and you don't need to graduate early. You should drop them and pick them up in the fall."

Henrik nodded in agreement. Finn watched me for a reaction.

My throat went dry. I'd kept quiet about my grades since my sophomore year, when things began going downhill. Flunking two classes and barely passing the others for two semesters was enough incentive to keep my mouth shut. I got by with simple throwaway comments about getting Bs on exams. Or Cs on papers. Nothing too fancy or absurd enough to warrant a closer look. Because we were all adults here, it was much easier to keep your spiraling under wraps when you were an adult.

"I want to take the classes," I said.

"You want to take classes," Grandma repeated. "In the summer? My Lincoln wants to take classes in the summer."

"Oh, come on," I said, taking on a lighter tone. "You know I love education. I can't get enough of it. And something about Mendell just makes me want to learn about everything. I'm hungry for knowledge."

Finn chuckled at Henrik's scoff of disbelief.

Grandma was quiet for a moment. She had to rely on Henrik's intuition. And she did as much by simply asking, "Henrik?"

Henrik looked at me. I knew I wouldn't win this battle, so I appealed to his soft spot for me.

"*Come on,*" I mouthed. I softened my expression and gave him a shrug. It was enough to get him to at least back off while on the phone with her.

"He's really into this volunteer course," Henrik said with a sigh because he hated lying. He'd trained himself out of doing so years ago; now, he only took part in lies when he deemed them part of the greater good. He gave me a look that said he'd expected a hearty excuse for pulling back.

"Volunteering?" Grandma laughed. "Maybe a summer session is what you needed."

She and Henrik talked a bit longer before she ended the call with her typical invite to stay with her whenever we were free on the weekend.

"Things are getting hectic around here," I said.

"We'll be there next weekend," Henrik said simultaneously.

I glared at him when we hung up.

"What?" he asked. "I miss home. And Grandma. And none of us is getting any younger."

I looked to Finn for help, but he offered, "I would like to see her. I want to get to know her again. She seemed like she liked me before."

"She liked you a lot," Henrik assured.

"More than me," I grumbled as I opened my phone to take note of all the assignments I had due this week. My calendar was bloated with obligations between classes, Anthony, and the musical. I highlighted everything I had to do with Celeste in pink and marked them as a high priority. Seeing her in my calendar provided a sense of ease. If only I could find a way to spend a little time with her every day. Even if it was only for a few seconds. What I'd give for a second of her time.

"And still likes you," Henrik said.

I glanced up in time to see a rare smile from Finn. "I'm happy to hear it."

"Lucky you," I mused. "Because I'm unhappy about being railroaded into sharing all my business."

Henrik sighed. "Okay, first of all, it's your grandma."

"I don't see how that changes the fact of something being my business."

"I needed backup. You're all over the place. Messing around during practice. Taking on a sixteen-credit course load during your favorite time of year and then…this. It's all our business if you're going to mess around before the biggest year of your life, Lincoln."

He gestured to my art.

"Hey, this is a fucking masterpiece." I reached over, gathering my paper up in a messy pile. "It's not messing around. It's Celeste's life's work."

"She's twenty years old," Henrik said.

"You can be a twenty-year-old and have a life's work," I argued.

"Fine." Henrik shrugged. "But if that's true, then what's going on with your life's work? Why are you half-assing it in the mornings and staying up hours to do this?"

"It's obvious why," Finn said softly.

Henrik shook his head. "I don't believe it's all for a crush…Jesus, Lincoln, you're over-extending yourself for a crush?"

"I can make decisions without my heart and dick, thank you very much," I told them. "And you two are not the ones to cast stones. Mr. Panic Over a Doorknob. And Mr. Dear Eden."

Finn covered his mouth, chuckling, while Henrik remained unamused and on my ass.

"I'm all for your head over heels interest," Henrik said. "I am. But I'm more for you not getting in your own way and working toward your goal. Your dream. You told us you didn't know what to do after college, and now you're spending all your time working on someone else's goal. I'm sorry for roping in Grandma, but Lincoln, it's the only thing I can think of to trigger you to admit what's happening."

"Nothing's happening—" I tried.

"Could you just be honest for once?" Henrik asked. "At least with us. It's us, Lincoln."

"I am," I snapped. "What the hell do you want me to say?"

"That you don't want to play hockey," he said. "That you spent all high school and college following our dreams. Our footsteps. And now that the rudder is gone and the rest of the boat is splitting apart, you're looking for a replacement. You're looking for another guide. You can't decide without someone else leading the way."

I scoffed and looked everywhere but at them. "You think you've got everyone figured out."

"Maybe not everyone, but I've figured you out, which is why it's hard not to want to jump in and save you every practice. But I will do it. I will do it if you look at me and tell me hockey is what you want. We will fix whatever is going on if you want hockey."

"Of course, it's what I want." But I didn't look at him. I couldn't. My gaze remained on the marble countertop, tracing the cloudy shapes and wishing this were an easier conversation. Wishing I believed in myself enough to feel worthy of wanting anything, including hockey.

Henrik stared at me momentarily before shaking his head and getting up. "Fine, Lincoln. Have it your way."

He left the room. It was just Finn and me. The silence lingered until Finn cleared his throat and said, "Would you want to tell me? I wouldn't tell anyone."

I met his gaze and offered him a small smile. "I know."

"So?"

"So..." I shook my head and wiped my hands over my face. "I don't know what the hell I'm doing and..."

"It's okay." Finn nodded, patiently willing to wait all day for me to get this off my chest.

It was easier to talk to him. My friend didn't remember who I was. Who I said I wanted to become all those years ago. Finn didn't compare the past to the present. He was free to live without echoes of expectation.

"I'm not sure what's going to happen to me," I said. "After this year. I could go back home, but the thought of that makes me so sick I can barely breathe."

"But your grandma...she sounded like she'd love that," he said. "To have you home."

"She would." I nodded. "And I'd be okay for a while. But if I go back there, I know how my life will turn out. I know I'll let her convince me to work with her. It won't be horrible, but it wouldn't be mine, you know? I want something to be mine. Something that will stay. I thought that something was hockey, but..."

There was a clock on how long I'd have until the last time I was on the ice.

"I guess I've realized I'm alone," I said. "And I know you all will say I'm not, but... let's be honest, this is what life is. Families split apart. They find their way back to each other occasionally, but I will be away from everyone most of the time. Because of that, I wanted something of my own. I thought it'd be us, but that was wishful thinking."

I tried to laugh because it all sounded childish out loud. I didn't like the mushy layer of sentimentality that coated my every word. Being an emotional person wasn't something I avoided, but this was a whole different level of feeling. I wanted to put it somewhere I'd never have to interact with it again.

Finn didn't take his time like he usually did in conversation. He quickly said, "You're right; you're on your own. But I don't think it's as negative as you view it. It's not as lonely. I know you well enough to believe you will find something that feels like home. I know you enough to say don't discount the home you've already made with us. You're so focused on saying goodbye. Lincoln, we're right here. When the time comes to move on from Mendell, we'll still be right here. Families don't split; they explore. Then they return and share everything they've found in the world."

I studied my quiet, kind friend. "You know, you would have clowned me a couple of years ago for being this upset."

"I was an asshole then." Finn smiled and then tapped his finger on one of my drawings. "Look, I can't do half the shit you invented. But I can do this."

The drawing depicted a simple rocking bench adorned with vines and flowers. It was where Celeste's main characters fell in love.

"And my uncle can work on a few realistic modifications for the rest."

"You got yourself a deal," I said with a smile and held my hand for him to shake. "Welcome aboard. Honored to have you on our crew."

Finn accepted my handshake. "Honored to be here."

CHAPTER THIRTEEN
CELESTE

Lincoln and I decided to visit the Playhouse a few days before the rest of the cast to map out how we want our sets to appear on stage.

I spent an hour on my makeup before our meeting. Just the mirror and me. It was a meditation of sorts. The only meditation I experienced that breeds long-term results.

My makeup routine was sacred. The application process required consistent focus. Whenever I sat in front of my mirror and unloaded my supplies, I became grounded—in harmony with the present.

What I felt influenced which part of my face I emphasized. Tonight, I was hopeful. So, I mixed orange and red blush shades on my cheeks. I outlined my lips with my favorite brown and topped them off with clear gloss. My go-to getting-ready playlist filtered through my portable speakers. The playful hum of one of my favorite tracks, *The Flower Garden*, inspired a delicate floral pattern design on the corners of my eyes. It was more detail than I usually had energy for. But I knew I was seeing him. And I knew he'd notice. I wanted him to, and I didn't consider that too much until I was behind the wheel.

I wanted someone to notice me. Not my music, me.

Not someone. Lincoln. Just Lincoln.

What did that mean for me? Most days, I felt so in touch with my feelings I might drown in them. Right now, I couldn't untangle a single thread of the knots in my belly.

The car behind me beeped. My heart jumped. The light turned green, and I'd been daydreaming about Lincoln's hand on the small of my back as I read one of his mystery books.

My hands clutched the steering wheel. I kept my gaze straight when the car behind me merged into the lane next to me to pass. My chest tightened when they lined their car next to mine for the typical "What the hell are you doing?" stare before they sped off and cut in front of me.

I should let it wash off me. It was a stranger I'd never see again. Road rage that, in the grand scheme of things, would have no long-term effects on me. And yet, I let those two minutes consume me. I became someone unable to perform simple tasks, like pressing the gas when the light turns green, and understanding how a guy could make her feel.

When I pulled into the parking lot, a cloud of unworthiness seemed to hover above me. Who would want to work with someone incapable of being normal enough to go outside without spiraling into a self-loathing cyclone? Who would want to be with someone like me?

I tried to ground myself by swiping on another coat of lip gloss. I considered pulling out my liner, too, but a van pulled up a few spaces away, and I'd recognize that shade of yellow anywhere.

My stomach bottomed out. I topped off my lips once more before opening my door. I tried to smile and make my expression welcoming.

Lincoln smiled when he got out of the van. His expression faltered when he laid eyes on me.

"Hey," Lincoln said. "We're not doing that."

We met at the back of my car. He smelled of spice and sun.

The t-shirt he wore clung to his chest, revealing his ripple of muscles. I don't think I've seen him out of a long-sleeved tee and a Mendell sweatshirt. It was distracting enough to channel my nerves from the red light incident to when I helped Lincoln into his house when he fell. When my knee landed between his legs, his hand held onto my waist to keep me from falling on him. I'm oddly fond of the memory now. When moments from that day pop up, they're covered in this soft, welcoming haze.

"Doing what?" I managed to ask. I sounded like I'd been hiking for hours in silence, and I finally stopped to give someone else directions.

"Second-guessing." Lincoln used two fingers, gesturing at my face. "You've got 'abort mission' written all over you."

"Do I?" I raised a brow. I could have sworn I wore a look of displeasure. I would have sworn anyone else would have seen my expression and decided I wasn't worth the trouble. Not Lincoln. He moved within arm's reach. His smile was back, settled in its usual tilt. There was excitement in his movement as he rocked back and forth, unable to keep still as he told me, "I've been up all night working on the set designs."

I came down from my nervous high to rest on the soft cloud that was Lincoln's enthusiasm. I could burrow into this feeling, relax in its security. One of the things I'd come to appreciate about Lincoln was his familiarity with excitement. He found a way to water it, allowing it to grow into something he could survive on. "All night?"

"When I tell you this is going to blow your mind," Lincoln spoke with his hands, pulling them closer and further apart as he mimed his idea. "I'm talking towers, gazebos, gondolas."

My eyes widened. "You're going to make the gondola?"

"That's the easiest thing on the list." He nodded, eyes alight with thrill and confidence.

I would laugh, but shock stopped me. I'd figured Lincoln

and my job tonight would mainly consist of deciding which boxes to pick through in the Playhouse's storage room.

"I didn't...I don't expect you to make new sets," I said. "That's so much work. We could just reuse some of the stuff from previous shows."

"I want to do the work," he said. "Your story deserves personalization. And we'll still use some of the other stuff. I just wanted to ensure the big moments hit, capture your vision."

"I don't think this project will be worth all this effort," I said. "You working outside of the hours we're together is..."

"Is?"

"I just want you to get the proper credit you need for class. And if you're working on it outside of our time at the Playhouse, I don't know if you'll get credit for it."

"It's not about the credit," Lincoln said. "I'd work on this even if it wasn't for my course."

I blinked; my chest tightened with all kinds of emotion I didn't know how to translate. "Really?"

He nodded. "I like doing something besides a party or wondering when my next party will be. I had all this pent-up energy since our season ended. I need to let it out somehow. You're doing me a favor, Celeste. I promise."

I studied him. We didn't know each other well enough to understand our different types of smiles or which eyebrow tilt meant we were being honest. But somehow, I trusted how breathless he sounded. Lincoln wanted to be here. He was genuinely interested in my work. I didn't know what to do with the thrill overflowing in my belly. His joy was contagious. He was some new, bright sun, pulling things into its orbit and giving them much-needed life. I wanted to be the closest planet. I wanted to be near enough to be wrapped in his warmth.

"I have the form you need to fill out to get credit." I perked up with energy, hurried to the back of my car, and returned to the front of Lincoln to give him the folder. "You and Jack just have to fill out the time sheets and get the playhouse manager to sign them."

Lincoln accepted the folder. "Do you know if your aunt would be okay with doing it weekly? We have check-ins with our supervising professor every Friday."

"Of course," I said. "Aunt Robyn's good with keeping up with paperwork. She runs this place mostly on her own. You'll probably be able to meet her today. I think they're rehearsing for one of the summer shows."

Lincoln smiled. "Perfect."

"Should we…um, go inside?" I asked.

Lincoln nodded. "I'll follow your lead."

I resisted the urge to pick at my nails as we walked. The sun dipped below the mountains, leaving the air cool. Monroe's Playhouse was a historic building, featuring a brownstone exterior and an old, yellowed marquee. Inside, the walls were lined with red velvet, and the floor was an elegant marble, making everything feel far more sophisticated than a small college town had any right to be. Tinsel possessed a tiny, well-known community of theatre lovers. It gave birth to a couple of big names in Broadway today and continued to nurture smaller ones.

I started up the stairs toward the mezzanine, pressing my index finger to my lips when Lincoln met my gaze. He mirrored my gesture and winked. I swallowed a laugh, stomach fluttering from the smile he gave me. He followed me so closely that I felt the heat radiating off his body. I envisioned pausing without warning on the staircase. He'd bump into me if I did. I'd feel his hard chest on my back. My cheeks burned from imagining being pressed against him. Was this how others felt when indulging in fantasy? It was far more physically demanding than I had imagined.

I didn't get turned on by people. Arousal in correlation to someone else had been foreign to me. I learned about horniness by sneaking romance books into my library stacks in high school. I would thumb through the pages, wondering what it meant to have my core heat or how one's breast swelled at the mere sight of someone. I didn't like the thought of a stranger touching me. I didn't like the idea of someone I didn't know in my space. Except recently, every time we talked, something in me wanted to be closer to Lincoln: no needy core or pebbled nipples but a gentle want to feel his fingers against mine.

I hoped our hands brushed when we sat in the back row and both set our arms on the armrest. I wanted to test these new emotions, see if the desire in my veins would react to his touch and be satisfied by it. But our fingers were nowhere near each other when we settled. And Lincoln didn't seem flirty. He was a million miles away. His gaze was on the stage, his eyes wide and mesmerized as he watched the actors practicing below.

I also directed my attention to the practice. I pushed away my heart's unusual flutter when Lincoln leaned over to whisper in my ear.

"Is it always like this?" he asked, voice hushed with reverence.

"What do you mean?" I whispered back, refusing to remove my gaze from the stage because he was close enough for me to notice how he hadn't shaved in a couple of days. Close enough his deep voice vibrated at a frequency that made every inch of my body alert and in need of finding the right tune to complement his.

"Being in a theatre," he said.

"Is this your first time?"

"It is. I think you've ruined me, Celeste."

My breath caught in my throat, hands itched to reach out to his. He was so close, and it was dark, and I needed to feel someone solid. And here he was, the guy who had been so consistent in how he interacted with me. Steady in how he talked to me.

Lincoln was already looking at me when I turned to him. His smile was small, and his hand rested underneath his perfect jaw. How did I not notice how perfect his birthmarks were before now? They were arranged like a connect-the-dot image, ready for me to paint a million and one designs on. Butterflies. Stars. Flowers. Hearts. Lincoln was a perfect canvas, and I could decorate every inch of his skin.

"I don't know how someone experiences something like this and ever leaves." He looked back at the stage. The band started up their next song. It must be a sound check day because otherwise, the actors would have used a recording of the music. Live music always made the experience ten times more awe-inspiring. We could feel the swell of the cello in the air. Our eardrums trembled from the pounding percussion.

There was a special kind of beauty in falling in love with a song along with someone else. The intimacy of catching each other's gaze right when the music swelled was unmatched. Lincoln was quiet as he listened, eyes widening at all the dramatic moments. Shoulders relaxing when the string section offered a sense of peace. His enjoyment made the experience ten times more memorable. It was difficult not to stare, but I wanted to watch every change in his expression. Lincoln was fascinating, beautiful, and so honest. It was far easier to let my guard down around honest people. And, I realized, far easier to want to be around them.

"I think I'll pitch a tent right here," Lincoln decided. He kicked up his feet, resting the back of his heels on the chair in front of us. "Live here until I run out of food and water."

I smiled because I'd thought the same thing the first time I witnessed live music. "How long will that be?"

"Well, there was a water fountain in the lobby, so I'm good on that." He dug into his front pockets and retrieved a box of mints and a lollipop. "This is plenty of calories."

"For a guy like you?"

"I have way more willpower than it seems, okay? I could probably last a week on this."

"You're a hockey player," I said.

"Another indication of my willpower," he insisted.

I chewed on my bottom lip, holding back a laugh. "You'd be starving before midnight."

"I'll feed off the vibes," he said.

"Ravished."

"Don't underestimate the power passion has to satiate. You've never pulled an all-nighter thanks to desire alone?" He glanced at me again; the mischief in his eyes made his expression a little dangerous.

My skin heated. I got his meaning all mixed up because I was used to him flirting. And I was used to brushing it off. But today, I liked the idea of being teased. I wanted it.

I dipped my gaze down to my lap. "I haven't."

"I doubt that," he said. "Your music has to keep you up."

"My music?" Right. Of course, he'd been talking about music. Not sex. Why would he be talking about sex at a time like this? And why was I thinking about it when I wanted to avoid people like the plague?

Maybe that was never entirely true.

I swallowed the revelation. Everything's tangled, the knots getting tighter with every second that passes.

"Of course, your music...unless you have another calling you've been working on. I wouldn't say I'm not surprised. You're an incredible musician, composer, and writer." Lincoln held up his fingers as he listed everything off. "You can probably sing and dance. You probably passed all your courses with straight As. You volunteer on the weekends, create art on your skin, and charm your way into the minds of everyone you meet."

I was overwhelmed, taking apart everything he'd said, I could do. Everything he said I am.

"I don't make straight As. I'm behind in my courses," I

blurted. "Because I've been dropping any of them with a presentation requirement. I'm so off track, I'm set to graduate three or four semesters late."

I shared my shortcomings because I needed to break his illusion of me. The idea someone who writes good music, earns good grades, and is charming was a myth. A version of myself I would never live up to. A part of me was on the defense, too. I wanted to darken his idea of me so he might pull away. Because if he did, there was a decent possibility I wouldn't have to address his growing pull on me.

"I don't think I'll ever leave my parents' house if I don't get this mentorship. This musical is... It's my best shot at changing my trajectory."

The words settled between us, threatening to become a wall or a bridge.

"I'm not on track to graduate," Lincoln said gently after a short lull. "My trajectory is kind of shot, too."

I raised a brow, surprised by the confession. Honored he'd trust me with it. "Really?"

"I've failed more classes than I thought possible in a college career," he said. "And with the way last hockey season went, I'm not getting any more chances soon. So, I get it. I know how it feels like you're on your last chance. If you don't get this right, you're shoved into a lane of life you don't want to be in. One you don't have control over."

I nodded and dipped my gaze down to my lap because I couldn't stand meeting his gaze for longer than a few seconds now. The way he spoke to me, gentle and understanding, relieved the tension in my shoulders. I wasn't alone in my shortcomings. Lincoln didn't look at me as someone to pity. I don't think he ever had.

"We're in the same boat," he promised. "And I swear to you, Celeste, we're going to make this work. You'll get the mentorship."

Lincoln leaned on the armrest nearest to me. My breath

caught at the sudden closeness. It didn't last for more than a few seconds, and yet, I was left in a daze.

This is not good. I wanted to give him things: time or attention. I wanted to give him my space. My hands, cheeks, and lips. I wanted him to lean into me with purpose and linger.

But he was only leaning over to pull something out of his pocket. It was a red Moleskine that'd seen better days.

"Was it run over by a bus?" It was a joke. My smile faded when he nodded.

"Twice," Lincoln said, nonchalantly as he slipped off the elastic band and started flipping through the pages.

I laughed, waiting for him to elaborate, but he was already focused on the sketches on the pages. I got distracted too, impressed by the detail in the drawings.

"Did you draw these?" I asked.

"Only the shitty ones like this."

Lincoln pointed to a lopsided drawing of something I couldn't quite make out. Next to it was an intricate design for a column laced with flowers.

"I'm an ideas person," Lincoln said. "Not an artist. Which is why I like to hang out with people like you or Henrik."

"Henrik drew these?"

Lincoln nodded. "I told him what I needed, and he came up with the rest. When he didn't have the time, I did what I could. It's horrible, but enough to get my ideas out of my head."

"You're not so bad…" I paused when he turned the page to reveal a set of stick figures on a boat. It was comical in its lack of artistic merit. I bit the inside of my cheek, trying not to smile too widely. He was trying. And it was the sweetest thing. Although his drawing skills were severely lacking, I could see the immense effort put into the work, as evidenced by the numerous lines erased and redrawn.

"I have thick skin, Celeste." Lincoln chuckled. "You don't have to be so nice."

"I'm not being so nice..." I pointed to one of his drawings. "See, that's really cool. It's a great idea for...you know...what it obviously is..."

"I do know what it obviously is." He smiled at me, amused. "But do you?"

"Of course," I said. "It's on the tip of my tongue. The obvious thing you drew is at the tip of my tongue."

"Go on." He relaxed back in his seat. "We've got more than enough time for you to remember what it's called."

I laughed at how he wasn't going to let me off easy. Lincoln passed the Moleskine to me, encouraging me to look closer. He didn't care about being bad at drawing. Lincoln wasn't embarrassed in his lack of proficiency when creating, and yet, he did it anyway.

The music below us continued to play. The song was slow and cheerful. I wasn't looking at the stage anymore, and I didn't know what play they were putting on. But I guessed it was a scene that captured a cozy lull in the story. A pocket of time where the audience got the chance to get lost in the beauty of a fantasy world and forgot all about the world outside of the Playhouse's walls. I'm falling into a fantasy world of my own, too. One where Lincoln smiled at me as if I were the most interesting person on earth. One where he watched me with so much focus in his gaze, as if my company was more thrilling than anything he's ever experienced. Somehow, his attention gave me courage. His nonchalance tugged me closer. I straightened my fingers again and brushed against the side of his palm on purpose. Lincoln didn't pull away. His pinky finger flexed slightly, returning my touch. It was nothing. It was everything. It was a hint that maybe his crush hadn't faded after all my months of radio silence.

"I could give you a hint," he said.

"Would you?"

"It'll cost you," he sang, voice low and teasing.

It was hard to breathe in the best way possible. "You can't draw, act, or play any instrument. But you can sing. You lied. You said you couldn't."

He gave me a look.

"What? I'm serious," I promised.

"You shot a thousand arrows and then flattered me," he teased.

I chewed on my bottom lip, trying not to laugh. "Sorry, but are they really arrows when they're the truth?"

"The truth?"

"You can't draw, Lincoln," I whispered. "It's...actually kind of comical how terrible you are."

"Is that so?"

"Very much so."

"I like this biting side of you," he confessed.

I felt the comfort I'd exclusively experienced with Naomi coil around me. "I don't mean to be biting."

"But you're so good at it," he said.

There was a lump in my throat. I couldn't swallow it, so I remained silent, letting the music below fill up the space between us. I really wanted to be able to have a back-and-forth with him. Come up with witty things to say and flirt back. Instead, I hit a wall I couldn't climb.

"Look here." Lincoln broke the silence, pointing at the rounded end he could only reach by sliding his hand underneath mine. "And here."

He moved again, his fingers left hot trails across my skin. I still wasn't in warm core or swollen breast territory. But I did feel something stir in me.

"It's a balcony," he said.

"Why is it horizontal?" I asked.

"Because it'd be easier to build it sideways, and then we could get a rope to pull it up."

"Yeah, sure, but why'd you have to draw it sideways and not up? Wouldn't whoever was building it be able to concur they should build it sideways without the visual aid?"

He opened his mouth and closed it, trying to think of a decent response. I laughed again. This was more than I laughed in weeks. Maybe even months. The weight of school had made everything black and white. With Lincoln, I could finally see colors in between.

"I'm really happy we're working together," I said before I could overthink. "This project has felt so impossible for so long. But now with you…I can see it happening. And…thank you. For putting in all this work. It…thank you, Lincoln."

"I got you." Lincoln smiled and brushed his hand against mine once more. "You focus on getting all the music together, and I will do everything else. Don't worry about anything. This is going to be amazing."

CHAPTER FOURTEEN
CELESTE

Their overlapping voices formed a symphony of opinions that didn't intend to cause harm but still pierced me. Halle was right; the music felt short and the lines were too hollow. Ellis' point stood: live music would leave a more lasting impact, so I needed confirmation on whether we'd get an orchestra. Jack was worried about the sets and how long it'd take to assemble them since now we had so many pieces. Even Finn offered input, noting various backstage hazards.

I tried to keep up, reaching for my notebook only to remember I didn't bring my bag on stage. I hadn't thought I'd be up here this long under the burning lights. But our fifteen-minute pre-rehearsal meeting had turned into forty-five minutes.

"Alright, everyone!" Lincoln's voice possessed a sense of authority that called for more than attention, but silence. They stared at him, expecting him to chide them. And I expected as much, too, even though I wasn't the recipient of his scolding stare.

"Let's stop talking for a second and listen to our director," he said. "All your questions and thoughts can wait until you actually learn what it is she needs from you."

Lincoln's gaze found mine then, expression softening. I wanted to lean into him. He was a rock outside of the shoreline. I wasn't quite out of the high tide yet, but safe enough for the moment.

All eyes were on me. My fingertips tingled, and my mouth went hot with the familiar preparation of throwing up. Ellis gave me a subtle thumbs up, but paired it with his "this isn't going well" face. Not on purpose…I think. Regardless, it made my breathing shallow because my panic was now apparent.

"I…" All I had to do was debrief them. Explain to them what decision I'd made. And as easy as that sounded, it'd become a mountain. Every idea I'd had sounded useless.

We all stood in silence for what felt like a millennium. Lincoln, still next to me, turned so his back was toward them and his face was toward me. He leaned down slightly and whispered,

"Do we need a break?" His smile was small, unjudging, as if he did this all the time. As if he micromanaged panicked twenty-somethings regularly.

"Just a minute," I barely got out.

He nodded and ordered everyone, "Take five! Don't go far."

In a low voice, he asked me, "Do you know a private spot where we can talk?"

I nodded, numb as I turned to the curtain.

"I still think this part is a little out of your range, El," Halle said.

"You know a lot of range all of a sudden," Jack chimed in.

"She's not wrong," Ellis agreed. "How about you give it a try?"

"Funny," Jack said.

"Yeah, give it a try," Halle agreed, mocking.

"Finn, grab my phone real quick," Kaya said. "This is going to be good."

Conversation flowed back into its normal rhythm as if they hadn't been about to make my head explode with their arguing mere seconds ago.

The closer we got to the curtain, the less I could feel my legs. Lincoln took the lead, trying to open the curtain in one sweeping motion. He got tangled, and I stood in silence as he went toe to toe with the curtain. One might think the odds would be in his favor. I mean, playing hockey had to give one possession of some kind of agility, right?

It was when his legs got caught in the fray I decided it was time to step in.

"I think if you just…" I stepped forward and easily untangled the curtain from his legs, pulling it back. I didn't laugh until we were backstage.

"There she is." Lincoln laughed a bit, too.

"Thank you for that."

"That, unfortunately, wasn't on purpose."

I nodded. "I know. I meant you getting their attention. Trying to help me be a director even when… I'm so clearly not one."

I sobered, picking at a hangnail with nervous aggression. "I'm so sorry. I thought I was ready…I thought I'd be able to at least…say something. *Anything*."

"Hey, hey. Do not apologize. You've done nothing wrong." Lincoln reached for my hand, covering the irritated skin. "Breathe. Ready?"

I took a deep breath, and he counted for me.

"Again." He instructed, stepping closer so he could place my hand over his chest. I felt him expand and contract with each breath. We kept going, syncing up after a few breaths. We held one another's gaze as he brought me back down to earth. His hand remained gently on top of mine. I could pull away whenever I wanted…that wouldn't be anytime soon.

Lincoln's thumb massaged circles on the back of my hand. I leaned in closer, pressing my forehead against his chest just to feel more grounded, closer, and his. With my eyes closed, I imagined I was his, and I love the idea. Loved it so much my breathing hitched.

"It's okay," he soothed, not knowing that made things worse. "You're okay."

I didn't know how to do this. What was the next step after wanting someone? Surely not telling them. No, not immediately...but what if they'd wanted you first? He had wanted me first, right? That was some time ago, before this summer, before he got to know me. And since then, Lincoln hadn't flirted once. He'd moved on. And who wouldn't if the person you were texting ghosted you for months?

Why had I ghosted him? Why had I taken so long to get to this point? Why was I worried about this now when there were far more pressing issues to figure out?

"I'm..." I tried, pulling my head off his chest. "I'm so frustrated. "

"It's a lot of moving pieces," Lincoln agreed, of course, oblivious to the fact that he was the sole cause of my budding frustration. He continued to trace circles on my skin. My gaze dipped down to my hand underneath his. It was almost completely covered.

"Let's take our time," Lincoln said.

"Okay." I was too breathy and lightheaded. Lincoln was consistently here, patient, and interested. I'd promised him nothing. He didn't expect that to change, and yet, he was still here. And maybe that was evidence of lingering feelings. No matter how small, it was worth the risk. Taking a chance on Lincoln was worth the embarrassment of being wrong.

"What do you want them to do?" he asked. "Think of one thing you want from them. From me."

I shook my head, pushing away my evolving feelings for him in exchange for work. I needed to focus. Questioning the evolution of romantic feelings would be for the sleepless night I undoubtedly had ahead of me.

I tried to recall everything they'd suggested at the beginning of the meeting. "I don't know. I want to keep hearing their thoughts, I think. They had some good ideas for changes. Improvements."

"You want to implement their changes?" he asked.

I shrugged. "I think I should."

Lincoln gave a dismissive wave toward the curtain. "When they have their own musical production, we'll prioritize their changes. But right now, what does Celeste want to see on that stage? Block them out and listen to that voice in your head."

I chewed on my bottom lip as I tried to internalize his advice. My fingers drummed aimlessly on his chest, picking up a beat in my head from one of the songs I wanted to run today. I took a moment to think, shoving the feedback everyone had for me in the far corner of my mind.

"Tell me what to do," he whispered, trying his best not to break my concentration too much.

"Get them to run the final song," I decided.

Lincoln smiled. "Yeah?"

"I need to start at the end," I said. "I always do."

"Alright, perfect. Sounds like we're back in business," he said.

I nodded, matching his smile. Neither of us moved, though. My gaze slipped from his eyes down to his lips. I didn't mean for it to, but being this close for this long had made it nearly impossible to avoid. And Lincoln's lips were beautiful, with the slightest hint of a cupid's bow that curved out into full roundness.

His hand still covered mine. Something had changed, and it took me a second to realize it was his chest. It wasn't moving as much as it used to. While I still took deep, steady breaths, his had become shallow. His heart pounded.

Is it because of you? It could still be because of you.

"Should I..." he tried, clearing his throat and looking away. He licked his lips, trying to ready himself to finish his sentence. He was nervous. I wanted so much to help. I wanted to know what he was thinking. And I was finally calm and brave enough to ask.

"Is this because of me?" I brushed my thumb across his chest, referencing his racing heart.

"Always." He still looked everywhere but my face.

My stomach was overwhelmed with butterflies. "Still?"

He chuckled, embarrassed. "Yes. It never stopped. Never went away."

"Lincoln," I whispered.

"I didn't do this for that," he promised, matching my lowered volume. "I'm here because I believe in you. Not because I'm holding out for an 'us'. I swear."

"I know."

"Good." He finally met my gaze, and when he saw what was in my eyes, his forehead wrinkled in confusion. "Right?"

"Right." I nodded and lifted myself on my toes. The movement felt more natural than breathing. Being this close to Lincoln was as relaxing as an exhale.

"This is..." He couldn't finish his sentence. Our noses brushed. I felt his breath mingle with mine. I knew I needed to run the final song. I needed to finish my edits on the opening. I needed to get this mentorship. And I needed to kiss him. I needed it all and preferably not in that order.

"Good?" Lincoln asked a million things with one word.

"Yes," I whispered against his lips.

Lincoln closed the remaining space. His lips were soft and gentle against mine. I didn't feel any sort of uncertainty. I knew exactly what I wanted and how I wanted it to be. An unknown part of me opened, like unlocking some secret level in a game. I understood heaving breath and swelling breasts.

The need to be so close to Lincoln I didn't know where I began and he ended.

But his energy didn't match mine. Lincoln was timid, holding back in the kiss when I parted my lips, offering more. His hand over mine loosened to the point where I could barely feel it. He was the first to pull away.

My forehead wrinkled as I tried to read him. But the guy who had been a constant open book was back on the shelf.

"I...sorry." He tried to laugh, but nothing more than an exhale came out. "That was...sorry."

"No, it's okay." I shook my head, cheeks burning. I'd read that all wrong. He *had* been over me.

Not because I'm holding out for an 'us'.

His words repeated over and over in my mind, mocking me. I pressed my fingers to my lips, wishing the kiss could be wiped away. Wishing I hadn't stood on my toes and asked him to do it.

"Celeste—"

"Could you get them to run it?" I asked, unable to meet his eyes. "We're behind schedule. Let's just...run it. We've wasted too much time."

"You got it." He nodded. "But we're talking after because I need you to know, I fucking loved every second of that. And I panicked. That's on me, you haven't done anything wrong."

His assurance changed the tide. A part of me didn't believe him, but as soon as I looked in his eyes, I knew it was true. Now, my next question was why? Why had he panicked?

"You and me?" He squeezed my hand. "After?"

"Yeah," I agreed.

Lincoln let me go and went back on stage. I took a moment, still behind the curtain, my fingers on my lips as I tried to fix my face to something normal. Something that wouldn't give away that my world had shifted.

CHAPTER FIFTEEN
LINCOLN

Her music looped in my head throughout practice. The melody was almost as all-consuming as her lips had been on mine.

But it was safer to think of the soft notes instead of her silky skin. Or my hand capturing the warmth of hers. Her body leaning into mine. That very real look in her eyes, I once daydreamed of being there.

The first thought that came to mind when our lips touched was: I didn't think we'd get here.

The second: *had* we got here? Truly taken all the steps?

All my report cards labelled me a class clown (derogatory). I liked the attention the laughs earned me. Humor made people feel good, welcomed, and safe. I loved that those feelings could be wrapped up in something as simple as a joke. Something that easy could build bridges. Move mountains.

It hadn't worked like that with Celeste. Connecting with her was something I was still trying to master. But I'd been getting better and sensed when she needed 'serious Lincoln,' 'Take control,' Lincoln, 'Don't leave my side,' Lincoln. And I was more than happy to be any version she wanted.

I worked hard to earn her smiles. But I'd done nothing to be in kissing territory.

When I got over the initial shock, all I could think of was whether this kiss was happening because she felt overwhelmed. I grabbed her hand and placed it on me. We were close enough to hear one another's heartbeats. And she'd been so nervous, so panicked. I was the only thing keeping her calm.

Celeste hadn't given me a single hint her mind had changed about me before our kiss. And I had been honest in letting the idea of us go. Because being even a small part of her life meant everything to me.

The idea of her kissing me because of fear didn't sit right with me. Enjoying it felt like taking advantage. I'd pulled away. And instantly regretted it because of the look of hurt in her eyes.

A talk was what we needed. And something we didn't get. After hours of rehearsal, Celeste's aunt called her away at the end of it. A couple of days passed, and I replayed everything forward and backward. We texted and finally found a gap in our schedule to meet before the next rehearsal to figure everything out.

Celeste's music carried me through a warm-up and thirty minutes of my session with Anthony before he noticed. Before he realized mentally, I was nowhere near the ice and had no intention of being there anytime soon.

"Lincoln!" he shouted, pulling me back into this icy abyss. "What the hell?"

I stared at him, obviously missing something. It took me a beat to put together that he'd gotten his third puck past me, and I hadn't done much more than half-assed attempts at defense.

"You're good," I said. "Might even be a professional."

I could practically hear his teeth grinding from here.

"The plan this summer wasn't to use some guy's grandma as a cash cow," Anthony said. "But now, you're making this feel downright exploitative."

We're on our own today. No Henrik to be a buffer, sanding down our rough edges. I couldn't bury my lack of effort behind my friend's hard-earned skills.

"If it's any consolation," I said. "I plan to pay her back in full. So, you won't be exploiting someone's grandma but some jackass goalie."

"That so?" Anthony sighed, releasing the tension in his shoulders. At the beginning of every session, he was a walking and talking wall of nerves. He watched everything (including me) with such intense purpose that if I didn't know any better, I'd think he owed someone a ton of cash and was afraid of losing everything at the drop of a hat if things didn't go exactly as he had planned.

"I'm curious," Anthony said. "How exactly do you plan on doing that?"

I leaned on my hockey stick. "What do you mean?"

"Money. How are you making it? Because it's not going to be through any league I've ever heard of."

"I'm good at thinking on my feet," I said. "There's a plethora of jobs for guys who know how to do party tricks. Who knows, maybe I'll get into legal gambling. I do have firsthand experience on what not to do."

Anthony didn't crack a smile, just as expected.

"What a waste," he said under his breath.

I felt sucker punched. "What?"

"You," he said, louder and determined for each word to stick into me like push pins. "A waste."

He started to skate away, leaving me in the middle of the ice to wonder what the hell I did wrong this time. Out of all the other times I'd been a million miles away in some daydream, why was this time different?

"Hey!" I called after him, substituting my dismay for the frustration that was tearing me apart. I held out my arms. "What are you doing?"

"Salvaging what's left of my summer." He stopped at the exit to call back to me. "There's a guy in Wyoming. He's not as good as you, but he's been emailing me for months. No one will take a chance on him. He deserves a shot."

Because I've wasted mine.

My mouth was dry. He wasn't just thinking of leaving; he already had a plan in place. And it wasn't just the fear of disappointing Sam that threatened to swallow me whole. My own fear of failure was upon me.

I couldn't stomach this session ending like this. I couldn't imagine going into next season and semester the same way I left last: coasting.

I hurried over to Anthony before he could step off the ice, nearly tripping over my skates to stop him. Something in me knew if he left now, that'd be the last I'd see him. And my panic told me it'd be the closing of a door—the end of my chances. I'd run out of luck. Out of favor with fate.

"Come on, man," I said, focusing hard on making my voice sound normal. Making myself sound like I could survive another disappointment. "I can defend, you know I can defend. Give me another round and I'll prove it."

Anthony sighed. "It's not about defending. It's not about how many pucks I get past you."

"Then...what are we doing?" I asked.

"Exactly." Anthony pointed at me. "Have you done any of the outside exercises I've given you? Have you reviewed the videos I've sent? Really studied the techniques?"

I opened my mouth, ready to spout a lie or some joke to smooth this all over. But I couldn't. All lightness had been burned out of me thanks to the finality in Anthony's nod. Every moment outside of our practice time, I was doing something for the musical or lazing about the house.

"That's what I thought." He took a breath, slowly calming his voice down. He'd cycled out of the disappointment and now, all left was surrender. He unloaded his proverbial pack onto my back.

"You've got the kind of talent most guys dream of," he said. "Enough of it to go as far as you want. But you're satisfied with where you are, which is fine. It's good for you. But I can't do anything with good."

Satisfied? I mulled the word over, and it had a nauseating taste.

"I'm..." I was not satisfied. I hadn't been since...ever? What did satisfaction even feel like?

I'd faked satisfaction. I'd learned how to do so by watching Sam after a good game, Finn figuring out another piece of his fractured personality, or Henrik ensuring everyone in the house was fed. But I hadn't experienced it firsthand, and there was shame in that.

"You'll figure something out," Anthony said, his voice didn't have the sharp edge he'd possessed the entire time we'd known each other. I guess the hard exterior was reserved for people he thought could become something bigger than what stood before him.

"Good luck, Hill," he said before leaving.

I stood on the ice, unmoving. *It's not that big of a deal,* I tried to tell myself.

I'd still play next season. I'd still be the starting goalie. Still get to be with my team on the ice... one last time.

None of that comforted me. Instead, I was somehow burning from the inside out. Lungs full of nothing but regret and dread. Why didn't I try? Why couldn't I have just tried?

"Lincoln?" Her voice pulled me out of the flame.

I didn't see her come in. Or how long she'd been here. She stood in the bench area, wearing a pink dress, her hair pulled up on top of her head, and her beautiful eyes lined in purple.

"Hey, sorry, am I late?" I asked, confused and a million

miles away. I skated over to her, meeting her at the boards. She smelled like a fantasy, and I'd just fucked up my summer. How was I ever going to deserve a woman as talented, brilliant, and driven as her if I couldn't commit to making a future for myself?

"No, you're not late," Celeste promised. "I was...I didn't want to sit around the house when I could just hang out on campus... so I thought I'd come early to...see you. Are you okay?"

"I'm good." I tightened my grip on my hockey stick. "We ended early and I... I'm going to need a second to get showered and changed. Then we can head out and talk."

"We don't have to," she offered quickly. "I didn't mean to rush you. We could go straight to the playhouse. You seem... distracted?"

"I've been looking forward to seeing you all day, so even if I were busy with something, I'd drop it," I confessed. It was the one thing I can say with my whole chest today, tomorrow, and forever.

"You wouldn't have to drop anything. I'd never expect you to do that. Hockey's just as important to you as my music is to me."

I chuckled under my breath, not a trace of humor in sight.

"Hockey is just as important to me," I repeated, words hollow.

Celeste studied me, gaze shadowed with confusion about my tone.

"I'm not rushing, Celeste. I'm done with my session, and I'm very conscious of how behind we are in finishing the paint job on those buildings. I'm going to clean up real quick and be back." I said, ready to make my escape in a cold shower and wash away all the muddy emotion this day left on my skin.

I hated being like this. I wanted a drink. A party. A night

in a place where nothing mattered besides the next song on the playlist or the next nonsensical thing coming out of some stranger's mouth.

"I'll be here," Celeste promised.

CHAPTER SIXTEEN
CELESTE

sat in the stands, going back and forth on how to bring up what I saw in Lincoln's eyes. I'd been worried all day about what he had to say about our kiss. But the moment I saw him, all that 'what if' fear dissipated, replaced with concern.

Lincoln's practice hadn't gone well. But there was something more than disappointment in his tone when I spoke to him. Something so familiar, my heart ached when I recognized it.

I never could have predicted looking at Lincoln would be like looking in a mirror. Tonight, I'd seen a part of myself I'd known in my deepest isolation.

It's not your business. Don't put a spotlight on something that's obviously bothering him. Don't make him uncomfortable.

I almost listened to the warning, but then I remembered how light my chest was while I laughed with him in the theatre. How comfortably lost I got while listening to him explain the tabs in his worn Carter paperbacks. Whenever I found his gaze already on me, offering an encouraging smile at rehearsals, the knots in my stomach loosened long enough for me to breathe again.

Lincoln gave me comfort. Safety.

I couldn't gloss over how he looked. Wouldn't, because now, it was my turn to offer that safety.

Lincoln buried himself like I did. He'd done it far more successfully and with far more grace than I ever could. But that didn't mean it made him feel any less lonely.

When he came out of the locker rooms, I was quick on my feet, meeting him at the bottom of the stands. He smelled as fresh as the pine of the mountains. The shower had washed away his worried brow.

"When you're out there," I nudged my chin to the ice, starting the conversation immediately because I knew if I didn't get it out soon, it'd stay trapped in my throat forever. "What are you thinking about?"

"Today? Every single rise and fall in your finale," he said without missing a beat.

I smiled. "Now, for real this time."

"I wouldn't joke about that," he promised.

I was still not used to flattery, but I resisted the urge to dip my gaze. I wanted to stay connected with him.

"Why?" I asked.

"Was I thinking about it? Or why I'd never joke about it?"

"Former."

"Because it helps me feel close to you," he said. "And when I'm overwhelmed and don't want to be somewhere, I distract myself with something comforting."

How was I supposed to keep talking to him without stammering? Without feeling completely undone and put back together all at once?

"When you were out there," I said, quilling the buzzing warmth of his compliment by picking at my bag's strap. "I noticed you held back whenever it came time to...do anything really."

I didn't know hockey, but I knew what it looked like to hide and hesitate. It was in the simple adjustment of his hands, the way he pulled them to his sides too prematurely. He stopped trying before the puck even reached him. He assessed the situation, yet he didn't take any action to influence the outcome.

Lincoln tilted his head to the side, studying me. "What do you mean?"

I shrugged. "You've always seemed like a full steam ahead kind of guy. But not out there. It's unlike you."

"Just because we've been hanging out all summer doesn't mean you've seen every part of me, Celeste."

The response gave me pause. I swallowed, fighting the urge to retreat into the shelter anxiety provided.

"No, no, of course not." I shook my head, cheeks aflame. "I know I don't know every part of you...I just thought I saw some small part that I could understand. It was...almost like self-sabotage. Like you were purposefully trying to hold back."

I wanted to be there for him like he'd been there for me. I *would* be there for him. Anxiety could have a lot of things, but I refused to let it have this.

Lincoln's smile faded, turned into a ghost that haunted the rest of our exchange. "It's not that deep, I promise you. I'm not that deep."

"Everyone's that deep," I whispered. I've been bullied, overlooked, and underestimated since I was a kid who decided to remain silent for years. I believed in multitudes, had to. I believed in a person's ability to be more than the surface-level version they presented to the public. I couldn't fathom someone made of stardust not containing beautiful secrets. And if, for some reason, they held no secrets, then I assumed someone or thing burned them out.

"What you see is what you get, Celeste," Lincoln said.

I wanted him to stay with me, but he pulled away again. He was fortifying his walls as soon as I was curious to understand what was behind them.

"Let's get out of here," he said before I could probe a second longer. "The arena's eerie this time of year. Too empty, too quiet."

He waited till I cleared the stairs before starting toward the exit. I followed, my thoughts racing a mile a minute as I thought of ways to touch someone who was just out of reach.

———

Lincoln made an excuse to go to the playhouse early. Apparently, the set needed immediate attention, and Jack wasn't going to do it right without him. So, we left campus, the air between us heavy with the strange concoction that was our kiss and his withdrawal.

I put my ruminations about self-sabotage and the gentleness of Lincoln's kiss on the back burner once I was with everyone else. They knew their lines, and for the first time, I had a complete recording of the music.

We ran through each scene; everyone hit their marks. Halle made a small mistake on one of her lines, but she recovered in time to meet Ellis at center stage. Thank God for a figure skater's stamina and grace.

It was all coming together like the final strokes of a painting. The only thing lacking was the structure of the finale. I couldn't figure out how to make it land with grace in exchange for its current screeching halt finish. I'd spent most of the week revising, taking things apart, and putting them back together. The songs had been edited sixteen times since the last meeting.

"It's perfect." Lincoln rested his elbows on the piano, smiling down at me. His mood lightened when he was around everyone. I was happy for him, but there was a string of sadness coiled inside my stomach because I couldn't do that for him.

"I...sure," I mumbled as I undid everything we'd just done

with an aggressive scrub of my eraser. I got rid of last night's revision as easily as new wiper blades cut through rain. "Almost."

"Celeste?" he asked.

The others remained on the far end of the stage, lost in conversation and the joy of being done for tonight. Envy clawed at my throat as they made plans to go to some party. I wasn't just jealous of their social competence, but their ability to step into their next moment of the day without so much as the need to reflect. Without the incessant pull to nitpick every little decision they'd made with a fine-tooth comb until their soul bled.

"It's perfect," Lincoln repeated, firmer. He tried to catch my gaze, but I only had the capacity to digest my writing.

"It's missing something." I shook my head and scribbled notes into the margins.

Lincoln joined me on the bench, stacking the array pages I wasn't working on back into my binder. He knew the exact order I wanted each sheet to be in and placed a crease in the corner of the middle page because he'd seen me do it countless times.

"You have changed this over and over again. Every new addition is no more or less brilliant than the last."

"That's…" I sighed. "Easy for you to say."

"And why's that?"

"Because you don't have an ear for this stuff," I whispered, trying not to come off rude or cruel. But he didn't. Lincoln didn't know the ins and outs of composition. He didn't know how to use notes to evoke that tiny feeling I got in my stomach when I felt my world caving in and crushing me in the process. He didn't understand that not all of us could be naturally talented, do the bare minimum, and still have adoring friends, fans, and a lovely future laid ahead of us.

"I may not have an ear for it," he said. "But I do have emotions. And just because I'm into you doesn't mean I'm pretending when I say what you've written is moving. You have done something incredible, and you keep trampling over it like it's nothing. It's infuriating to watch, you know? Someone with so much talent and drive is getting in their own way simply because they can't see themselves clearly, due to a warped perspective. Do you realize how fortunate you are to possess both talent and drive? I'd give anything to be able to do half of what you've done. Anything to be brave enough to give it my all."

My hand paused. Heat traveled across my cheeks as I tried to digest his compliment and the contrasting frustration in his tone.

"You can tell me," I said gently. "You know you can. You know I'm not going to judge you for whatever's going on with you."

"I did hold back," he confessed, voice dropping in volume even though our cast was too loud to notice this new shift in Lincoln's persona. "At the arena. You were right. I self-sabotaged."

I lowered my pencil, giving him my undivided attention.

"I hate that you noticed." He laughed a little, nerves lacing throughout the sound.

"I hate that you notice me, too."

We shared a smile. Some of the rising frustration simmered.

"I don't put one hundred percent into anything," Lincoln said. "I don't believe I ever could. I don't feel like it'd be enough. And if I did try... I'd finally have tangible proof whatever I do will never quite work out."

My chest was heavy, honored he trusted me with a peek behind the curtain. I pressed my shoulder against his. "I get it."

He smiled, leaning into me, and we stayed that way, supported by one another for a moment. When I brushed my fingers against the back of Lincoln's hand, he opened his palm. I entwined my fingers with his without a second thought.

I loved how my hand fit into his, how his secured my fingers in his grasp. I loved how it felt like neither of us would ever let go, no matter what direction the other could pull us in? I wanted to be linked with him like this indefinitely. The thought of returning to an existence where there was a gulf in between us sent a gut-wrenching ache through my belly. Lincoln Hill was the only person I wanted to share my chaotic, concerning, and saddening honesty with. He was the one person I knew could keep my confessions safe while challenging me enough to question my beliefs.

Lincoln and I were building something. A world in which being seen wasn't synonymous with performing. Because that's who we were at the end of the day, two people trying their best to put on a show that would protect us from looming shame. The stage was much less intimidating with company.

"Just because you've cast yourself as the silly guy who doesn't have the drive to do something different doesn't mean you have to stay that way," I whispered and squeezed his hand. "Lincoln, you of all people are capable of being whoever you want."

He brought my hand up to his chest, pressing it there like he'd done the other night. His heart was still racing like before. "Thank you. Really…thank you. I haven't been feeling like myself today."

"Be whoever you need to be."

Lincoln studied me for a second, searching for something. "We should have that talk—"

"You two in?" Ellis interrupted, standing at the other end of the piano.

"What's that?" Lincoln asked. He didn't take his gaze off me, but I removed my hand from his, still not comfortable enough to be showing public affection to him when we didn't know what we were yet.

When I looked away from Lincoln, my gaze met Naomi's in an instant. She knew. She didn't have to give me more than a small smile to tell me she knew. Without a word, Naomi understood I couldn't keep a wide breadth anymore because no part of me wanted to.

"Party at Noel's," Halle said. "They have food and a pre-screen copy of that new superhero movie. Noel's mom's the producer."

Lincoln looked at me. I didn't want to say no, but going out would be a lot of work. I'd spent the last few hours with everyone. I liked how comfortable I was getting with our small group. But something more could push me on the cusp of burnout.

"We could do something just you and me." Lincoln's voice was lowered so only I could hear.

"Really?" I asked, unable to mask the excitement in my tone.

He smiled. "Would you like that?"

"I would," I said. "But I know you like... people."

And with all the work we'd been doing together, he hadn't been around them much.

"I'd rather spend a night with you," he promised, and before I could protest, he said to everyone else, "We're out. You guys have fun though."

"Damn," Ellis said. "You sure? Half your team's going to be there."

"Group chat says they're dying for you to bring your game," Kaya said, trying her best to sound uninterested. I'd gotten used to her enough to notice she only brought up things when she really wanted to do them.

"You love facilitating your game." I nudged my elbow against Lincoln's side.

"I'd love being with you even more," Lincoln countered.

I chewed on my bottom lip, unable to hold in my smile or maintain his gaze.

"We'll send plenty of pics in the group chat," Naomi said before anyone else could protest. She steered the conversation away from Lincoln and onto how they were divvying up the ride situation. Our bubble reclosed as Lincoln said, "I say we stop working on this tonight and do something fun."

"Your kind of fun?"

"Or yours?"

I shook my head and laughed. "My kind of fun mostly consists of solitary acts."

"I don't mind a quiet movie night. Or reading session"

"No," I said as I looked over at how excited his friends were. "I want to do something you think is fun. Something exciting. Just us, but exciting."

He raised a brow. "You sure?"

"I…yes, I think so." I crossed and uncrossed my ankles, trying to calm myself with movement. Was this going to be a date? My excitement multiplied at the thought. Anxiety made itself known, too, but didn't linger for more than a couple of seconds.

"Do you have something in mind?" I asked.

"I always have something in mind."

"Should I be prepared?" I looked down at my skirt and sandals. "Dressed a certain way?"

He looked down too. "Maybe some walking shoes?"

"Where are we going?"

"Ever been on a ghost tour?"

CHAPTER SEVENTEEN

LINCOLN

The line outside Tinsel's Ghost Tours booth was long enough for me to breathe a sigh of relief for a good season ahead. Winter was Tinsel's tourist season, thanks to the ski slopes and an impressive number of Christmas-themed shops. Summer still attracted a crowd, but most of it focused on camping and holing up in fishing cabins until August rolled around.

"Mr. Hill." Abel Johnson was an old, quiet man who owned most of the Ghost Tour buses (despite the different-named tours). His family bought up a host of tour companies after decades of working for them.

"I haven't seen you in so long, I was starting to think you moved on," he said.

"Just a busy summer," I promised. "I'll be here to use up all my membership points once fall comes around."

Abel smiled. All his children had moved out of Tinsel, and his grandchildren didn't come to visit. He spent most of his days selling tickets and driving tour buses. I'd made a habit of taking tours any free chance I got. He was so used to my presence that he created a membership card in my honor. He claimed it was a good business move, but I think he was trying to help me save some money. I countered his generosity by stocking up on Tinsel Ghost Tour merch any chance I got.

"I need two tickets." I scanned the new product display behind him. Abel loved a quirky design. He'd hired a comic artist who went by the name kraken to draw all the illustrations for the exclusive merch. "Two of those baseball caps, a large and medium tee, and what's that…? A water bottle?"

"It's horrid," Abel warned. "Tastes of plastic, no matter how much you wash it. Bad investment, I've been meaning to take them down but haven't got around to it."

"Put me down for one." I wouldn't subject Celeste to microplastics, no matter how much of a super fan I was. The bottle could be transformed into a pen holder or a flower pot.

"Where's your buddy?" he asked. "The nice one with the cookies?"

I smiled. Henrik usually accompanied me on tours. He'd ask the tour guide millions of questions and marvelled at the answers as if half of the responses weren't ad lib.

"He's actually doing something young people like to do for once: going to a party."

Abel scoffed. "I think he's better at baking."

I chuckled. "I'll tell him he owes you cookies."

"So, did you buy another ticket for one of 'em ghosts?" Abel collected my merchandise, taking his time to fold the t-shirts neatly before tucking them into the paper bag.

"Nope, I got a new partner in crime," I said. "She's using the bathroom before we head out."

I was an amalgamation of energy and nerves anytime I thought too long about Celeste being there with me. It was still unclear whether her agreeing to go out was a dream. Regardless, I was determined to make sure I enjoyed every second, even if the edges began to blur and I woke up in disappointment.

Abel raised a brow. "She?"

"We're working on a project together and decided we needed the night off for something fun."

I tried to keep my voice steady. Cool. I could be chill about this. Or, at least pretend to be, while internally I couldn't stop repeating, *she's here, don't fuck this up. She's here and we're not going to fuck this up.*

He smiled. "Oh yeah?"

My stomach dropped for a second, fearing I had shared my mantra out loud. "What?"

"This is the same girl you talked about in the book club?" he asked.

"Yeah." My amusement bloomed when Abel nodded with a sense of pride.

"Was it the flowers?" he asked.

I'd convinced Abel to join the Pinewoods Bookstore mystery book club last semester (in secret hopes Lenny and him might have some sparks). He didn't like the books, but he could stomach the company (more interested in Lenny than Lenny was interested in him). I suppose we were alike in that way, obsessed with ghost stories and prone to falling first.

Besides Lenny, Abel loved post-book club gossip. And all the attendees were old enough to offer advice to someone young enough to be still stumbling over their toes in the dating world. Our talks often led to my cider-drunk confessions centering on Celeste.

I'd come away from book club with a million suggestions. I ignored all of them in favor of not coming on too strong. Everyone had been helpful, don't get me wrong, but most of what they'd suggested would have been too overwhelming for Celeste.

"Kind of," I said, not wanting to disappoint.

Abel's gaze flickered over my shoulder, distracted enough for me to turn around. Celeste had exited the bathroom. My heart hammered in a familiar yet still disarming rhythm when I met her gaze. She smiled at me, her brow relaxing when she saw me, and started our way.

"That's her?" he asked.

"Yeah." It was hard to breathe in the best way possible. "That's Celeste."

"You should get more flowers," Abel murmured. "Every day. A woman like her deserves flowers."

I smiled and nodded. Because that was the least a guy could do for a woman like her. Celeste deserved all the flowers on every inch of the mountainside.

"Hey, sorry I took so long," she said when she got to my side.

"No worries," I said. "This is Abel. My friend. He owns the tour company."

Abel tipped his nonexistent hat to her. Celeste smiled and offered him a shy, "Nice to meet you."

"We should be heading out soon," Abel said. "In the meantime, why don't you two get yourself something on me?"

He dug out a couple of free coupons for cups of frozen lemonade and ice cream sandwiches to redeem at the cafe across the street.

"*Flowers,*" he mouthed before we could set off.

I laughed as I led Celeste to the cafe.

"What?" she looked up at me, already amused despite not knowing what I was laughing about.

"Nothing," I said. "Got you some things."

She peeked into the outstretched bag. "You didn't have to. Tourist souvenirs are a fortune in this town."

"When I go on a tour, I always like to experience it in full." I pulled out the cap and raised my brow, asking if I could put it on her.

Celeste nodded and stood still while I slipped the cap on. She repositioned her two braids so they hung over her shoulders. My fingers lingered on the rim of the hat, an excuse to stay as close to her as possible.

"Does it look okay?" she asked when far too much time was spent adjusting a simple baseball cap.

"Looks like you're ready to go ghost hunting."

Her forehead wrinkled. "I thought this was a ghost tour."

"Little column A, little column B."

"Is there a pamphlet or something?" Celeste wondered, gaze straying back to the tour booth. "So, I can get a rundown?"

"You don't need a rundown—" I tugged on the t-shirt and clipped my water bottle to my belt loop. "—when you have a seasoned professional right next to you."

She tilted her head, studying me. "A seasoned professional?"

I was still getting used to that teasing glint in her eyes and the slight hitch in her voice, which I found happened whenever she tried to flirt with me.

"Questioning my qualifications?"

She shrugged. "I'm more of a seeing-is-believing type of person."

The space between us had shrunk. I was close enough to grab her waist if I wanted. Kiss her lips. Whisper how much I wanted her.

Instead, I settled for grabbing the bottom of her shirt and gently tugging her close enough that there was nothing between us anymore.

"Want to talk?" I asked, feeling more levelheaded and ready to clear the air.

Celeste swallowed, nervous as she nodded. "Okay… explain yourself. You have five minutes."

I laughed. "I never thought I'd see the day you'd be bossy."

It's sexy and now, I'm desperate for her to tell me what to do and how to do it.

"I've waited long enough," she said. "And also, the time limit is because the tour bus boards in ten, and I really would like that frozen lemonade."

"I will make sure you have your lemonade."

"And my explanation?"

My gaze fell to her lips for a second. They're red, covered in a gloss that sparkled in the light. Had I really been lucky enough to have a taste of her?

"You'd been so anxious and stressed," I started.

She smiled. "When am I not?"

"True." I chuckled. "But I didn't want to kiss you when you were in the middle of that kind of storm. I wanted to be sure you wanted it to happen. I wanted to be sure you weren't holding on to me in fear of getting caught up in something else."

"Lincoln… I'm pretty sure I kissed you," she said. "So, yes, I wanted it to happen. Did you?"

I scoffed. "Of course, I did. And *I* kissed you."

"I stood up on my toes," she said. "Why else would I do that?"

I frowned, trying to remember. "But I leaned in."

"After I leaned in."

"Are we arguing?" A very low-stakes and arousing argument.

"We are. And you deserve it after how you pulled away." She playfully stepped back, putting unnecessary distance between us. "I panicked, and it was all I could think about, but couldn't talk about for days."

"I'm sorry." I moved closer. "I was playing it safe."

"Ask me next time," she said, distracted by my lips this time. "If I want it safe… don't assume just because I haven't… done this that you know what I want. Or need."

I nodded, breath caught in my throat, skin on fire with the need to touch her. "What do you want? What do you need? I'll make it up to you."

She stood on her toes again, and I was so hers I don't know how I'd lasted that long without her.

"A frozen lemonade," she whispered against my lips before lowering herself.

My head was buzzing from the suddenness of expectations rising. It took a moment for me to get my bearings once again before saying, "Whatever you want."

———

With our frozen lemonade in hand, Celeste and I boarded the old tour bus that would drive us around Tinsel. The sunset painted our seats a fuzzy, warm orange. The bus was half full of tourists, most of whom were Americans because Tinsel wasn't popular enough to attract much international attention.

"How often do you take these tours?" Celeste asked once we had settled into our seats. I wanted her to have the window so she could enjoy the scenery.

"Every other week," I said. "It's a two-hour ordeal, quick enough to do after lunch or sometimes before games."

Celeste raised her eyebrows. "Every other week? You have to know every ghost tale this town has to offer."

I chuckled. "I do. But each group has a different vibe. Plus, the turnover rate for tour guides is impressive, so each time feels like a fresh experience. And ghost stories never get old."

I held out my cup for her to take while I dug my phone out of my pocket.

"Look." I opened my notes app for this tour. We exchange goods: my drink for my phone.

Celeste's mouth parted as she scrolled through paragraphs and paragraphs of my notes on the tour. I'd written down everything I learned, making edits whenever I found something in books that contradicted what the tour guide said.

My knee bounced up and down as I waited for the ride to start and for Celeste to finish scrolling through my writing.

"You're in love," she said and handed me back my phone.

My knee paused in mid-bounce. For a moment, I thought she was talking about us, and I didn't know what to confess other than, *yes, of course, I've been marching toward that for quite some time when it comes to you. Thank you for clearing the air.*

"What are you going to do with it all?" she asked.

"I use it to help come up with new ideas for mystery dinners," I said.

"Your famous mystery dinners," she mused and relaxed into her seat, favoring the armrest closest to me. "People talk about them on campus all the time. Even in the music department. You know everyone, don't you?"

I leaned back too, resting my arm right next to hers. "Not everyone. I just invite everyone. Most come at least once."

"And they have a blast."

"Not you," I said.

"I.... wanted to. I did, but you know…"

"What can I do to convince you to try again?"

"I'm already convinced. I know I want to go because it's… another chance to be close to you." She picked at her nails. "Which is something I really want."

"How close?" I asked because I'm over guessing and wondering if this was just a summer fling she wanted to get out of her system before moving on to bigger and better things once she secured the mentorship.

"Close enough that…" She held onto her necklace, rubbing the star charm like it'd grant her a wish. A frown appeared on her face, deepening wrinkles in her forehead as she struggled to press forward. But Celeste was a fighter. She waded through all her doubts and found the strength to say, "You're the first person I talk to in the morning and last at night. You're the person who's in arm's reach whenever I feel like I'm drowning. The person I want to kiss because it makes the world feel less scary and lonely…. sorry, that's… a lot for the beginning of this... I'm being weird. I haven't learned how to flirt without using music yet. I'm working on it…among other things."

I chuckled. "I happen to like how you flirt, Celeste."

"Oh. Good," she whispered and sniffed. The bus AC cut on as the tour guide climbed in to do a head count. Everyone around us chatted, excited for the trip. We were humming on a different frequency.

"I like that you're quiet," I whispered. "That you care about what you say and how you make people feel. And that's when we're close now, you always want to hold hands. I like that when we kissed, you felt less scared and alone."

"Yeah?"

I smiled and set my cup down between my legs. I'd need two hands for this.

"I like your nose and the way it wrinkles when you don't believe what someone else is saying." I traced my index finger down the bridge of her nose. "I like your graphite smudge fingertips and constant stream of ideas.

"I like how you understand music more than you do people. I like that you believe in the power of stories. I like that when you look at me, you don't see someone who's at the end of his luck. You look at me like I can create as many beginnings as I want."

"Of course, you can. You will."

I shook my head, not wanting to argue and not needing to because none of that stuff mattered right now. Not probation, not hockey, not the future.

"I like it when you look at me like this," I said. "Because when you do, I feel like we're something that'll eventually spill off the pages we've been scribbling on."

"And you still want that? Us?" she tried to confirm. "After how long it took me?"

"I will always want us," I promised. "Doesn't matter if it's today, months, or decades from now. I will always want you."

Celeste tried to close the distance between us, stopping when her cap clashed with mine.

"Sorry." She laughed nervously. I laughed too, but reached up and removed her cap.

"Alright, folks," the tour guide started.

Celeste's eyes flickered to the front of the bus. I gently grabbed her chin and turned her face back to me. "Just stay with me here for a second?"

She nodded. I positioned the cap so it blocked us from the outside world and everything that'd dare to make this moment anything other than ours.

CHAPTER EIGHTEEN
CELESTE

Lincoln held the baseball cap in front of us as we leaned in to kiss each other. He was sweet from the lemonade and warm from the summer sun. I parted my mouth, my tongue sweeping across his bottom lip, and he followed my lead. It wasn't as gentle as our kiss backstage. I was hot with the need for his mouth to be on more than just my lips.

I knew Lincoln. His love for his friends. His want for excitement. His fear of working so hard and not living up to expectations. Every little piece of him I'd seen this past year had built this growing fire I possessed for him and only him. The burn ignited the feelings I'd read about in books. The feelings Naomi whispered about during sleepovers. Or students talked about during classes. I felt the heat now, the desire to never disconnect from a man I wanted to call mine. I'd gone from unable to look in his eyes to unable to pull myself away. But we did manage. The kiss couldn't have been for more than twenty seconds because when we broke apart, the tour guide was still getting through introductions.

Lincoln lowered the hat and offered it back to me. I finished off the rest of my lemonade, hoping the sugar would hit my dopamine receptors like Lincoln's lips did. It was nowhere close, and for a second, I panicked that nothing ever would get close again. That I'd forever need a high only he could give me.

Would that be so bad?

Lincoln's gaze flickered between the front of the bus and me. He traced his bottom lip with his thumb, mouth parted as if he were going to say something, but couldn't figure out how to say it. I smiled because he had way more experience in this department than I did. And yet, he quickly downed his drink like me, desperately trying to keep his attention on the tour guide.

The bus jerked forward, setting us off to the first stop. As much as I tried to listen to what was on our agenda, my mind wouldn't center itself long enough to remember what our tour guide said. I opened the brochure, scanning its pages as I brushed my fingertips across my mouth.

"We'll start at the center of downtown." Lincoln's voice was low and soothing. Our kiss had left me wide awake, but it seemed to do the opposite to him. Lincoln sounded calm enough to drift off into a carefree sleep.

"Here." He pointed to the map on the brochure. "And then they'll take us around in a circle, which they call the Haunted Circle —very original. It's on this stop we'll get to see a haunted house."

I chewed on my bottom lip and nodded. "Sounds fun."

We were still close enough that a lean in wouldn't take more than a second. My eyes flickered to his lips, but he didn't move. Didn't take the hint. So, I shocked us both by closing the remaining distance. This time it was a quick peck because I was too nervous to linger.

Lincoln chuckled under his breath when I pulled away and leaned back into my seat like I hadn't just given him the world's shortest kiss.

"It'll be very fun," he promised.

Tinsel was a coal mining town founded in the 1700s. Its legacy was a mix of gritty labor and folktales.

"When the need for coal declined." Our tour guide stood on a step that led up to a statue I had passed a million times, with a stone plaque I had never taken the time to read. "The town lost almost half of its residents in a mass exodus. However, those who stayed behind began to experience strange occurrences. And the first one documented was right here, on the steps of our old city hall. An apparition of the first mayor appeared here with a warning to all: *never mind the coal, we need to go deeper.*"

The crowd oohed and ahhed. I raised my brow, less fascinated, more creeped out.

"You good?" Lincoln had his mini notebook out and been scribbling in it since the tour group started walking. I tried to stay quiet while he wrote, not wanting to derail his train of thought. But he seemed to master the art of writing and talking because he consistently whispered other facts into my ear whenever he felt the guide glossed over something. I leaned in more than I needed to whenever he whispered, causing his lips ever so slightly to brush across my skin.

"I'm fine," I said. "Just...I wish someone had listened to him and dug deeper, you know? Now, it's going to haunt me —no pun intended—not knowing what he was talking about."

Lincoln smiled. "Do you believe in ghosts?"

"I don't think so." I paused to give it proper consideration. "But I think I'm going to for the next few hours, so it gives more weight to the stories. Feels more exciting that way."

He chuckled and nodded in agreement.

"Do you?" I asked.

Lincoln shrugged and wrote something else in his notebook. "They're an amusing story device. I believe in them for that reason alone."

"But we're talking in real life," I reminded him with a gentle bump of the shoulder. I lingered a bit, blaming it on his warmth rather than the immediate calm I felt from being so close to him. "I would have bet my last dollar you, of all people, would say yes without any hesitation."

"Well…" Lincoln leaned into me too, prolonging the gentle touch for another couple of seconds. "There was a time when I thought I lived with one."

I raised a brow. "Go on. Don't leave me hanging."

Our group started following the tour guide down the sidewalk. We'd visited a few sites on foot before heading back to the bus to our next stop, closer to the mountains, where we'd find the haunted house. Lincoln and I fell behind the others for the sake of privacy and my splintered interest in lore outside of Tinsel.

"I grew up with my grandma." Lincoln snapped his notebook closed and tucked it into his back pocket. "She has this huge house on the hill, it's called Marble Manor."

"You grew up in a manor?" I asked. "So, you're fresh out of one of those spooky books for children with black cats and uncles who murder next of kin?"

He scoffed. "If only I were so lucky. No animals of any kind because my grandma thinks they're the spawn of Satan. And no murderous uncles because my mom's an only child. And all my dad's folks live in France."

"Your parents. What are they like?" I asked, realizing I didn't know anything about Lincoln beyond what happened here at Mendell. I never considered asking about his family because of how he was with his friends. The guys' lives seemed so entwined it was almost as if they'd been born together. A family of their own choosing since they took their first breath.

"My mom's an animal photographer." The back of

Lincoln's hand brushed mine. Once. Twice. Thrice. "She's obsessed with the job."

"Your grandma must love that." I flexed my fingers, my knuckles pressed against his.

He smiled. "She loves to brag about Mom's work but hates the content, so she has bed sheets she uses to cover the photos whenever no one else is around."

"And your dad?" I asked, swallowing a sigh when his hand caught mine. The grip was loose enough to pull away if desired. When I didn't, he held on tighter, tugging me close enough I'm sure he heard every thunderous beat of my heart.

"My dad's a filmmaker. Or, at least, trying to be…for decades now. They travel all the time together."

"Is that why you lived with your grandma?" I asked.

He nodded. "And that's why I thought I lived with a ghost. My grandma runs a candy shop, which needs far more attention than one might think. So, that meant I was home alone a lot. And what does a lonely kid with a weird obsession with mystery novels do?"

"Accidentally scare yourself?"

Lincoln laughed. "You know me well."

"I'm getting there. "

We fell further behind the group now. Not that it mattered to either of us. I was here for *his* stories. His dreams. His smile. Those lines around his eyes when he was genuinely amused and not just looking for a laugh. It was hard to make a person who always laughs, actually laugh. I'd learned as much from being friends with Naomi. People like Naomi and Lincoln knew how to find the funny, even in the dark spaces. If you managed to get an unplanned laugh out of them, then it felt like you could offer something new and special to them.

"Have I told you this before?" he asked. "Sometimes I tell people the same thing because I can't keep track of who knows what."

"Nope, I would have remembered if you told me about being haunted as a child," I assured.

"Good because it's my favorite story." His free hand ran across his jaw, a telltale of blooming excitement. "Picture this: You're ten years old and just dying to talk to someone your own age. You've just learned what Ouija boards are, but only through the grapevine of kids in your neighborhood. The kids who only talk to you on the weekends at your grandma's shop because they know they can get you to sneak them free reject lollipops and chocolate bars."

It was odd to imagine a young Lincoln having to grow up as isolated as I felt. If I'd been without my brothers and Naomi, I would have been more afraid of people. Isolation had had the opposite effect on Lincoln.

"You cut out the back of a cereal box and write the questions you have for a new best friend," Lincoln continued. "Because how else will the other side know what kind of friend you're looking for if you don't give them the exact criteria of who you're looking for?"

"Making sense so far," I said.

"You write down all the obvious questions first, of course."

I nodded. "Duh."

"Do you like wrestling?" Lincoln held up his fingers as he listed each one. "Which Power Ranger do you want to be? How long can you hold your breath underwater?"

"Only if it's cartoon wrestling," I answered. "I never watched *Power Rangers*, so I can't give an honest answer there. But I did watch *Powerpuff Girls*, that's almost the same?"

"Oh, sure." Lincoln shrugged, expression amused—and perhaps a bit surprised—at my chattering. But our kiss and every second we'd spent together had woven this tapestry of security. There was no expectation to say something wildly meaningful with him. I was all relaxed, limbs at ease, unhurried thoughts, and deep breaths. I was in the present moment, and it was liberating. It was what I imagined a healthy home should feel like.

"I wanted to be Bubbles. And I can hold my breath for about a minute."

"You do have Bubbles' energy," he agreed.

Our group stopped in front of an abandoned building that used to be a furniture shop. I caught bits of information on how the family that moved there had only been seen at night. Now, every Halloween, a small candlelight could be seen flickering in the window on the second floor for a few minutes. Because, for some reason, all ghosts agreed to sync up on the same holiday to do their essential business.

"I left the cereal box in the attic for a couple of days," Lincoln said. "No answer. One night, I decided to stick around in case the ghost needed to suss out my vibe more. Personally, I wouldn't want to befriend someone I'd only heard live a life below me and had left me three questions to answer—no matter the importance of those questions."

"Fair enough. I respect a ghost with standards."

"It's admirable." Lincoln nodded. "I stuck around and talked for a few hours. This ghost has heard my whole life story."

"You were ten, though, right?" I imagined a tiny version of Lincoln full of wonder and the constant need to chatter. "Couldn't have taken more than a few minutes."

"One decade holds a lot of content, Celeste."

I smiled, amused at his insistence. I loved how dramatic this man could be. "You're only conscious of maybe six of those years? Seven if you're like a really self-aware three-year-old."

"I remember things from as young as two," he said.

My brows raised as I tried to recall my childhood and kept getting stuck at a four-year-old me collecting rocks at the base of a mountain. "Man, what I'd do for that kind of memory retention. I bet that's a lifesaver when it comes to studying."

"I wouldn't bet on that."

"Why not?"

"I'm one failing grade away from being on academic probation. From the results of my first few assignments this semester, the chances of probation doubled," he said. "Memory doesn't do much for me these days."

I tried not to show too much shock or concern at the comment. The confession was far more significant than his nonchalant tone suggested. When I met Lincoln's gaze, I saw nerves there. He hadn't meant to share that tidbit. He wasn't using his failure as a setup for some punch line. His jaw tightened when he looked away from me and back to the tour guide, like he was finally interested in the information he'd digested a multitude of times.

"This potential probation," I started, voice low as I treaded carefully. "Do your friends know?"

He let out a dry laugh. "Nope. This was something I was going to take to the grave. Or at least keep under the radar until they started doing their big things and I stayed at Mendell for another year or so without them."

My chest tightened at the thought of him on his own. The strings between us strengthened because, despite being opposites, we'd buried something similar. We were afraid of the same kind of failure and loneliness.

"Do you want—"

"This is my favorite part," Lincoln interrupted, moving closer to the group.

I watched his back as he turned his attention to the tour guide's explanation of our empty bell tower and the secrets it held.

CHAPTER NINETEEN
LINCOLN

My skin continued to burn in embarrassment after we boarded the bus to head up to the abandoned mines and haunted house. The ride took us twenty minutes outside of town. Our tour guide spent the entire time going through repurposed jokes and setups for tourists' questions. I tried to listen in because even from those recycled talking points, I gleaned inspiration. But the twisting feeling of shame weighed heavily on my shoulders.

I'd done well with keeping the vital things under wraps. So, letting my potential probation slip left my system stunned. This day wasn't supposed to end with such a thud. We'd been wonderfully high off over-sugared lemonade and first kisses.

I'd never been properly introduced to embarrassment. I didn't understand the intricacies of this spiral of regret. Now that Celeste knew about my failure and had seen me trying to press forward without much explanation, I was anxious about what would come next and how I could shift her attention to something lighter and less about me.

"It's not a big deal," I said once when I deboarded the bus and stepped into the dusty, abandoned mining town.

Celeste looked up, quiet as she waited for me to continue. Her eyes were soft with understanding for a story I had yet to relay and with empathy I'm not sure I deserved.

"Not to me," I said.

The tour guide moved toward the boarded-up mine entrance. Cameras flashed, lighting up the dim space. Everyone took photos of remnants of lives we'd never really know and stories that got more fictional with age.

"And so, what if it was a big deal?" she asked. "What's wrong with things being a big deal?"

She rested her hand on my bicep. It was barely any weight, but it was an anchor holding me in place. It was a connection I didn't want to sever.

"When things become a big deal, they become out of my control."

We'd fallen behind the group again. I suggested this tour to distract Celeste from the stress of work. Now, I'd pulled her into my own twister of fear and uncertainty. I've never even cracked the door open for someone to see the storm. I wanted to shut it now, but she'd already slipped inside.

"You don't have to keep glossing over the hard parts with me. I know I'm anxious and worried about everything, so if you're hesitating because you think I can't handle it, don't. Please, let me decide what I can handle."

It was dark enough that the solar lights lining the mine's entrance flickered on. A soft blue light bathed Celeste, highlighting her beautiful eyes and cooling her skin. Despite everything she battled on her own, Celeste was willing to jump into the deep end and face my shit too. It was an honor and privilege I knew I didn't deserve. I was desperate to be deserving, though. To figure out all my bullshit and be someone worthy.

"I keep it from everyone," I reminded her. "Because I'm not good at the more serious stuff. It makes me feel..."

Useless. I liked being the entertainment. I liked if the room was heavy, I could lighten every load in under a minute. The ability to do that was far more addictive than anything I'd ever taken. My identity was intrinsically tied to being someone no one had to worry about.

"It's not because of your anxiety I'm holding back. This sharing stuff is new to me." I looked toward our group starting to the bus once more. "It's going to take some time."

Celeste nodded, understanding. "But you'll try? With me, at least?"

I smiled, fingers aching to take her hand in mine. "Of course."

"Now?" She beat me to the hand grab, braver and more sure in this moment. Her delicate fingers felt strong wrapped around mine.

My forehead wrinkled, confessed at her request. "Now?"

"Now," she confirmed. "Well…after the tour bus takes us back to town."

I laughed. "As long as it means I get to be with you, I'm in."

———

The night's alive with a humming of cicadas and the glow of billions of stars. Celeste turned off her headlights before we turned onto her street and parked her car in the driveway. She placed a finger to her lips when I opened my door.

"My brothers are home for the summer," she explained. "And I've never brought anyone…I like home."

"I'm good with families," I promised when we'd softly closed her doors and met at the front of her car.

"To be honest, I want to be selfish and keep you for my own a little bit longer," she confessed. "You'll undoubtedly think they're cooler than me, and I'll probably never get you back."

"Do you ever think there will come a day when you understand the magnitude of how much I'm into you?"

Celeste pressed her lips together, trying her best not to smile too much. Instead of answering, she grabbed my hand and tugged me behind her toward the backyard. She had a hard time opening the gate, going slowly so the hinges wouldn't squeak. I took over after watching her struggle for a minute.

"First time sneaking someone in?" I asked, using my old trick of shutting the gate completely.

"I do this all the time," she said, confused when I gestured for her to step back. "I have an entourage of lovers."

"Figured." I swing the gate open quickly, minimizing the squeak.

She clapped silently, impressed.

"It's all about accepting it'll make noise no matter what and knowing all you have to worry about is how much."

"A philosophy for life, truly." She grabbed my hand again, pulling me into the backyard. I took a deep breath, trying to calm down at the sight of the woman of my dreams leading me somewhere new. Her hair was bathed in moonlight, appearing softer and more heavenly than ever. I tugged her to a stop for a second, earning a confused eyebrow raise.

"What's wrong?" She turned to me, framed by the hazy glow of fireflies buzzing behind her.

"I just..." I shrugged. "Wanted to see you."

"Were you not looking this whole time?" she teased, dipping her gaze down for a second. I tucked my fingers underneath her chin, coaxing her head back up.

"I was, but it didn't feel like enough." I kissed her and we melted right into each other. Every one of my nerve endings was on fire, longing for the incredible relief only she could offer.

"Was that enough?" she whispered against my lips.

I swallowed and shrugged. "Getting there."

She laughed under her breath and resumed tugging me through the yard. The grass was overgrown. There was an old shed on one side and a small bird bath tucked underneath some trees on the other end. The main event stood in the middle, built on a large oak tree, which I was confident possessed some sort of magic. Everything around it seemed to be dying, but the tree was teeming with life.

I followed her up the ladder. She turned on soft, pink lights and shut the curtain. There were blankets scattered all over the floor, and a box overflowing with CDs lay open in the middle. While I had to kneel, Celeste could almost stand at her full height.

"Sit, sit." She gestured for me to take a place among the fluffed pillows.

I lowered myself down. "This stuff of childhood fantasy."

She laughed and joined me. "You grew up in a candy store."

"When I was a kid, I'd give up all the candy in the world for a treehouse." I leaned all the way back, taking in the glow-in-the-dark stars on the ceiling. Someone had arranged them to mimic a few constellations.

Once she grabbed another pillow and made herself comfortable, she joined my stargazing.

"These are impressively accurate," I mused.

"Can you name them?" she asked.

"Some." I nodded and reached for her hand. She watched as I folded all her fingers except the index. I used her as my pointer.

"Ursa major," I said.

"Easy," she teased.

"Orion, Leo, Cygnus."

She hummed, a little more impressed.

"Aries," I said. "Gotta know that one."

"Your sign?"

I nodded. "What's yours?"

She directed my hand to the crab.

"No way. That means your birthday was recent. Or is it soon?" I pushed myself up on my elbows, shocked when she nodded.

"It was recently," she confirmed.

I frowned, damn near heartbroken. "Celeste, you didn't say anything."

"Purposefully, would you believe it?" she teased.

"I would have loved to celebrate. Everyone would have."

"I know, which was why I swore Naomi to secrecy." She played with the edge of my sleeve, her long nails grazing my skin now and then.

"Have you always been like this?" I asked on a more serious note. "So hesitant to be seen? Celebrated?"

She nodded, not meeting my eyes. "I can't tell you why. It's probably a combination of things. Being the youngest and the only girl in my family. Being naturally more nervous and cautious led to all my family members doing everything for me. I started depending on it and, at one point, couldn't imagine living without it. And then, when I became a teenager, everything was heightened."

She laughed a little to herself. "I started becoming acutely aware of how I affected people. And I really didn't want to offend them because…"

"What?" I prompted. She was the closest she had ever been, and I didn't want her to start drifting away.

"I just remembered something." Her brow furrowed as she revisited the memory. "That's so weird…my parents used to be so upset when I talked back."

"You? Talking back?"

She smiled, tilting her chin up a bit because she was proud of the fact. "I went through that phase like most teens do. But I wasn't too forceful. The few times I was tough didn't end up well. And my brothers weren't around, so when my parents were mad at me… the house was quiet."

I nodded, knowing all too well how silence could make a home in one's bones. "Sounds lonely."

Celeste shrugged, her smile fading. "By that point, I had plenty of practice dealing with that feeling."

I watched as she traced lines over the veins on my arms. I wanted to make up for all those quiet years. Wanted her to know she could speak her mind without fear of being iced out and abandoned on some island. There were healthy ways to discipline a kid. Kinder ways. But between how they took care of their properties and the small things I continued to learn about Celeste's childhood, I figured whatever discipline that'd been given had been unfair and neglectful.

"I shared a secret." Celeste's voice was soft. She relaxed on the pillows, gazing up at me, guard vanished. I brushed my thumb across her cheek. No matter what happened out there in the world, past, present, and future, she'd be able to find this kind of peace in my arms.

"Now, it's your turn," she said.

"You're not going to wine and dine me a little?" I was joking, but Celeste sat up and crawled over to a mini fridge. I'm ashamed to admit how much I admired her ass while doing it.

"Ask and you shall receive," she handed me a bottle of water. "Wined."

And then, a bag of pretzels.

"And dined." She smiled, very proud of herself, and cuddled right back next to me, pressing her cheek against my arm.

"Be still my beating heart," I said with a sigh because she smelled so good and felt so right next to me. "Seriously, be still. This is kind of getting embarrassing."

Celeste raised a brow and pressed the back of her hand to my chest. "You weren't kidding. You do like to be wined and dined."

"Honestly? My heart's rarely not doing this when I'm with you."

"You're joking."

I shook my head. "Celeste, everything about you makes me feel like I'm taking both my first and last breath. Every semblance of chill doesn't exist when I hear your name."

"You're so dramatic," she said, trying her best to keep her voice light, but I could see the change and realization in her eyes. I was serious about this. About her. This wasn't some fling or crush I'd move on from after some time.

"But you like it," I said, hopeful. "Don't you?"

She bit on her bottom lip, trying to tame a smile. "I…"

"I won't judge," I promised.

"Yeah?"

"I can't get you out of my head, no matter how much time and space stretches between us. And I've tried. Before this summer, Celeste, I tried *very* hard. I'm not and will never be in the position to judge."

I think there were tears in her eyes, but I couldn't confirm before she tugged on my shirt, pulling me in for a kiss. The world outside the treehouse might as well have faded into nonexistence because nothing else felt as real as being here with her.

Our kisses became urgent. Neither of us interested in oxygen if that means parting from one another. Her body was soft underneath mine. When she hooked her leg around my waist, her skirt fell above her thighs. I've experienced a lot of things, but none can compare to the simple pleasure of my fingers pressing against her thighs.

"I hadn't told anyone about the probation," I confessed when we took a breath. I'm disconnected from the most critical parts of myself, lost in a maze, and trying to get every hang-up I have out of my way because, like our clothes, it's a bunch of nonsense keeping us apart. "Because it's not something I can talk my way out of, and I don't think I'll be able to recover from how they'll see me. The disappointment and..."

"And?"

"Resignation," I said. "My parents once said I was a lost cause. And I've been trying to bury that idea ever since. That's the haunting I should have been worried about."

She pulled away a little to get a better look at me. Concern casted a shadow over her face. Celeste brushed her thumb across my cheek as if my hurt were something she could wipe away.

The heat between us faded as she seriously took in my confession. I followed her lead ruefully, even though I wouldn't mind letting my wound fade into the ether.

"You do know that isn't true. That it never was," she said. "And no one in your life, no matter what mistake you make, is going to believe that."

"Mm." I hummed and tried to pull her back into me.

"Lincoln," she protested. "At least, some part of you knows that that wasn't your baggage to shoulder?"

"I want to, I really do," I said, knowing after all this, I couldn't lie to her. I didn't want to after being completely seen by her and having the chance to be wholly known.

She nodded, ever gentle and understanding. "We'll get you there. Just don't hide it anymore. None of us can help if we don't know what's going on."

"I don't plan on hiding," I promised. "Not when I'm with you."

There was no reason to hide from Celeste. When she looked at me, she didn't see one part. I wasn't the class clown. The hockey goalie. The party guy. I was everything I wanted to be, and more.

When Celeste looked at me, she expected me to have more to offer and to be unfinished, which she saw as something good. And inspiring. And hopefully, as something that was hers.

CHAPTER TWENTY

LINCOLN

"You know how I hate to be dramatic," I started. "But this fucking sucks."

Henrik snorted, shoving past me to get a box into the van. "Don't start. This whole carting sets across town was *your* idea."

"Maybe this'll make it better? Or at least more fun," Naomi said as she tugged a cap onto my head, pulling the brim so low I couldn't see for a second. I laughed and readjusted it in time to see her skip over to do the same to Finn. He was entranced with something on his phone. But before Naomi could move on, he grabbed her waist, holding her still for a kiss. She ruefully pulled away, out of breath as she offered Henrik his cap.

Henrik studied the embroidery on the front. "What's this?"

"For our production team." Naomi beamed, made a show of slipping hers on, and moved her fingers around it with a flourish as she modeled for us. "I know it's our final rehearsal —I meant to get them sooner. But it's better late than never, right? I did the design and everything."

"You designed this?" I pulled off the cap and studied the

logo, which featured flowers and musical notes. The words, Celeste's Crew, were sewn in cursive.

"I wanted us to have something to remember it by," she said. "It's the first time I'm on a team with you guys, too. You all get to have the jerseys, I wanted something to commemorate, since this'll be our last summer together on campus."

My chest tightened at the idea of next summer. The lease on this house would be over, and even if Naomi and I wanted to stay, we'd have to find new roommates. I'd have to figure out if I'd be able to continue playing for Mendell.

After deciding to recommit myself to training, I thought I could dodge most of the emotion that surfaced when faced with the reality of my situation. If I pulled myself together, with a full course load and excess hours on the ice, I wouldn't have to deal with being left behind. Wouldn't have to deal with the change of any season. I had to focus and be who Celeste believed she saw when she looked at me.

"These turned out incredible." I pushed down everything I couldn't control now and proudly tugged on the cap again. "I love them. Celeste will too."

"Yeah, thank you, Naomi," Henrik said, clearing his throat a few times. "A perfect way to remember the summer."

We all paused, watching as Henrik turned red.

"What?" he asked.

"Are you…?" I started.

"Getting emotional," Finn finished with as much confusion in his tone as I felt.

"Yes, I've been known to care about the people I spend most of my time with," Henrik joked. "And I just binged a ton of my favorite childhood movies, so I'm in a strange headspace."

"You know how you get when you revisit those movies. Why would you do that to yourself?" I asked.

"I had a lot of baking to do. It all took forever," he

defended. "Those movies are the best kind of background noise."

"Background?" Finn asked with a furrowed brow. "We sat through three entire movies."

"*Three*?" I asked. "Holy shit, where was I?"

"Sleeping," Henrik said.

"And you didn't wake me? Some friends."

"It was like a six-hour ordeal because he kept pausing," Finn said. "You didn't want to be up, trust me."

"I only kept pausing because you kept missing the turning points," Henrik defended. "You were constantly putting your head down."

"I was at a very critical point in my pattern," Finn said. "I've never done cables before."

"You're doing the cable sweater for me?" Naomi perked up. "The pink one?"

"Trying," Finn nodded. "Don't get too excited, I think it's going to take me a few decades to get it right."

"I'd wait forever," she promised with her hands clasped and pulled to her chest.

A car pulled up right outside our driveway, interrupting Naomi's attempt to convince Finn to show her his progress so far. It took us all a moment to realize who it was before Sam stepped out.

"What do we have here?" he asked. "How many hockey players does it take to load a van?"

"You're late," Henrik said with a smile, and was the first to pull Sam into a hug.

"Strategically," Sam said, voice briefly muffled by Henrik's shoulder. "I thought you'd all have everything loaded by now."

I got in line for a hug after Naomi placed a hat on his head.

"Thank you." He leaned in so their brims bumped into each other. As nervous as I was to tell him about Anthony, having him here was worth it. No place felt home without everyone present. And our tapestry was almost complete.

"Where's Aderyn?" I asked, giving him a shoulder squeeze after our hug. "I thought she was coming down with you?"

"She's coming down next week to help me move Eden in," Sam said. "For now, there's a girl's trip to the mountain. Last week of summer, you know? Gotta make it count."

"Which is why we need to get this show on the road," Henrik said. "It's an hour drive there and back. We want to be back in time to watch the final rehearsal."

Sam smiled. "That's tonight?"

"You're going to love it," Naomi said. "Celeste's music is magic, Halle's voice is breathtaking, and the sets Lincoln and Jack worked on are incredible. "

"Jack?" Sam chuckled. "The Jack I know? He's working on this musical?"

"I didn't give him much of a choice," I confessed. "But when school starts, I owe him a favor. Fair trade."

"I am so ready to see this," Sam said. "But first…Lincoln, isn't today a practice day? With Anthony?"

And there it was. The anvil on my foot. The cliff on which I should jump off.

Sam raised a brow expectantly.

"You're right. It's Wednesday." Naomi's smile faded.

Henrik had to check his phone to be sure. "I completely forgot to set my alarm. Sorry about that, Lincoln. I was so caught up in the prepping."

Sam and I watched each other, waiting for a crack in the dam. I didn't have to tell him; he already knew. He'd possibly known right after it happened and hadn't said a damn thing.

"What's going on?" Henrik asked, taking note of our quiet staring.

Sam shrugged and gestured to me. "Ask him."

I sighed and confessed, "Anthony dropped me last week.

He walked out because I wasn't focused. He didn't think it was worth the effort—"

"He told me he gave you multiple chances," Sam cut in. "You do realize it took incessant convincing to get him to come down here and invest in a guy who maybe, kind of, sort of wanted to be a free agent. He did it because not many people who look like you and me have the means and resources to be in this sport, and then you just don't put in the work. For what?"

When it was all laid out before me, the shame may as well have swallowed me whole. My knees were weak, my body half-turned away from my friends, prepping for a flight reaction.

"I don't have a good excuse, Sam," I said, shame morphing into frustration because I felt guilty enough without him throwing salt in the wound. "If that's what you've come all the way down here looking for, you're not going to get it."

"I'm not looking for anything. I just wanted you to be honest with me. Serious, for once in your life. I was trying to help you. We both were."

"I know." Breathing was laborious. So was standing, talking, and simply existing in this moment. "And I'm sorry I wasted your time and his. If you want honesty, I'll let you know, I didn't think I was worth it. I didn't think I'd make it this far."

Henrik frowned. "Make it this far?"

"What the hell does that mean?" Sam asked.

They all waited for my response. I could spin this. I could keep pretending I was fine. Heaven knew I was good at faking it. But last night, Celeste poked holes in my plan. She offered me some of her strength, and I felt how good it was to be seen for all that I was. And I couldn't hide anymore without the risk of shoving a wedge between the people I loved most in this world.

"For the past few semesters, I've been struggling with

maintaining my grades. I'm not on track to graduate in the spring." I said. "And if I don't bring up my GPA with this semester's grade, I could be on academic probation... It's pending review."

They were silent. Sam frowned, jaw tensed as he undoubtedly tried to come up with a plan before I could even finish explaining. Finn and Naomi exchanged looks, trying to see if the other knew.

I didn't want to look at Henrik. I knew his response would be filled with hurt. We were best friends, and I hadn't once hinted at a struggle.

"As you all know, my attention span isn't the best. It's gotten better with volunteering. Yay," I tried to smile, but they weren't biting. Being this serious for this long made my skin itch. I could barely stand still as I said, "But it's getting worse when it comes to school and hockey. Bad enough that...like Anthony, I'm starting to believe I'm not worth the investment."

"Lincoln," Naomi tried.

"It's fine," I stopped her, mainly because I was embarrassed about how much care was in her tone. "Discovering hockey and playing for Mendell has been one of the best things that's ever happened to me. Being with you all has meant everything. But when Sam moved, it shattered this illusion I'd bought into by no one's fault but my own. I remembered this isn't our life. This is the prologue to some story I'm not sure I want to read because when we leave Mendell, and this is all over, I don't think it's going to get any better than this. I don't have much more to offer. I'm not the brightest of the bunch – though we all know I am at least runner-up."

"You should have said something," Henrik finally spoke up. "I could have helped with classes."

"Me too," Naomi chimed in. "You know I don't mind, it's literally my job."

"We still could," Finn said. "It's a pending probation, not suspension. There's time, and you don't throw in the towel just because there's a limited amount. I'm down for extra practices. I like being on the ice with you."

"As far as being worth the investment goes." Sam's steady voice called for all our attention. "Who the hell convinced you of that?"

I swallowed, trying to figure out how to explain how deeply rooted my belief was. It was so far down it didn't seem worth digging. Unearthing the roots felt impossible.

"My folks did," I muttered. "I guess. A long time ago. Honestly, I forgot about it until recently. Somewhere down the line, their voice morphed into mine. And I've been telling myself this whole time, I'm not worth it."

"Where's your proof?" Sam challenged. "Because I don't give a damn about what your parents said or what the voice in your head adopted. I don't know them; I don't know that voice in your head. And honestly, after hearing this, I have no interest in it. I know you. And I need you to give me proof that you're not worth it."

"Well, I can't commit, I can't focus. I didn't choose hockey, I followed the leader all the way to Mendell." I counted my many flaws on my hand. "And here I don't know what the hell I'm doing half the time. The one thing I want is Celeste and me, but even in that aspect, I don't know if that's going to happen because if there's one thing for certain, I'm going to find a way to fuck it up."

"My god, you talk so much." Sam rolled his eyes. "And still, you can't give me solid evidence."

I let out a dry laugh. "Is the failure of my academic career, being dropped by my personal trainer, and not being able to match the energy of the woman I'm in love with, not enough proof for you?"

"Not even close," Sam shut me down. "Want to know why?"

I scoffed. "Enlighten me."

"You haven't even tried. You shut out all of us," Sam said. "You listened to a part of you led by fear instead of listening to the people who know that when Lincoln Hill puts his mind to something, it's game over."

"You really don't see it?" Finn's forehead wrinkled. "How much you mean to us? How much we see in you?"

"I don't hang out with losers," Sam agreed. "It's depressing and leads nowhere. You think I would have driven hours to confront a loser?"

Despite all nerves, sorrow, and embarrassment twisting in my stomach, I laughed.

"I can't stand you," I said.

Sam smiled. "Likewise."

"I do have a plan, a sort of plan." I scratched at my brow. "My last-ditch effort to fix everything. Figure this all out by fall."

"*We'll* figure this out by fall," Sam corrected. "Because you are stuck with us, whether you like it or not. And investment is our top priority."

My throat tightened at the firm, unrelenting look in his eyes.

Naomi nodded. "I've got tutoring covered."

"Same here," Henrik said. "Your paper writing skills are… wanting. I need editing practice anyway."

"As far as the ice goes," Finn said. "Do you remember I'm one of the top scorers in the league?"

"Vaguely," I teased, still trying to mask the overwhelming feeling of having my six covered four times over.

"I'll put you to work," Finn promised.

"You don't have to figure out where you fit, Lincoln," Sam said. "Because it's here. With us. No matter where we move or how we change, this right here is solid ground. Understood?"

There were no words for the eclipsing relief I felt at hearing those words. Letting them sink into my skin and become a part of the story I told myself. Accepting they're forever part of my story, regardless of how my jaded emotions attempted to convince me otherwise.

I was no longer some kid in the attic counting days until I had someone to talk to. My body had been unknowingly stuck there for almost a decade. My reality revealed the door to something brighter had been opened a long time ago.

"I do," I told them. "I understand."

"In love, huh?" Naomi appeared at my side, offering me a paper cup filled with lemonade.

Finn's uncle, Aaron, had prepared us a whole spread of snacks and drinks to keep us fueled during the unloading process. We'd spent half an hour getting the pre-cut wood from the van into Aaron's studio. Now, Henrik, Naomi, and I were trying to catch our breath, lounging in the old lawn chairs set in front of the house. Sam and Finn were in Aaron's studio, asking a million and one questions about his work. Finn's interest in building had been growing over the past year. And Sam's interest in people was ever constant.

"You caught that?" I accepted the cup and patted the chair beside me.

Naomi smiled and relaxed beside me, sipping her own drink and holding a napkin filled with cheese and crackers. "Of course."

"It's the first time I said it out loud."

"How did it feel?" Naomi asked.

"Like it's been on the tip of my tongue for ages."

"Celeste means the world to me." Naomi picked at her food as she spoke. Her expression was a mix of a kind of solemn seriousness I didn't realize existed in her repertoire. "She physically has a family, but... they're not really there, and that leaves a hole, you know? I've spent years watching that hole grow, watching her become more isolated. Close off because nothing really fits. And people don't often give her a chance."

"I understand," I said.

"But she has me." Her voice softened. "For a while we just had each other."

"I wouldn't say that's just. You two fill up too much space to be "just" anything."

They'd created things in a world that wasn't always kind and hardly ever accepting. But they managed to be both those things and so much more.

"I'm rooting for you, Lincoln. I'm rooting for you two together. I love how you love her. I see it in everything you do for and with her."

"But," I prompted with a knowing smile. I didn't underestimate Naomi because she was nice and sweet. She was a woman who would ensure, no matter what, her friend would be safe.

"If any of this ever changes, trust she has someone else who loves her as much, if not more than you ever will. Regardless of what happens between you two, she will be okay, I'll make sure of that. But be good to her, okay?"

"I promise, with every ounce of my being, I'm going to take care of her. There's nothing I won't do to take care of her."

Naomi nodded and offered me her cup to 'cheers.' "Here's to loving the sweetest person we know."

"Here's to making sure she's happy." I touched my cup to hers. "Forever and always."

"Forever and always," Naomi agreed.

CHAPTER TWENTY-ONE

CELESTE

Dress rehearsals at the playhouse were a physical slog because the AC broke down on us. My speakers output too much static. And the sets still weren't completed and returned, so Halle and Ellis had to mime most of what they interacted with on stage.

It should have been a nightmare. I should have been a bundle of unconsolable nerves.

I wasn't.

Because I maintained enough calm to remember there were extra fans in the community center's storage. Lincoln promised the sets would be back this weekend; his assurance helped me let that stressor go. And Aunt Robyn convinced the musicians at the local seniors' center to not only learn all my pieces but play live for opening night when Ophelia would be in town—and maybe, just maybe, she'd be in the audience.

"Are you doing okay?" Naomi stopped next to my elbow after she got back from bringing in the fans with Sam and Finn. She'd made a habit of hovering, never more than a few feet away. She understood the importance of getting everything in order today.

"I'm good." I kept moving as I set up the tripod. "Nervous, of course. But I'm going to finish this."

Everything was slowly but surely coming together. And I could relax more knowing I did all I could to breathe life into this project.

"What sets we do have are set." Lincoln joined us with a big smile on his face. His presence was the catalyst for my quiet, calm sigh.

"Halle and Co. are ready. I got the lighting to work and taught Sam and Henrik how to operate the controls."

I chewed on my inner cheek while doing a final check of my notes. "I think we're ready to go."

"Really?" Naomi asked, brows raised, impressed and excited.

"Really." I nodded to Lincoln to give everyone else the green light.

"Alright, guys," Lincoln spoke through a mini megaphone he'd gotten from heaven knows where. It did wonders in projecting his voice, but it also morphed it into a high-pitched tone. He sounded like a tiny version of himself. It was hard to take him seriously whenever he spoke, but we all gave it our best effort. I personally love fighting off a laugh; it's a great distraction. Infinitely soothing for the nerves.

"Places," he said. "Let's put on a show."

Finn and Sam didn't have any issue dimming the lights. Jack and Henrik easily opened the curtains. And as soon as Halle came on stage, I was lost in the production like I would be in any other show.

It wasn't perfect, but somehow, it was right. In all its flaws —because of its flaws—it was right. And it was me. I was threaded into every part of the lyrics. It didn't matter that it was a small glimpse into a world that may never fully come to life. My voice was loud enough to carry through, making everything feel whole.

"Well?" Lincoln looked at me when it was over.

I blinked, trying to see through the watery blur of my exhaustion and happiness. My cast directed their attention to me, waiting for my approval. The ache in my throat made it hard to think, let alone speak. For the first time, I didn't need to ask for someone's opinion. Everyone else's thoughts didn't matter right now. I'd spent so much time swimming in other realities, I'd forgotten mine could be as bright if I'd just given it a chance.

"I love it." My gaze broke from the stage, meeting Lincoln's. "I can't believe I love it."

And I had another revelation that made it difficult to breathe: If I could love this piece with all its rough edges, I, in turn, should be able to love the person who created it.

I'd found a way to love me in all my misshapen, not fitting in, on-the outside-looking-in glory. In this little life, that's all one could ask for.

"It's ready? We're ready?" Lincoln asked, looking for the go-ahead to tell everyone else.

I nodded. "Yeah, this is it. We did it."

"It's a go!" Lincoln called to the others with his hands in the air.

They cheered. Naomi hugged me from behind before going to celebrate with everyone else on stage.

"I'm so proud of you." Lincoln remained at my side, voice low and nearly drained out from the excitement of everyone else. They'd dove into plans of celebration at the end of practicing and the end of summer.

"I wouldn't have made it this far without you." I slipped my hand into his, squeezing to communicate my overflowing gratefulness. "And I'm not just talking about the musical."

"You would have," Lincoln promised. "You shine too bright not to."

———

The house burst with music, laughter, and the scent of sugar. The windows were open, letting in a comforting cross breeze that was starting to smell more of fall than summer.

Naomi and Finn worked side by side, pulling clean dishes from the washer and placing them in the overhead cabinets. Halle had volunteered to mix drinks, and Jack had protested, citing a lack of skill. Sam suggested they both be put on the task. And Aderyn — who'd dropped by earlier than we expected—suggested she film it for documentation's sake.

"Trust me, girl," Aderyn told Halle. "When you win, you're going to want proof."

Halle nodded. "Good looking out."

I sat at the kitchen's island, sandwiched between Ellis and Kaya. My cousin was trying to sell her on possible cross-promotion plans for next year. Last semester, Mendell's women's and men's hockey teams collaborated to develop a brand and promote their games. Ellis wanted to work with Kaya on expanding their reach into the world of figure skating.

"I promise you, I have more to offer than these puck-slinging guys," Ellis joked, jerking his chin toward said puck-slingers. "Our audiences have a lot of crossover."

"Maybe." She looked at me and asked, "What do you think?"

I blinked, quiet for a moment, not sure she had addressed me. "What do *I* think?"

Kaya nodded, placing her hand on her chin as she looked at me. She genuinely wanted my opinion.

"I think..." I paused, giving the question the time it deserved. I didn't feel the need to rush because everyone here was used to waiting for me to gather my thoughts.

I surprised myself by not attempting to figure out what Kaya wanted me to say. I wasn't in the business of mind-reading anymore.

"From what I know about hockey and figure skating—

especially when it comes to the women's team, there's definite crossover appeal. You guys could do those videos of hockey players trying a figure skating routine and vice versa. It'd be entertaining," I said. "And Ellis is good at entertaining a crowd."

Kaya nodded, face solemn, but there was a small spark of curiosity in her eyes. "Alright."

The one word was downright enthusiasm when it came to her. Ellis laughed and asked to switch seats with me so he could further explain what he thought next semester could look like for them.

"Thirsty?" Lincoln appeared behind me and set down a grocery bag on the counter. He'd disappeared as soon as we'd gotten to the house, claiming he'd be back in the blink of an eye.

"That was more than a blink." I teased.

Lincoln placed a hand on the small of my back and kissed my temple so gently I barely felt it. When I smiled and leaned in, he gave me a longer kiss.

"Is that okay?" he asked in a whisper, referencing the public display of affection. He pulled back just in case.

I nodded, heart fluttering. "It's perfect."

"I got you some non-alcoholic beverages," he said. "Didn't know what you might be in the mood for, so I grabbed a little bit of everything."

I smiled. "I see."

The grocery bag held ginger ale, lemonades, and those fancy, fizzy, health-boosting drinks that weren't exactly sodas.

"Wanted you to have options." Lincoln unloaded the bag. "Whatever you don't drink we'll put in my mini fridge upstairs and whenever—if ever you come over--you'll have something."

"Whenever," I confirmed. "Thank you."

He kissed my forehead this time. "Now, what do you want

me to use for your mocktail? Lil lemonade, some ginger ale, grape juice?"

I laughed and shook my head, overwhelmed with the options. "Surprise me?"

"You sure?"

"I trust you."

Lincoln's smile grew. You'd think I'd given him the world. I smiled back, understanding the feeling.

Lincoln joined Henrik on the other side of the counter, setting my drink supplies down before asking his friend if he needed anything.

"Grab the cake for me?" Henrik pulled out covered dishes from the refrigerator, each one more elaborate and beautiful than the next. The food set out before us drew everyone's attention.

"Now, this is for Celeste," Henrik announced as Lincoln set down a two-tier, star-shaped cake. The base icing was pink, and its corners were overflowing with delicate frosted flowers. In gentle cursive, Henrik had written,

For our brilliant songwriter, Celeste.

"Henrik," Naomi said, voice soaked in the same emotion that made my throat tighten and my eyes water. I couldn't speak just yet. Thank God Henrik had more to say.

"This is my grandfather's lucky recipe." Henrik pulled out spoons from the drawer and started handing them out to everyone. "It's lavender with rosemary and vanilla. And before we dive in—" Henrik stopped to give Ellis a warning look when he noticed my cousin trying to swipe a bit of icing onto his spoon. "—there's a bit of tradition we must uphold."

We all stood (or sat) at attention for Henrik's explanation.

"In my family, you bake this kind of cake when someone is starting a new chapter of their life. So, we bake it with intention. And I intended to make something that'll bring you peace, Celeste. I hope when you submit this project, no matter what happens, you'll know you did everything you could and you deserve to enjoy it."

Everyone's gaze turned to me, and there was a familiar need to perform rising in my belly. Lincoln was at my side in an instant. He slipped a spoon in my hand, keeping his fingers wrapped around mine so I was steady.

"And my intention—" Lincoln started.

"You helped make this?" I asked in a whisper.

"I did." Lincoln smiled. "Couldn't let Hen have all the fun."

"He did the flowers," Henrik said.

"They're stunning, Lincoln," Aderyn said as she leaned on the counter to get a closer look.

"Incredible," Naomi agreed and gave me a look that seemed to ask, "*Do you see how much they love you? I love you, we love you?*"

I blinked, trying to keep back the tears. I held onto Lincoln's hand like it was the edge of a cliff.

"Who would have thought you could stay still long enough?" Jack said, ruefully admiring the design.

"Knew someone could bring it out of him." Sam nodded his approval at Henrik.

"I'm a very proud teacher," Henrik said.

"Alright, alright," Lincoln said. "Yes, I'm capable of doing a detail-oriented thing. Now, can I share?"

"Go for it." Henrik gestured that the floor was his.

"My intention," Lincoln started, voice softening when his gaze met mine. "Was that you find a way to accept you are a light. A star—which is rather on the nose, I know, but I couldn't let Henrik's design skills go to waste."

I laughed despite the lump in my throat.

"I'm not saying this because I'm in love with you," Lincoln continued more seriously.

My heart stopped. He continued talking, and I didn't

think he knew what he'd just confessed. But a couple of people exchanged knowing smiles, which assured me I hadn't imagined it.

I was a bundle of the lovely kind of nerves. The type of energy that made me restless with the need to do something like play my favorite album front to back, sing every lyric, and compose my own addition to the soundtrack.

"I'm saying it because it's true," Lincoln said. "And whatever happens with your musical, you've already shifted the balance of the universe. You've already made your mark. You don't need proof of that."

"You all are sickeningly sweet," Halle said with her chin resting in her hand as she admired everyone in the household.

"I really want to fucking hate it," Kaya chimed in. "But I can't."

Halle sighed. "I know."

"It's easier said than done," Jack agreed.

Henrik laughed. "Alright, we'll wrap it up. Lincoln?"

"Right," Lincoln said, having to tear his gaze away from me. "We all have to dip our spoons in at the same time. When you do, you make a wish for Celeste."

"It's vital that it's at the same time," Henrik said. "Otherwise, it won't work and we'll be cursed forever."

"Jeez, no pressure," Aderyn said.

"Okay, focus, you guys." Sam held up three fingers, ready to count down. "Ready positions."

They all held the spoons out, reaching over the counter to claim a spot on the edge of the star.

"Me too?" I asked Henrik.

Henrik nodded with a smile. "Of course."

Lincoln placed a hand on my back, holding me steady as I reached a shaky hand forward. Sam counted us down. We all dipped into the cake. I had no solid evidence, but a part of me knew we'd taken our spoonful at the same time. A part of me understood every single person in this room wanted the best for me. They'd do whatever they could to make it happen. And I'd do the same for them in a heartbeat.

I was a part of a tapestry. A string of thread in this complicatedly beautiful design. And as we all ate our bites, the reality of being connected washed over me. Their wishes became cloaks over my doubts. The good intentions burned out the darkness.

"I'm so much better at music than words, so I know this might not...communicate everything I want," I said softly, forcing myself to talk because I needed to try to get them to understand how they'd changed a part of me forever. "But this summer has meant everything to me. What you guys have done... I'm never going to be able to thank you enough, but... I won't ever stop trying."

"Celeste." Naomi smiled. "That right there is more than enough."

"A little post-partying could also show us how much you love us," Lincoln teased, breaking through the heaviness with ease.

"Oh, this is going to be good." Ellis smiled at the idea of me at a party.

"Let's get it started," Sam said, picking up a shot glass and holding it towards me in a salute. "To new friends, good music, and dreams coming true."

We cheered, downed our respective drinks, and the room became alive again with overlapping voices.

Lincoln hugged me from behind and kissed my cheek before asking, "You okay?"

"More than," I promised, covering my hand over his and finally feeling like it for the first time.

CHAPTER TWENTY-TWO

LINCOLN

The plan for the night was to bar hop, and Celeste surprised us all by agreeing to join. Sam, Naomi, and Ellis pulled out their phones, narrowing down the list of places to visit. Since Celeste was on board, they dedicated themselves to crafting the best experience for her. She wasn't drinking, so I busied myself making her a mocktail and then a cup of tea before we headed out.

"Might help some with the nerves," I offered her the warm cup.

"Thank you." She tilted her head up for a kiss.

"It's better this time," I promised with a knowing smile.

She laughed. "I'm sure you've been practicing hard."

Being hers was so easy. We took care of each other as if it were second nature.

"Alright, carpool situation?" Halle asked, loud enough to be heard over all the conversations. "I'm not driving because I'm drinking."

"Same," Ellis said.

"So, I'll take your car," Kaya offered. "And you two can come with me."

"The rest can pile in the van," Finn offered. He rarely

drank since his accident. The disorientation of drunkenness had become triggering for him.

"Want to ride together?" I asked Celeste, wanting a little extra alone time after sharing her with everyone all day.

Her smile let me know she'd been thinking the same. "I do."

It took us all an hour to eat, get ready, and head out. By the time we got on the road, it was ten, and all the best spots were just starting to come to life.

Celeste rummaged around in her bag when we got to a red light, letting out a sigh when she couldn't find what she was looking for.

"What is it?" I asked.

"My phone." She shook her head, still digging through the bag with one hand. "I think I left it at the house."

"U-turn up here," I said.

"Sorry," Celeste whispered, shaking her head as she turned on her signal. She chewed on her bottom lip, the telltale of her feeling guilty about producing even the smallest amount of inconvenience to someone.

"Hey." I placed a hand on her thigh, giving her a gentle squeeze. She released a sigh, relaxing into my touch. "It's fine. We'll get there when we get there. No rush. And, I wanted an excuse to be alone with you, remember? There's so much talking happening when everyone's around."

Her smile was back. "You love talking."

"Obsessed," I agreed. "But I love it on a whole other level I never thought existed when you're the one doing it. And you do it less when other people are around, so I'm starting to make a list of ways and excuses for us to find pockets of alone time. Wanna hear what I got so far?"

She smiled and covered her hand over mine just as I was about to pull it away. "Definitely."

"Losing a phone." I held up a thumb and counted. "A very believable late excuse."

She laughed. "You said you made this list. That one's stolen from me."

"What can I say? You're a constant inspiration."

She rolled her eyes. "What else?"

"Need your help with that thing I was talking about," I said, playing up the fake-acting. "You remember the thing?"

"What thing?"

"See, you can't say that or people will know we're lying. You just nod and follow me, and voila. We're alone."

Celeste gave me a look. "Seriously?"

I laughed and had the urge to cup her chin in my hand and pull her closer. But she was a cautious driver, and I wouldn't distract her. And her free hand was still on mine, so I was basically in heaven.

"What? It works," I said. "It's best to keep these things simple."

"It's not that creative, though," she mused.

"Ouch." I held my hand to my chest. "Tell me what you really think."

"Sorry, sorry."

I leaned over and kissed her cheek and my favorite spot on the corner of her jaw because I couldn't resist before pulling away. "I'm kidding. I can take a punch. Hell, I can take a whole-body check."

"I would hope so."

"Give me your best shot," I dared.

"Alright. I think that guy who writes weekly 'who dun it' has a lot more to offer."

I blinked, surprised at the ease with which she shared. "You believe in me?"

"Of course, I believe in you," she said thoughtfully. There wasn't an ounce of doubt in her dark eyes. There was a lump in my throat born from gratefulness.

"I was sad when you told me you didn't think you're worth the investment," Celeste continued. "There are so many paths for you to take, and I think all of them begin with that entertaining brain of yours."

"I'm giving hockey a fair shot," I shared. "I've been working these last few weeks to train and win back Anthony. I'm going all in."

"Lincoln, that's incredible. And that's what you want, right? Not Sam, or Henrik, or Finn. You?"

I nodded and looked down for a second with a smile on my face. It was scary admitting it, but it was the truth.

"Perfect." She squeezed my hand. "As long as it's what you want, it's perfect."

We were back at the house before we knew it, beginning the search in the living room because that was the only place she'd been.

"I don't get it." Celeste tossed a couch pillow back into place. "It's not here."

"It's here," I assured, opening the refrigerator.

Celeste let out an easy laugh. "Really?"

"Hey, one time I left a whole tablet in this thing overnight," I said. "It happens."

She kept laughing. "Could you call me? My ringer's off, but maybe we'll hear the vibration."

I nodded. As soon as the call went through, something buzzed nearby. I found her phone tucked under the cushion of the barstool she'd been sitting on.

"Thank you." Celeste smiled and hurried over.

"When did you add this?" My stomach jumped at what I saw on her screen. I turned the phone to her, pointing to the pink heart she'd placed by my name. I couldn't not ask when all the excitement in my body turned into a buzz far better than any I'd find at the bar tonight. Thank God I hadn't taken a shot. Being sober left enough headspace to get drunk on the shy smile she offered me.

She reached for the phone, but I didn't let go.

"It was after that first practice when I panicked and you listened," she said, leaning into our tug of war.

"So, before the kiss backstage?"

Celeste pressed her lips together for a second, trying to read my face. "You seem surprised."

"I am. I mean, I fell for you the moment I laid eyes on you, but I know it's not the same for you."

She stopped tugging, brows raised, and her eyes went big. "At the arena. You fell for me at the arena? Over a year ago?"

I laughed at the shock in her voice. "Of course."

"Lincoln." She scoffed. "Seriously? Let's be…serious."

"I'm being serious," I promised. "Come on, you know this."

"I didn't know. I thought you were exaggerating."

"Celeste." I tilted my head to the side. "I came to that community every weekend for months. I called your dad a chill dude. He is not a chill dude; I ran out of material because I was panicking about talking to you. And I never panic. I could give a TED Talk in the nude and not blink an eye. But I couldn't breathe when I was in the same room as you. That's very serious. None of my friends know CPR—that's actually very concerning, considering I live in a household where no one knows a life-saving technique. We should fix that."

"Lincoln," she warned.

"Sorry, right, focus," I said, bringing myself to center. "I know it's taken longer for you. And I figured nothing strong enough to warrant a heart beside my name had happened before our kiss. Before the treehouse."

"That day…I don't know, something just unfolded," she said. "It kept unfolding, and it felt like a pink heart, so…you got a pink heart."

I'll never forget everything about her in that moment. The soft way her brown hair curled around her shoulders. How her wide eyes search mine, no longer trying to read my thoughts but instead, trying to connect.

I closed the remaining distance between us, leaning down

and letting her have her phone. Our noses brushed, and I closed my eyes, getting lost in her scent and warmth. Celeste tilted her head, hands holding my face, and she kissed me. Her hips were soft under my grip, shirt slightly ridden up so I felt the heat of her skin.

"Are you okay?" I asked, a little worried about how warm she was.

"I'm okay," she promised with her eyes still closed. "Just really thankful we got this creative excuse to be alone."

I chuckled and pulled her feet on top of mine because it was easier to kiss her that way. She smiled against my mouth.

"This is impressive," she whispered against my lips.

"You haven't seen anything yet," I teased, kissing her between every word. It was hard to stop once I started.

Celeste laughed between our kisses. "Yeah?"

I hummed, too turned on to verbally confirm.

"What else you got?" she asked.

For the first time, words didn't feel like enough to me. I kissed her until we're both heaving for breath. She wrapped her arms around my neck, holding on tight as I walked her backwards. As soon as we reached the back of the couch, I lifted her onto it. My hands were free to hold onto her face while I kissed her, thumbs rubbing circles on her jaw.

"What else do you want?" I pulled back enough to get a good look at her and let her have the chance to see me. "I'd give you anything. Everything."

"You. You're enough." She tugged on my shirt, gentle in how she pulled me back into her. Despite the tenderness in her grasp, her mouth sang a different tune. She was more comfortable with taking the lead. Celeste arched her back, pressing her chest firmly against my body. I was grateful the couch blocked her from feeling how hard she made me.

"Well, here I am," I told her. "Yours. For as long as you'll have me."

"Or as long as you'll have me," she said.

I shook my head. "There is no scenario in which I wouldn't have you, Celeste. It's the one thing I know for certain. It's written in the stars or etched in some stone on a remote island. It's all ancient and mystic and true."

"We're two college students who just decided what we want to be for the rest of our lives," she reminded me with a smile. "You really think this is ancient and mystic and true?"

"I know it, Celeste," I promised with a grin. "There's some painting about us on a cave wall somewhere. Or an oral story passed down through the ages. A ballad about a beautiful flute player and a head-empty goalie."

She tilted her head back when she laughed. I kissed her neck, my lips feeling the fast and steady drum of her pulse. Celeste's laughter faded into a small sigh. It was soaked in eroticism, and I was harder than ever—I didn't even think that'd be possible at this point. I found my way down to her collarbone and to the space between her breasts. She pressed herself into me, her breathing labored and as longing as I felt.

"Maybe one day you'll know it too," I said. "Feel all these connecting dots and overlapping strings. It's incredible to be so entangled with you."

"I feel them," she insisted. "All the dots and tangles...and now, I'm realizing something."

"What's that?" I lazily pulled myself up so I could meet her gaze. All this kissing and realizing was torturous, but to be honest, I could do it forever and never tire of it.

"I've never seen your room."

"My room?" I raised a brow, unsure why she'd brought that up now.

Celeste chewed on her bottom lip and nodded as she watched me. I waited for more. Some further explanation. It took me a bit longer than I'd like to admit to realize what she meant.

"Oh, damn, my room," I said. "You want to see my room."

She smiled, relieved at not having to expound.

"It's not in the best shape," I warned, straightening to my full height. I kept my hands on her waist as I talked. "I wasn't planning on showing you so…early."

"Oh." Her shoulders sagged. "Do you not want to show me? You don't have to—"

"No, no," I said quickly. "I want to show you, trust me. I just want you to want me to show you."

"Lincoln, I asked." She laughed and rested her hands on my chest.

"I know, I'm just trying to be sure," I said. "Trying to let you know that I want to go at your pace. Room reveals are a big thing, you know."

"Are you trying to talk me out of it?"

I shook my head and pressed my forehead against hers. "If you're sure and willing to give me two minutes to clean up, then let's do it."

"You got it."

"Four minutes," I corrected and shook my head. "No, maybe five."

She laughed, that light, musical, beautiful laugh that I will always strive to hear. "How about you take all the time you need and call me when you're done."

CHAPTER TWENTY-THREE
CELESTE

ran my hands under cold water in the kitchen, an attempt to ground myself amid mouth-drying panic.

I'd fumbled through sex once in my life. During my first year at Mendell, I decided I wanted to experience what everyone else did. I wanted to experience the act people deemed life-altering. Did I have a desire to be intimate? No. But I figured maybe it'd come during the moment. The urge, the longing, the lust, the world-shattering orgasm would help me finally understand.

But a post-sex epiphany wasn't anywhere in sight with the guy I'd been with. He was a violinist (almost as anxious as I). We had a handful of classes together, so we easily bonded over music and assignments. When the time came (a small window one weekend when his roommate went back home for the holidays), we had an awkward exchange I'd since pushed into the farthest corner of my mind. There had been no earth-shattering realization. I was plunged further into confusion over how people truly bonded when sleeping together.

Now, I knew the reason: I needed a connection before the physicality factored into the equation.

It felt silly to rejoice at this tiny realization, and yet, I couldn't help but smile to myself. I was getting closer to the woman I wanted to become and figuring out all the things underneath anxiety's hard surface. To be anxious for so long was to look at myself through fog. I'd been a blurry, amorphous being.

I shut off the tap when the stairs creaked under Lincoln's footsteps. He stopped in the entryway of the kitchen with his hands stuffed in his pockets. His voice was gentle when he said, "So, what are we thinking? Give me more time to prepare the room?"

Another out. I smiled. "I'm sure it looks great."

I pushed away from the sink and went to him. He wasted no time, taking my hand and pulling me in for a long kiss.

"Let's go up," he whispered, his eyes barely open.

I nodded and followed him upstairs. I hadn't been on the second floor of the house in ages. There were new paintings in the hallway and a collection of framed photos of the guys placed on an end table. I spotted Naomi and the guys in the middle. The picture showed them in the living room, with a board game on the table and a few girls from the hockey team present. Everyone squeezed on the old couch, and you could practically smell the heater and hot chocolate that'd warmed the air that night. I smiled, remembering Naomi had asked me to take the photo before I planned an escape.

"If I knew that would be the last night I talked to you for months," Lincoln said after he noticed I lingered to look at the photo. "I would have tried even harder to shut up and listen to whatever you had to say."

"I had nothing to say."

"You don't believe someone can be shallow," he said. "And I don't believe it's possible for someone not to have something to say."

"Nothing interesting," I corrected.

"Half the shit I say isn't interesting," he countered.

I smiled; my gaze still locked on the photo. "The plan wasn't to ghost you by the way…"

"No?" he teased.

"Of course not." I looked up at him, trying to see if he really believed otherwise.

"Figure it was a very gentle way of telling me to fuck off." Lincoln chuckled. "Which was fair."

"Every time you texted, I thought for ages about a decent response. And then, when I finally sent it, you'd reply in no more than a couple of minutes, and I'd go into my spiral again. And I started wondering when you would figure it all out. See that I wasn't some mysterious girl but a theatre geek who couldn't order her food in person or make a phone call."

"So, it wasn't how much I wanted you then?" His gaze was questioning, shadowed with a hint of relief.

I shook my head. "No, it was never because of anything you did."

"If it's any consolation, I happen to think you're very mysterious, theatre geek and all," Lincoln said. "But that's not why I'd wait forever and a day to get a text back."

He reached up to cup my cheek, thumb tenderly painting circles on my skin.

"I'd wait till the sun burned out for a simple response because you are one of the most genuine people I've met. You think your quiet's a flaw when all I see is a person who doesn't put on a mask to entertain people. So many people make noise, but you, Celeste, know how to build something in the silence."

I didn't know what to say, so I just held my hand on the back of his and turned to kiss his palm. Having my greatest weakness seen as a strength was like being permitted to look at myself in a different light. To claim that light as my own.

He kissed my forehead and then asked, "After you?"

I nodded, taking the lead the rest of the way to his bedroom. As soon as I walked in, his scent enveloped me: a faded spicy cologne and fresh laundry. The smell triggered a sense of calm; its familiarity was a reminder that I was exactly where I wanted to be.

Lincoln's bed faced the opposite side of the window that looked out onto the backyard. He had a nice view of the thick, green forest behind their house and a glimpse of the old bell tower in the heart of Mendell's campus.

The floor was clean, home to a few overlapping earth-toned carpets that were cotton-like soft between my bare toes.

Weathered paperbacks with cracked spines, waterlogged notebooks, red yarn, and fountain pens overrun Lincoln's desk.

"Wow, these are..." I ran my fingers over his collections of notebooks, all of which seemed stuffed to the brim, bending in ways only a constant companion could.

"I fall asleep at the desk a lot and tend to knock over my water," he explained.

"You write a lot."

Lincoln scratched the back of his head with a sheepish smile. "It's a way to continue talking without completely irritating everyone around me. Plus, I'm a sucker for a good journal, and empty pages make me sad. I get through one a month."

I hummed, impressed. "And here I am thinking I'd done my big one, finishing the one I've been using since middle school last year."

I stopped in front of a corkboard above his desk. It had a million and one red strings pinned across it like a map of highways across the U.S. "What's this?"

"It's another hobby." He joined my side. "For this event, I'm obsessed over in a way that may be worrisome, weird, or valid. I haven't decided on which."

He started fidgeting with some of the notes on his desk, shoving things into drawers and tossing other items into piles that would minimize their presence. The shy side of Lincoln came out when he felt safe and comfortable. I loved that we were opposite in that way. I was honored that I was the person he could be shy around.

"What's the event?" I asked, too curious about what made him this bashful.

"It's a murder mystery dinner," he said. "Sickeningly exclusive. They only have two a year and offer ten spots each time. It's hosted at a bed and breakfast. They pick customers through raffles."

I raised a brow. "That's intense. You think it's worth it?"

"I know it is," Lincoln said without missing a beat. His voice returned to its typical upbeat cadence. "They release all the info of the story online so people who weren't lucky enough to go could play along. This is their upcoming story. I'm trying to solve it…"

I studied the print-out photos, scribbled words on blue sticky notes, and endless strings of yarn held up by black push pins.

Lincoln cleared his throat. "This… isn't exactly a winner in the foreplay department."

"Says who?"

He chuckled, a little shocked at my challenge. "Just a feeling."

"I think it's fine foreplay," I said, leaving out the fact that I had little to no experience on that front.

"Yeah?" He moved closer, wrapping his arms around me from behind. Relaxing into him was as easy as sinking into the snow to make angels.

"Good even." I bit my bottom lip when his lips pressed against the side of my neck. Lincoln traced warm kisses across my shoulder. He tugged my spaghetti strap down a bit so he could kiss every inch without the slightest bit of obstruction.

"How so?" He moved up my neck again, kissing behind my ear. My lips parted as I let out a heavy exhale. His gentle touch sent sparks down my spine, warming my entire body. Every inch of me begged for its turn next. I needed his lips on my fingers, thighs, and belly.

"Shows you have a knack for small details," I whispered and closed my eyes as his mouth kissed the nape of my neck before moving to provide much-needed attention to my opposite shoulder. My heart's a deafening drum, drowning out my anxieties and replacing them with desires.

"I suppose I do." While Lincoln's mouth painted invisible tattoos on my skin, his hands slipped underneath my top, massaging circles on my waist. Arching into him felt as natural as picking up my instrument and hitting my favorite note. He pressed back, meeting my demand with an offering.

"Want to know what kind of details I've been dying to get from you?" he asked.

I couldn't speak. My throat held onto a moan I was too shy to let out. I opened my eyes; the world was now a perfect, soft haze of blue and white from the moonlight outside. A soft melody flowed into my brain, delicately opening with a flute and joined by the steadiness of the piano. Whenever this happened, I usually needed to get to a notebook quickly and jot down the idea. But I turned around to look up at Lincoln instead, knowing this won't be the last time he'd elicit this kind of music from me.

"What kind?" I asked.

He walked me backwards until we reached the bed. I sat, and he surprised me by kneeling. His hands disappeared under my skirt, fingers circling my thighs.

"The kind that helps me make you unfold for me," he said. "Let go for me."

"I let go plenty." I circled my arms around his neck, brushing my nose against his. "I'm in your room because of my own suggestion."

He chuckled. "Sure, but this is just a start."

His thumbs kept circling but remained in place. There was

an ache between my legs that grew ever wanting with every second he didn't make a move.

"I've found my first clue," he said, and before I could ask what he learned, he kissed my neck and the space right under my ear. The arch was instant and embarrassing. I laughed.

"An amateur sleuth could have deduced that one," I teased.

"Hey, give me a second," he whispered into my ear, voice low and deep. My smile vanished, the aching evolving into something dire.

"This kind of stuff requires time." He pulled back enough for me to see his face. His fingers hooked the strap of my top, raising a brow to ask permission. I nodded, and he slipped both down my shoulders. Lincoln urged the shirt down until it pooled at my waist. My cheeks burned as the cold air hit my breasts.

"Everything…okay?" I asked when he paused for a second, interrupting the momentum.

He nodded. "Sorry, it's just… you're the woman of my dreams and I'm trying hard to remain present and not think of all the ways I could screw this up."

My muscles relaxed when I remembered Lincoln had his own set of fears. Fears that occasionally intersected with mine. "I'm trying too. We're doing it together."

He smiled, placed his hand on the back of my head, and pulled me in for a kiss. It was a comforting sidebar that had nothing to do with satisfying sexual desire and everything to do with making sure we felt safe.

"You okay?" He pulled back, making sure he saw my face as I offered him confirmation.

"I'm perfect." I kissed him again.

"Want to be my right hand?"

I tilted my head to the side. "What's that?"

"Someone who helps gather clues?"

"Are you trying to shortcut your way into solving a mystery?" I laughed when he shrugged.

"I just think you'll be good at it," he said. "Something tells me you're a natural."

"Your instincts are wrong." I sobered a little.

"Never about stuff like this," Lincoln promised.

"I…I don't have much experience with stuff like this." My voice naturally dropped, seeking privacy in the quiet, as if someone were around to witness my lack of experience and offer me pity and comfort. "The physicality. The finishing."

Lincoln nodded. "I hear you. Any fantasies?"

I shook my head.

"No scenes from movies or books?"

"None I can recall," I said.

"Any about me?"

His question gave me pause. My grip around his neck loosened as I recalled something I'd thought of just a couple of days ago. My skin burned, and I considered not telling him. But the door was open and Lincoln stood on the other side, completely willing to make sure I was okay once I cross the threshold.

"I've never had anyone go down on me," I said softly. "And I'm…curious how it'd feel if you were the one to do it."

Truthfully, I was more than curious. I couldn't put into words how a dream of his mouth on me had filtered its way into my repertoire multiple nights in a row. The memory of him had woken me up with enough longing to grind against my pillows for an unsatisfying release.

"How do you want me?" he asked with no hesitation.

"How…?" I blinked, confused, thrilled, and overwhelmed.

"On my knees or back? In a chair?" he asked.

"Chair?" I whispered, thinking of the possibilities I hadn't considered.

"I could do it from the front or back," Lincoln offered. "Till my lungs give out. In any way you want me."

I took a deep breath, thinking of everything and wondering if any of my choices would please him. "I don't know. How do you usually like to do it?"

He shook his head. "Celeste, I want you to tell me what to do. That's my only ask. I know what I like and it's being bossed around."

"You may have the wrong person for that," I said, unsure and nervous at the thought of being more dominant than him in a situation that required so much confidence.

Lincoln shook his head. "I don't think so. But I'll make a deal with you."

"Okay?"

"If you really hate it," he said. "I'll lead."

"And if I like it?"

"You get whatever you want, whenever, however," he promised. "I could walk away from this without finishing once, that's how much control I want you to have over me. How much control I've wanted to give you the moment I laid eyes on you."

There was nothing I could say to communicate to Lincoln how every nerve in my body was aflame for him. I wrapped my legs around his waist and pulled him towards me so I could feel his body between my legs as I kissed him. It was a soft kiss that grew rough and messy with every passing second.

"Tell me," he pleaded between kisses. "What to do?"

"Take...off my underwear?" I asked, feeling silly and needy at the same time. It was a discomforting combination that made it hard to swallow, let alone order.

"You sure?"

I nodded. "Yes."

"So be sure," he urged. Lincoln's fingers burned the skin on my thighs, but he still didn't move. He wanted a confident leader. It couldn't hurt to try.

"Take them off," I said. "Please."

He smiled and kissed me before reaching up to my waist and slipping the underwear off. "You're so polite about it."

"Should I not be?"

Lincoln kissed me and playfully bit my bottom lip before letting go. "I love it."

"Now my skirt." I took his hands, guiding them back to the zipper. He had it from there, and my last piece of clothing was gone in an instant.

Without a barrier between his bedsheets and me, I became keenly aware of how messy this could get and how messy I already was.

"Should I get a towel?" I asked, already feeling the spot underneath me getting wet.

"Unless that'll help you get more comfortable, don't worry about it. Because seeing you like this on my bed is making me unbearably hard."

My gaze strayed to his pants, where the firm imprint made itself known. I tilted my head to the side, studying it. "Take yours off."

"You sure?"

"Yeah, now," I said, only slightly firmer than my previous order. A spark flowed through my veins when he listened. There was a thrill in getting him to remove his shirt and underwear as well. I tested the gift of control by leaning back on my elbows and saying, "Kneel in front of me again."

He followed, trusting the surety in my tone. I could feel his heart hammering when his chest made contact with my knees. I nodded permission when he reached for my thighs.

"You can part them," I permitted after a few seconds of melting under his massage.

He followed the instructions, exposing me slowly.

"Fuck," he groaned, gaze entranced by me.

I burned at the show of pure, unfiltered admiration. Never in a million years did I think someone just looking at me would warrant such a reverent stare.

Lincoln pressed his lips to my thighs, kissing up and down as if he couldn't wait for another command but would in favor of his kink.

I sighed, body swimming in a new sense of pleasure and power. "Closer, but not completely there."

He hummed, thankful for the request. His kisses moved further in, mouth grazing the point where my thigh stopped and the soft hair began.

I hadn't trimmed in weeks, but it didn't seem to bother him. In fact, Lincoln's fingers brushed their hair, playing with the wispy strands as if any touch would give him the satisfaction we were both currently after.

"Could you..." I swallowed, anxious for a second before pushing myself to be brave and ask, "Taste me?"

He smiled and trailed his kisses closer to the spot that was desperate for him. I laughed when his initial kiss tickled. His touch was so light, nearly nonexistent. I laughed again when he continued the featherlike kisses.

"Lincoln," I said around my laughter.

"You're so ticklish," he mused, still coaxing me on with a grin.

"I know." I gasped for air. "It's...no one's ever been down there...so... It's very sensitive..."

He chuckled. "I see."

I kept laughing, a part of me afraid this wouldn't work. I'd never heard of anyone not being able to receive oral because of being too ticklish, but it could be a thing. And if that were the case for me, then we'd have to—

I stopped thinking when Lincoln's tongue pressed onto my clit with firm determination. All softness and playfulness washed away. My laughs faded into the moan I'd been holding onto. Lincoln responded when his own sent a vibration through my body, and it made staying in contact both the best and worst possible experience I've ever had.

"Lincoln." I looked down at him to find he was already

looking up at me. His eyes were questioning, in search of his command.

"Don't stop," I said.

He nodded without breaking contact. When I started to squirm from the overwhelming spikes of pleasure, he gripped my thighs, tugging them against his shoulders. My hands found his head, and instinctually, I pushed him into me as I rocked my hips back and forth. Lincoln moaned into me again, his brows wrinkled and fingers digging into my thighs as if pleading for more.

I didn't care about being good, sweet, or agreeable. I cared about the man between my legs, bringing me to a finish. I cared about the guy who'd supported me in every way he could, seeing me become completely his. I want to make him completely mine.

"I'm close," I said, my climax a breath away. But right before I could tip over the edge, Lincoln repositioned his mouth. The climax moved into the distance. I let out a breath, thinking it was an accident and thinking his excitement was getting the best of him as he tried to make this a perfect finish.

It didn't take me long to get close again, but once more, Lincoln changed his pace.

"Focus," I said, half-teasing, half-frustrated.

He hummed into me, his mouth still busy.

"Are you focused?" I propped myself on my elbows, meeting his gaze.

He nodded, eyes big, feigning innocence, and that was when I knew he was doing it on purpose. I laughed and said, "I thought I was in control."

Lincoln pulled away from me. I was all over his lips, and his smile couldn't be happier. "You are."

"Doesn't feel like it."

His deep chuckle pierced me. "I'm just having a little fun, sweetheart."

I felt myself tightening, needing something inside to calm

the want. This was fun. This was why people moved mountains, skipped meals, and lost track of time. In a world where Lincoln existed, I never wanted to be alone again.

"You can't have it both ways," I said.

"Can't I?" he teased, nipping at my thigh.

"Lincoln." I put my hand on his cheek, urging him to face me.

"Yes?" His voice strained after he saw the seriousness in my expression.

"Make me come," I said. "And maybe I'll consider doing the same for you."

He tried to laugh, but my words had reached the part of him that'd been waiting for this kind of energy from me. I guided him back to my clit, and that sealed the deal. He was one thousand percent committed. His tongue oscillated between quick, needy licks and slow, careful ones. My nerves couldn't take more than thirty seconds of Lincoln's focus. I came with a moan louder than any word I've ever uttered.

I found my voice between Lincoln's sheets with his head between my thighs and my body in ecstasy. It was a kind of power I'll never give away. A type of power I knew he'd want me to keep forever.

CHAPTER TWENTY-FOUR

LINCOLN

Celeste tasted like those moments between wake and sleep. When life was flawless and without anything weighing you down. I prayed I'd get to do this forever. Prayed that time would expand for me to spend every waking moment between her legs.

I'd been hard from the moment she asked to see my room. And I nearly finished when she placed her hand on the back of my head, holding me steady against her as I had the best fucking meal of my life.

She'd come twice, and I was still going. Still tasting every drop she had to offer. I glanced up at her, finding her eyes closed and mouth parted as she let out moans that made me hungry for every inch of her. She'd gotten lost in the feeling, more comfortable in her body than I'd ever seen her.

A sense of pride overtook me. I'd been able to give her an escape. Made her feel safe enough to let go of everything outside of us.

Her pleasure became my reason for breathing. I was put here to satisfy her. I paid attention to every moan and whimper. Every time a shiver ran through her. I was hyper-aware of all her reactions, cataloging them to understand how to be better for her.

She preferred when my tongue made bigger, slower circles. She loved when I pressed harder against her. Her strongest reaction came when I moved my tongue back and forth instead of up and down.

Her orgasms were soft explosions, fingers threading through my hair, tugging on me for more. Celeste's thighs tightened around my head, holding me in place in case I had any plans on teasing her again. I smiled through her climax, amused at how bossy this woman could be when she was sexually frustrated.

She let out a laugh once she recovered from her third climax. Her thighs fell away from my head, permitting me to regain my range of motion. But I longed for the restriction.

"How was it?" I murmured, kissing her clit once more.

"Earth-shattering," she said, her voice breathy from fulfilled desire and fading laughter. "You're incredible."

I shook my head. "It's all you. You demanded. Took it."

Her eyes were half-opened, so I couldn't tell if she believed me. By her lazy smile, I'd say not entirely, but I did notice something clicked in her. It was in the way she moved, no longer hesitant but sure in where she wanted to put her hands, how she wanted to receive her pleasure.

"On your back." She patted the spot beside her.

I crawled onto the bed, landing on my back with a hard enough thud that made her bounce up. She laughed and turned over to kiss me. I had a few kinks, one of which she'd offered me perfectly when she wouldn't stand for my playfulness at a certain point. Being under her command had me stiff and aching to please.

Another was her tasting herself on my lips. She was shy about it, but still so curious. Still so willing to try.

"Condom?" she whispered against my lips.

I nodded, about to sit up and reach for my drawer, when her hand urged me back down.

"I'll get it."

My breath caught in my throat when she reached over me, opened the drawer, and pulled one out. When Celeste moved back, she straddled me, studying the condom's wrapper.

I held onto her waist, trying not to lose the final bit of calm I still possessed, even though I could feel the warmth of her on my stomach. She was wet still, clit swollen from my mouth and her orgasms. I gave in to the call, my thumb circling her as she opened the condom.

"You want to put it on?" I asked, oh so turned on.

"Mm." She nodded and moved so my length was within reach. "It should be easy…right?"

I chuckled and nodded, my fingers still playing with her. She closed her eyes for a second, getting distracted by my teasing. I slipped two fingers inside, earning a head tilted back and a mouth parted.

"This is what you want?" I asked. "This is how you're going to take me?"

She nodded, placing her hands on my shoulders, steadying herself as she moved in tandem with me. She was a bit tight, which made me a little concerned about her comfort.

"You sure you're ready?" I asked, serious about the inquiry.

Celeste opened her eyes, gaze confused. "Do I seem like I'm not?"

"You do." I slipped another finger inside, briefly pulling our attention back toward the beauty that was her pleasure. She pulsed around me, and I wanted to take her then and there. Wanted her to ride me until every part of me gave out.

"Are you?" she asked, the first to come back to center.

"Of course."

She raised a brow. "You sure?"

"Never been surer in my life," I promised.

Celeste nodded and lifted herself so my fingers slipped out of her. I groaned at the sight of her sticky, wetness, leaving behind a thin string that connected her to me for a second longer. She became entranced by it, too. There was something in her eyes. After being her right-hand man all summer, I knew it was a want for something she didn't yet dare to ask.

"Tell me," I whispered. "I won't judge. I never do."

She smiled, her eyes softened as she remembered our constant promise to one another. "I've never... there's so much I want to try now that I'm doing this. Now that I'm into this."

"You can try it all with me."

She leaned in for a kiss. It's slow, on the hunt for comfort rather than pleasure. I gave in without question.

Celeste pressed her forehead against mine, gaze directed down as she rolled the condom onto me.

"You aren't going to tell me, are you?" I sighed, mourning the loss of her unvoiced desire.

"Another time," she said with another kiss. "Now, lie down. I want to be on top."

The command was music to my ears. The second I felt her on my tip, I knew holding off my orgasm would be a feat.

I recited the titles of my favorite novels in my head when she leaned over me. I counted the number of strings tacked on my wall when I was completely inside of her, and her hands found my chest. I ran through every drill I'd memorized that summer on the ice when Celeste started rocking her hips back and forth.

"Look at me?" she asked, grabbing my hands and putting them on her breasts.

I took a deep breath, knowing looking at her could do me in and ruin a good thing before it even started. "You feel so fucking good, sweetheart."

"So look at me."

"I don't know if I can without finishing."

"You can." She laughed, moving more slowly, probably thinking it'd make things easier. I got harder. "Please? Look at me."

I gave in. Celeste was everything and more. The moonlight from the window highlighted her dark skin. Her round lips were bare from all the kissing we'd done, and her braids were in a state of unravel with coils escaping to give her a halo effect. This woman was an angel. Seeing her in this state, so brave and beautiful and perfect, had me come undone.

This couldn't be real. She couldn't be mine. I couldn't be inside of her, feeling every damn pulse and grind.

"You did it," she said in a soft, sweet cheer.

"Barely." I chuckled through a heavy breath.

Celeste smiled. "How long do you think you can last?"

"As long as you need," I promised, fully prepared to suffer. "I won't finish without permission."

"Good." She kept my hands pressed on her breast. "I want to go a little longer."

Her stamina was unmatched, but I was more than willing to keep up. Celeste grinded against me, testing different speeds and angles. I wasn't sure if I was the first person she'd shared an orgasm with, but I was cocky enough to believe I was the best person to give one to her.

Celeste's curiosity was sexy. I watched her test out movement and sensation, feeling as if I was experiencing it for the first time, except there was no awkward fumbling. Exploring with someone I trusted my soul with was a dream come true.

"Holy," she whispered when she realized she could stimulate her clit against me if she leaned forward enough. I pushed into her, and she nearly cried from the pleasure.

"How long can *you* last?" I teased when her hands clung to my headboard as she found a way to steady herself.

"Seconds," she confessed, chasing her high faster.

True to her word, she came in seconds. In the midst of the

wave, she begged me to, "Come with me. Would you do that for me?"

"You know I'd do anything and everything for you."

She nodded with a devious look in her eyes. "I've known for a while now, yes."

She leaned in to kiss me, and I couldn't hold back any longer.

As soon as I went over the edge, I flipped her on her back. With Celeste beneath me, I found my preferred rhythm. The headboard banged against the wall as I gave her what she asked for and what I needed.

"Lincoln." She'd tightened around me, every inch of me squeezed inside of her.

My taking the lead had surprised her and been rough and fast. "I'll be good next time, I swear. I'll let you take it from me however you want. I just needed to give it to you for the first time. I had to let you know I want it to be yours."

She was cognizant enough to nod. Her fingers trailed down my back, nails leaving faint scratches. The mix of slight pain and an overwhelming amount of pleasure made me lightheaded. It was a long, needy finish that left me spent.

"Shit," I groaned, still locked in the haze of post-climax bliss.

"Good?" she asked, her voice returning to its cautious tone.

"So good. I never want to live a life outside of this room," I said. "Everything I could want is right here."

She nudged her nose against mine, asking for a kiss that I happily provided. "My thoughts exactly."

———

The night's extended test of endurance. Celeste and I dedicated ourselves to memorizing every inch of each other.

Our break came when she asked for a cup of water. I grabbed a warm towel to help clean her up.

"There's more if you need it in the closet. And there are wipes and other things you're free to use in my bathroom," I said before finding my way downstairs. I grabbed an assortment of juices, fruit, and small sample sizes of the meals Henrik made for us to try for the beginning of the semester party.

"That smells good." Celeste sat up when she saw me. The sheets hugged her lower body. She—thankfully—remained shirtless as she leaned back on my mountain of pillows. I wanted to linger in the doorway and admire her in the warm light of the bedside lamp she'd turned up. Wanted to capture this moment perfectly so it never faded from memory, no matter how much time passed.

"I didn't realize I was so hungry," she said around a yawn. "Or sleepy."

"Yeah, the best sex of your life will do that to you," I agreed as I reclaimed my position beside her.

She snorted, her eyes half-closed. "So presumptuous."

"Alright, giving someone the best sex of his life," I offered.

"I was kidding. I came like five times. It was hands down the best." She snuggled into a pillow and watched as I created a makeshift table using last semester's hardcover textbooks.

"You came up with a six-course meal in the middle of the night?" she asked.

"Seven if you count the shrimp puffs," I said.

"Man of my dreams."

"That would be Henrik." I picked up a puff and held it to her mouth. "He's the man of all of our dreams."

She laughed before taking a bite. I held my hand under her chin as she took another mouthful. When she reached the last bit, her tongue briefly flicked across my finger. I was hard again in an instant. It wasn't just the physicality of it all that was a turn on (though that could never and would never be denied). It was the opportunity to be close enough to take care of her in more ways than just one.

"What's that?" Completely unaware of how irresistible she was, Celeste moved her attention to a bowl of dumplings.

"I got it," I said before she could reach for the fork. I fed her two of them, marveling at how erotic feeding someone could be. Celeste could have me (and probably would have me) coming up with a whole new list of kinks by the night's end.

"Mm." She lay back, chewing the last of the dumplings. "I feel like a princess. I haven't lifted a finger yet."

"You never will whenever I'm around," I promised.

She smiled lazily at me and watched me for a bit as I ate a couple of bites of chicken pot pie.

"What?" I asked when I realized her gaze had become distant.

"Before this..." she began, her smile fading slightly. "You and me. Us...I was so confused about myself."

I frowned and set the fork down. "What do you mean?"

"I never thought about having sex with people." Her voice got lower as she came back to who she was outside these four walls. "Not like how most people I spend time with seem to... like, everyone I know seems to fantasize whenever they have a crush. Imagine that person there with them doing...this."

I nodded, leaning back on my elbows so that my face was close to her knees and vice versa. "That's how it works for me."

"And it's never been like that for me," she confessed. "When I realized that, I considered maybe sex wasn't for me. Which would have been fine, of course. I felt fine about that. But then...us."

"You enjoyed tonight, right?" I asked to be sure I hadn't overstepped in any way. My stomach twisted at the thought of her feeling any kind of discomfort.

"There has to be a bigger word than enjoy." She smiled.

"And it's because it was with you. I know you and like you and...I started thinking about sex after I started feeling close to you. I started wanting the things everyone else seemed to want... does that make sense? Sorry if this is weird. I'm just excited, you know? It's all fresh and new."

I smiled and pushed myself up so I could grab her hand. "It makes perfect sense. And don't apologize. I love that you've discovered something about yourself with me. I love that you're letting me be a part of it."

She bit down on her bottom lip, trying to hold back her growing smile.

"Celeste?" I took a breath, wondering if I should leave it be or dig a little deeper. Give her something more to consider.

Her smile disappeared as she defaulted to worry. "Yeah?"

I brushed my thumb across her cheek, trying to remind her that everything was okay.

"Have you ever thought about your sexuality? Ever considered you may be demisexual?"

Her brow furrowed. "I don't think so. I... I'm not sure I know what that is."

I shrugged. "I didn't either until a couple of years ago. My grandma—love her to the moon and back—isn't exactly educated on sexuality. Or gender. Or much of anything outside what goes on in her world. After Henrik came out—it'd been hard for him—I realized I had blind spots. It was another mystery I wanted to solve. And I wanted to learn how to be there for him. So, I researched. Fell into a lot of rabbit holes."

She sat up. "So, what I explained is what others have felt? I-I mean, I know I'm not unique enough to have an isolated experience, but... there's a word for how I feel?"

I nodded and massaged circles on the back of her hand. "You should look into it for yourself. Make sure it feels right. But you said you needed a connection. And other people experience desire in that way. It's not an anomaly. You're not an outlier. Celeste, everything you feel and how you feel it is perfect. It's you."

She pushed the covers off and carefully made her way over the makeshift table to crawl into my arms. Celeste buried her face into my neck as I squeezed her tightly into a hug. We stayed quiet for a while, enjoying each other's warmth and energy.

"Thank you," she whispered. "For making me feel safe."

My arms tightened around her, one hand on the back of her head, the other around her waist. "You'll always be safe with me."

CHAPTER TWENTY-FIVE

CELESTE

I didn't know how we strayed so far off the beaten path, but somehow I convinced Lincoln to unwind by watching a Barbie movie.

"You said this is your comfort movie?" he asked for the second time.

I poked his side. "Yes, why?"

"No reason..." Lincoln rubbed slow, soothing circles on my lower back. "So, this sidekick."

"Bibble," I reminded him, relaxing into his arms. Watching my comfort movie with my comfort person was a dream that left me feeling high on satisfaction.

Lincoln pressed his nose into my hair, which was his way of quilling laughter when he thought he needed to take something seriously. It was a new habit I loved being a part of.

"We like them?" he said once he pulled away from my head. "Like, Bibble's not some sleeper agent. Or a weird distraction to teach us the woes of judging a book by its cover?"

"We like Bibble," I confirmed. "Could maybe even love him, you know?"

"Definitely...but just in case I didn't know," he said. "Just theoretically, if I come across someone one day who doesn't know. What should I tell them?"

"That Bibble's Bibble and we love him for it."

"Truer words have never been spoken," Lincoln agreed. "Never mind the fact he looks like he could stab someone in the back at a moment's notice—"

I playfully backhanded his chest.

"We love him and his design so much," he finished. "It's not creepy at all."

"What do you have against good art?" I asked.

"I love good art. It's the reason I live and breathe. For Bibble, actually, is who I live and breathe for. I want to thank you for this moment. For reminding me why I'm here, living and breathing for Bibble."

I snorted. "You do too much."

He squeezed me closer and whispered, "You love it."

"I do." Because his "too much" was just right.

We watched the rest of the movie before I reached up to pull my braids out of their bands and consider twisting my hair up for the night.

"It's late." I looked at my phone. "I should probably head out soon."

"Stay?" he asked, a simple tug at my heart. "I can't stand the idea of you leaving."

I considered how easy it would be to remain by his side. Because I knew as soon as I stepped away, I'd count down the seconds until I heard his voice again.

"I have a meeting with my mentor tomorrow. I need to get an early start. Plus, I have a whole nightly routine." I swallowed a sigh, trying to stave off internal protests. Being the voice of reason after a night like this was torture. "Starting with my hair and ending with meditation. I need to make myself as ready as I can be for tomorrow."

"I could help," he offered. "You'd have plenty of time to do whatever you'd need right next to me, and you're already in bed, so wouldn't it be easier to start getting ready for bed here? Driving would just wake you up. And relocating to a bed warmer and more attractive than this one…well, let's be honest, it's impossible."

"You're very tempting."

"I'm willing to be even more tempting," he murmured before kissing me.

"You're making this very difficult."

"I'm sorry," he said before kissing me again. "If you really have to go, I'll walk you out to the car. I'll drive you home myself if you need. And pick you up tomorrow to take you to campus. But if you stay, I could help you wind down. Ensure you're well-prepared for your meeting. You'd be so relaxed with me, Celeste, I promise."

I sighed into another kiss. "You drive a hard bargain."

"Mmhm?" he hummed between kisses.

"But I don't know if…I mean…look at my hair."

"It's perfection," he said. "And?"

I snorted. "I need to twist it up for the night. I need my products for that."

"I could do that."

"Twisting?" I asked. "Or products?"

"Both."

I pulled back a bit to get a good look at him. "You're going to twist my hair?"

"Celeste." He gave me a look. "You know I'm very gifted with my hands."

I snorted. "That so?"

He sat up to meet my challenge. "I'll show you."

I squinted at him. "Fine. Let's do it. Trial run."

"One sec." Lincoln climbed out of the bed and disappeared into the bathroom. He came back a few seconds late with a spray bottle, oil, and a green hair product. I eyed the products, poking my bottom lip out in approval.

"This is some grandma's kitchen stuff." I leaned in to smell the grease. "Literally. I remember her putting this on my head after she'd fried my edges with a hot comb."

"My grandma thought it wise to teach me how to take care of my hair when I started growing it out during the summer," he said. "She said I'd probably have a daughter one day, and she couldn't stand when she could tell when a Black girl had depended on her father to do her hair…Also, I think she just wanted someone to do her hair for free."

"Valid." I sat up taller so he had easier access.

"How many?" he asked as he picked up the spray bottle.

"How many do you have in you?"

He chuckled. "As many as you need."

"We'll start at six and then, if you're good, we'll move you up. Hopefully, we'll get to micro twist level so I can wear it out."

"We will," Lincoln assured, and carefully wet my hair. He was a gentle and slow worker. I kept closing my eyes, missing most of the movie because of how soothing his fingers were on my scalp. He gave me a massage that had me releasing a moan reminiscent of earlier.

"Sorry," I mumbled, embarrassed. "That was a lot."

He laughed and kissed the back of my neck. "Glad you're enjoying it."

Once the twisting started, I was impressed with his ability to maintain tension. It wasn't so tight that I'd have to battle a headache later, like it typically happened whenever my mom tried to do my hair. But it was tight enough that I wouldn't have to worry about it coming undone while I slept. He didn't have a head scarf, so I settled for one of his durags.

"Good?" he asked when finished.

"So good." I sighed, leaning back into his chest. "Lincoln, if I wasn't into you before, you have me hooked, line, and sinker now."

He kissed my cheek. "That's what I like to hear."

"How much do you charge for washes?"

"For you?" he asked as he tightened his arms around me. "A couple of nights like this."

"You've got yourself a loyal customer."

———

I woke up alone in Lincoln's bed. At first, I was unsure of where I was, and then I panicked because something was off.

Not now. Please.

I winced when my lower body tensed from a cramp. I lay still for a moment, hoping that it was a fluke. But, when the next wave rolled through, I knew I'd need to go into clean-up mode, stat.

Of course, this had to happen after the night we'd just had. After I'd finally felt comfortable enough in my body with someone else, it was as if life was determined to move the goalpost of comfort. *Did you enjoy a sweet night connecting with an incredible guy? Wonderful. Now try a bloody morning and see how that works out.*

Lincoln came back into the room right as I sat up to assess the damage, which was a decent bloody stain on his gray bed sheets.

"Morning, gorgeous," Lincoln greeted with enough energy and excitement to indicate he'd been up for quite some time. His eyes brightened when he saw I was awake. He started to climb onto the bed, but before he could reach me, I held my hand up.

"What's wrong?" Lincoln froze, sitting on his knees at the bottom of the bed. "Did you sleep okay?"

"I..." The only way out was through. There would be no hiding the blood on my underwear and the blankets. "I just got on my period."

"No worries." The concern that'd stiffened his brow melted in an instant. Lincoln nodded as if I told him it was going to be a little chilly outside, so he should bring a jacket. "I'll start the shower and get a change of clothes. You could wear some of my things, or should I grab something from Naomi?"

I blinked, surprised and a little put off by the nonchalance. Did a part of me want this to be weird? A part of me wished to confirm that I couldn't maintain a normal, kind, supportive relationship. Wanted to wade through the discomfort because, in a way, it was all I knew how to navigate?

"Something of yours should be fine." My voice was low, barely audible to my own ears. "My skirt's still good, so all I'll need is a top and some shorts underneath."

"Top and shorts. I can do that," he promised. "Do you have your products? I'm sure Naomi has extras I could grab from their bathroom."

Lincoln got up from the bed and started digging through his drawers, pulling out some boxers and an oversized Mendell's hockey team training long-sleeve shirt.

"It's on...your sheets." I winced, apologetic. Eye contact became a temporary impossibility.

"No worries." Lincoln shrugged and set the clothes on the nightstand beside me. "I'll get us some new ones while you're in the shower. Are you in any pain? I have a couple of heating pad options." He gestured to his shoulder. "Recurring injury, so I always keep a few handy. The plug-in is one of the best, in my opinion. But I could warm one in the microwave. I think that one's safer to use."

"No, thank you, but...um, but could you grab me an Advil?" I asked.

"'Course." He kissed the top of my head. "Hey, look at me?"

I took a deep breath and did as he asked. It was embarrassing to be that embarrassed. I was caught in a weird, cramping infinite loop.

"Don't worry about this. You're not going to freak me out." He kissed my forehead this time. "I can handle blood. This is as natural as breathing. And you're as beautiful as the sunrise."

I nodded, my cheeks burning, but the tightness in my chest dispersing.

"I'm going to start the shower, get you your Advil, and then, I'll fuck off for a bit while you get ready," he said. "Sounds like a plan?"

I nodded, laughing a little, and watched him disappear into the bathroom. It took a few minutes for the water to get hot. Once it did, Lincoln gave me the all clear and left to find some meds.

He laid out a couple of towels, body wash, and lotion for me. Being taken care of to such an extent had every ache in my body loosening before I even stepped foot into the steaming shower.

I smelled of him as I scrubbed the night away. I felt wrapped in his arms when I tugged on his shirt that nearly reached my knees. I caught a glimpse of myself in the mirror hanging on the door of his closet. My hair remained in the perfect twists he'd done for me last night. I drowned in his clothes, looking like a woman in love. It was a realization that made me smile. I was falling in love. It was a feeling that was neither scary nor complex, as I had thought it'd be. Falling in love with Lincoln felt like reaching my natural state.

Lincoln knocked before coming in. "You okay?"

"Yes." I glanced at the door, trying to fix my face to something not so lovestruck. It was one thing to admit being in love with him to myself. And another to share it with him. Yes, he'd already mentioned love last night. But Lincoln was the kind of guy who got an idea during breakfast and made it his personality by dinner. He was ever-changing and quickly evolving. I loved that about him. However, it also meant that it was best for me to take things slow. Keep us grounded. Because maybe once we started dating for real, he'd get another idea. Find someone new to obsess over. Be ever-changing and evolving far quicker than I could keep up.

"This is for you." Lincoln joined me in front of the mirror, encircling me between his arms as he offered a hot mug of tea and a couple of Advil. "Made it myself."

"Oh?" I accepted the mug, bringing it to my nose to catch a whiff of the contents. It smelled of ginger with a hint of vanilla.

"I've reached perfection," he quickly assured as he rested his chin on the top of my head. "Promise."

"I liked it last night," I said before taking a shy sip.

He chuckled. "You don't have to be so nice to me. I saw the look on your face when you took your first sip."

The tea he'd given me now was noticeably different. It was smooth — no renegade tea leaves—and with just a hint of sweetness. Not enough to make me need a sugar detox like last time.

"Well?" He watched me drink through the mirror, genuinely worried he'd messed it up the third time around.

"Honest?" I asked, drawing it out to tease him.

"Always."

"It's amazing and exactly how I'd make it." I held the cup close to my chest. If all my mornings started like this, I think I'd eventually be able to take on the world. "I love it."

Lincoln kissed behind my ears and neck, coaxing me into a fit of laughter.

"Okay, okay," I said. "You're tickling me, you're going to make me spill this."

"I've been practicing for weeks," he said, excitement making him talk so fast it was difficult to keep up with what he was saying. "Trying to get it right for you. I just have one problem."

"What's that?"

"I don't know what the hell I did to get it right this time," he confessed. "I was just panicking, mixing shit, trying to make sure it was ready for you when you got out of the shower. There are six variations of this downstairs. I had to choose between them, and in the end, just went with the one that called to me."

I laughed. "Lincoln, when you want to, you really know how to dedicate yourself to something."

I turned around so we were face-to-face when I said the next part, "Remember that, okay?"

He sobered a bit and pressed his forehead against mine. "I will."

"When are you talking to Anthony to ask him to come back?"

Lincoln shrugged. "Tomorrow."

"Oh, wow."

"Too soon?"

"No…" I shook my head, unsure. "I don't think so. I just thought you were going to give it a couple of weeks. Train with the guys, you know? Spend some time to show you're dedicated."

"I know what I want to say and what I can do," he said. "There's no use in beating around the bush and dragging this out. I just want to get back out there. Start over and work toward improvement. I don't like wasting time, you know? I've made up my mind, and now I want to take action. I want to move forward."

"I get that, I do…" I bite on my inner cheek.

"Say it, Celeste." Lincoln smiled down at me. His hand massaged the nape of my neck. "What are you thinking?"

"I don't know…I think taking your time could be good for you," I said. "It shows you're patient and willing to put in the work."

"I am only one of those things."

I smiled. "Could you try to be the other?"

He took a breath, considering. "One day, sure, I'll give patience a go. But with the new season right around the corner, I don't think I can afford it. Besides, patience on the ice could be the reason you miss a winning play. Most winners aren't patient."

"I don't think you're giving yourself enough credit. You've been plenty patient with me."

Lincoln shook his head and leaned down for a kiss. "Because you make everything feel whole. There's no amount of time I wouldn't wait for you."

I kissed him this time, parting my lips slightly as a reminder I've let him in once and I would continue.

"It's up to you ultimately," I said once we pulled away to catch our breath. "Regardless, I'm rooting for you. And if you need anything from me, just let me know."

"I will," he promised. "You let me know, too. I'd push it all to the sidelines for you. In a heartbeat, I'd drop it all for you."

"I'm not asking for you to drop it all," I assured. "But I will ask you to bring in the castle set pieces before next Friday. My aunt's been asking about it. She's getting nervous. We really need it for opening night."

"I got it taken care of," Lincoln promised. "It's as good as done, so cross it off your to-do list."

"Thank you." I forced myself to step out of his embrace. "I need to go now if I want to make my meeting on time."

"Alright," Lincoln said, disappointment making his voice quieter. "When will I see you again?"

"I'm free after." My cheeks burned at how eager I sounded. "Too soon?"

He shook his head. "I'll start the countdown. "

My hand trembled as I knocked on the door of Professor Nola's office. But there was more excitement than anxiety flowing through my veins. She welcomed me in with a smile and immediately pulled up the email with my video attachment of the final practice. We watched in silence. I was so focused on the stage I didn't notice Nola's worried brow.

"Celeste," she said as soon as the music faded out and the video cut to black.

I sat up straighter, my smile disappearing. I was out of the foggy bliss of last night. Now, the world felt brighter and once again, as dangerous as ever.

"Yes?" I managed to ask, sounding far more stable than the trembling hands I tucked underneath my thighs.

"It's not just an audio recording," she said, trying to laugh to lighten the mood.

"Right." I swallowed and willed myself to elaborate. "I wanted to do something bigger. Something that'd help me stand out from everyone else."

Nola watched me, expression blank as she waited for me to say something more. Something that made sense.

I couldn't make much sense, but I could be honest. "I wanted to do a production."

"A big job," she noted.

"Yes, but not unlike what Ophelia Lawrence did during her time here." I tried to smile, but Nola stared back at me blankly. My gaze became flighty, unable to hold eye contact as I realized she wasn't the slightest bit impressed. I tucked one hand around my midsection and slipped the other underneath my thigh. Sitting here, confessing I was trying to be like Ophelia—and had so clearly failed in the eyes of a professional—made my insides feel ready to spill out.

"Everything fell into place over this summer." I'd given up eye contact altogether, staring at the back of her computer instead. "Some of my…friends didn't mind pitching in. And I figured this was a perfect opportunity to really see my music come to life. To show what it'd look like and feel like…a musical isn't at its fullest if just on a page or recording."

It was quiet for too long, the suspense more discomforting than my shame. So, I dared to glance up and look for some sign that maybe it wasn't as bad as I thought. Nola twisted her mouth to the side as she considered my explanation. I could hear water dripping from the AC. A hum of a microwave coming from the lounge next door. Music of everyday life, taunting me in its ability to be loud and consistent. Everything else was ever in motion, when I felt as though my world had stopped.

"I don't think you should submit this," Nola finally said. "In fact, I'd strongly suggest you don't."

"Okay..." My stomach lurched at the confirmation of failure. I was surprised I didn't start to cry on sight. But if there was one thing social anxiety was good for, it was saving face. Crying would lead to more shame. I tucked my emotions up in a tiny box that would eventually burst open at the seams.

"The set design isn't strong," she continued. "It pulls from the music."

"The sets are still...being worked on."

"And the lyrics need edits. Your peers, the ones submitting against you, won't have full productions—I'll give you that. But they're work is tighter because they don't have to worry about multiple issues that come with working with a cast of inexperienced singers."

"Yeah, I thought of that but..." I shook my head, trying to block out shame, if only for a second, so that I could explain my vision. "I think this would be a perfect representation of who I am and what I hope to be capable of one day. A project like this demonstrates an interest in collaboration and an ability to develop a voice. Since Ophelia did a similar project while she was here, I used that as inspiration."

"Maybe," Nola agreed. "But do you really think your voice is strong enough? In its current state? You're not Ophelia."

"I...I know that." My throat tightened. Her words settled on top of my skin, a hot branding that would scar me for heaven knew how long.

"Celeste, I think you're a very talented musician," she said, voice softening as she noticed the sag of my shoulders and sensed my overall utter devastation. "And you will be a talented composer and songwriter. But I also feel I'd be doing you a disservice if I didn't warn you that your voice isn't particularly strong or intriguing. There's fear in how you write music. That can be overcome. But because you haven't had the right amount of experience yet, do you really want to risk wasting a chance like this? You could submit something safer and get to the next round in a heartbeat. You'd get the feedback you need to start tackling some of your fears."

My jaw tightened, but I nodded, trying to swallow every bit of thick feedback. This was what being an artist was, right? If I couldn't handle this, I surely wouldn't hack it in the professional world.

"I'm speaking from experience," Nola continued. "So, please, trust me. A rejection at this stage of your growth could do more harm than good. Play it safe. Submit a simple composition. Something from last semester. Your final piece was gorgeous."

I nodded, too numb to speak but lucid enough to smile. It was a good smile, I think. All soft and grateful. I could taste the bile rising in my throat.

"Does that sound like a plan?" she asked.

It took two deep breaths for me to get out, "If you think this is for the best. Then, yes...I can pull something from my old projects and submit."

Nola's expression brightened. "Perfect. I'm so glad we're on the same page."

I wanted to sink into the folds of my chair, drown in the leather. All that work for this. To be back at square one.

———

It took twenty minutes. The overwhelm, disappointment, and embarrassment consumed me for twenty minutes. I made it to my car, let out a river of tears, struggled to breathe, drank half a hot bottle of water, and pulled up last year's composition notes on my phone.

I found one of my old pieces, ready to tweak a few things, attach it to the rest of my application, and be done with it, when I realized I couldn't do it. I wouldn't do it. I'd rather not submit if I wasn't able to submit something I was truly in love with.

My embarrassment and shame morphed into something hotter. A type of annoyance I'd never felt before. I replayed all the feedback Nola had given, trying to pick out what was valid and what was wrong.

I pulled out my laptop, balancing it on my car's console as I reviewed the musical's video before I called Naomi.

"I need you to tell me if I'm going off the deep end," I said.

"You got it," she said in a heartbeat.

"Nola doesn't think the musical is good enough to submit," I said.

I waited for my throat to constrict with emotion, but it was unresponsive. I'd cycled through the stages of grief at three times speed, arriving at acceptance sooner than I'd ever anticipated.

"Celeste," Naomi said, voice quiet with empathy. "I'm sorry."

"No, it's..." I was going to say fine, but it's not fine. It doesn't feel fine. I didn't feel fine. "I'm scared because...I think I'm going to ignore her."

"What?"

I switched the phone to the opposite ear, feeling excited about my small act of rebellion. "I've studied, implemented my professors' and peers' notes, and completed projects catered to everyone's preferences. I've molded my music into what Mendell's program has told me it has to be. When I lean into my voice, they say it doesn't fit, and that's fine. Fine for them. I've guided myself back onto their path. I've followed it quietly. Just like I always do, but this time I want...I really want..."

I didn't know why I wanted to cry again when I finally started to feel like I could breathe. I was finally brave enough to accept that whatever I said or did or felt didn't have to be the right thing. My decision to do this musical didn't have to be right or good. All it had to be was my vision. My voice. "I really want to be like Lincoln."

"Lincoln?" Naomi asked, and I could hear the smile in her voice.

"To do something and not look to my left and right, asking everyone around me, 'is it okay'?" I laughed. "And, I'm already messing it up by calling you."

Naomi laughed too. "Maybe."

"Definitely." I took a breath and accepted I would have to do this next part on my own.

"So?" she asked, ever patient and willing to let me be whoever I needed to be when I was ready to be it. "Do you need me to tell you what I think? If you're going off the deep end?"

"No," I said without hesitation. "I'll dive off on my own this time."

"I'm proud of you," she said.

"I love you," I said before hanging up.

Without any more what-ifs or catastrophizing, I reached for my laptop and pulled up my application. It took me a second to connect to my phone's weak hotspot, but I eventually did. As soon as the page loaded, I clicked on submit.

CHAPTER TWENTY-SIX

LINCOLN

t's shameful admitting up until now, I couldn't say with my whole chest I experienced the authentic, metallic taste of hard work. Sure, three seasons on the hockey team at Mendell meant I was no stranger to a decent grind. Long gym sessions left my muscles feeling worn down and run over, while hard collisions on the ice caused bruises and scars that didn't respond to ice baths or heating pads. But (any athlete could vouch for this) there was always a point in a workout, practice, or game where you could decide to push or pull back. To take yourself well past your limit, knowing you're more than willing to face any and every consequence. Or, to stop right when your body requested.

I'd always given in to the ask without challenge and always pulled back because who cared what was on the other side of trying when I knew for sure what was right in front of me?

Training without holding back for two weeks left me in the kind of exhaustion that made blinking a laborious task. It was the first time I allowed dissatisfaction to breach my walls, leading to frustration with my limitations, which had become bold enough to begin haunting me in my dreams. I'm not sure how others deal with hitting wall after wall consistently.

"If we had the chance, I don't think we would have won nationals," I said through a heavy cough.

Henrik filled my ice packs, and Finn checked an old blister on my hand. I was a warrior coming back to base camp, having my comrades attempt to patch me up for tomorrow's battle.

"Not with how I was playing," I said.

"Well, lucky for us, one person's not a whole team." Sam lounged on the couch opposite the one I sat on. He stuck around for moral support and to cash on his last decent, 'I told you so.'

"Is this how it always is?" I rubbed my hand over my chest. "Working hard for something? Truly wanting it? It's draining."

"You'll develop a tolerance for it," Henrik promised as he placed an ice pack on my knee.

"The pain never really goes away," Finn mumbled, still laser-focused on lining up my bandage. "You just learn how to live with it."

"I'm going to call Anthony tonight," I said.

"And say what?" Sam asked, but not even a small part of him took my declaration seriously. "All it took was a few independent practices for you to become the player he's been trying to make you all summer?"

The guys already convinced me not to try persuading Anthony to take me on as a client again. But now, I felt like more than enough time had passed. I knew what it'd take (my screaming shins were proof). And I had another driving force: Celeste and her unwavering belief in me. I was determined to live up to the man she thought I was.

"Not in so many words," I said.

Sam chuckled and shook his head. "I don't think you should bother."

"Why not?" I asked. "I want to work with him. And he said to call him back when I got serious."

"I think what he meant was, he wanted you to prove you were serious." Henrik sat on the couch's armrest, watching Finn's slow, meticulous way of wrapping my wrist.

"I am," I said. "I have."

"You've verbally committed to a change. And have actively stuck with that commitment for less than a week." Sam rested his phone in his lap, focusing his gaze on me when he realized I wasn't budging on my plan to speak with Anthony. "It's been *twelve* days."

"Less if you count rest days," Finn said.

"And actual practice time." Henrik looked up at the ceiling, trying to do the math in his head. "So, maybe, around thirty hours? Forty tops?"

"That's not even two days when you break it down like that," Sam said. "A commitment of two days isn't going to change someone's opinion. Especially not a guy like Anthony."

I scoffed. "Oh, come on. We all know no one breaks stuff down like that. I've been working for almost two weeks. That's commitment."

"It's progress, definitely," Henrik said quickly. "We're not trying to discount that."

"Sounds like you are," I said with a shrug that made me wince. Finn frowned with a look that told me to keep still.

"We're being realistic," Sam said.

"What's wrong with just starting this season without a personal trainer?" Finn asked. "You've done it before."

"This is different," I reminded him. "It's senior year. I want to get it right."

"You want to fix something you've messed up over the course of months in a matter of days," Sam corrected. "You want results right after you've made the decision. You're conflating instantaneous gratification with right."

"I'm sorry, I thought you guys were encouraging this?" I frowned. "Isn't that the whole reason you agreed to help me with training?"

"Of course, we're encouraging," Henrik said. "I think it's a good idea."

"We're just adjusting your expectations," Sam added.

"So, you got me an in with Anthony, but don't think I should use that in anymore?" I asked.

"Correct," Sam affirmed.

I blinked, surprised at how easily he answered. "Then why encourage me to do it at all?"

Sam sighed and exchanged a look with Henrik. I couldn't decipher what passed between them. Still, they reminded me of parents looking over their kid's head because the kid was too young and naïve to understand. My jaw clenched.

"Hey, I'm not some kid you have to protect from the dangers of the world," I said. "Don't look at each other like you're trying to decide which one has to be the mean parent."

"Lincoln, we all know you work better with external motivation," Henrik said.

Sam nodded. "And an opportunity at a second chance is a pretty damn good motivator."

"But in reality…" Henrik shrugged.

"Anthony's not even glancing in your direction for another few months," Sam said. "Maybe not even until we're well into the season."

I scoffed. "What would be the point then? It'd all be over."

And then, I'd be back to square one: aimless in a sea of possibilities that never called to me like hockey did. I hated being this aware of a clock. It was almost as if I could hear the seconds ticking off, time slipping into a bottomless pit, never to recover.

"There's still plenty of points," Finn chimed in. "You'll be able to hone your skills."

"Just in time for me to never play again? Sure, sounds like an incredible use of my energy."

"You can't rush this, Lincoln," Sam said, tone clipped and annoyed. "You can't talk your way out of it. You can't cram all the work in the night before. This is your problem. You think once you decide something, the stars will align. That's never how life worked. Grow up."

My laugh was devoid of any humor. The pain in my joints suddenly couldn't hold a candle to the piercing headache nudging against my skull. I didn't mind a mirror; a hard truth staring back at me. I did mind when the truth had been held behind a door, waiting for the right moment to make its appearance and put me in my place.

"I would have loved to know all these opinions weeks ago. Because it feels like you guys dangled a carrot, knowing it would distract me. And that's fucking condescending."

"Lincoln!" Henrik called out when I got up from the couch and started out of the room.

"Leave it," Sam said. "Give him space. "

CHAPTER TWENTY-SEVEN

CELESTE

"You should come out with me tonight." It was hard to hear Lincoln over the already large crowd of whatever house party he'd found himself in. "I want to introduce you to some people."

I only hesitated for a second. "Alright."

The smile in his voice made it even harder to hear him. "Yeah? You sure?"

"Positive." I tried to smile at myself, flooding my brain with thoughts of positivity and feigning self-belief in an attempt to outdo the twisted, cruel beliefs.

If Lincoln and I were going to have a real chance of lasting, I'd have to try to exist in his world. I'd have to meet him where he was, like he'd met me. So, I ignored the butterflies wreaking havoc in my nervous system. I focused hard on keeping my hand steady as I applied makeup, ensuring my pink and purple eyeshadow blended seamlessly. Lined my lips with a nude color and swiped on a couple coats of clear gloss.

My high anxiety outfits consisted of tops with sleeves long enough to hide my fingers (just in case the trembling was too frequent). The white, flowy one I chose provided the right amount of warmth for the chill of a late summer night. I slipped on a pair of wide-leg jeans that Naomi had painted butterflies on the back pockets.

Naomi video chatted with me when I got to taking down my twists. She sat in Finn's car with her hair up and a pair of hoop earrings on (the telltale sign she'd also agreed to a night out).

"You look adorable. You're really coming?" She tried to balance the phone on the dashboard. It fell a few times before she gave up with a laugh. I smiled too; my chest felt a bit less like it was underneath a twenty-ton weight.

"As soon as my hair's done." I could hear the buzz of people outside her car.

Her smile grew at my words. "I can't believe he convinced you to come."

"I want to be there for him. Trying to," I said. "And who knows, maybe I'll like going out and being around people?"

"Sure. Or maybe, you'll hang out for a bit and go back home because being here for even a minute is more than enough."

"You think so?" I asked, unable to hide the hint of hope in my tone.

"Even a second of Celeste is enough to make me happy," she promised. "I know Lincoln feels the same."

My chest loosened, breathing becoming obtainable once more. Feeling enough and being enough were two separate things; Naomi always managed to sew them together for me in less than a minute.

We talked until I was in my car. Once on the road, I got through my playlist of comfort musicals—a little *Phantom of the Opera*, *Wicked*, and *Hamilton*. By the time the *Prince of Egypt* began, I pulled onto the noisy block. My window vibrated from the music outside, disrupting my listening party with much more bass and intensity. Since on-street parking was full, I found a spot a block away at a park. It was late enough that mosquitoes were buzzing about. I saw a few fireflies too, hovering around the trees in the neighborhood.

Music vibrated through my chest as I approached the house. The two-story ranch-style house stood behind an iron gate, left open so people in the yard could filter in and out as they pleased.

Unlike the neighborhood Naomi and the guys rented in, this one was a well-known area for college students. The street was within walking distance of campus. Older cars, with the occasional flashy one, lined all the driveways on the street. With the fall semester around the corner, Tinsel was about to become crowded once more. I wouldn't be able to find quiet corners as easily, but hopefully I wouldn't need them as much. That hope was tied to Lincoln and the smile he gave me the second he saw me coming up the walk.

He'd been waiting for me on the front porch, surrounded by a group of guys who looked vaguely familiar (more of his teammates).

As soon as he saw me, he broke away from the group. Lincoln wrapped his arms around me. I could barely hear what he said between the music, people, and the fact that he'd buried his face into my hair.

"What did you say?" I pulled back enough to glance up at him.

Lincoln's eyes were a bit red with exhaustion. But his smile and the energetic kisses he pressed against my forehead led me to believe tiredness wouldn't be much cause for concern. He was in his element once more. With hockey season right around the corner, Lincoln seemed infused with energy from the people around it again.

"I'm happy you're here." Lincoln kissed my lips this time. He tasted sweet and smelled of alcohol. The drink in his hand was half full. When he saw me eyeing it, he offered to grab one for me.

"I'm good," I said.

He nodded and kissed the top of my head before asking, "Can I introduce you to a few people? I've been telling some of the guys on the team about your music and how brilliant you are."

"Oh...sure, of course." I tried to keep my voice steady. There was no reason for me to devolve into panic yet. No reason for my chest to sting with burning air, or my throat to swell from the anticipation of 'hi' and 'my name is' and 'whatever I have to say to help you think I'm a normal human being.'

Lincoln grabbed my hand and said, "Squeeze if you want to go, and we'll leave in a heartbeat."

I took a breath and smiled, grateful for some sort of plan. Heavens knew my brain wasn't exactly in the state to come up with one.

Lincoln led me up the stairs and to the group of guys. There were six of them, and I started forgetting names as soon as Lincoln began introducing them. I smiled, or at least tried to smile. I didn't have much control over my face. As Lincoln went on about the musical, my hands started to tremble. The one linked with his was relatively stable thanks to his secure grip. But I tucked my free hand into my sleeves, clutching the fingers into a fist.

I tried to find something to focus on during the conversation, an external life jacket when my internal one of positive affirmations deflated.

The guy on our left said he'd grown up in New York. His parents would often take him to the theatre.

I built up the courage to ask, "Do you miss it?"

He looked at me blankly and asked, "What did you say?"

Between the music and the people, even my "loud" voice had no chance of being heard. I tried again. It wasn't successful. All the guys looked confused, and my skin was so hot I was surprised Lincoln's hand didn't have third-degree burns. It wasn't a question worth repeating. No depth or substance to it to warrant this amount of time spent on recovering the words. It was as if I'd stopped us to admire a small hill when the view of majestic, snow-capped mountains was right around the corner.

"Do you miss New York?" Lincoln gave my hand a comforting squeeze as he repeated my question for me.

I couldn't even pay attention to the full answer because the guy started with, "No, never. Like I said, I was counting down the seconds until I was out of there."

With all the overstimulation, I hadn't remembered him saying that before I asked the question. It was a small mistake that catapulted me into the depths of embarrassment. I tried to anchor myself by focusing on how my hand fit in Lincoln's, with a perfect overlap of fingers and alignment of palms, and how I was close enough to smell the warmth in his cologne and the spice of his aftershave.

Our group kept changing throughout the night. Most of the people Lincoln spoke to, I didn't know. Naomi and Finn migrated in our direction for a little bit. She took one look at me and leaned in to whisper, "Finn and I are heading out. You want to leave with us? We could hang out back at our place."

I forced myself to smile; it worked this time. "It's okay."

"You sure?" She pulled back to get a good look at my face.

I nodded and glanced over at Lincoln, who was completely enmeshed in a debate he started on whether childhood is better with chemical-colored cereal. He kept switching sides, mostly to annoy his fellow debaters.

"I'm going to stay a bit longer. Try to challenge myself." I hadn't been part of a conversation I started on my own. And every discussion Lincoln managed to rope me into had my senses too overwhelmed to process in time to formulate something worthy of saying. Coming here had been solely for Lincoln, but somewhere after the fifth or sixth experience of my throat becoming too tight to share my name, I decided I needed to be here for me as well. It'd taken me a summer to become brave enough to click a submit button. It'd take even longer to develop a voice strong enough to withstand my cyclone of social inadequacy.

"And I need to talk to Lincoln before the night's over," I added. "Check in about sets for the musical."

We looked over a Lincoln who was in a deep one-on-one with a guy on the football team who swore he also grew up with a ghost. Apparently, his family had hired a team of ghost hunters called the Jones Family back when people used landlines and phone books.

"It might take me a month or two to detangle him from all of this," I joked.

Naomi smiled and nodded in agreement, "Okay, but if you change your mind and get tired of waiting, let me know."

I hugged her goodbye and watched as she made the escape I so desperately craved since I'd set foot inside the house.

As the night stretched, I managed my anxiety by doing breathing exercises and gradual body relaxation. The ground techniques worked until another wave of worry breached my walls. The house got more crowded, bloated with students and older people from town. The music got louder, and people got drunker. Conversation became looser, so one would think it'd be easier to weave in and out. One would be wrong. One would be me.

I took my first leap with a group of women who were on Mendell's softball team. Their conversation had broken off from the hockey guys, venturing into the realm of a dating reality TV show I'd binged (and loved) whenever I couldn't manage to get to sleep. Two of them hated the obvious scripted nature, while the other two thought that's what made it fun.

"It's almost the best of both worlds," I'd spoken up, inserting myself into the back and forth like I'd seen Lincoln do a dozen times tonight. Like he'd done ever since I'd known him. The initiation's not as terrible as I've built it up to be. It was everything that followed.

"How so?" All the softball girls had a blinding level of beauty, but the one who asked this was the kind of breathtakingly beautiful I believed could start wars. Her jet black, tight coils, dark skin, and round eyes would be the muse to some oil painter one day.

The beauty and inquisitive gazes sent me into another panic. I tried to build on my previous conversation skills: no awkward staring, no sudden pauses, and no weird stumbles (like when I couldn't pronounce 'school' earlier).

"Having people follow a script but somehow always make it their own. It's a compilation of happy accidents," I managed to get out seamlessly. Pride swelled in my chest because I hadn't had to look at Lincoln once. In fact, I didn't know where he was. I stood on my own, articulating my genuine opinions. The balloon of joy that'd begun to inflate in my chest popped when they stared at me for a moment in silence and exchanged the kind of looks only people who had known one another for years could. A silent conversation proceeded, and a subtle judgment was made.

"Right," one with long legs and a short, blonde pixie cut said after their judge, jury, executioner sidebar. "Interesting take, I guess."

One of them scoffed, as if she disagreed. The others remained silent, as if waiting for a train to pass before they could continue exchanging ideas in peace.

It was a lackluster response. Nothing groundbreakingly horrible, and yet, I felt the need to apologize for interrupting and inserting myself into an established friendship that wasn't currently open to applications.

They eventually continue their conversation as if I hadn't said a thing. And the kicker was, they ventured into the realm I'd been trying to go. Theorizing on the merits of the blending of fact and fiction in a world where, thanks to social media, we have to exist in both constantly.

I didn't know how to stand. How to untangle myself after having said one thing and being edged out of the conversation in a heartbeat. I turned my body away from them at least, understanding social cues enough to know hoovering would be foolish. My gaze scanned the room, heart racing in hopes of finding a lighthouse before the storm got too heavy. Everyone I knew had gone home or somewhere else. My need for escape was dire.

I eventually found Lincoln in the crowd. But when I managed to catch his gaze, he gave me that 'I'm so happy you're here' smile. His 'I'm so proud you're standing on your own right now' smile. The 'aren't you excited to be here, like this, with everyone' smile.

He would leave in a heartbeat, at the slightest inkling of my unwarranted discomfort. I couldn't manage to convince myself to ask for his assistance on escape. Not when his eyes were so bright and everyone around him seemed to want to talk to him. I found a corner, pulled out my phone, and refreshed my email as if it were the most fascinating thing on the planet. As if I was too busy to talk about my favorite reality TV show anyway.

Once it was too dark to see out of the vast bay windows in the front room of the house, I decided I waited long enough to pull Lincoln aside for a quick update.

I found him doing shots in the kitchen. His smile was wide, and his cheeks were red from the heat of what I would swear was a hundred people crammed into the house. We were all elbows and knees, knocking into each other, trying to get drinks and air.

"Hey." I held onto his shoulder, trying not to get pulled back into the current of people migrating. "Can we talk?"

He leaned in close enough so I felt his lips on my ear to ask, "Right now?"

I wanted to burrow into him and forget all the nerves clawing at my insides. I wanted to be back in his bedroom with his arms shielding me from every uncertainty life has to offer. When I met his gaze, I saw unfiltered happiness. Before now, I thought I'd seen him excited and present. Tonight was different. Tonight, Lincoln was weightless. And maybe a little drunk. Very carefree.

Despite his smile, something was different about how quickly he was drinking. He could be easily distracted and quickly jumped from conversation to conversation.

"Or could we wait one second?" He held up a finger and took another sip of his drink before adding, "Someone found an old Wii. We're going to set it up. Do you want in?"

I glanced at my phone. "It's midnight."

"Yeah?"

"I—"

One of his teammates called him over — the guy from before who'd looked at me weird ever since I brought up New York twice. He was giving me that same look now.

Sorry for not hearing you say you hated that city, I wanted to snap. What was his problem?

"You in?" Lincoln asked.

I shook my head when I noticed the softball women gathering to play. My lips trembled as I tried to smile. "I'll watch."

"It'll only be a couple of games," Lincoln promised, giving me a quick forehead kiss, lips barely making contact.

A couple of games expanded into seemingly endless mashing of the "play again" button. Everyone with a controller agreed to turn it into a drinking game. And as good as he was at hockey, Lincoln wasn't great with game reflexes. Or maybe it was all the alcohol. The point was, his response time was horrible, the house became a sauna, and I couldn't breathe. By the third round of golf, I would bet my life there wasn't enough air left in the room. I tugged on my collar, trying to manufacture some sort of breeze that could cool me down. But the burning heat was coming from within as well. The longer I tried to hold out, the lighter my head became.

I got up without saying anything (not like anyone besides Lincoln would care). Going outside didn't immediately cure my lightheadedness, but at least the cool air provided solace. I bounded down the porch and outside of the iron gate. In the privacy of a dark, empty night, I stopped trying to keep my hands from shaking. As the noise of the party became quieter, my breathing became louder. My mind decided to run through every little interaction, dissecting my responses with stinging criticism.

You think you can survive writing in New York City when you can't even hold a conversation with your peers?

I squeezed my eyes shut, trying not to cry in the middle of the walk like the small person I felt like I'd become.

"Celeste!" He sounded a million miles away. Lincoln jogged to catch up to me.

He tried to reach for me, but I stepped back, too overstimulated to process touch. Hurt and confusion flashed across his face, but he stepped back, giving me space.

"What do you need? Water?"

"I'm fine." I waved away the question. "I think I just need to go back home."

His nod was slow, brows knitted with lingering confusion. "Sure...you weren't going to say goodbye though?"

"It was loud in there." Talking through residual panic made my voice breathy and strained. "I didn't think you'd hear me or..."

Honestly, I thought he was too drunk to even register my absence. And if I was lucky enough, maybe he'd forget my arrival, too.

But now, Lincoln looked steady and alert. Which meant maybe he was capable enough to maintain an awareness of time. Maybe he did remember we were supposed to talk, and he kept going on and on anyway.

I didn't know which would be more frustrating: him being too drunk to remember or him being sober enough to care. I didn't know if I was allowed to be frustrated. This night was supposed to be for him. And if he didn't need me, then that should be fine with me. I preferred being on my own anyway.

You don't prefer it. Not if the alternative is being with him. Even when you don't feel like enough, you want to be with him.

"You wanted to talk about something?" Lincoln asked.

He did remember. I waited for frustration to rise to the surface, but tasted sadness instead.

"Let's talk," he insisted, swaying a bit so he had to grip onto the fence to keep himself steady.

"You sure you can?"

He laughed, unable to detect the thick seriousness in the air between us. "I'm not that drunk."

I gestured to his hands on the fence. "You're not able to stand up straight on your own."

"I can." Lincoln let go, held his hands in the air, and made a show of spinning around. He stumbled, and I reached for him. He laughed with his arm around my shoulder. The memory of us at the beginning of summer, when I was too afraid to respond to his text message, flashed in my mind. Despite my frustration, I smiled. "You seem happy."

Lincoln raised a brow. "Happy?"

"Yeah, in there with everyone. I thought I'd seen you happy, but that was a whole other level."

Lincoln laughed. Or tried to laugh. It was the kind of amusement someone feigns when they're unsure whether they should be offended or not.

"What does that mean?" he asked.

"Nothing." I stepped back, out from underneath his arm. He didn't reach for me; instead, he shoved his hands into his back pockets. Lincoln tilted his head up for a second, staring at the sky like his last straw was floating amongst the stars.

The air between us was heavy with dissonance. It was him

at the hockey rink all over again, but instead of having to contend with blocking a puck, it felt like he was blocking me. I was at a loss, combing through our conversation like all the others I'd had that night. I hadn't had to do that for our interactions for over a month now.

"Is this what you wanted to talk about?" All amusement drained from his tone.

"No, not entirely." I folded my arms over my chest, and one hand massaged circles in my side. "Not at all, actually."

His eyes softened a bit when he noticed I was hugging myself. "Then what was it?"

"I wanted to ask about the...sets," I said. "My aunt said you hadn't dropped them off yet. I thought you'd done that last week."

He sighed. "I got it, Celeste. I told you, I got it."

"I know. It's just that the opening show is tomorrow. And I'm kind of worried. Do you know if it's completed? Will you have enough time to pick it up and put it all together?"

I didn't know all that went into putting the pieces back together because I'd completely given up the responsibility. Lincoln had assured me I could afford to with him in charge.

He took a deep breath and ran his hand over his head. "I'm sure it's ready."

"Sure?" My forehead wrinkled. "Wait, you haven't confirmed with the person you have working on it?"

"He's going to have it done."

"He's going to have it done," I repeated, more to myself and the knots in my stomach.

"Yeah, he is," Lincoln said. "Trust me. Try to relax. Don't let your anxiety win."

At any other time, I would have let those words wash over me. They were common enough to be ineffective. But right now, in this conversation, I didn't believe my anxiety was an issue. My nerves were burned through, replaced with annoyance.

I didn't appreciate the idea of my disorder being brought up when I responded in a perfectly normal way to something that would cause anyone concern. Cause anyone to question.

"Lincoln, those sets have been gone for almost a month," I said, voice hard and steady. "You said they'd be done in time for the show—a show where someone I really need to impress will be. I'm sorry, but I don't think this is an anxiety issue. I don't think most people would be relaxed."

He leaned his head back for a second. "Celeste, I swear I will get you those sets."

I couldn't believe the slight hint of annoyance in his tone. "Sorry, it's been such a bother. But...you do remember you volunteered, right?"

Lincoln laughed dryly. "A bother? What's going on right now?"

"I'm trying to hold you accountable for something you promised you would do." I blinked so fast, my body oscillating between the need to cry and scream. "I don't think... that's too much to ask."

All this time, we'd kept a couple of feet between us. The distance felt like it stretched with every word we said. And those words started to become bricks on a wall.

"I think I should go." I tugged on my sleeves, giving my trembling hands something to hold onto.

"*Now*?" He shook his head in disbelief. "Right now?"

I nodded. "I should have left earlier. Nothing either of us says is going to change anything. I'm exhausted, you're drunk. A back-and-forth is pointless. I can't do this."

Lincoln blinked as a shadow of confusion crossed over his face. He studied me, trying to figure something out, but couldn't because the alcohol hindered him from coming to an understanding.

"Can't do this as in the party?" Lincoln asked. "Or as in us?"

I hadn't even considered us. Not consciously. But a small

part of my brain had poked at the idea. We had considered our differences to be novel and never thought they could turn into roadblocks later.

"This is new and different," I said.

"Fun," he offered, almost hopeful.

I tried to smile. "Sure, sometimes."

"And other times?" His brows furrowed as he forced out the question I'm sure he didn't want to ask.

At other times, our relationship felt like a mirage. A fantasy of what could be if we had our lives figured out.

"Sometimes you party as if tomorrow doesn't matter. I…I thought you were going to be there. Like, really be there for me."

"Of course, I'm going to be there. This is just one bad conversation. One uncomfortable party. One long, uncomfortable night." Lincoln tried to laugh as he glanced behind us at the loud chaos of the house. "One delayed pick up."

"I'm not sure this will work all the time," I confessed and gestured behind him. "I'm not sure I want to be the person pulling you away when you could easily enjoy your night. The person waiting for you to remember a commitment. I'm not sure you want someone you have to keep an eye on. To constantly worry if I'm okay in a crowded room when that's the most natural thing for most people."

Surely he'd tire of running out of parties after me. I couldn't promise complete separation from anxiety. I couldn't stomach being the one gray cloud on his otherwise sunny days.

"I'm not worried. You're not pulling me away." His voice was firm, gaze unwavering. "You don't pull me anywhere, Celeste. I willingly followed you out here. I would follow you anywhere and everywhere, every single time. I can barely see straight, and I still followed you."

"I'm saying you don't have to follow me." If he continued, it could eventually ruin us. I could subsequently ruin us.

"I know I don't," he said. "I *want* to. That's the one commitment I won't ever break. I've proven that, no? When have I ever given you evidence otherwise?"

He hadn't directly. But in other aspects of his life, Lincoln clearly struggled to maintain his course. I'd been okay with that. I wanted to help him with that. But the decision to party when something so big and important to me loomed over us both gave me pause. I couldn't force him to change. I couldn't get him to take the right things seriously if he wasn't yet ready.

"Look, it's been a long day and an even longer night." I swallowed and brushed at my cheeks, swiping away unshed tears. "And...I really need some sleep. I need to be up tomorrow so I can figure out how to do a show without sets."

Lincoln pinched the bridge of his nose. "I told you, I'm going to handle it."

"No, I know." My anxiety was diluted with frustration. "But I've been quiet for days thinking you'd already done it. Those sets weren't mine to keep. My aunt has worked hard for everything at the playhouse, and she's trusted me enough to handle things. And I trusted you enough to do what you said you were going to do."

Lincoln looked at me, expression unreadable. For the first time since I'd known him, he was quiet. And remained so while I continued, "All I'm saying is maybe it's time to do what you say you want to do. Be responsible. Find some sort of balance. Stop treating everything like some game, especially when someone wants to trust you with something important and special to them."

There was nothing left for me to say. And for once, I didn't feel the need to endure the silence in hopes things will get better. In hopes I'd find a way to smooth everything over and make someone want to find merit and worth in my words. That was not, nor had ever been, my job.

I walked away. And Lincoln didn't follow.

CHAPTER TWENTY-EIGHT
LINCOLN

watched Celeste leave, too ashamed to call after her. But not so far up my own ass I didn't make sure she got inside her car. I wiped my hands over my face as she drove off, trying to ground myself enough to think clearly. The buzz I'd embraced only a few minutes ago was now an aggravating blocker.

It had all spiraled so quickly. At the beginning of the night, I'd convinced myself I had a handle on everything, that the drinking wasn't a reactionary response to all my disappointment, but a celebration of my choosing to be my own person.

The look of hurt in Celeste's eyes was a stab to the chest. The tension and pain lodged inside, burning as it melted.

My immediate instinct was to call one of the guys. Ask them to pick me up and help me sober up in time to drive across town and pick up the set pieces. But as soon as I unlocked my phone, I hesitated to pull up anyone's contact. It was past midnight, and they'd been firm on their stance of how I should have handled my failure this summer. I couldn't stomach another disappointment from people I knew wouldn't give up on me (no matter how much they should).

Frustration at every single decision I'd made to get to this point boiled to the surface. Why did I come here tonight?

I knew Celeste wanted to leave. I knew that hours ago. She'd been so patient.

Something in me needed to prove I could still live life if hockey weren't on the table. I needed a good enough distraction, so I didn't sit and ruminate on everything I'd ruined.

I hadn't left because the noise and drinking were the pause button I needed on life. And a small part of me, a part that seemed to feed off my budding insecurity, wanted to show Celeste who I really was. How careless I could be, just so she completely understood what she was getting into.

So she had a reason to leave you. So you didn't have time to screw it up any more than you already have because you're not worth it. You're a lost cause.

The thought began as a whisper, expanding with every second that ticked by. I was doing it again, self-sabotaging when things had started to get good. Ruining something that was working because of a belief that'd attached itself to me over a decade ago.

"Shit," I breathed out, trying to contend with my growing headache and the knowledge that this was a cycle I'd built and fed into. And when everyone in my life mentioned it to me, I ignored them. Convinced them, with hollow words, I could maintain control.

I didn't know how to fix myself, but that wasn't the top priority tonight. The sets were. Celeste was. She'd given me every ounce of her trust, and I'd tucked it into the back of my mind, forgetting it was the most valuable thing I possessed.

Without wasting another second, I pulled up navigation on my phone and typed in the nearest gas station. Thankfully, the campus was close, which meant the most essential places were within walking distance. I alternated between jogging and walking, acutely aware of the ticking clock. The opening show was today at three PM. That meant I had fifteen hours to pick up the set pieces in the next town over, drive back to Tinsel, figure out how to get the keys to the playhouse, transfer everything inside, and put it all together before the curtain rose. Exhausting but not impossible...for a sober person. For a drunk asshole? Time would tell.

The gas station cashier looked concerned when I stumbled inside.

"Can I help you?" he asked, voice gravelly.

He watched as I made my way to the back wall, set on grabbing every cold bottle of water I could carry.

"I'm in some deep trouble, Dave," I said. His name tag had been upside down on his shirt, nearly faded from what I assumed were years of wear and tear from his shifts.

"What kind of trouble, kid?" He glanced outside as if he'd find someone strapped up and waiting for me at one of the empty pumps.

"The kind that will determine the fate of my entire existence." I pointed at the steel tin of coffee. "How much?"

Dave scanned me, wary and unsure if I was a threat or a joke. My look of sheer exhaustion convinced him of the latter.

"Two fifty," he said.

"And how much if I use one of those?" I pointed to the jumbo-sized slushy cup.

"Six and a free call to the ER," he said. "Aren't you one of those Mendell kids? Hockey player, right?"

"Guilty." I dumped my water bottles at the counter and headed for the coffee.

"Yeah, I thought I'd seen you in here before."

"You're usually on the morning shift. Your kid is in high school, right? You said he wanted to run for Mendell. Cross country," I noted while trying to decide if I really wanted a 32-ounce cup of coffee. I needed enough fuel to stay up until I installed the sets.. Desperate times.

"That's right." He huffed, surprised I remembered. "He got a scholarship."

"Congrats." I swayed a little but managed to catch myself on the counter, resting my forehead against the cold surface. "Great school. The athletic department is in shambles, but by the time he's a junior, I'm sure they'll have it all figured out."

"Yeah, I heard about all that on the news. Last season was unfortunate. Sorry, you all's season was a bust."

"It happens."

Dave started checking out my supplies while I went for the coffee. "Hey, hey, hold on!"

I stopped mid-pump. "What?"

"I thought you were joking," he said. "You can't put coffee in that thing. You'll burn your hand off."

"Listen, Dave," I said. "I've spent most of my summer blowing up the rest of my runway. And the woman I fell for over a year ago finally liked me long enough to almost fall for me. Except I fucked it up by making big promises and waiting until the night of to fulfill them. So, unless you have another way to keep me alert and semi-sober—"

"Coffee ain't going to make you sober." He finished putting my waters in a bag, then came from behind the counter and grabbed a couple of cold sandwiches, which he tucked into the bag too. "Nothing but time can do that. Food and hydration help."

"I need the caffeine. In an IV drip, preferably. You wouldn't happen to have one of those?"

He scoffed. "Does this look like a hospital or a ritzy clinic to you? "

"Had to ask, you never know these days. I don't plan on sleeping for the foreseeable future, so I'm dedicated to offering my body to science. Maybe I could be your first drip patient? It can't be that hard. Hot water, coffee grounds, and a needle."

"I don't see how that's going to help you win a woman over."

"The big promises, Dave," I reminded him. "Big promises."

He raised a brow, unconvinced, but gestured to a thermos. "I'll let you fill that for the price of a small one if you promise you're not driving tonight."

"Never intended to." I hurried to fill the thermos. I gave him a twenty and waved him off when he tried to hand me change. "I appreciate you."

"Good luck," he said. "And try to get a bit of sleep. I'm sure she'll forgive you if you're a little late on that promise. We all fall short one time or another. Best not to beat yourself up about it."

I nodded, trying to smile. He didn't know what I'd done and who I was. How careless I'd been with someone else's dreams. How much I didn't deserve to rest until I made things right.

As I waited for the ride I ordered, I guzzled two bottles of water and half of the coffee. I'd requested an XL ride and got a guy in a SUV with chipped blue paint and magnetic signs promoting a car detailing company.

"You Lincoln?" he asked when I climbed into the back seat. It smelled like cigarettes and Clorox. "Are you going to New Dane?"

"That's the goal." I slammed the door behind me and ripped open my sandwich. My headache grew, piercing enough to make the small bit of light pouring in from the gas station sickening. I needed to focus. Needed to center myself enough to stay alert and ready for the next steps in my plan: making sure Uncle Aaron would open the shop for me. And convincing this driver to do this trip back while carting the sets.

"That's over an hour's drive away," he warned, voice hesitant as if he was half-hoping I'd put in the wrong location.

"It always is," I assured.

He sighed and pulled out of the gas station. "Alright then. Let's get this show on the road."

"Full transparency."

The words made him glance at me through the rearview, eyes squinted in suspicion. "I don't care what you rate me; I'm not above leaving assholes in curbs in the middle of nowhere."

I laughed despite feeling like something had chewed me up and spit me out. "I'm on a tight deadline. I'm locked in. Laser focused. And I need to know if you're with me. Willing to do whatever it takes to get a job done."

"My man, you're paying me over a hundred dollars." He chuckled, relaxing into his seat now that he realized I wasn't going to try to do something chaotic like grab the wheel. "I'm with you."

"There and back again?" I asked. "With cargo."

He frowned, guard going up once more. "What kind of cargo are we talking about?"

"The kind that will hopefully right one wrong, thus setting me on the course to righting every wrong." I stretched out on the backseat because holding my head up had become too strenuous. Were heads always this heavy? Or maybe the neck was the bigger culprit?

"I'm not interested in carting around any drugs," he said. "Unless you're willing to pay me under the table. I have a sliding scale. It's in the passenger's seat back pocket. Take a look."

"No worries, no worries," I said around a mouthful of ham and cheese. "No drugs. It's all fairy dust and wooden towers."

"Huh?"

"She's going to end things, I think." I sobered, resting the sandwich on my chest. "And then, I don't know what's after. I...I don't even like thinking about before because I now know how black and white it's all been."

"This is for some girl?"

"I need a drink," I mumbled.

"I think that's the last thing you need."

I grunted in agreement and finished off my sandwich. My

phone buzzed in my pocket. I ignored the first time and then the next four until it started making my headache worse.

SAM

You good? Do you need me to get you?

HENRIK

Everything okay? I thought you'd be back by now. I'm sorry about earlier. We were trying to help. I know these past few months have been hard for you. Don't shut us out, though. This is the time to make a change.

NAOMI

Worried about you! Text back when you can. Love you!

FINN

Hey.

I responded to the 'hey' because, of course, I did.

hi

FINN

How are you, Lincoln?

on top of the world. you?

FINN

Good, thank you for asking. Where are you?

why are you texting like that??

FINN

Like what?

Like some 65-year-old who's just gotten their first flip phone

FINN

Feels the most natural to me, I suppose.

you're something else.

FINN

Thanks. Where are you?

My driver made a sharp turn, abrupt enough to make my drinks topple over. The coffee spilled a bit from the half-opened lid.

FINN

I went back to the party looking for you.
Everyone said you disappeared.

Off to New Dane. gotta get those sets and bring them back before the first show tonight

FINN

It's 1 AM.

Celeste needed them weeks ago. I kept dragging my feet. It's brunch time.

*crunch

FINN

I could have taken you. I could still leave now and meet you. Bring you back.

no, don't. I didn't ask because I knew you guys would offer and do all this last-minute running around

FINN

What's wrong with that?

I need to fix this myself. It's my own mess.

FINN

We'll never mind helping you clean things up.

Despite my headache and the looming possibility of losing the woman of my dreams, I smiled. I found brief comfort in the fact that when I went home, people who cared waited for me.

I really appreciate that. But I have to get this done myself. I can't keep phoning a friend.

There was a pause in our conversation. My driver turned on some smooth jazz, making a bumpy ride a little more peaceful. My stomach was turning, so I sat back up, rolled down the window, and finished another bottle of water.

FINN

I understand. It's very respectable. I'll tell everyone to leave you alone. If you change your mind, let me know.

I let out a breath of relief and responded,

Thanks. Wish me luck; I'm not sure this is going to work.

FINN

You don't need luck. You just need to stop getting in your own way.

———

"Keep it running," I said as I hopped out of the SUV and onto the wet sidewalk. It had started raining on the ride up.

"That's not how it works," my driver, Lucas, said. "You gotta put in another request on the app."

"Right, right." I hurried to do that before jogging up the walk to Aaron's front door. I called him twice before resorting to the dreaded doorbell. His voice came through on the door camera.

"What?" he asked with a valid level of grumpiness in his tone.

"Sorry to do this to you so late," I said.

"Then why are you doing it?"

"I need the set pieces."

"The ones I asked you to pick up last week?"

"I'll owe you big time." I stepped back from the door ring camera to make sure he could see the promise in my eyes. "And this'll never happen again."

He was quiet for a second. Just when I started considering whether I should have asked for forgiveness instead of permission, he told me, "There's a spare key to my workshop taped on top of the door frame. You can start loading up. Give me a minute to get dressed, and I'll come and help."

"Thank you, thank you," I said. "And don't worry about it. You've done more than enough."

"Trust me, you're going to need help... There are some things I need to explain to you. It gets a little complicated."

I frowned. "Complicated?"

"I'll explain."

His ominous warning left little room for confidence. But I refused to panic too much before seeing what he meant.

I shot Lucas a thumbs-up before heading to the back of the house to Aaron's workshop. I got a splinter when grabbing the key. The pain of it barely registered as I unlocked the door and remembered how large the set pieces were. They were all scattered, unpainted wooden blocks that resemble children's toys.

"What happened to the..." I folded my fingers together as Aaron came in. "Easy assembly."

"That's what I have to explain," he said, still adjusting a half-on sweatshirt. "For easier transport, I took the pieces apart. It's how the original designer made them, so it wasn't difficult. Fortifying was the difficult part. As I was adding in all your notes."

"You added them all in?" I asked in awe.

"It was a nice departure from everyday work." He tugged at a sheet covering the main parts of the balcony. "You're going to have your work cut out for you when it comes to reassembling. Your friends here, too?"

"It's just me." I held my splintered hand to my chest while running my finger over the floral-engraved detailing on some railing. "This is incredible."

"Just you?" he asked at the same time.

I ignored the concern in his tone, too over-extended to manage any panic outside of the ticking clock in my head. "Tell me what I have to do."

"This is a four-person job at best."

"Well, I'm a one-person operation today, so lay it on me and I'll figure out the rest."

He stared at me for a second but eventually shrugged and went into detail on how I'd have to reassemble everything. It was mainly about clicking things into place and tightening them. Lots of pieces and lots of screws that were vital to the entire operation.

"Whatever you do, don't rush through it," he warned. "One mistake and this whole thing could come toppling down."

I nodded. "I got it."

There was no room for any mistakes. I couldn't afford them, and I would do everything in my power to ensure the results were perfect. I would do everything to show Celeste that letting her down wasn't a habit I planned to form.

CHAPTER TWENTY-NINE
LINCOLN

t took us an hour to load everything back into the rideshare. Lucas helped after I ended the current ride with a substantial tip and promised to do the same once he took me back into town.

"You sure you got this?" Aaron asked before I could hop back into the SUV and hurry back to Tinsel.

"Not at all." I flashed him a smile and cracked open my last water bottle. The buzz of alcohol had worn off, replaced by a headache akin to what I'd imagine the sensation of someone drilling directly into my skull would feel like. But I was still standing and still committed.

"I'm going to give it one hell of a shot," I said. Celeste was my main driving force, but there was also a small hope I could prove myself wrong. That I wasn't a lost cause.

The ride back to Tinsel took longer because the rain picked up once again. This time, it became a full-on storm, and Lucas became a timid driver.

"Is it too much to ask you to pick up the pace to a steady, I don't know, twenty-five miles per hour?" I sat in the front this time, obsessively watching the clock. It was almost 3 AM. We had to stop at Celeste's aunt's because I had no way of getting into the playhouse without a key. I'd texted Ellis, who was thankfully up. He was a night owl who liked me enough to push off his sleep a bit longer and pass off a set of keys.

"You alright for one more stop?" I asked, wary when Lucas swerved around a pothole that couldn't have been larger than a mixing bowl.

"Yeah." His knuckles were white from his iron grip on the wheel, gaze never straying from the torrential downpour.

I wanted to offer to drive, but I still wasn't entirely sober, and there was no chance in hell he'd let me bend the rideshare rules.

By the time we reached Celeste's aunt's house, I'd concluded I was not taking the quick nap I thought might be on the horizon once everything was unloaded. And I was okay with that because every time I thought about how Celeste looked when I confessed I hadn't done what I promised, I felt like throwing up.

"Celeste's going to be so nervous about this." Ellis answered the door, dressed in all-black and tugging on a pair of sneakers.

"I just need the keys," I said.

"I'm coming with you. This musical means a lot to me, too. Plus, I really like you for Celeste. You challenge her without being overbearing. She needs that. And you're very close to fucking it up. I'll feel guilty till the end of time if I don't do something to help."

I sighed. Even though I was still adamant about fixing this on my own, every minute that went by felt like a crushing weight. I had to be smart about this if I really wanted to finish in time. If I didn't complete this task, it wouldn't matter whether I did it alone or not. Celeste's trust in me would plummet. And who knew how long it'd take to get it back. Or if I'd ever get it back.

"I'm going to see this through," I promised. "And not just

today. Because losing Celeste isn't something I'll ever be able to live with."

Ellis smiled and clapped my shoulder. "Let's make sure it doesn't happen."

The rain finally stopped once we got to the playhouse. It was still dark outside while we unloaded everything. At night, the playhouse felt eerie and smelled stale. The moment we placed the last display on the stage, I slipped into autopilot. Lucas wished us good luck, leaving Ellis and me exhausted on our own.

"Let's catch our breath for a second." Ellis practically crawled to a chair in the audience, resting his head back onto the cushion and closing his eyes.

"You rest a bit," I offered. He'd started huffing and puffing on our third trip to the car. By the fifth, I knew he wouldn't have enough energy for the mountain we had to climb.

"How are you not knocked out?" Ellis asked with his eyes closed.

"I've got a pretty consistent third wind."

"Huh?"

"If I'm focused on something, I don't just have a second wind, but a third." I clicked a few pieces into place, just as Aaron had shown me.

"Lucky."

"Very. It's twenty percent genetics," I said. "Eighty percent Celeste. I keep imagining a scenario where I did everything right. And it's constant fuel. Like trying to push myself onto a different timeline. A preferred timeline. A place where I'm not so dead set on ruining everything before it's begun."

"I love ruining things. Self-sabotage is my favorite hobby. My therapist says it's a coping skill from being expected to deliver a perfect routine before my brain developed. What about you?" Ellis asked around with a yawn.

"I don't have a therapist," I said. "Yet."

That would be going on my list of high priorities. No more

managing my emotions with only mystery novels...even though it didn't seem like the worst way to cope.

"No, why self-sabotage? You figure it out yet?"

I opened the box of screws and sat down on the cold, dusty stage as I sorted them. "My parents told me I wasn't worth it. From what I can remember, it was a joke. But it stuck."

"Damn, sorry," Ellis said, voice quiet with sympathy. "It's the little stuff sometimes. Things people don't mean anything by."

"Tell me about it." I nodded, thinking about what had happened and how I hadn't even remembered what my parents had said until talking to Celeste. She'd broken that spell. When she asked for my help, she'd expected more from me. She'd trusted me to deliver. She believed.

A stab of pain shot through my chest, and I picked up the pace. Ellis' soft snore and the scraping of wood against the floor were the only things left to keep me company. I stuffed all the doubts into the depths of my mind, replacing them with the reminder Celeste had believed. Hopefully, that meant somewhere deep down, I could pull this off.

My hands were dry from paint, my arms ached from rearranging, and my legs were ready to give out from dragging myself past my threshold. I hopped off the stage to get a better look at how the lights shone down on set. The sun came up a couple of hours ago. Warm light stretched in from underneath the entrance door, trying to wake the dark theatre.

"Well?" I asked Ellis, who had also gotten off the stage, to join my side as we took in our work. He'd slept for only an hour before getting up and getting to work. Since Ellis wasn't motivated to make the woman he was in love with happy, he moved at a slower pace than I did. Despite that, I appreciated the company.

"Does it look okay?" I examined our handiwork. Despite this being a rush job, I'd done everything possible to make sure the details were correct. The paint job had been meticulous, resulting in clean lines and no smudges. I'd rigged up the backdrop so the crew backstage could easily change it with a tug of the rope. It took a good half hour to retrieve decor from storage and figure out how to arrange the flowers, bushes, and wicker baskets in a non-distracting way.

"Do you think she'll like it?" I asked, reconsidering my arrangement, wondering if the banister needed a fourth coat of paint. I debated whether I'd given enough attention to the balcony positioning because if it were a little more to the left, the lights above would hit the actors more easily.

"She's going to love it." Ellis nudged my arm when he noticed my brow was tense. "You did an incredible job. It looks way better than I thought it'd be."

"Really? No notes? Don't hold back. I need this to be perfect for her." I crossed my arms over my chest, trying to quiet my critical thoughts. I'd reached the point of fatigue where opening my eyes from blinking felt like pulling a boulder from the bottom of the ocean.

"Lincoln, it's perfect," he assured. "You've been up for over twelve hours. Even if there was something to fix, I don't think your brain would be capable of doing it well. You need to get back home and get some rest."

"What about the bench on that side?" I pointed. "Don't you think it'll look better in the middle?"

"Lincoln," he said, serious. "Have you been diagnosed with ADHD?"

I blinked (it took my last bit of willpower not to knock out while standing). "What?"

"You've never mentioned it, so I thought maybe you

hadn't. And then, I wondered if maybe you didn't even recognize your symptoms."

"I'm…no, I haven't gotten tested." It'd been something my teachers considered when I was in elementary school. But somewhere along the way, my grandma brushed off testing and instead decided TV and the internet were the problem. And books were the solution. I stayed still long enough when I got caught up in the *Hardy Boys* series, thus satisfying the adults around me.

"You should consider it," Ellis said. "Meds help me a ton."

"I'll add it to my growing list of concerns," I promised, tucking the information in the back of my mind to revisit when I wasn't challenging the earth to a race around the sun.

"Good. But for now—" Ellis grabbed my shoulder and gave it a tight squeeze. "—*sleep*. You need it. We could nitpick right into next week; it doesn't matter at this point."

"This just…it all has to be perfect for her," I said. "If I ruined this—"

"Celeste is the most forgiving person I know."

"I know, and that's exactly why I don't want to even ask that of her." One night of hard work wasn't going to change me fundamentally. I had to do better consistently, and I would keep doing so. In the meantime, I wasn't expecting forgiveness. But a small, selfish part of me hoped she'd be willing to give me a chance. That she'd be willing to wait for me while I removed my roadblocks and untangled my hang-ups.

"You won't have to ask," Ellis said.

I smiled. "Thanks for being here."

"It's my mom's set and my cousin's dream," he said. "I'm biologically obligated to be here."

I chuckled. "That doesn't make any sense."

"Sorry, I'm not as alert as you after this long," he said. "You must be incredible during finals week."

"It's typically my best week," I confirmed.

"Let's go home." Ellis's shoulders relaxed, relieved he was finally able to step away.

I shook my head, mind still racing and stomach twisting at the thought of forgetting something. There would be no stone unturned, especially this close to the finish line. The joy of finishing the set was temporary, overshadowed by one final task. "Not yet."

"Lincoln." He groaned. "The bench is fine where it is. Everything's fine where it is."

I laughed. "No, I know. I just have to pick up some flowers. That's tradition, right? Opening night flowers?"

"Celeste will understand if you forgo tradition."

"I want her to have it all. She's going to have it all."

"Fine." He sighed and pinched the bridge of his nose. "And then, sleep?"

"Then sleep," I agreed.

CHAPTER THIRTY
CELESTE

There'd been nothing I could do to fix what happened, so I'd gone to bed as soon as I got home from the party. I spent most of my time lying awake, replaying the whole night from beginning to end. Once my brain grew tired of that, I replayed the small moments, every tiny detail, until my stomach churned. I couldn't change anything, but that never stopped me from wondering if I could think my way into a better outcome. Force the past to rewrite itself, so I didn't walk away from Lincoln. So we didn't leave all these dangling threads between us that felt far more painful than him forgetting to do what he said he would.

In the morning, I avoided my phone, embarrassed at how I reacted. During the little sleep I did manage to get, I dreamt of a far kinder way to have responded. Even though I had every right to feel emotional and frustrated, I jumped from point A to Z. A jump from disappointment to break-up consideration wasn't fair. Lincoln had made a mistake. That wasn't unforgivable. I didn't want him to feel like he had to reach perfection or risk our relationship ending.

When I finally checked my phone in the afternoon, my

heart sank straight into my stomach. No messages from him. No messages from anyone.

It could mean nothing. A coincidence. And yet, I wondered if he was angry with me. Maybe everyone was furious with me because maybe Lincoln had told them about how I walked away, how I didn't let him defend himself. And perhaps they thought I was horrible for it. Maybe I was horrible.

No.

Breathe. You're safe. You haven't done a thing to warrant such a reaction.

I repeated the mantra until the weight on my chest began to loosen. There was nothing from last night that would make my friends (and yes, I could claim them all as my friends) think I was horrible. They wouldn't write me off. And even if Lincoln was upset with me, he didn't hate me. I hadn't earned something as strong and cold as hate.

I got ready for the playhouse, self-soothing with constant repeating of my mantra and my makeup routine. My theme was pink, the soft color that brought me comfort. The pink silk dress I wore clung to my skin and paired well with an oversized white cardigan.

On the car ride over, I stopped wondering why no one had contacted me and decided to make the first move. Naomi answered on the first ring.

"I was just about to call you." She was out of breath. A door creaking open and closing blocked out what she said next.

Despite my success in calming myself down, I found my lingering bits of anxiety melt out of me when she spoke.

"Are you on your way?" I asked, unable to mask the hope in my voice.

"I am," she said. "Just about to hop into the car. Is Lincoln with you?"

I frowned. "No. Why? Is he not at the house?"

"No one heard him come home last night."

I forgot the nerves and embarrassment, exchanging them for worry. "Has anyone heard from him at all?"

"Yeah, he talked to Finn," she quickly assured. "And Finn told us not to worry."

My shoulders sagged as I drove into the playhouse parking lot. "Good. I…I left him at the party last night, and he was pretty drunk. I was upset. It was a whole thing."

"I know," she said. "Finn told us that too…. I think Lincoln spent the night at the playhouse."

"What?" I got out of the car, looking up at the marquee. *An Original by Celeste Able* had been put up. I smiled up at it. This was happening.

"He told us he wanted to get all the set pieces last night," Naomi explained. "He wouldn't accept anyone's help. If he managed to get inside the playhouse, he's probably still there."

The comment made me walk faster. My aunt was already at the front desk, settled into her seat, and sorting through printouts for this month's events.

As soon as she saw me, she waved me over with a look of concern darkening her eyes.

"I have to go," I told Naomi.

"Let me know if you find him," she said quickly. "And good luck! It's going to be amazing. I love you!"

"Thank you," I said. "Love you too."

"We're all ready." My aunt shoved a stack of flyers into my hands.

"What?" I frowned, looking down at the print colors I'd okayed at the beginning of summer. That felt like eons ago, back when this whole musical thing was something I thought would die before it got started.

"Put those at the table by the front door," she instructed. "That's the last thing on my list. We're all set for tonight and even sold a few tickets online. Ellis set it up for me. He was right, I need to get online more for marketing."

"Everything's ready?" I was scared to ask, but needed to know. "Even the sets?"

"Yeah, they got dropped off and assembled last night." My aunt frowned. "Lincoln didn't tell you?"

I shook my head.

"He came by last night," she said. "He picked up Ellis, and they finished everything together."

"Lincoln was really here last night?" I asked.

"More like this morning," she said. "It must have been 3AM when Ellis and him headed out."

"Is he here now?" I asked, looking around the lobby as if I had missed the one person I wanted so desperately to see, to be held by, to be on the same page with once again.

My aunt nodded. "Found him sleeping backstage."

I started to go to the theatre, but she stopped me, saying, "But he's not there anymore."

My hand froze on the door handle. "Do you know where he is?"

"Left about ten minutes before you got here," she said.

I sighed. "Did he say where he was going?"

"Said something about flowers."

He'd spent all night driving around Tinsel for the sets. All morning putting everything together. And now, his afternoon consisted of flower shopping for me? It was utterly ridiculous. His priorities were once more out of order.

I pulled out my phone, ignoring the anxiety that would come with talking to him. The call went straight to voicemail. When I tried again and got the same result, my aunt reminded me, "You'll see him in a couple of hours. The curtain opens at three. He promised he'd be here. And guess what?"

"What?" My stomach dipped, expecting a last-minute crisis.

"Ophelia confirmed." Aunt Robyn squealed along with me. "I got her a seat right up front. Very VIP."

"Thank you." I burned with hope Ophelia would see even the smallest amount of potential in my work.

"I'm so proud of you, sweet girl." Aunt Robyn came closer for a second to hug me. "You've done so well, I hope you know that."

I nodded, my stomach all mixed up with butterflies that sourced their flutters from excitement rather than dread, a feeling that had been absent this morning.

People were actually coming to see my work. After everything my mentor said, I was still going to share my work with my hero… And Lincoln Hill was somewhere, severely sleep-deprived, looking for flowers.

"He didn't say what store he was going to?" I tried to put a little pressure on my aunt. The sooner I saw Lincoln, the better. I needed him to know I was okay. That we were okay.

"Girl, why would I ask that?" My aunt pinched my cheek before going back to the front desk to answer the ringing phone.

My cheeks burned, but I smiled anyway because maybe this would all work out. Maybe I hadn't ruined what Lincoln and I had.

I got busy helping my aunt with any last-minute things she had to do to prepare for the matinee. Once cars started filling the parking lot and my performers came through the door, my attention swung backstage.

"Hey," I greeted Halle, who sat in the dressing room, working on her makeup. "How are you?"

She smiled at me while keeping her hand steady to create a perfect black line across her eyelid. Halle made the other one match with little to no effort. "I'm perfect. Ready."

"Do you need anything?" I asked. "Water? A warm towel? Something to eat?"

She shook her head and exchanged eyeliner for blush. "I'm all set. Do *you* need anything?"

"No, I'm good."

She gave me a sympathetic smile. "Your hands are shaking."

I tucked my hands behind my back and moved close enough so I could lean against the wall behind her mirror. "They tend to do that."

"Big night for you," she said, understanding.

"For you, too."

"Yeah, but I'm used to performing."

"You don't get nervous anymore?"

She laughed. "Oh, I feel like I'm going to faint. I always feel like I'm going to faint."

My eyes widened. "You don't look it."

She didn't have a hair out of place or a wrinkle in her outfit. Her voice was as steady and soothing as ever. "It's because my belief that I'm going to crush it is stronger than the need to rid my stomach of breakfast."

"Wow, any tips?" I asked.

"She'll keep the best ones to herself," Jack warned from where he stood in the doorway with his gym bag slung over his shoulder.

"You're late," Halle noted, losing her smile.

"And whose fault is that?" he asked.

She bit the inside of her cheek, something unspoken settled between them. I knew in an instant I was intruding, so I pushed off the wall to make my exit.

"Lincoln said he'll be a little late," Jack told me. We switched places. I lingered in the doorway while he went next to Halle.

"You saw him today?" I asked, my heart jumped in my chest.

"Yeah, I came in early this morning," Jack said. "He'd forgotten to seal his paint job, so he called me to finish it. "

Halle and I exchanged looks of surprise.

"What?" he asked.

"You two aren't exactly buddy-buddy," Halle said. "I'm not sure what's more surprising: him calling you or you showing up. "

"You don't know the ins and outs of all my relationships," he countered.

"How was he?" I interrupted before they got too deep into bickering. "How is he?"

"Running on fumes. And guilt." It looked like hard work for Jack to pull his gaze away from Halle, but he eventually managed.

"Don't worry about him, though," he said. "He's fine. And he really wants to see you."

I nodded numbly. Grateful for the assurance.

"I'll let you two get ready." I did my best to smile. "Break a leg."

There were still things to do before we opened the doors for seating. I'd have to wait a little longer to talk to Lincoln. I looked at my phone every few minutes and watched the door of the theatre so much my neck started to ache.

Once they set the stage and patrons filtered in, I decided to stop looking and waiting and focus on being present. My music was going to be played in front of an audience. Our musicians were already in the pit warming up. The conductor was at their stand with the sheet music. I pressed my shaking fingers to my chest, closing my eyes for a second as I took deep breaths. This was the finish line, and amidst all the anxiety, there was a comforting promise of an ending. Regardless of how this turned out, I'd survived to the end. And a smile played on my lips at the thought.

I stayed backstage as the lights dimmed, watching the front rows of the theatre fill. The opener was a solo for our flute player. As soon as that first note pierced the air, I closed my eyes to soak in the feeling.

The audience wasn't large. We weren't anywhere close to being sold out. But people were here. They were here for the music. To see what I had to say. And as soon as Halle's voice filtered through the mic, I remembered I had so much to say. The one musical couldn't cover it all, but it was a start.

When I opened my eyes and tried to peek at the audience without attracting attention, my gaze immediately found Lincoln. He'd slipped in the back quietly, his arm full of pink and yellow tulips. I covered my mouth to suppress a laugh when he took a photo with a disposable camera, and realized it had a bright, distracting flash. He instantly shoved it into his pocket and slouched into his seat, embarrassed.

Halle got through the opening seamlessly. While everyone watched her, I watched Lincoln, my heart racing a mile a minute when I realized how he was the first person I wanted to call when I got good news. The only person I wanted to curl up with after a long day and share all the truths I'd been too anxious to admit.

Lincoln must have sensed someone watching because his gaze strayed from the stage to where I stood. As soon as our eyes locked, the world went silent. His smile was bright, and his eyes came to life when he saw me. Whatever sleepiness lingered in his body from last night faded for a moment.

"*I'm so sorry,*" he mouthed.

I shook my head and mouthed back, "*It's okay.*"

I pulled out my phone and gestured to it before texting. He shook his head and held up his phone. The screen remained black.

"*After?*" he mouthed and held up the flowers.

I smiled and nodded before pulling back from the curtain. I pressed my hand on my chest, breathing to slow down my heart rate. Whatever lay ahead, I would be okay.

———

The crowd wasn't large, but the noise from their standing ovation made the place feel packed. My lungs were sore from how long I'd been storing emotion in them. Obtaining a dream was unlike anything I could have imagined. It tasted bittersweet. Gratifying.

As the clapping went on, Halle turned to look off stage, where I stood, and gestured for me to join her. My stomach did backflips, and I shook my head. Ellis caught on to what Halle wanted and moved from his spot next to her to come to me.

"It's your show," Ellis said, voice muffled thanks to the applause. Our musicians were getting their acknowledgements now.

I shook my head, knees nearly giving out at the thought of moving. "It's your show too."

"It's *yours*," he insisted. "None of us would be here without you."

He offered me his hand. When I hesitated, he added, "Just see what it's like this one time. If you hate it, you'll never have to do it again. It's better to hate something and know for sure than to live a life wondering. Better to feel it all firsthand than listen to someone else tell the story."

I glanced at the audience again, gaze falling on where all our friends stood. I could focus on them and only them, and maybe that would keep most of the stage fright at bay.

"Okay." I breathed out and accepted Ellis' hand.

He led me out to the stage next to Halle, who also took my hand. I stood between the two of them and followed their lead into a final group bow. My skin was on fire. I could barely see the audience because of the lights beaming down on us. But the cheers and extra whistles when I came onto the center stage were enough to trigger overwhelm. Halle and Ellis stepped back for a moment to give me a few seconds of solo spotlight. I didn't die like I theorized I might. But I also didn't know what to do with my hands, face, and all this joy coursing through my veins.

The prolonged attention was blinding. I never wanted to stand on a stage again, but Ellis was right; it was better to know. Better to feel it firsthand.

I found my friends right after. I shook so much I could barely hold onto Naomi.

"It was perfect," she repeated in my ear while she hugged me, knowing my mind was running a mile a minute with doubts.

"Thank you." I could barely focus on anything or anyone. Being on stage had been overstimulating. And now, I was surrounded by people congratulating me. I was grateful for the love. But my body felt like it crossed the finish line of a marathon. Everything around me was blurry, and I wanted to collapse into a thousand years of sleep.

"Celeste," the voice I wanted to hear since the moment I woke up, greeted me. Lincoln opened his mouth to say something else, but was cut short when I immediately wrapped my arms around his neck for a hug. He returned the hug in an instant, picking me up off the ground so I wouldn't have to stand on my toes. Everything faded until it was just the two of us.

"I'm so sorry for last night," he said once he set me down. "For being so late. For being such an asshole. For letting you down."

"It's okay," I promised, squeezing his biceps in the hope he could feel my honesty. "I'm sorry for walking away."

He shook his head, voice firm as he said, "Don't apologize. You did nothing wrong. You should have walked away earlier. I should have known it was too late, and I was too drunk, and I was ruining it."

"You haven't ruined anything."

Everyone still moved around us, talking excitedly among

themselves to give us as much privacy as possible in a public space.

"How did you get the pieces here? You didn't drive...did you?" I asked.

"No, I ordered a ride share," he quickly confirmed. "Got really friendly with my driver. He invited me to a barbecue."

I laughed. "Of course he did. And you assembled every-thing? In one night."

"Ellis helped some. When he wasn't sleeping. So did Jack, later."

"My aunt said you stayed here all night."

He looked down at his feet, sheepish. "I screwed up so badly, I was trying to make sure everything was right on time. I didn't want to waste a second."

I brushed my thumb across his cheek. He leaned into the touch, planting light kisses on my palm.

"I won't ever do something like this again," he whispered. "I won't ever ruin something this important to you. That party was a mistake."

"And it's okay to make mistakes," I said. "I should have been more concerned about why you wanted to be there for so long. Lincoln, I didn't mean what I said about us not fitting."

I couldn't think past how happy he seemed and how horrible I'd been at talking to people. The insecurity made everything black and white.

"I was miserable, not happy," he confessed. "And being surrounded by people was the only thing that used to help when I got this way. I had forgotten I had other ways to cope. That I could choose better ways of coping."

"You can make a mistake," I repeated because he needed to know he deserved grace. "Sometimes I might need a break. I might need to walk again, but I won't leave you forever, Lincoln."

He nodded, closed his eyes, and pressed his forehead

against mine. "I was so afraid you would. All night and morning. I was in the parking lot for half an hour before this started, terrified I was walking into the end."

"You should have picked up your phone," I said. "I called you like five times."

He sighed and laughed. "It's dead. I lost my charger while gallivanting all over town for your flowers."

I smiled. "Gallivanting?"

He gave a signal behind his back, and Henrik placed the flowers in his hand. They fumbled the hand-off, and I laughed. He offered me a bouquet that was almost too big for me to hold. I cradled it to my chest, completely in love.

"Gallivanting seemed like the only word that fit," he said. "I'd gallivant all over the world for you. The universe, too. Whatever space station'll have me."

"You're so silly."

"I know. But you love it," he teased.

I nodded. "I do."

"You love me." There was a hint of uncertainty in the way he grabbed my hand and brought it to his cheek. Lincoln kissed the middle of my palm before holding it in place.

I smiled and, without hesitation, said, "I do."

CHAPTER THIRTY-ONE
LINCOLN

efore I got too far from my reality check, I forced myself to keep pushing (after a decent night's sleep that turned into ten hours of rest, resulting in a concerned Henrik checking in to see if I was still breathing).

"You never make a sound when you sleep," he said when I finally woke up and dragged my way to the kitchen. "I had to get a mirror to check if you were breathing."

"Such a worrier," I teased before grabbing an orange and starting back upstairs.

"Are you busy?" he asked, because our early mornings usually consisted of hanging out in the kitchen or near the pool, posing scenarios to one another, and being infinitely curious about how the other would react.

If the zombie apocalypse happened, but you were in space, would you try to come back down or live out your days exploring space? What if we found a door at the bottom of the ocean with the words "don't open"? What if, all this time, a higher being has been trying to combine different DNA to remake one person they lost? Once they found them, would this human experience cease to exist?

"Got to get organized before practice," I explained. "Lots of catching up to do. We'll scenario later, I got plenty of good ones for you."

He didn't say anything, but from the delayed nod, I figured he was impressed their feedback hadn't rolled off my back. Or that my photo finish with the sets hadn't lulled me into a false sense of security.

With the playhouse set priority crossed off my list, it was vital I began this whole betterment journey, or else live with the cyclical nature of my avoidance. I wasn't sure how to change everything about how my mind reacted to struggle, so I started with familiarity. I started with red strings and far too many notes.

Developing a decent plan took hours. I sat on the ground in my room, putting everything I hoped to achieve in life on blue lines of paper. I avoided fear the best I could because after a few hours of writing, I realized somewhere along the line, wanting things had become embarrassing. Almost shameful. Because what lost cause dared to want?

My handwriting was abysmal, and the effort, herculean. The entire morning and afternoon passed, resulting in a three-year plan that didn't make me want to throw up. The work would be brutal, and sinking that much time into myself would be risky. But if I'd learned anything from being with Celeste, it was that even with all the uncertainty and doubt, trying was better than standing still. Seeing the plan laid out before felt like stepping on solid ground after being at sea for years.

HENRIK

It's almost time. You coming down soon?

I frowned and responded,

What?

HENRIK

Did you forget about presentation night?

I checked the clock and laughed to myself. Since the abrupt end of last season, I had been the only one to remember the tradition I started. So, I was shocked to find everyone in the living room with the TV already on and Finn fiddling with the HDMI cord that's plugged into Naomi's laptop. It was her night and mine to present a PowerPoint of our choice.

"Hey," I said when I saw Celeste on the couch. Any lingering stress filtered out of me, replaced with the solace of her presence.

She sat underneath a blanket, her fingers tangled in a black string Aderyn adjusted. "I didn't know you were here. Why didn't you come up?"

"It's because we intercepted and wanted her to hang out with us. You're going to have to get used to shared custody," Naomi teased from her spot in front of the TV.

Celeste smiled at me and leaned her head back on the couch, so I'd have an easy time planting an upside-down kiss on her forehead.

"I came over to surprise you," she said. "I didn't know you guys had plans tonight."

"So, they lured you in?" I placed my hands on either side of her shoulders, watching Aderyn show Celeste how to make a ladder.

"You're a natural," Aderyn encouraged, her string art a bit tighter and cleaner.

"Thanks." Celeste smiled shyly, unable to make eye contact but able to take a compliment. Progress. Slow and steady progress. I admired this woman for it. Loved her for it.

"Want to try a shooting star next?" Aderyn asked.

Celeste nodded, bottom lip tucked between her teeth as she listened to Aderyn's instructions. I placed one more kiss on top of her head before venturing into the kitchen, where Sam and Henrik were.

"They're getting along," I said to Sam as our girlfriends laughed at their tangled fingers and impossible shapes.

"Aderyn's already kicked me off another trip to the mountain," Sam said, pretending to be bothered. "The house is too crowded, and she wants to prioritize the girls, she said."

"Boohoo," I joked. "You're stuck with your house in the mountains with your friends."

"Talk about torture," he grumbled.

A crash from the oven drew our attention to Henrik. He cursed under his breath as he picked up the dropped rolls.

"You good?" I asked, going over to help clean up the mess.

"Great," Henrik said half-heartedly. He didn't even meet my gaze as he tossed the rolls in a bag and moved to take the non-floor snacks into the living room.

"Great?" I asked Sam in a low voice as I watched our friend automatically give everyone food.

"Eden's upstairs," Sam whispered, giving me a look.

"I see."

Sam chuckled into his cup and took a few sips before asking, "Do me a favor?"

"Sure, I'm in your debt, aren't I?"

He smiled, remembering. "Don't let those two get too cerebral while I'm gone."

"Huh?" I frowned, confused.

"Henrik and Eden," he said. "You know how they get; all lost in the weeds. On the hunt for deeper meaning and poetic purpose."

"It's kind of endearing," I said, recalling high school and Henrik and Eden's letters.

"It's kind of concerning," Sam said. "Do your own thing. But whenever you can...I don't know, get them out of their heads. They're bound to put Finn there, too. And all that will be left is you and Naomi trying to nudge them outside to touch grass and experience life as it is and not imagined."

"Unromanticize the romantics." I nodded. "Got you…question though."

"Uh oh."

"What happens if I, too, fall into romanticism? Theoretically?"

Sam frowned. "Resist, Lincoln. You must resist."

My gaze strayed to Celeste. I didn't mean it to, it just happened. And so did the confession that fell from my lips. "It's just, I think I get them more now. The letters and emails. All the writing is because there's so much to say and not enough time to say it. And putting it all down somehow immortalizes it. They have years of shared ideas forever preserved and accessible. Who wouldn't want that? I want that with Celeste. I want everything with her."

Sam stared at me blankly. I raised a brow, waiting for the disapproving response. Instead, I got a half-hearted sigh and an amused smile.

"I think I'm just too…physical for all this," he decided. "I don't get you guys and your need to talk about your feelings constantly."

"I was next door to you for a year," I said. "I know all about your physicality and talk second mentality."

He laughed. "Shut up."

"How are you two?" I asked, nudging my chin toward Aderyn. "How's the adjustment to moving been?"

Sam looked at his girlfriend, who was still trying to teach Celeste (and now, Henrik and Naomi) how to make Jacob's Ladder. "It's different from what I imagined. Leagues better and brighter. Hard. Very hard but…good. I get to be Sam with her. Every side of me fits with her."

"See, you're not too bad at this talking about feelings thing," I teased.

He shook his head, and I added, "I promise I'll get them out of their heads. It is my sworn duty, being the only trusted form of entertainment and all."

"I appreciate it." He held his cup up toward me in salute. "It's nice to know they're in good hands."

Right on cue, Eden appeared in the doorway, taking stock of the room before joining us in the kitchen.

"How's it going, Lincoln?" Her smile called attention to the piercing in her dimples. Eden's free-form locs had gotten longer and thicker since I'd last seen her. And her wardrobe had gotten baggier. The oversized black T-shirt she wore hung low enough to hit her knees, which was saying a lot considering she was my height.

I crushed her into a hug, surprised at how nostalgic the sound of her husky voice was. At one point, I'd considered her my older sister, too. I'd begged her for car rides, she tutored me in science, and we'd shared copious amounts of vacations in which we'd take turns getting Sam to face his fear of the water, animals, and anything else that was new.

"I missed you," she said, with honesty in every syllable as she took a moment to look at me and then tugged on my hair. "Why did you cut it? It was beautiful."

"Got too annoying to deal with." I laughed. "Wash days were heinous."

"Tell me about it," she lamented.

"Are you guys ready?" Naomi asked. "Finn's got the HDMI working!"

"Ready?" Eden asked.

"PowerPoint night." Her brother explained. "Join us. You'll need to learn for later."

"Do I?" Eden looked unconvinced but curious, nonetheless. She grabbed a ginger ale and joined us in the living room.

I sat on the ground in front of Celeste. She immediately placed her hand on my cheek, thumb rubbing circles on my jaw. I closed my eyes for a second, enjoying her touch and turning in to kiss her palm.

Sam took his place by Aderyn, teasing her with the strings by loosely wrapping them around her wrists.

"Me or you first?" Naomi turned to me from her spot on the floor. Finn held out his hand to her, offering to work the laptop and click the next button on the slides.

"Me," I said. "Mine's boring, so best to get it out of the way. I'll shoot you the email now."

Henrik took his time closing the curtains. I could tell from how he was dragging his feet that he was waiting for Eden to take a seat. She found a spot on the recliner, tucking her long legs underneath her, popping open her soda, and squinting at the TV.

"What am I looking at?" she asked.

"It's PowerPoint night," Naomi explained. "We make PowerPoints on things we find interesting, or want to convince others to find interesting."

"Lincoln wanted to convince us to watch the *Banner Chronicles* last semester," Sam explained as he stretched his arm out over the back of the couch. "So he made us sit through a presentation on its merits."

"It was shockingly convincing," Naomi chimed in. "I felt like I'd be missing out if I didn't watch."

Aderyn leaned into Sam's side. "Doesn't that series have like thirty-five movies and a dozen spin-offs?"

"Two dozen," Finn corrected in a low voice as he pulled up the email I'd sent to Naomi.

"You convinced them to watch over sixty movies?" Aderyn whistled, impressed.

I shrugged, still pleased with the accomplishment. "What can I say, I'm persuasive."

"We're on the twentieth," Naomi said. "Going strong."

"Some of us are still strong," Sam noted. "Others grow weary..."

Celeste continued to massage my cheek, her movements

gentler as she listened to everyone go back and forth. I tilted my head back for a moment to get a good look at her. She smiled down at me, pride in her eyes. Making her proud took over the prideful spot of convincing everyone to watch all those movies in a heartbeat. If I didn't accomplish anything else in life, I'd be happy knowing I'd made her look at me like that.

However, I would still strive to accomplish more. My hastily made PowerPoint presentation appeared on the scene. I pulled out a red laser light and pointed it at the title.

"Where do you get these things?" Aderyn wondered under her breath.

"The Journey to an Impossibly Bright and Brilliant Future (or a three-year plan that doesn't completely suck)," I read.

"I need one of these," Eden mumbled under her breath.

"Slide, please," I directed Finn.

"It's very minimal," Sam teased, aware of my usual flair.

"I was pressed for time," I defended. "For good reason."

Celeste leaned forward so both hands were on my jawline as I went through my plan with everyone.

"Graduation," I started. "Realistically, it will take a semester and a half longer than projected. But if I want to avoid burnout and still commit the right amount of time to practice, then slow and steady wins the race."

"Words I'd never thought I'd hear from a hare," Henrik said, finding his voice once again as he settled on the floor next to Naomi. He took in each of my bullet points with far more attention to detail than the others.

"What are those?" Naomi pointed at the little drawings.

"My side quest. You two inspired me," I said, referencing Finn and her shared interest in gaming. "I'm embracing the fact that I should be well-rounded. And perhaps I can channel my interest in mystery into something post-college. As I wrote this out, I wondered if it was okay if my end goal wasn't fully figured out yet, or if it would naturally fall into place. But, trying to improve doesn't come naturally, so I figured, why would my purpose?"

Even naturally gifted, brilliant people had to wake up every day and get to work. Celeste, with all her talent, kindness, and strength, still worked for it. Every day, she faced a fear, whether it was editing a lyric, believing she deserved friends, or talking to a stranger. No matter how large or small, she showed up. I wanted to take a page out of her book. Be as brave as she was.

"This is impressive, Lincoln." Henrik glanced at me. "You did all this on your own?"

I gave him a look and smiled when he realized how it sounded.

"Sorry," he added quickly. "I didn't mean you weren't capable...I just..."

"You just used the data you had to make an accurate assumption," I said. "That makes perfect sense."

He smiled, grateful for the understanding and the knowledge I wasn't nursing some silly grudge. He wanted what was best for me. And now, I felt daring enough to imagine what that might look like, too.

"I know this is all words on a page," I said. "But it's a start. I'm committed. And...well, I won't try to bite your heads off this time if you have any tips."

It was only quiet for a second before the room came to life with their praises, thoughts, and suggestions. We spent over an hour carefully reviewing my plan, examining the fine details to make it more fleshed out and manageable. With their help, my dreams seemed to take on a more solid shape, the abstract fading thanks to deep-rooted care.

"What do you think?" I asked Celeste in a low voice when the others got caught on a tangent about my approach to next semester if Anthony would agree to my request in a few months.

"About Anthony?" she whispered back, her hands on my chest now, thumb absentmindedly drumming a beat.

"About all of it." I looked up at her, taking in her beautiful smile and those wondrous stars.

She traced the edge of my jaw, studying me as if I were as exceptional as she was. "I think you're an incredible dreamer. I think it's amazing how much you're showing up for yourself. I think wherever you end up, it will be wondrous."

"Wherever we end up," I gently corrected.

Her smile lit me up from the inside. She wrinkled her nose, obviously wanting to lean in for a kiss, but was too nervous to do it in front of everyone. I covered my hand over hers, promising her that and so much more whenever we had privacy.

"We," Celeste agreed.

CHAPTER THIRTY-TWO
CELESTE

The loss of summer hit me harder than ever before. Though the season was home to my birthday and guaranteed escape from the pressures of school, the long, warm days never settled well on my skin. I preferred the cold, gentle urge of winter. Even the crisp air of fall. But this summer had claimed my favorite beginning. It was where I fell for Lincoln Hill. When I discovered all the things I believed would keep me trapped were actually the keys to setting me free.

"Here?" Lincoln whispered, words mixing with the singing crickets, fingers holding onto the day's heat and painting it on my skin.

Nights were colder, making the treehouse less appealing to be in. But I could stretch out its use with another body's warmth. Lincoln was a willing tribute.

"Here." I nodded, slipping my hand underneath his shirt. My fingers played with the line of hair under his belly button, teasing him with chaste brushes above his belt.

We'd spent the beginning of the semester as entangled as we could. I was fascinated with exploration. Testing my bounds, learning my desires, satisfying his.

"You're supposed to be studying," he said, trying his best to be the responsible one.

Lincoln stuck to his plan with rigid determination. He'd also committed to developing coping skills in managing his ADHD. Not every day was a winner—a complex reality he lamented over and was struggling to get used to after years of avoidance. Most days were full of effort. And that was more than enough.

"I didn't come here," he said between kisses. "To distract you."

"Well, I invited you here to distract," I whispered against his mouth. "So where does that leave us?"

"Leaves me being used." He chuckled when I frowned in disapproval. "Use me as much as you want. I don't mind being here for just that."

"Just what?" I teased.

"Everything," he promised and cupped my head, pulling me to his mouth again.

The weight of the new semester melted to the wayside. I forgot about scheduling my new mentor appointment, prepping for my audition for the school's symphony, and the phone call I'd been waiting for about my mentorship application.

I hadn't gotten to talk to Ophelia while she was in town. Rumor had it, she'd been front and center with a smile on her face the entire show. But she'd disappeared after, and it'd been radio silence since. I'd gone through the five stages of grief, settling into acceptance when I decided to register for the fall semester with just six credits and a new job to help pay for them. It wasn't the dream, but it was a step in the right direction. An independent direction.

"I've been thinking," I confessed when Lincoln gave me a break and kissed down my neck so I could breathe.

"Mm," he asked, focusing on unbuttoning my dress.

"There's this..." I sighed when he kissed my nipples

through my thin bralette. Lincoln parted his mouth, teasing the swollen tip with his tongue.

"Shop not far from campus," I managed. The need to address the ache between my legs made my thought-process foggy. I wasn't sure how people who experienced this for years and years managed.

"The Field," I said, struggling to get air in as Lincoln took turns circling his tongue around my nipples.

He pulled away from me, meeting my gaze with a curious smile. "The sex shop?"

My cheeks burned, but I nodded. I was close enough to him now to understand I may never completely shed shyness. Still, I would always have the courage to push through it in favor of connecting with him.

"I've never been to one," I said.

"Oh, yeah?" He leaned down to give my breasts a couple more kisses before directing his full attention to me. "You want me to buy you a toy, beautiful?"

I nodded, my clit swollen with the need for his attention as he stared down at me with that dark, knowing look.

"I'll buy you anything you want. But would you play with them in front of me?" he asked, fingers pulling my panties to the side. "Let me watch you?"

"I want to. I want to do a lot of things." I reached for him. Lincoln pulled up, so I only made contact with his chest. His fingers tease my entrance, not going further, not paying any mind to my clit.

"Hold on," he said. "I want to hear what else you want to do."

I arched for him. "I'll tell you."

"*Before* I touch you," he said. "I can't have you getting all quiet on me again."

My skin was aflame with longing. I had brought up wanting different things in our sex life. And I had gotten too afraid to go into detail whenever I climaxed, and the safety haze of desire washed away in place of severe self-consciousness.

After being with Lincoln, the floodgates had opened, and I was what Naomi would refer to as a beginner-level kinky. I wanted Lincoln's hand on my neck when I finished. His cum on my clit. His mouth on me while he cleaned it up.

"It's normal to want to try stuff," Naomi had insisted. I hadn't told her the details, but I had confessed my shame because I'd been bursting with it and had no idea where to put that energy. "Have fun with your sexuality. You have a partner who's safe and wants your pleasure. Have fun."

Lincoln leaned down, placing the lightest of kisses on my clit. I sighed, arching into the cold air.

"Why did you do that if you're not going to continue?" I complained.

"A little incentive never hurt anyone," he teased.

I huffed but gave in. "I want to try those remote-control vibrators."

"The ones where I can change the pace?"

I nodded, biting the inside of my cheek, nervous about continuing.

"Go on." Lincoln offered a thumb on my clit, circling me slowly. I closed my eyes, swallowing a moan so I could continue speaking.

"Clamps, maybe," I murmured.

"You'd look so beautiful with those on," he agreed and leaned in to tease my nipples by gently raking his teeth over them.

"I want to be...on top..." I swallowed, gathering the last bit of courage. "Inside of you."

Lincoln met my gaze, eyes unreadable but hand speaking volumes. He slipped two fingers inside and his thumb firmer as he massaged my clit.

"Say that again?" he asked. "And look at me while you do it."

"I…Lincoln…" I couldn't. It's too new and intimate.

"Celeste," his voice had as much fire in it as my body did while fantasizing about this. "I'm into it. This. But, if you want to do it, I need you to look at me while you say it. Because that's what I want."

I forced myself to meet his gaze. The cold of the night was no more, burned away by my confession and his insistence I stand on it.

"Lincoln…" I released a soft moan when he added a third finger, more incentive, more longing.

"I'll keep going, but I won't let you come," he promised.

"You could never."

He smiled. "Want to find out?"

From my trembling thighs and soaked core, I most definitely couldn't afford to test him. Here was the thing about Lincoln: when he put his mind to something, nothing could hold him back.

"I want to buy a strap-on," I said, breathing slowly to calm my nerves. "I want to be on top and make you come."

"Fuck, Celeste." He groaned and pulled his fingers out, replacing them with his mouth. I rocked my hips, matching his rhythm and meeting his gaze.

"Have you ever done that?" I asked through labored breath. "Has anyone made you finish like that?"

He shook his head, not parting from me once. I smiled, thrilled to be the first.

"And you want it?" I asked to be sure. "You said you want me to do it, right?"

Lincoln closed his eyes, moaning into me as he nodded. My orgasm was on the horizon. I weaved my fingers through his hair, riding the high of the present stimulation and our (now shared) fantasy ahead.

"Celeste," Lincoln repeated when he finally pulled away, successful at giving me two climaxes.

"Come here." I undid his belt.

He reached for his backpack, pulling out a condom.

"On top," he requested, lying on his back and holding my hips firmly as I climbed on.

I ground, rocked, and used my knees to get every bout of motion I could in.

Lincoln stared up at me, eyes half closed and thumb lazily circling my clit. "You're my world, you know that? Everything that matters is all wrapped in one. So, I'm going to need you to always remember that, especially when every part of you is wrapped in every part of me. Fucking claim me, Celeste. Tell me what you want to do, and it will be done. From the moment I met you, it was done. I was meant to be yours."

"I know," I whispered, my hips making small, lingering circles. My acceptance of my power and his desire had us both seeing stars. I wouldn't deny what I did to him no more than I'd deny what he did for me.

We were a collective of heavy breathing, drumming hearts, and delicate satisfaction. Lincoln pulled me into his chest, kissing me gently as we lowered back down to earth, where the crickets were still singing and the stars were taking turns on the center stage.

The ringing of a phone interrupted our slow descent back to our bodies. Lincoln groaned when I pulled away to check my screen.

"Just a second longer," he asked, his hands pulling my hair off my neck so he could playfully bite me.

"It's...someone from New York," I whispered, stunned.

Lincoln pulled himself out of the sleepy world of post-sex. He sat up, holding me steady against his body so I wouldn't fall, as he reached for a blanket to cover me. He understood if I was going to talk to someone, even if it was on the phone, I'd want to be semi-decent.

"Answer it," he urged.

"New York," I repeated, as if that'd change anything.

"Celeste, answer it." He pushed the phone up to my ear.

I laughed, humorlessly, and swiped to accept the call. "Hello?"

"Hi, is this Celeste Able?"

I knew that voice like the back of my hand. The slow, confident cadence. High octave. Tell-tale smile.

"Hello?" she asked, confused by my pause.

Lincoln hugged me, trying to offer strength and support.

"Y-yes, this is—I'm Celeste," I confirmed while grinning widely at Lincoln. "Able. Hi. Hey."

"Hi." She laughed at the evident excitement in my voice. "I'm Ophelia Lawrence. You applied for a mentorship with me a few months back. And I was lucky enough to catch your project at the local playhouse."

"I...yes, you're...my hero," I said, too in awe to cringe at myself just yet.

She laughed again. "I was calling to inquire if you were still interested in the position. Usually, we go to interviews next, but I've seen enough of your work to know it'd be a waste of the other candidates' time. I think we should work together. How about you?"

I had a million and one things to say. It was a new problem: figuring out which idea to share first. Lincoln nodded, encouraging me to speak, to share, to take up space, to leap. And I did because I knew it'd be okay. He'd be there to catch me if it wasn't.

"I would love to work with you," I said.

"You don't know how excited that makes me," she said, sounding so genuine and honored. Ophelia Lawrence was honored to work with me. "I'll send you a follow-up email, and we'll coordinate an official meeting. Sound good?"

"Sounds perfect."

We said our goodbyes, and I barely remembered hanging up the phone. I found myself in Lincoln's embrace, him squeezing me tight.

"Lincoln?" I asked, dazed. "Did I just talk to Ophelia Lawrence? Did she invite me to work with her?"

He pulled away to look at me, his smile so bright it outshone the moon and stars. "You did. She didn't just invite you, beautiful. She asked you. Wanted you to say yes."

"So, it was real." My eyes got misty, and I held onto his shoulders to steady myself.

"How does it feel?" he asked, brushing tears off my cheeks. "To know your work matters? Your hero loves it."

I laughed and shook my head. "Weirdly enough...not as good as the moment I saw you in the theatre with those flowers and that camera."

His brow furrowed, confused.

"That was the moment I knew I'd never have to wonder if my quiet would continue to hinder me from belonging," I told him. "The moment I knew, despite my quiet, I'd always have someone around, ready and willing to listen."

Lincoln smiled, brushing a few stray coils out of my face. "I didn't mind the wait, but damn, I'm glad we finally made it here."

I laughed, nodding in agreement. "Here's the best place I've ever been."

ALSO BY DEANNA GREY

Mendell Hawks

Sunny Disposition

Team Players

Standalones

Outdrawn